Harry Warne came to South Africa in 1993 to help with military integration after apartheid. He was a career soldier before diplomatic life in Pretoria. He then farmed and ran businesses in Natal and Zululand. He lives near Durban, anxious as South Africa's sand trickles through its time glass.

To Jeannie, Alexander and Lucy.

Harry Warne

SAVING SIYEZA

AUSTIN MACAULEY PUBLISHERS™

LONDON • CAMBRIDGE • NEW YORK • SHARJAH

A CIP catalogue record for this title is available from the British Library.

ISBN 9781398410770 (Paperback)
ISBN 9781398411036 (ePub e-book)

www.austinmacauley.com

First Published (2021)
Austin Macauley Publishers Ltd
25 Canada Square
Canary Wharf
London
E14 5LQ

Chapter One

Maddox Illingworth had compromised. He had not wanted a birthday celebration at all, having become worried about his curmudgeon image. Everyone had Big O parties these days and as an employer, he had not wanted to be a killjoy. When all the staff assembled like this, he felt responsible, rather than in charge, wishing others took the lead. He would force himself to enjoy it.

'Can I have your attention, please? Bernice, Chavi? One moment all of you, please...' Gary was doing his best, tinkling his glass with a spoon. The women were already raucous, some unsteady on pencil heels, short skirts creased across heavy hips. There was a purple sari, magnificent woven hair, dazzling beadwork and several glistening black wigs. Maddox managed a smile at Gary, who was making a sporting gesture with a Mandela shirt in pink and lime green, knowing that these occasions were uncomfortable for him too. He had been Maddox's right-hand man since the detective agency began and although he knew what the boss expected, it didn't make it easier. A pleasant breeze wafted through the hired restaurant balcony Gary had booked at the popular Escargot, off Simon's Town's main square, where the thin streetlights were playing second fiddle to the deepening dusk.

'Come a bit closer so I don't have to shout,' Gary began hesitantly, beckoning them from around the balcony. 'That's it, thank you, ladies. Now then. You know we had to bully the boss to come out tonight so don't expect a big speech from me. All I want to do is welcome you all and wish the boss well. It's the first hundred percent turn-out we've ever managed, which says something, I think.' Gary turned to face Maddox as a few light cheers were raised.

'It's the good weather, mate, not me!' quipped Maddox cheerily. 'Maybe the free booze helps?' Good old Gary, this was going to be bearable.

'Not a bit. None of that, boss. We're here because we want to be. Everyone knows that we're a happy outfit, doing well. I must admit we're all on edge about the ownership share agreement but let's face it, it's a wonderful prospect to make us even happier!' Maddox stayed implacable, not expecting nor wanting the Trust issue to be mentioned now. The buy-in share scheme had been floated six months ago, hopefully to be finalised by his birthday but these days, so-called wealth managers were as prickly as lawyers.

'The boss and I began Maddox Private Investigators in 1998 – just the pair of us! And now look, there are seventeen here today. The locals are still suspicious and worried, so there's plenty of business! To begin with, we were all ex-coppers but the youngsters joining now are all graduates, which is great. And we're a no messing Rainbow Nation operation too – I don't know what this racial minorities fuss is all about!' A subdued ripple of laughter greeted this.

'So on your sixtieth birthday, Maddox, we thank you and wish you continued good health. May I ask you all to raise your glasses to our boss? To Maddox!'

As a thin chorus of "he's a jolly good fellow" began, Maddox's mind wandered. After those sixteen years mentioned by Gary, he felt a Capetonian. Long since a dual citizen, Maddox had been responsible for tempting Gary to join him as he began his company. Their hair had thinned as their midriffs thickened, their hearts became a little harder and their attitudes more cynical as they went about their business, investigating strange people and odd things in Cape Town's Mediterranean-style metropolis. They had known each other for over ten years in the Royal Military Police's Special Investigations Branch in UK, Cyprus, Gibraltar and Germany, with Gary seemingly coat-tailing Maddox in their specialised trade.

But at that moment, it wasn't his redcap days with Gary, busting import-export fiddles, knocking off tax-evading car syndicates, infiltrating right wing extremist parties or exposing licence counterfeiting that flitted across Maddox's mind. Instead, he was further back as a Royal Military Police recruit in the Chichester depot, falling in love with Sandra and waiting until he could afford to marry her. Not much celebration there either, with no money. And definitely no Big O palaver at thirty, because Sandra was already going off the rails. Jasmine and Celia were small then and farmed out around the family in UK, which was a misery.

And what about forty? He was commissioned from the ranks by then, living with Terri. A terrible tug of love between his job and her expensive tastes, but foolishly, he'd married again. It hadn't worked for a moment, with her attraction for senior officers and clubbing, ten years his junior and childless. She drifted away during one leave in Brussels and never came back. He'd heard she'd married a club owner – best of luck to the poor devil. He was left with two washed-up marriages and two grown daughters rarely in touch.

'Did you hear that, boss?' Gary was leaning towards him.

'Most of it, Gary, I think. Sounds like a bit of choral practice might go down well?' Maddox injected spark into his voice, refusing to be maudlin – Cape Town had yielded great returns.

'No, I'm saying, they've had a whip round – I know you said it was forbidden but that's that, I'm afraid – so I'd like young Karin to present you with something.' Gary stepped back, pleased it was over but feeling he'd done Maddox proud. They'd had some stormy times and split up on a couple of occasions but having committed himself to the firm for the last ten years, Gary was content with his lot. Being five years younger, there was every chance that he'd become a major shareholder, with downstream dividends if he consolidated things after Maddox departed, ensuring him a pleasant retirement in the Cape.

Karin was a perfectly proportioned Cape Coloured mobile dispatch clerk. That meant she drove a scooter around the city, serving and collecting documentation, attracting business as well as wolf whistles. Her outfit left little to the imagination with a pelmet mini and aggressively uplifted breasts popping out of her low-cut white T-shirt. She was overcome with embarrassment, steeling herself to do nothing other than hand her parcel to Maddox. She clicked on the large flag tiles in her sawn-off bootees to stop in front of Maddox, rising from his chair. He was concentrating now, again mindful of being more relaxed but enthusiastic. The parcel was large and heavy, preventing him doing anything other than dutifully peck Karin on the cheek. He knew he had to open it then.

'Well, what a surprise! Very many thanks to you all. Let's just have a look inside – have we put this through the metal detector, Gary?' Maddox willed himself to slow down, slicing the colourful wrapping paper with his faithful Swiss Army penknife. The paper wrapping images of the Eiffel Tower and Big Ben fluttered to the floor, revealing a gleaming beige and black Nespresso Coffee machine, with two hundred capsules to set him on his way. His sensitivities were still alive as he wondered why this gift had been chosen. It could only be for the private and lonely perfectionist – maybe even a curmudgeon?

'You know, this is so kind? I've always stared at these things, wondering whether I'm technically up to it! Many thanks to everyone. There's no excuse left to raid the office coffee machines now. In fact, maybe we should start a "Nespresso of the Month" prize, with the winner having as many capsules as he or she can manage in a day?' Maddox placed the machine on a nearby table to free his hands. 'Yes, well, Maddox Private Investigators is indeed going well and I'm confident about the future. There's so much talent and loyalty here and I'm blessed to watch things grow the way they have. But look – all of you – I might be sixty but mercifully, I feel fit and full of ideas. Today's sixty is yesterday's fifty, they tell us! It's you who keep me young and bring the success. As Gary mentioned, I'm going to motivate us further through an employee buy-in ownership scheme which I'd hoped you'd all have signed by today. My broker is still tinkering with it, so I'm sorry about that, but don't worry. I'm told it's one of the most adventurous labour relations agreements that they've seen, so I'm as keen as you to get it finished.' He'd said more than intended but felt confident that he'd begun to resist the Mr Grumpy tag.

*****

Maddox was dropped off by Joost, the latest and youngest in a stable of five qualified detectives. He had volunteered to bring him back, Gary having completed the outward trip. Maddox had been increasingly impressed by the young Afrikaner, who came from a Karoo background but also spoke good English and isiXhosa. He had spent six years in the South African Navy as a dockyard policeman at Simon's Town and Durban. Unlike the Indian and African younger detectives with degrees, Joost had graduated from the School of Life and seemed steady and methodical.

'Would you like a nightcap?' Maddox asked but was politely refused. Joost had a girlfriend in town and it was getting late. Maddox was not put out, since he knew it was high time he spent some time alone reviewing his investments and reading what the city's experts were saying about the project in the Cape Flats. He noticed the cascading pink Cape Sweet Pea crowding out his stoep entrance as he climbed the steps to his solid Wynberg house. They'd come on with a vengeance since the rains had returned to Cape Town in April and it was now mid-winter. Maddox undertook to get a grip of his house and garden. Did his position justify a housekeeper perhaps or would gardening go hand-in-glove with Operation Curmudgeon Eradication? He rarely allowed himself to think of living with a woman again but there was no doubt about some disadvantages to the bachelor existence, two of which were being miserly and critical.

Having changed into more comfortable trousers and jersey, Maddox poured a mild whisky and soda. It was nearly midnight and things had gone really well. But he had held back with festivities, partly preoccupied by Siyeza. The scheme had been germinating for twenty years. It was the earliest township modernisation aspiration in the Western Cape as Mandela came to power in 1994. But the gargantuan Cape Flats project had withered in the face of tourism and CBD development around Cape Town's Waterfront in the early post-Apartheid scramble. Along the way, the Cape Flats had passed through corrupt hands as a money-spinning pawn, with no intention to see things through. Being acknowledged as the traditional dumping ground for the Cape Town's coloured masses, it fell between two stools as white Apartheid government handed power to the ANC. But recently, Maddox was noticing the project's rejuvenation, albeit as an investment enterprise rather than social upliftment programme.

His mind had been drawn to Siyeza before setting out for the Simon's Town dinner. He had received a glossy brief from his stockbroker, Richard Kirkside, suggesting that Siyeza would dwarf any previous Cape Town development plan if it ever took root. An impressive list of blue-chip foreign investment names dripped from the brochure. With an eventual target area of a hundred and thirty square kilometres, and a downstream investment estimate of R200 billion, it had continued to excite but baffle an overawed South African government and public. He sipped his whisky, his eyes flicking to and from the local TV station pictures. Even with the sound turned down, Maddox could see how Siyeza was building up a fast head of steam. As usual, the ambiguous language in the brief failed to pinpoint dependable investors but the drift was clear enough. It aimed at securing overseas confidence to underwrite the largest funding venture for renewed development in modern South African experience. He would talk with Richard in the morning about his own paltry portfolio, which admittedly had quadrupled during the last three years through expanding business. He could kill two birds with one stone by urging Richard to fast-track his employee ownership scheme. He smiled as he pushed his Ginger Tom through his kitchen door cat flap; true Curmudgeon's colours! He clambered upstairs, circumnavigating a watchful Jack Russell. Like himself, neither pet required another name.

*****

As Maddox went about his business the next day, fixing a meeting with Richard Kirkside, he wasn't the only man in Cape Town, or indeed in several further-flung spots, to be pre-occupied with Siyeza. Easily the most notable was the nation's Deputy President, Jabu Nhleko, as he was driven in his customised Mercedes with three escort vehicles at 180 kph in the N1's overtaking lane. His driver and bodyguard sat in front while his staff assistant and latest mistress, Nozipho Ndlovu, slept in the corner, lightly snoring with open mouth. Nhleko was making his way out of Cape Town for a meeting organised by his ex-wife, Lindiwe, now enriched to ministerial status through his sponsored appointment as Minister of Women in the Presidency. The gathering had not been promoted by her Ministry but for the last month, there had been detailed preparation at the luxurious winelands farm venue near Paarl. For those who enquired or needed up-front payment, or for the many municipal services involved, they were told that it was all about "Gender and Race in Post-Transitional South Africa". Lindiwe's Director General had signed off a vote of R3 million to fund it, but Nhleko was never interested in such detail which merely made success possible. He would have lunch with the foreign trade missions.

Jabulani Bhekizifundiswa Nhleko had done well. Like all advanced ANC politicians, he knew where his bread was buttered. The party had advanced his life as a youngster in Kwa-Zulu-Natal. He had won a sponsored scholarship to Hare University in the Eastern Cape from his humble Nomgomo High School, through good matric results and membership of the Youth League. As a fourteen-year-old, he had campaigned for the ANC in Zululand against the formerly omnipotent Inkatha Freedom Party in their own back yard. A typical weekend foray by several hundred boys had left hilltop villages strewn with bloodshed and even corpses. They then trembled, expecting a revenge visit the following weekend – a free but deadly Saturday home-and-away football programme.

Their local ANC masters encouraged them to march, hill by hill, to "total victory". Later, Jabu's ilk stopped calling themselves "struggle heroes" because of the term's hijacking by Mandela's children – young, slick political officials who had always had meals and shoes. Nhleko's breed showed undeviating adherence to the party diktat. The Comrades were loyal to default, there to be counted, supporting the President in public. If they won ministerial rank, it was customary to flex a few muscles to see where the really big favours lay. But for the last twenty years, this was not necessary, with hand-outs being guaranteed for all levels of the hierarchy.

Upon graduation, Jabu was made Deputy ANC leader in the Uthungulu Municipality, aged just twenty-three. He had fathered two children but had no wish to stay with their mothers – future partners would be party functionaries, sharing the spoils on offer. He attracted criticism in Richards Bay regarding contracts for mining and port enterprises. But he soon became accustomed to sitting in the back seat of powerful cars, with nothing to fear. He was appointed to the State and Allied Workers Union [SAWU] in Jo'burg, where he attended South African Communist Party gatherings and learned about the Tripartite

Alliance. He made no enemies, raised no eyebrows and attracted no media scrutiny – the voice of moderation on TV news channels.

He actively sought the trappings of success that came the way of an ANC rising star. He took the simple advice from Robben Island veterans: stay awake, spot a traitor, take the rewards and dispense favours carefully. This was a measured exercise involving firstly family and clan, secondly ANC party faithful and family friends and lastly those outside who oiled the wheels of government – the Indian middle men, the clever specialists, the networking agencies, the inconspicuous links to foreign funds. With the public servants who ran your department, the rules were black ANC first, Indian or white ANC thereafter. A partisan legal and accounting rump had attached itself to the ANC over a generation that made this easier.

Nhleko acquired a ruthlessness as SAWU president. Steering clear of Umkhonto we Sizwe veterans, he rose to be the Trades Union Federation Vice President as a young man. But then, after ten years spent in Home Affairs and Economic Development, he realised his miscalculation. The bountiful new ministries with rich rewards were beyond his influence until he became Deputy President. In his favour, he amassed a spectacular assortment of overseas contacts in inward investment.

'Two minutes, sir,' murmured the bodyguard in the leading Mercedes. Jabu pressed the button to slide the glass partition aside in the car.

'We will be met by Mrs Nhleko at the door. There will be others. Drop me off and a guide will take you to the rear entrance where you will look after Miss Ndlovu. This will not be a busy conference and I think we will return to Cape Town by midday tomorrow – okay?'

'No probs, sir.'

It happened as he thought. Lindiwe, now vast and corseted, with an extravagant bandanna and electric colours in a gown to her ankles, was among a clutch of ANC apparatchiks at the lodge entrance. As his wife, she had produced three children while being the fierce Chairwoman of the Democratic Nurses Union, which propelled her to high office. Jabu's increasing obedience to the party machine encouraged her to strike out alone. He had a second wife and several mistresses, but she knew that he was as unappealing as he was greedy. The young "Barbie Dolls" would get jobs with their names on their doors, but not many favours beyond the bedroom. Her best bet was to stay influential in his life, while he stood an outside chance of succeeding to the Presidency. What pre-occupied her more as she waited for his arrival was the full story behind the whole gathering. As a traditional Zulu, Jabu did not care for gender equality. So what was going on, with all the inbound foreign interest?

*****

Ravi Chetty stared at his accountant. They were in the fifth floor of Amalgamated Holdings' glinting office block overlooking the Waterfront. Ravi did not hold standard board meetings unless the outside world was invited for publicity purposes. So although this represented an annual presentation by the country's foremost auditors, formality was at a minimum. A scattering of half a dozen men in short sleeved shirts, one or two with a tie, sat around a gleaming mahogany table.

'Stop there please, Edward. I want to pause there because there's a danger of you overrunning your remit, if you follow me?' Ravi had a smooth face of medium coffee colour and thinning, greased, jet-black hair that showed no grey. His thin gold-rimmed spectacles gave him an air of establishment, an Indian of wealth and consequence. He was slight and stationary in his chair, his hands playing gently with some worry beads strung along a leather lace. He wore a monogrammed brown silk shirt above tapered black Italian cotton trousers, a plaited crocodile belt around his slim waist that matched his pointed shoes. A simple necklace of Zulu beads seemed out of place alongside his encrusted Tagier wristwatch, which seemed too heavy for his thin arm.

The respectful and unsmiling accountant drew breath. He thought Chetty was a slime ball without peer and hated the whole Amalgamated Holdings experience. Any of the Chetty accounts were a nightmare and it was public knowledge that it was impossible to trail the Black Economic Empowerment handouts that were distributed into holding companies in Jersey, Zurich and the Cayman Islands. Now and again, a senior partner would enjoy a week away, showered with luxuries and favours while conducting rudimentary account checks, but for Edward and the junior accountants, it was an excruciating annual charade, with in-depth briefings by senior staff upon submission of reports, resulting in an immaculately presented leather-bound brief, couched in anodyne and soothing language.

'You're wasting my time with the Phalaborwa and Ukahlamba accounts now. I've agreed with the Revenue to present them later, because they're too active with major inward investment right now – all this Siyeza fever heating up. So let's just get the main drivers in the frame for this audit, heh? You know, the Tubatse Development Group, Hlabisa Brabazon and maybe even Chetty Barbizon Bang Bang – the ongoing city stuff we own? Otherwise, it'll be a fuck-up. The Revenue and government will be jumping on me – another death by tribunal. I just can't have that, man. I want you to show the nice BEE story, okay? How can I talk about starting a thousand jobs in the city when the books ask questions, heh? Get real, Edward, right?' Chetty hardly shifted as he spoke quietly against the room's air-conditioned silence. His staff relaxed, twiddling pens and wondering when the message would sink in. A sallow Afrikaner with a skeletal face was the only one looking alert as Chetty's bodyguard and strong-arm fixer, sitting forward with hands lightly clasped between knees, washed-out and frayed jeans ending in bare ankles and deck shoes. It seemed this accountant oke had a lot to learn and must tell his bosses that Chetty wanted a clean and simple audit, without the offshore clutter, which would be fixed later at a private level. Chetty stayed silent, staring at his victim, who had shuffled his papers together and disconnected his laptop. There would be no problems with this kid but he needed to learn the background music.

'Edward, no offence, heh? Maybe I should've said this before but it's not too late. Siyeza is the biggest money spinner the Cape's ever seen. There's a long way to go yet but take it from me, my friend – it'll happen! Some guys are saying the DA want to hold it close to their chest and dribble out a township renewal plan over the next ten years. No bloody way – that's bullshit man! You take it as a given that it will be run from the top, and I mean top, okay?' Chetty tossed his beads on the table and straightened in his chair, his voice rising. 'The media don't know half and maybe they never will, which is fine by me. But we're looking at R200 billion – I said billion, Edward – being channelled here, mostly from abroad. Okay? There's no way that the ANC can manage that, period. It's too hot to handle and they can't even count their fingers. Besides, they'll screw it with family favours before it hits the bank floor. Who does that put in the frame, heh? I've spoken to your chief and warned him off, right? In six months from now, Amalgamated Holdings will be the government's preferred handling agent. That means we need an easy audit, Edward, my friend, do you follow?'

*****

Kobus Labuschagne wasn't idle either. As Mayor of Cape Town, he had an uneasy feeling about the forthcoming meeting at his offices. The DA were in reasonable spirits after a series of headline-catching political successes in the Western Cape but as he knew better than most, the success story did not reach too far beyond the city's boundaries. It was many years since a rejuvenation plan for the Cape Flats was first floated, but as fast as the metropolitan fortunes grew, so did the sprawling population of the entire Flats, now spreading over an area approaching two hundred square kilometres. Kobus knew that open plots were selling in Philippi for R5 million a hectare, so those early ideas were no help. He had summoned players interested in the Siyeza vision for two reasons. Firstly, he wanted to put a DA stamp on the enterprise and secondly, he needed to identify the mushrooming political and business groupings. His recent local TV and media profiles had made him nervous; there was a vortex swirling around the city without any obvious propulsion and Kobus felt under pressure to be the commonly accepted focus and leader. He had asked Moses Sithole, the newly appointed manager at the Cape Flats model project in Rocklands to spend a few minutes with him before the meeting.

'So what are the Gammatjies saying about all this, Mo? It would help if we could put out a line before the community forums and do-gooders start spreading shit?'

'Nothing new, boss. It's still all crime and more crime, drugs and more drugs. There've been stories before about industry coming in with new schools and clinics. The Rocklands people are happy enough to see us, but the gangs are watching too. The clothes and shoe factory builds have started and we've marked out the first sewage grid for western Mitchells Plain. There's fighting about the contracts before it begins, as you could guess.'

'Do you think we'll have to clean up Rocklands crime before anything serious starts? What are the police doing about the button-kops?'

'There's a Capey poephol running the local cop shop. He's on the take from the gangs so it's getting worse. Soon Rocklands will be no different from Mitchells Plain or Khayelitsha.'

'Okay, it's time – we'd better go in,' said Labuschagne, glancing at his watch. 'Now look.' He paused to jab the air in front of Sithole's chest. 'There's going to be hand-wringers in this meeting, even tree huggers, Mo. Also financiers and developers. There's a rumour that Jali might come too, because of the Dutch and British trade missions. The media will be there of course and most of the service departments. And Nhleko's invited himself to lunch. We must put over a strong message Mo! If we decide – not the media or the criminals – that Siyeza is a goer, it must stay ours. We're not ready to say that yet but this meeting will get us a lot nearer, hopefully.' The burly Afrikaner rose and gave Moses a rough hug with his right arm. 'Make no mistake Mo, Siyeza will keep the DA in power and bring hope and jobs to the Flats.'

He propelled the plump and amiable Moses along the corridor towards the babel that always surrounded such gatherings, with visitors arriving late but insisting on wolfing down the buffet before assuming their places. Kobus steeled himself at his charismatic best, greeting them all individually before inviting them to sit at the huge Cape Dutch oak table. He noted some interruptions to upstage the briefing as his staff gave a succinct power-point introduction. The gist was that, contrary to media and local speculation, Siyeza was still an unborn child, with much preparatory work needed before it could be reliably costed and staffed. Cape Town Municipality must remain the project's focus and control, reinforced by existing Parliamentary support. Kobus was at his affable best as he invited comment.

'Mr Mayor, may I?' The first person to push back his chair was Benny Solomons, a well-known local businessman and charity entrepreneur. His jewellery shops were spread throughout the city and Province, having grown from cut-price offcuts and baubles in the Sixties to being equal to the city's best foreign jewellery chain stores. Nobody begrudged Benny his wealth because he gave the impression of giving most of it away. There were Solomons Hospices, Solomons Discount Stores and Solomons Children's Homes. He numbered himself among the earliest champions of Cape Flats revival and had recently reaffirmed his willingness to establish outstations for all his charities as a Siyeza pace setter.

'Go ahead, Benny. We always welcome your views.'

'I appreciate that, Mr Mayor, thank you.' Bent now in his late seventies, with a genuinely pear-shaped figure, Benny's reputation nevertheless commanded respect. The brightest colour he wore was khaki, with his wide sleeves leaving plenty of room for his lank, sun-spotted arms. His voice was still strong: 'As you've suggested, nothing's a done deal yet so we need to agree, or at least remind ourselves of Siyeza's history?' He smiled disarmingly, arms widespread. 'The Cape Flats have caught the Capetonian imagination for two generations but nothing has been done. It's an in-house joke.' He paused, guaranteed attention. 'But here's the rub. Sixty years on and all I read or hear about is the promise of the entertainments and retail industries. If I'm getting it right, it seems that overseas investments will help create casinos, clubs, pubs, gymnasia, cafeterias and theatres?'

Benny paused, looking around with mock incredulity. 'This can't be true? Theatres in Cape Flats? With a hundred thousand unemployed? What comes first then? Somewhere to work, somewhere to live, somewhere to contact government services, a clinic, a school?' He looked around with open arms, ushering in a sense of helplessness. 'The people there are turning to prostitution for a taxi ride into town, not a ticket to the casino!' Benny stared over his glasses at Kobus. 'And I have to say this. The politicians will kill this overnight if they play the crony card again. I pray to the Lord that we will stay focussed on doing well for these souls, two-thirds of them Coloureds, who have been neglected and ignored for so long.' His theme was inescapable; by all means bring employment and then township replenishment but only in tandem.

He had no time to sit before a functionary called everyone to order to listen to the Right Honourable Malusi Jali, Minister of Trade and Industry, who had appeared mysteriously through the back door. This was the moment that Kobus awaited, since the DA knew little of the ANC's interest in Siyeza. Jali had a survival pedigree, married now to Lindiwe Nhleko, the current Deputy President's ex-wife who still used his name. The hot money was on Jali to replace her late husband as Deputy. The DA knew that it faced an uphill battle to maintain ownership and credit for Siyeza.

'Comrades all, and beloved friends from overseas, my close brothers!' Jali looked like all the ANC's leading brotherhood: heavily overweight, sweating profusely, out of place in a Boss suit, squinting behind thick lenses, invariably with neighbouring seats reserved for fawning sycophants, who whooped in the style of Hollywood-sponsored free guests. This time though, he was on his own and it showed. 'We are so lucky today to witness the launch of Siyeza by the government who are grateful for the co-operation of the Democratic Alliance. It has been a long time coming, but now we have sufficient support and funding, making it impossible to go backwards once more on this great community project.'

Jali began to run into trouble, realising that he was not making the important point about control mechanisms. 'It is a humbling moment. I commend the work of Mayor Labuschagne and I'm sure we'll see more new faces and influences very soon. If I'm right, the size of the inward flow of revenue will demand the personal and on-the-spot management of those closest to the Treasury. Naturally this will require a special ANC dispensation, without interfering with the day-to-day practical administration of the overall project by the Municipality and Provincial Government.' Waffling now, Jali ran out of steam and received nodding gestures to sit down, having introduced and congratulated the overseas observers from the Netherlands and Britain. Neither of those visitors chose to speak at that point, which unsettled Kobus. Without external funding, Siyeza remained the same dream first mentioned in the mid-Sixties.

Kobus bobbed briefly from his chair. 'Gentlemen, I realise this is unscheduled but would either of you like to say anything at this very early stage, please?'

A tall, urbane Dutchman rose. Bram De Vries had the permatan of the first-class traveller. He wore a buff cotton suit and fashionably puckered and collarless white shirt. He glanced over spectacles that seemed fixed too low, his white teeth picking up the overhead lights as his brushed-back thin hair moved gently in the air-conditioning flow.

'Hello everyone. For those I did not meet beforehand, I'm Bram De Vries, Chairman of African City Development Industries, based in Holland. In brief, we're in twenty countries, with an operating capital outlay of R600 billion, concentrating on upliftment, environment and in-country sponsorship. We're based in The Hague but our associated charities account for fifteen percent of our gross profit, all re-invested back into Africa or Asia. You might have heard of *Umuntu othembekile* – that's 'honest person' in isiZulu – that we run in Cape Town? Like the Minister and Mayor said, it is early days but you've been listening to dreams about Siyeza for a long time now. We want to say that we're ready and waiting! If it's finance, co-operation, service delivery, professional technical advice or hardcore development operations, then here we are, keen to join in, with a generation of African friends and achievements behind us.'

Even Kobus shivered. His meeting had brought the worms out of the woodwork. Bram De Vries, rarely seen heading up his enterprises abroad, made his skin crawl. Where did he fit in with the local ANC beneficiaries and benefactors? He planned a buffet lunch afterwards but didn't want this to go on beyond an hour with the media in order to feature on the six o'clock news both in Europe and Cape Town. There was one last voice that he wanted to hear – Harry Reynolds from Trustcore Development Corporation [UK], whose industry and township regeneration group activities had listed on the JSE earlier in the year. Reynolds acknowledged his pointing finger and stood up in a business-like fashion. He was a leathery Englishman in his late forties with a reputation for delivering what he promised.

'Last before lunch – is this the poisoned chalice? Look, I hope I don't need to introduce TDC. We're firing on all cylinders in South Africa right now and Siyeza looks just the sort of undertaking that we'd love to take on. The figures aren't clear yet but we're ready with a substantial inward Sterling offer to kick-start the whole road show. We're looking at five years flash-to-bang but await government guidance. I know you're ready for a lunch break, but I'd like to underline the sentiment expressed earlier by Benny Solomons.' Reynolds' quiet demeanour was deceptive, as he summarised his objectives with a clearer grasp than the previous South African speakers. 'South Africa has a mixed reputation abroad, which is where most of the funding will come from, of course. If, and I say again if, TDC was to consider a sizeable funding position – say thirty percent– then we would like a clean and level playing field not just for Rocklands but all the sub-divisions – Athlone, Ottery, Hanover Park, Philippi and Manenberg. And beyond – we think the synergy will roll on to Mitchells Plain and eventually Khayalitsha, either sequentially or even concurrently as we near completion?'

The assembled listeners seemed impressed by the Englishman's no-nonsense straight talking. 'TDC see this as a life-saving opportunity for behaviour, attitude and economic dispensation. So please!' Reynolds gave an engaging smile and raised his hands above his head. 'No more yellow cards, no more constitutional hearings, no more convoluting tenders, rate of exchange tinkering or tiers of ill-qualified middle men. I hate to appear a Prophet of Doom but my gut feeling is that if Siyeza goes down the tubes, then nothing of substance will replace it in existing memory.'

Kobus ended the session and led them to the sagging buffet tables. He knew that the Deputy President, Jabu Nhleko, had arrived to host this and wondered whether there would be the usual contradictions with Minister Jali's comments. He felt that Reynolds had rebutted any criticism against the TDC but that Jali had appeared hopelessly out-of-touch. On balance, it looked like the DA would get a favourable media report. If he hurried through their question-and-answer session after lunch, there would still be plenty of time to pick up his friends and get to Newlands for the Stormers match.

Chapter Two

Ami Kirkside was always rushing. To work, to schools, to shops, even to bed. She claimed that it kept her fit and away from the gym, with all its costs, time and frantic culture. This was dubious, although there was no denying her trim and youthful appearance. The students at the University of Cape Town ogled her in lecture theatres and refectories but soon learned that unless you were prepared to take in a flood of molten intellectual lava and admit defeat in debates, Ami was not much fun. She was an unapologetic blue stocking, now in her tenth year's lecturing in the Politics Faculty. She was three years older than the faculty professor, a thirty-eight-year-old Indian called Ashwin Chetty, who in turn was the UCT's youngest head of department and an acknowledged authority on Politics and International Strategic Relations. There was a positive symbiosis between them, making the lecturing standards formidably high.

She was rushing out of her grand mansion in its curving lane, high among the elevated Hout Bay dwellings, as Maddox arrived for his appointment with Richard. Known affectionately as "the Republic of Hout Bay", there were few properties that sold for less than eight figures and the Kirkside's was no exception. They knew each other only in passing, so Maddox was surprised to see Ami pause as he approached the house from his car.

'Good morning – it's Ami, isn't it?'

'Well done, yes. And you're Maddox, aren't you – or that's what Richard calls you?'

'The very same, yes. I lost my other name years ago and only need it for the Revenue Service.' They shook hands, Ami's pleasant scent in the still air.

'Look, I know you're busy now but do you mind if I call you quite soon please? I've got something I'd like to talk about, which involves you professionally. Since we sort of know each other, I'd be happier if I dealt directly with you?' Ami summoned a smile with closed lips. 'It's a bit personal and private, obviously.'

Maddox was taken aback but did not show it. Richard Kirkside was a rich stockbroker and although Maddox would have expected such a request to be made by him, it was not unknown for wives to request security business with their own, or their share of amassed fortunes.

'Of course, any time.' He made a quick appreciation. 'You know where we are, don't you? If you prefer, I can come and see you wherever you wish?'

'That's lovely, thanks. If not this evening, I'll call you tomorrow. We can swap details later?' Ami was on the move again, half-skipping in her thin-soled flat shoes to the white Mercedes Coupe.

At the sound of the four-litre beast surging from their forecourt, Richard Kirkside appeared through the opening porch way, hand outstretched as he sauntered across the gravel.

'Maddox, welcome! How good to see you again! Would you like some tea or coffee – I've got both warmed up?'

'Tea, if you would. Thanks, Richard.' Maddox followed him through broad corridors, across thickly carpeted and well-lit rooms, to end in an office suite overlooking the tennis court. Beyond was a sauna house, a thatched boma and entertainment decking with sunken indoor swimming pool alongside. A gentle breeze blew through the opened lattice windows, swaying the drawn curtains.

'You wanted to talk about your own portfolio, I assume? And, of course, we want to finalise the employee ownership scheme, don't we?' There was a firm knock on the study's heavy door. 'Come on in, Lesebo!' The door swung inwards, with a statuesque African girl pushing it open with her backside while negotiating a tray with their tea and light refreshments. Kirkside gave a manufactured laugh. 'Maddox, this isn't my housekeeper by the way – it's Lesebo Bafokeng, who's been tutoring my son for a couple of months.'

Maddox stood to take the tray but was rebutted.

'No, leave it please! Otherwise, we won't be able to shake hands!' Maddox remained on his feet. The tray was put on Richard's vast desk and Lesebo stood up, eyes almost level with his own. Maddox had never lost his appreciation of lovely girls and remembered the rare jolt caused by a remarkably beautiful woman at first sight. Such was Lesebo with plaited lines holding tiny beads, crossing a perfectly shaped skull, with a large full forehead above a retroussé nose and full curved lips. Her glistening bramble eyes were alive beneath gentle eyebrows. A dazzling smile showed large and uniform teeth and her speech seemed very English. She wore a light blue cotton shirt, without collars or sleeves, worn outside a pair of fawn, tapered culottes. There was scarlet in her earrings, necklace, fingernails and strappy shoes. She looked in mid-twenties, full breasted, with a flat stomach between narrow hips but with a curvaceous backside. Maddox saw her shapely calves and slim ankles as she left the room, her centre point swaying gently, her strides reined in to keep her tall frame feminine.

Richard noticed Maddox staring at the retreating girl and savouring her lingering scent. He smiled and broke the awkward silence. 'I might have told you that I was married before and have two daughters – they're both in London? Ami is a Rhodes Scholar and lectures at the UCT. She and I have just the one child, Tristan, who's a bright kid himself.' Richard had an engaging side to him that made Maddox comfortable. He wanted his savings to be in safe and steady hands!

'And Lesebo?'

'You want to know why I have Naomi Campbell living with me?' Richard was laughing too, as he came from behind his desk to sit closer to Maddox. 'Ami asked on the UCT grapevine about a tutor for Tristan – we're thinking about him trying for a Cambridge scholarship, using the baccalaureate entrance. Lo and behold, Lesebo drops out of the sky. Lesebo means "whispers" by the way – isn't that an inviting name? She's a chief's daughter from Lesotho and has just passed out top in the Maths Faculty finals. She's waiting six months before beginning a sponsored doctorate with Investec. Ami grabbed her, just like that – what better solution for finding a live-in tutor – manna from heaven?' Richards threw his hands in the air, his eyes wide as he delivered this rhetorical question. Maddox shuffled as he smiled. Maybe life was best decided by picking horses for courses, with Ami theorising loftily at UCT and Richard squirrelling away cash on other's behalves while making himself extremely rich. But the detective in Maddox thought that Lesebo would bring trouble, rather than benefit, to the Kirkside household.

'Well, I hope it all works out well for you all. Now can we look at the Employee Ownership Scheme please, and then perhaps you could run through the investments?'

'Sure.' Richard clapped his hands together and wheeled behind his desk once more. He glanced briefly at a file before pushing himself back on his chair's wheels and clasping his left leg with his hands, his tan moccasin showing its new sole. 'Okay, let's refresh ourselves. What you've preferred, Maddox, is a hybrid that satisfies most of the conditions for Black Employee Economic Empowerment and a broad-based workforce buy-out. All the South African models come from the American Employee Stock Ownership Plan or ESOP, as you know. We've formed a Trust, we've decided on the size and origin of the loan to it and I can now recommend the loan commitment fees for all your staff. All of them will have two years to repay that loan, although they benefit faster by paying earlier. Happy so far?' Maddox nodded approval.

'Right. You've invested half a million in the Trust, which will be paid back by all employees, including yourself, on a pro rata basis. This will not change when stocks are distributed once the Trust is active and trading. So typically, your employees will find R245 thousand between them, or forty-nine percent as fast as they can, tax-free. You cleared around R700 thousand in the last tax year, didn't you, so once the Trust is distributing, you're looking at a five percent entry level dividend, or shares issue of about seventeen thousand. That's a healthy little earner really, isn't it?' Maddox was no financier but he was keeping up so far. He had waited until business improved and it was looking like a good time to start. But now aged sixty, he had to think of retirement plans.

'Yes, that's about what I thought. I'll feel much happier when they all get used to it. Obviously, I'll leave it to the accountants from now on, but thanks for the advice. When will it be ready to go?'

'No more than a month, I'd say. Quite a bit of bumph to wade through and sign and a bit of last-minute tinkering with the tax stuff.'

'Excellent, thanks. We'll run a Familiarisation Day at work with the lawyers and accountants but they're all looking forward to it, I can tell you! For all the crap you read in the press, I'm told that ESOP is getting the thumbs up for work and attendance rates, retention, and genuine shareholder benefits. Anyway, Richard, how about my portfolio?'

'Very healthy indeed, I'm glad to say! Since we met six months ago, it looks like an end-of-year eighteen percent growth. If you do your sums, that's more or less paid for the ESOP Trust loan account!' They both laughed. Kirkside was a natural salesman – the portfolio had comfortably outmatched his ESOP outlay, which satisfied Maddox on his timing.

'That's marvellous. Absolutely – it's the right time to splash out, isn't it, although I don't think I'll be feeding it so much with only fifty percent of future profits! Are you happy with conservative growth or should we think about being a little bolder?' Kirkside got off his seat again, pointing at Maddox meaningfully.

'You spooks are paid to be psychic, Maddox! It's funny you ask, because I was about to end up with a "look forward" review for you anyway. What I'm saying to investors in your position is "be just a little bit bolder". You'll have heard about Siyeza, of course – you can't avoid it at the moment? Well, like it or not, it's going ahead, starting with a trial development around the edges at Rocklands. But they're stumping up serious cash now and some mega overseas players are chipping in – European companies and banks. Kobus Labuschagne, the Mayor, and Malusi Jali, no less, are both clients of mine and without divulging confidences, I can tell you they're voting with their feet! Kobus is drumming up a huge Stocks Issue funded by all sorts of blue-chip entrepreneurs which will be available soon. Would you like me to look out for you – it looks like a buy-in at around a quarter of a million, which will double overnight and hopefully stay up as the project runs for several years. I was thinking about a thousand shares for you? I could double it by switching portfolio stocks if you prefer – we're selling your commodities all the time – and sell half at the right time?'

Maddox was getting quite animated about his anti-curmudgeon drive. A lively, forward-thinking entrepreneur like him would always take a decent risk, wouldn't he? 'I'm in that sort of mood, Richard – make it two thousand. That'll give me my profits back, having paid for the Trust!'

*****

There was little to prepare Maddox for what happened during the rest of that day. He was at home, having completed further work on the office ESOP. Everyone seemed happy to sit it out for another month or so and from a straw poll, it seemed that even the least-paid juniors were planning to pay into the Trust within a year, probably by borrowing. He tried to avoid work at home but unless he took up gardening more seriously, or became a bookworm, there was not enough to distract him from the dreadful television menu that only became worse. Instead, he was reading a business assignment file about a bank messenger's suspicious itinerary when his phone rang. It was Ami Kirkside.

'Maddox? Hello, it's Ami.'

'Hello, Ami. You said you'd ring, thanks. I spent a very pleasant hour with Richard after seeing you earlier.' Maddox rearranged his space around his desk, picking up a jotter pad and pencil.

'Really? Yes, well, it's about Richard that I'm ringing, actually. I think he's having an affair.' Maddox was no stranger to direct outbursts such as this but somehow the blue stocking Ami seemed the wrong person to say it. Maddox's mind went immediately to the eye-catching Lesebo Bafokeng.

'I'm sorry to hear that. Have you proof or any idea of the partner?'

'Not as such. But he's doing so well these days he lives like Hugh Heffner – all of Cape Town's great and good are flooding to be on his books because he's the fashionable choice in this roaring bull market. All the society deb types have to be seen there and I just know there's something going on. Have you ever married Maddox?'

'Twice.'

There was a brief pause. 'Ah, okay, well, in that case you'll remember how one develops a sixth sense about these things.'

Ami Kirkside was as subtle as a Serengeti wildebeest so Maddox risked exposing his first thoughts. 'But you have no idea? I was introduced to the most attractive live-in tutor, Lesebo Bafokeng, I believe, whom you've hired for Tristan. Forgive my impertinence, but is there any possibility that he's involved with her?'

'Get real, Maddox! Richard hates the whole idea. Says it's a social embarrassment, bad for business. Besides, black women, or indeed people – aren't his strong point. We have a white housekeeper and gardener for example. So hardly. If you delve around all the meetings, he's having these days concerning this Siyeza hysteria, I think you'll come across the femme fatale. Start with the *Country Life* garden party piccies...'

'But what are you going to do with any incriminating evidence?'

Ami didn't appear distraught or vindictive towards Maddox. 'I might leave, I might not. Or he may have to. It depends. I don't need money and there's no other man. I just don't like being taken for granted or cheated when I'm more than his equal. We're not at war or even quarrelling. But depending what you find out, moods and impressions may change rapidly.'

'Yes, I see. One more thing, Ami. I'll come round with a contract and terms of reference to agree and sign before we begin. But how important is this? Is it urgent, important or casual? Do you want it quickly? Do you want intensive surveillance that's expensive, cameras, recordings, confirmatory evidence? Do you want the evidence to support follow-on litigation? Do you want it presented privately to you or can we use police or other security company resources and so on and so forth?'

'I never thought this would be easy! You make it sound like a bit like a TV cop series! I think best speed, privately conducted with unambiguous evidence. If that's expensive, so be it.'

Maddox undertook to draw up a contract within twenty-four hours and arranged to meet Ami at a Constantia shopping mall Mug and Bean coffee shop the following day. He found it hard to shake off a conviction that Richard and Lesebo were the cause of Ami's suspicions.

*****

'Good serve!' Ashwin Chetty acknowledged Richard Kirkside's only fluke ace. When it came, it was good but Richard's erratic play made him mediocre opposition for the nimble Indian, who played in a weekly foursome and was a consistent performer. They were playing mixed doubles at the Wynberg Tennis and Bowls Club, where Ashwin and Ami were getting the better of Richard and Lesebo.

Ashwin had seen Lesebo playing before at UCT and knew her skills. The word was that her father had built a squash court and two tennis courts to give his Maletsunyane Falls hotel in towering Lesotho an upmarket racquets club atmosphere. Lesebo was excellent at both sports, emerging as a ladies' double winner at the UCT tennis championships the previous year. Ashwin's quality managed to produce an even contest, with both the Kirksides being casual social performers. Seeing her husband across the net, Ami's mind wandered back to Maddox's suggestion that they might be having an affair. Richard was certainly more civil with Lesebo than she imagined but he had taken some persuading to play as her partner. As the evening shadows drew in, Ami watched the tall Basotho girl move around the court, beautifully lithe and supple, with a long and graceful reach, always in time to make a considered stroke. Lesebo wore a grey tennis skirt, trim and straight, pleated across the front, accentuating her narrow hips but full backside. Her high young breasts moved slightly under her sleeveless cream top, her slender muscled arms lightly moistened. Ami had been told that she had not had a regular boyfriend as a student, cloistered in libraries and seminars to gain the top academic honours.

Ashwin was having a chance to see Lesebo and Richard together for the first time. The thirty-eight-year-old bachelor egghead somehow found time to run a successful department, give advice to the UCT Council on many topics, thrill students with his unconventional approach to teaching and be seen frequently on television as the leading authority on strategic analysis. Ami had been entrenched as the brilliant but literal lecturer when he arrived from Wits and they bounced off each other perpetually as inspired academics. She was three years older and married to a multi-millionaire; he was single and drove a battered Toyota Tazz, which further endeared him to his students. She had learned how he nursed a major anxiety regarding his infamous brother, Ravi Chetty, commonly held to be the leading drug and crime baron in Cape Flats. She had learned to avoid this in conversation.

Ashwin's cross-court volley followed some deep serving to clinch the match for the academics at two sets to one. Richard was probably the weakest player and had not looked forward to the encounter but now it was over, with the prospect of a stiff drink in the club room, he felt relaxed and contented.

'Lesebo, if you have trouble with Tristan, bring him here and run him around the court. Let's get him a tennis scholarship to Harvard instead!'

'No time for that, Richard! You should see what I've set him for tomorrow's seminar – we discuss his five hundred words on "maths providing the ultimate definition of truth", would you believe?'

'Hell's teeth! Is that why I'm employing you? A Cambridge scholarship will do!'

'Well done, Lesebo! Next you can ask him to confirm or disprove Goldbach's Theorem which if I remember correctly is all about "every even positive integer greater than three is the sum of two prime numbers".' Ami beamed at Richard. 'You're the only one here who is out of his depth, darling!' Richard was visibly annoyed.

'You might have noticed how many intellectual giants end up as dysfunctional cripples as well. Meanwhile, I'll keep making money, sweetheart, before some bloody mathematician tells me to slow down so he can explain to the world what I've done!' It sounded brash and unpleasant, which made Richard feel worse: how can a man live with a woman who has invisible chips on her shoulder and ridicules one's success?

It was a party killer. Ashwin made excuses, saying he'd meet Ami later at the Faculty staff braai and Lesebo looked at Richard, expecting a lift home. Upon arrival home, Ami and Richard went different ways. After showering, he heard her Mercedes thunder into the gloom. Tristan was at home, worrying about food. Lesebo promised to cook him some supper if they didn't talk about maths. Richard made himself a sandwich and having poured a beer, went to his study to finish the Siyeza presentation he was making the following day at the City's Chamber of Commerce's luncheon.

*****

Joost van der Merwe eased back along the rear seat in the Isuzu Double Cab, pausing for the first time on his shift. In the previous three hours, he had covered the Kirksides playing tennis at UCT, trailed them back home, followed Mrs K back to UCT to a braai gathering of some sort and was now back at the Kirkside place with Mr K and Lesebo within. Maddox had told them that in his view the investigation would be best solved by keeping a watch on these two, but it was too early to hope for decent evidence. There was no doubt that the black girl was a good-looking piece but Joost wondered whether Richard would bother with her, with all the obvious dangers, when he had the pick of the bored rich wives who pretended they needed their money massaging? If nothing came up tonight, he'd recommend they stick a few tails on the more likely regular visitors to Richard's office.

'I'm letting you into a secret, Ashwin.' Ami didn't look in the slightest confidential, as she clutched a beef burger in one hand and a bottle in the other. Her hair had blown across her forehead and she looked as dishevelled as Ashwin ever saw her. The braai smoke gusted around them as they stood on the fringe of a dull academic staff gathering at the edge of the sports fields. It was a fresh evening, with more chinos on parade than shorts.

'You really do know the answer to Goldbach's Theorem, don't you?' joked Ashwin.

'Of course. Only a Russian could con us for over two hundred years! But no, I'm being as serious as I hope I sound. I've hired a detective agency to see whether Richard is having an affair.' Ami gave Ashwin a mock smile, intent on shocking him into reply.

'Really? I'm sorry to hear that obviously.' Ashwin stared hard at Ami, who took another bite and chewed away without further clues.

'What is it that's going on when you say "see whether he's having an affair", what do you mean – you're not sure or what? I don't understand.'

'There's something going on. Late nights at no warning, no sex, furtiveness, putting back plans. And getting very arrogant and bad tempered.' Ami gobbled her last mouthful and took a swig from her vodka mixer. Ashwin felt she was less stable than normal, since despite her good looks, she was not a natural party animal.

'But you suspect someone at work or a new acquaintance, or what?'

'I don't really know to be truthful. Richard is seeing so many rich, spoilt madams these days. They're queuing up to buy his Siyeza shares. It could be one or any of them – maybe six romping in a vast bed!' Ashwin didn't laugh, but having taken a sip of his soft drink, he looked at her carefully.

'Look, Ami, I've got to say this. Watching Lesebo on the court earlier, my God, she's something! And you leave her alone with Richard all day long! Could that be the problem?'

'Oh my God, Ashwin! First Maddox and now you. You're all the same – just dirty old buggers who can't take your eyes off sexy young girls! Of course it's not bloody Lesebo! She's too smart and managed three years without a man at UCT, hasn't she? And I'm talking about "bored housewives", Ashwin. Cape Town is full of them, all after a little bit on the side while hubby makes his next billion and screws the secretaries. Life's changed Ashwin. Maybe bachelors don't notice but its girls who have the fun these days! One of these man-eaters has got her claws into Richard who is making a perfect arse of himself. Maddox will tell me who it is and I'll move out with Tristan. I'm going to shack up with you and ruin your reputation – another UCT grand scandal! Take me seriously, Ashwin – what else do you expect me to do?'

As sometimes happens, the highly intelligent fail in their everyday human perceptions. They lack judgement; the brilliant inventor who forgets to patent or the visionary plutocrat who believes everything can be bought. So it proved with

Ami, who not only emphasised Richard's temptations but stared through them, oblivious of the effect that Lesebo had brought to her household. Half of her had sensed that her relationship with Richard was changing or adjusting, but her helter-skelter brain that never slept, guided her elsewhere instead, into unknown shadows and bizarre possibilities. While those aware of her suspicions assumed that the femme fatale was Lesebo, Ami was angry that others approached problems so directly or simply, implying that she had an inferior intelligence. And so the dismissive response to sharing her conviction, engaging Maddox and the undoubted high costs, while her near-and-dear could have led her instantly to the true cause, free of charge.

*****

It was eight o'clock and Joost stirred as his cell phone purred by his shoulder. His military training, although rough and ready, had been enough to instil a choreography at such moments. He had dozed with some thoughts uppermost which were instantly in charge: was his weapon loaded but made safe and his holster free of snags, what was the weather like, was the camera battery fully charged, was his link to the base active and what was the current office updating readout on his tablet? These took seconds – it was a dry night with a half-moon and his camera was ready. He glanced at his tablet in the green glow of the Isuzo cabin:

Achilles 1950. Subject A at braai with AC. Party going strong. Looks intoxicated. Might be driven elsewhere. Departure and car details to follow. Target not alarmed – might be waiting for Subject A's return. +

Joost munched some dry fruit and finished off the soda water. He tidied up the cab, checked lights and alarms and slipped into the bushes by the verge. He eased his bladder, switched on his link to base and sent the "operational" message by the pressel switch under his black jacket. He strolled silently across the lane and vanished into the shrubberies at the bottom of the Kirkside estate. He crouched near the driveway wrought iron gates and confirmed the inactive alarms. The garden cameras were not switched on either. Zipping his jacket equipment pockets, he was over the gate in seconds, heading out of the circle of light into the shadows of a tree copse, still thirty metres from the house. He crept forward and zipped the grey balloon mask at the back of his head, checking his camera lens and earphones were uninterrupted. He checked his holster; the threat was assessed as low and his weapon was a precaution against intrusion or emergency. He brushed his microphone diaphragm and heard its magnified rasping. He was ready to identify what the office had judged to be Lesebo's bedroom in her spacious quarter in the top near corner of the mansion.

*****

'Where's Tristan?'

'Not sure. I think he's asleep. He exhausts himself watching those porn films. Why?' Lesebo had wandered into the kitchen as Kirkside put the finishing touches to two large plates of canapes. He had changed since Ami departed, now barefooted and wearing a collarless floral shirt over baggy khaki shorts. A wine cooler contained a misted bottle of Chenin Blanc, sitting lop-sided on a bed of ice. He turned to face Lesebo.

'Now why do you think? Man's deep yearning, my dear! I thought I'd make us a little snack and sip some special chilled wine – you won't have tried this Spier 21 Gables?'

'I rarely try any of them, Richard, as you know. If it's special, I might be tempted but it's got to be special to me too!' Lesebo stopped halfway across the kitchen floor, leaning with a hip against a tiled preparation surface. She folded her arms, pushing breasts that were free underneath her loose saffron top with an embroidered neckline. The shirt hung around some brief glossy shorts that reminded Kirkside of those worn by girl sprinters before they invented Lycra. She too was barefoot, somehow accentuating her real beauty.

'We have an hour or so before Ami comes back. Shall we sit down or do you want to go somewhere else?' Richard stood at arm's length, a plate in each hand. 'I'd prefer you, I must say, but just in case, we can fall back on these – Mozzarella, mint and mango skewers, or smoked salmon crostini – straight out of the Woollies fridge – or good old pear, camembert and prosciutto wraps? What do you say, Lesebo?' He paused, feeling excited that this was getting out of hand. 'You know, you're very beautiful.'

'Richard, you've got a lot to learn about me. I rarely drink but I never flirt either. My father could buy and sell even you, Richard. He's a traditionalist who likes everything his way. So he sent me to Cape Town because he knows I'm clever but he's promised me a very large amount of money if I'm a virgin until twenty-five. I'll be tested. I'm already a freak as a twenty-three-year-old virgin so what's another two years?' Lesebo smiled dazzlingly and put her hands on Richard's shoulders. 'On the other hand, a rich man like you can offer my father a lobola of one hundred Charolais cattle – a million and a half Rand or thereabouts, which is peanuts to you? Am I worth it?'

Richard could not remember being more immediately excited. He turned to put the plates on the sideboard, one crashing to the floor, shattering and spilling the canapes. As the lean tabby cat leapt off his chair to smell the prizes, Richard drew Lesebo towards him, slipping his palms against her cool and smooth back. She did not pull away but let him do all the moving, as he pressed forward, clearly ready for her.

'Lesebo, you little beauty, you blew me away when I first saw you, you know? I think Ami's brought you here to pep me up! But I can't believe you're a virgin?' Richard's hands were feeling her urgently, softly but undisturbed. Lesebo's eyes were closed as she stayed still but flinched now and then as his hands and fingers found sensitive parts. She met his kiss with an open mouth, allowing her fleshy lips to become part of a growing heat.

Richard had not behaved this way for half a lifetime. He had never played the Lothario at school or university in Britain, somehow skimming the hedonism of an engineering degree course at Manchester. He had hunted as a pair with his oldest chum, Harry Reynolds, finding girlfriends in pairs and later joining him in the same engineering conglomerate. But it wasn't a quest. And having a black girlfriend wasn't on the cards. He had preferred to keep a girlfriend as long as he could, like Harry, who went further by marrying a girl, to whom he remained married now, although long since separated. Richard married early too, because of an unplanned pregnancy, which more or less settled his lot. It was an unhappy marriage and two daughters later, he had divorced and drifted to Cape Town. The arresting and brilliant Ami had been a wonderful salvation, although true to form, the impulsive lover yielded Tristan, another early child.

He dropped his shorts and wrenched hers downwards, with their miniscule thong accompaniment. He felt her warmth against him. Her breasts stayed still, the nipples wrinkled within tawny circles. He knew she was a stranger to all this but her failure to resist urged him on.

'God, you're beautiful, Lesebo,' his voice coarser, his strength summoned from nowhere as he held her close while dropping to one knee. Lesebo seemed limp, her body following his strong directions. She lay on the cold kitchen tiled floor and looked up at him, face swollen and flushed, eyes wild. 'Open a little wider. I won't hurt you.'

'Richard, I don't do this. Get off now! I don't, stop! Don't hurt me. Don't do that! Richard! Stop!' Her head stretched back as she lightly screamed, his hands pinning her narrow waist as he drove into her, a mumbling, fumbling thrusting within the shining pink lips with scarcely any surrounding undergrowth – did she do that fancy shaving? They writhed briefly, she inert, he vigorous and rushed. As he pushed his head downwards, moaning exultantly, they were wrenched into another terrifying world. There was a momentary flash of light which both mistook for ecstatic pleasure. The cat was snarling at Lesebo as her flapping arms threatened his salmon treat but worse, Tarquin the Rhodesian ridgeback arrived on the scene, barking gruffly and pointing towards the kitchen window. Richard was on his feet at once, scooping up his clothes.

'Quick, come on. Go to your room. Quick! Ami's back – the dogs have heard her.' Lesebo was a fleeting nubile shadow, gone from the floor in a flash with her skimpy clothes. Richard pulled on his clothes, swabbing the floor and throwing away the broken plate. He listened carefully but could not hear the garage doors moving. He peered out and saw no car. It had been a false alarm. Now unnecessarily worried, Richard released the dog who pounded down towards the gate, barking furiously. Richard left him outside and checked the kitchen more thoroughly, the chenin untouched alongside an unused plate of canapes, which would be a perfect greeting for Ami upon return. He made his way to Lesebo's flat and knocked softly on her door.

'Lesebo? Hello, Lesebo are you there?' He tried to open the door but it was locked. 'Lesebo, it was a false alarm. It wasn't Ami. Can we talk?' There was no reply although Richard thought he heard a stifled whimper from the room. He traced his way back to the kitchen, shocked and shaking. What had he done and what the hell for? With the world crashing around his befuddled head, he poured himself a glass of wine with a shaking hand.

*****

Joost arrived back safely at his Isuzo, breathless and alert after his near miss. The big dog had leapt at him as he cleared the gate but there had been no damage to himself or his kit. He removed his mask and unstrapped the camera and microphone wiring. He checked his tablet and saw that Ami was not coming back tonight.

Achilles 2125. Subject A heavily intoxicated. Drove with AC. Housed AC. Subject A's car at UCT. Will cover AC house until you leave Subject B. +
Joost jotted a quick reply:
Archimedes 2155. Ack. Departing Subject B house now. Mission successful. Positive visual and sound. +

He ferreted for the remaining dried fruit as he released the handbrake to roll a few metres before jump-starting as quietly as possible. As he trundled through the city's party-going traffic, he reflected on his own private life. Kirkside, worth billions, was shafting a Basotho girl brought in by his wife to tutor their genius son. Bloody madness! It seemed as near to rape as the equipment could prove, although her resistance was lukewarm. He didn't want a court appearance and nor would Maddox – publicity, costs and down-time at the court. It would depend on what that black girl said and if she made a complaint. No doubt Kirkside would try to buy her off? Would he ever do that sort of thing himself? Joost's relationship with Eloise was going well and he planned to move into her place shortly. But would she ever try to get away with this sort of stuff with a rich oke? No bloody way.

Chapter Three

It was the most grotesque murder ever witnessed by Khanyisile Mthembu, the Deputy Commissioner of Cape Town South African Police Service. She had been called to the scene an hour after the first police had arrived. It was normally a mayhem no-go area ruled by infamous youth street gangs – the surrounding graffiti gave a clue with "Americans", "Hard Livings", "Wonder Kids", "Junky Funky Kids", "Nice Time Kids", "Junior Mafia" and "Bostons". But there was an eerie calm as the dawn broke around the derelict and battered township of Manenberg in the Northern Cape Flats. A silent crowd were there, faces lit fleetingly by the flashing blues and yellows from police vehicles. Already, armed police were taping out a large area and pushing the crowds beyond it.

Benny Solomon's wife Ruth had been led away by an ashen-faced and bearded rabbi, having confirmed what those present already knew. The elderly property and jewellery chain magnate had been viciously assassinated. His body lay crumpled at the foot of a roughly hewn log crucifix that served as a focus for worship in the rudimentary Fusion Manenberg Truth building. It was a centre for guidance, care and rehabilitation of Manenberg's lost young generation, condemned to join or be ruined by the drug gangs in the district. Behind the crucifix the words '*Your Kingdom Come*' were painted crudely in rust paint as the official explanation of the cross' purpose. It looked as if Solomons had been nailed to the cross by his wrists, having been shot in the side and through his forehead. His weight had torn the wrists free, leaving him an unnatural pile on the dust and rubbish below.

Once upon a long time ago, Manenberg had something to recommend it. With a view to the north and seaward to west, there seemed possibilities for an eventual better life and some imaginative planning. It had been a coloured district suburb since 1966, when the Apartheid government conducted their infamous forced removal policies from District Six and elsewhere. It was not so much submerged but hemmed in forever by the subsequent growth of other townships around it, including the neighbouring black district of Gugulethu. Eventually, a railway servicing Menenberg and Gugulethu split it in two, further compressing its space and options for redevelopment. With a population of around seventy thousand, its characteristic semi-detached rows of houses and flats were joined by ugly "maisonettes" in the 1980s. It began an early resistance movement, accelerated by the 1976 riots, with an armed struggle movement core within its social structure by the mid-1980s. But progressively, with organised crime pressures and an ambivalent law enforcement policy, it had become an ungovernable haven for drugs, prostitution, enforcement agencies and all illegal tendering and informal trading.

Khanyisile Mthembu did not know the area well. Indeed she did not know Cape Town nor the SAPS modus operandi too well either. She was the natural sister of Lindiwe Nhleko, now married to Malusi Jali, Minister of Trade and Industry, but equally impressively, the ex-wife of the country's Deputy President, Jabu Nhleko. For her pains, Lindiwe had been appointed Minister of Women in the Presidency – nobody better qualified, the cynical white press had remarked. So Khanyisile approached untouchable status, having risen through the police ranks faster than a ball on a rubber string. She was aware of the power and influence that Jali was bringing to Siyeza as an ANC project objective but warned her sister continually of the strength and determination of the Democratic Alliance and its incumbent Mayor, Kobus Labuschagne. Siyeza was the last great political battle of the Western Cape and the party that took the credit would rule the Cape for another generation. It was those sort of thoughts that filled Khanyisile's mind as she waited for early reports from the Scene of Crime Officer and his forensic team.

'Very macabre. Probably died soon after the gunshot wound to the head but my unproven guess would be five to seven hours ago – probably around midnight.' Khanyisile knew the city's head coroner and trusted his apolitical professionalism. All she needed were the headline points for discussion to release to the press now, ahead of a press conference that afternoon. 'They used a small calibre handgun – probably a Mauser or the like, looking at the gunshot wounds. He wasn't killed here – there are signs of being dragged and thrown around, so he was probably brought here in the early hours. They tried to hang him on the cross and bodged it badly – probably too heavy, made too much noise and not properly equipped with hammers and stepladders. They gave up when his wrist wounds enlarged. It looked like they planned to nail the ankles as well – they were bound but not pierced. Obviously, a crude enactment of Christ's Crucifixion for whatever assassination symbolism. I'll leave that one to your boys. The forensic lads will be here another hour or so. I won't have the cadaver until ten-ish. I wouldn't recommend any statement before eleven or a press conference before three – I know that you'll want an unambiguous story before the six o'clock news, so I'll do my best. Goodbye, General.'

Khanyisile could see Mayor Labuschagne approaching on foot and noticed a calvacade of Mercedes hurtling through the dust with flashing lights and blaring sirens – that would be Jali. She summoned her driver and beat a hasty retreat north through Heidevald. She knew in her heart that the eventual investigation and report would be heavily conditioned by political spin. For reasons she never knew, she made an impromptu decision to run a clandestine parallel inquiry free of state interference. She experienced conspiratorial excitement, squinting at her cell phone contacts list to find the name she wanted.

'Hello? Brigadier General Mthembu of the SAPS headquarters here. May I speak to Mr Maddox please?'

Deputy President Jabu Nhleko paced Malusi Jali's office floor. He had flown from Jo'burg at his own initiative, having heard about Solomons' death. He had overruled his staff who wanted a Cabinet briefing instead at Pretoria, but he knew better than them why Siyeza mattered most. And he also knew that Solomons had been murdered because he opposed the whole ANC strategy behind the project, having got wind of the assorted and competing financiers and developers who were lining up to force the issue.

'Malusi my friend, you're not getting the main point. We are running out of everything – money, brains and friends. We are running out of ideas. If you read the predictions, even the *Sowetan* says we will lose four out of every ten municipalities next year, country wide. The ANC has got it badly wrong about helping 'your party first, your brother second, your friend third.' The party is now totally criminal and all our brothers are brainless and rotten. We will never change the President because he hides behind steel doors and gets his security thugs to do the hatchet work.' Nhleko stopped, arms out wide in his shiny suit with tapered legs that were puckered under his fat knees, exposing shrunken socks and hairless calves. He looked comical but Jali knew better than to annoy or ridicule the man his party caucus were trying hard to undermine and remove from office.

'I agree, Comrade. So do all us old-timers behind closed doors. But we live in the real world and Siyeza offers hope.'

'No, it's more than that. Much more! It's a last chance.' Nhleko crept softly for a heavy man, leaning forward on Jali's desk with his knuckles bunched. Jali resisted telling him his ornate jewelled ring might scratch the French polish. 'First, before all else my friend, you must get wise about the Who's Who of those who pull the strings. Then you must make it happen and leave the DA and Labuschagne dead in the water. I'm going to tell you the home truths – are you listening hard?' Jali objected to being treated like a child by a man he did not admire. But if this was the only way to learn the inner machinations behind the Siyeza story, then he would grin and bear it. He nodded with as natural a smile as he could manage.

'South Africa has to come to this party with half the food already on the plate – you know that, don't you? Don't worry about the big stuff downstream, just think about the throwaway estimates. The chatterboxes are settling on R200 billion but how do we get even fifty? There's only one skellum that can raise that sort of capital, as you know. Ravi Chetty. We all hate him but the President owes him, we all owe him and he gets the job done. He says he can handle the private and overseas half himself – that's R100 billion, which of course is bullshit. He can probably put up collateral for a few billion, if that, but these Indians weave wicked webs, heh?'

Nheklo turned away from the desk, took off his tight jacket and sat in one of Jali's comfortable armchairs. His eyes were protuberant and he was sweating visibly, continually wiping his face with an ironed and folded handkerchief. 'But he's wheeled in some frightening numbers. I'm told to go ahead so I have to back them. There's this Dutchman who gives me bad feelings – Bram De Vries. He runs an international group called African City Enterprises who seem to raise cash, build and get-out-fast, all over the world. He's saying he's good for R30 billion, which I don't believe. That's a third of the total foreign estimate but he says he wants nothing to do with Chetty. He's already talking direct to the President.' Nhleko waited for this to sink in Jali's mind.

'And then a really big one, Trustcore Development Corporation, whom you know about? They're well established here already and are big-time in Kenya and Uganda. Their boss Harry Reynolds knows our mutual money guru Richard Kirkside very well. They trained as engineers together in TDC apparently and Reynolds ended up as the CEO. So he's getting a fast track entry. Trustcore are all smoked mirrors but they're not shying away from a minimum R50 billion share, providing the field is eliminated. Does this lift the scales from your eyes, Mr Minister?' Jali was keeping his composure. He did a few shrewd calculations without touching his keyboard.

'But who's the ringmaster, Jabu? How will I get burned? We've all seen our comrades go to the furnaces in the last couple of years. All of them thought they were allowed to do what they wanted. When the party's bankers caved in, maybe a year after the white press fingered them, they were left to dry out man! Nobody cared. They had taken as much as they could but once the game was up, there was no protection. What about now? Will the fucking Indian or Dutchman care if I go down for them?' Malusi Jali was shouting now, driven to outburst because of the despair his comrades felt about being ANC donkeys: they were identical to a young mother caught by Indonesia customs with a kilo of heroin, in that they took the risk but forgot about the death sentence rap.

'That's exactly what happens Malusi. Always has, always will. After playing denial to stupid extremes, you're tossed to the judiciary. Luckily that's changed now, with our comrades wearing the wigs, but now and again, my brother, you tumble an umlungu judge! And then you wait patiently for readmission. If you're not a young lion, like you and me, that's the end.'

'Okay, Jabu, I've got the picture. I'll handle Labuschagne, who's no pushover, let me tell you. It sounds like that British group needs neutralising against the Dutchman. There's nothing I can do about Chetty, is there?''

'There might be. Fight fire with fire!' Nhleko waited for this comment to sink in. At last Jali was talking the talk. There was one important message left to put across.

'Malusi. About Solomons' death. We don't dwell or have second opinions about the reason, the cause and the culprits, right? You understand that don't you?'

'Ya, okay, okay. But is that the way we're operating from now on? Is it Chicago 2020? Is Chetty our little Al Capone and Labuschagne the white sheriff? What about the real drivers in the Flats today – the barons, the drugs trade? Do you think they'll lie down?'

34

'Maybe not lie down my friend. But when you do my job, which I know you want to do, you'll learn to grease the wheels in big bad cities like Cape Town. The drugs warlords make the headlines here but in the fullness of a deal like Siyeza, they become chicken feed, heh? They all sell or belong to someone who can stand in front of them and say, 'Okay, listen in. I run all your supplies, pushers and distribution links. Do you want to work for me properly now, or do I rub you out and start again with my own guys?' So don't worry about them. They'll lose their bottle quickly, once these big boys start prowling around. They'll be some bar-brawls but that's everyday Manenberg, heh?'

*****

Kobus Labuschagne kept striding through the Waterfront as he spoke into his cell phone. He was one of those shameless social beasts who shouted and gesticulated in public while using a phone. This made him unwelcome in crowded places and suicidal while driving alone. He was a large and energetic man with a definite presence. He dressed snappily, although conscious of his increasing girth, which had crept on him slowly because of his height. Now he was a formidable one hundred and twenty kilos and looked all his forty-eight years.

'Of course. But I'd like you to be there with me, because all our friends are wondering about us and saying we've split. Well, we haven't, have we? I know we've had an argument and I'm sorry if I was bad-tempered about it. You know I never wish to hurt you? So let's at least meet up and talk things through again. Look, I'm so busy right now but how about next week? I'll get Lisa to squeeze us in. Lief vir jou, Rita!'

He was a well-known face about town and a popular choice as the DA mayor. Until recently, the pretty and demure Rita Marais had been his constant companion at all official events but had been absent for the last few months. Kobus and she were at odds about their public face and circumstances, she wishing to settle down as proper partners, possibly to marry. At thirty-five and after two long affairs, she still hoped to have a child.

Kobus was heading for the Café Coco Bana for coffee with Sonny Chopra, the slippery boss of Cape Show Time, a PR and advertising company. Any simple audit trail exposed it as the frontispiece agent for Ravi Chetty's main Cape Town construction, insurance and property development enterprises. Labuschagne kept a strict discipline about partisanship and although a sworn DA man and their likely future party leader, he did his best to hear approaches and views from across the political and social spectrum. Sonny was the face most seen when Ravi Chetty was making major moves and Kobus judged it important to afford Chopra a fifteen-minute discussion over coffee. He spotted him already at a corner table, Buddha-like, crouched with his hands around his coffee mug, surveying the scene behind fashionable sunglasses.

'Hoe gaan dit, Sonny? It's been a while man – are you well?' Kobus made hand signals to a waitress for a coffee, shook hands with Chopra who stayed seated and sat down himself. 'I haven't got long I'm afraid but you said it was important. So we'd better do the business straight away, heh?' Capetonians around were recognising him and he made a gesture to an acquaintance. It was always the best policy – meet the dodgy ones in public view to avoid media misinterpretation.

'No, it's good of you to take the trouble, Kobus. I know you're busy but since the DA got my vote last year, I'm after a bit of service!' Sonny had a cackle of a laugh, although Kobus knew there was no laughter in the eyes behind the shades. 'Okay, well as we all now know, there's already real blood on the floor over Siyeza. That was a shocking thing, that Solomons murder, heh?' Kobus nodded emphatically but said nothing. 'My guess is that it was a turf war killing and maybe Benny had stumbled into some local racket? Terrible. It doesn't help everyone who is trying to make things work, heh?' Chopra paused, sipping his coffee and not seeming to be in any particular rush to unburden himself. Kobus had no time to waste.

'It showed us all how criminals are influencing our everyday lives, Sonny. Benny Solomons was a rich but honest trader and gave back a fortune to the Cape Town poor. He was top of the class as a charity dynamo and was busy launching a huge anti-drugs drive in the heart of Siyeza country.' Kobus thanked the girl for his coffee and paid for them both, not wanting the meeting to drag on.

'As it happens though, what you say links with what I want to tell you.' Sonny shuffled in his chair and pushed back his shades on the bridge of his nose. 'We've been contracted to promote Siyeza big time. This is on behalf of private finance, not donors, some overseas, some local. They're confident about the returns. But there's confusion about the control of the whole operation. Certainly the big Dutch investment is being paid into the ANC fund that's been set up by the Deputy President, no less. I think the local punters will go that way too. But the recently preferred main construction contractor, which is British, has withheld funding so far and is maintaining that Cape Town Municipality is where it all began and is the natural caretaker for the project. Mr Chetty, who is one of Richard Kirkside's clients like you, I'm told, tells me that you've initiated a Rights Issue, hoping for mega billion for an account linked to DA funds? So we're all a bit lost about the facts before we launch the promotion.'

Kobus anticipated this moment from some organisation linked and loyal to Ravi Chetty. Chopra was no fool and was sailing as close as he dared to embarrass him. The Municipality had rolled out the Siyeza model at Rocklands a year before and despite considerable civil disturbance whipped up by the drug lords, had made decent progress. Three hundred houses would be handed over shortly and infrastructural upgrading was due to follow, with roads, clinic, and school finished within the following three months. Using funding from the Province and the new Trust, Kobus hoped to launch the next phase in Manenberg shortly. He noticed Chopra's "currently preferred" reference to Trustcore Development Corporation, who had no serious development competitor, when measured against the national government's tender that had expired recently.

'Not really sure why you've asked me along Sonny, to be truthful!' Kobus finished his coffee and pushed his chair back, both fists on hips, ready to walk away. 'The government's tender was quite clear. They'd publish the requirements and select the contractors but throughout, and please note this, Cape Town Municipality was to be the operational focus and oversee all aspects of project management, including funds. That's what we've prepared for and that's what we're doing. We await the contract decisions but Trustcore is head and shoulders above its competitors. As for your alternate funding, I can't help you. The government has made no mention of a ring-fenced arrangement at Treasury level, although I must say, we're getting worried now about top-up funding for the next phase. That's it, in a nutshell – you sound like you've been sent along by Chetty to put the frighteners on me, by the way?' Kobus smiled broadly and rose. He held out his hand across the table.

'Not at all my friend. We're about to launch and I wanted to ensure that you knew where most of the force lies…I'm saying that the Municipality is going to feel uncomfortable if they try to make political advantage out of Siyeza. I think the ANC think that everything that's happened so far is irrelevant. There's global interest and funds are flowing now, which is a national responsibility to handle. They'll pick who they want as their agents in the Flats and the DA will be told what to do every step of the way.' Sonny stood up and drew himself as high as he could against Kobus' bulk. 'That's politics, I guess. But what a proud Mayor you'll be, whatever the in-fighting along the way?' They strode off in different directions, Sonny in earnest conversation on his cell phone.

*****

Maddox was looking out of his drawing room windows, thinking how business and life seemed to be picking up. His half-hearted gardening excursion had yielded small dividends already, with some previously smothered *chrysanthemum frutescens* he had discovered from his recently bought book of garden flowers – he suspected his were "ruby reds". It suited his enquiring nature to pin down another tall flower he'd previously called "yellow broccoli", which the book told him were *achillea filipendula*. He mused about inviting guests over to show off his knowledge. Maddox sensed other changes too, due surely to his anti-curmudgeon drive. He had visited a Virgin Active gym as far away from home and work as possible and although he hated the whole idea, it had at least convinced him that he needed to get a grip on his physical well-being. Another sign had been his introduction to sending SMS messages on his cell phone by the shapely Karin. She had promised a second lesson to introduce him to Facebook and Twitter to see whether they were his cup of tea. 'You could join my special group boss – my friends would love to talk to you!'

Maddox abandoned his reverie to consider Ami Kirkside. He knew she would not welcome the bad news nor begrudge the amount it had cost to gather the evidence. He was contemplating the timing and venue for giving her the news when he received a call from Brigadier General Mthembu, the city's Deputy

Commissioner. She wanted him to visit her at his earliest convenience. She gave no clue for the request. Maddox had met her often enough and had felt sorry for her being given an appointment she couldn't handle. Twenty years ago, the new inexperienced chiefs were catapulted from nowhere and given a dependable pair of white hands to bed them in and if necessary to do the job for them. Now everyone was inexperienced because the name of the game was career planning, with no connected appointee spending more than a year in post. They were even spared the form-filling these days, apparently, since the chief dispensed a pro rata largesse every six months that pre-determined their overtime and reimbursement totals. Maddox mused that today's police would give short shrift to his timid ESOP idea.

Khanyisile Mthembu was a buxom woman who showed little femininity trussed in her light blue SAPS uniform. She had few social graces and was jerky and unwelcoming to Maddox. She pointed at a chair she wanted him to use and retreated behind her government desk with courtesy panelling to preserve the incumbent's modesty. A young and slim policewoman brought them both coffee and some toffee crunchies, which pleased Maddox.

'Thank you for coming Mr...er Maddox? Is that your second name? Some say you have another name!'

'No, that's fine. If you'd stopped me for speeding, I might give you my proper name but everyone calls me just "Maddox" – even the company is called "Maddox Private Investigators", so you've got it right from the start!' Maddox smiled at her and leant forward to pour them both tea and steal a crunchie for himself.

'Good. Well Maddox then, I have heard how well you're regarded by the SAPS. They tell me you're an ex-policeman yourself?'

'Yes. I served in the Royal Military Police in the British Army for over twenty years. I came out here when I retired and started up the business.'

'That's good because you are sympathetic to us for the difficult job we do. Not all of us are good policemen and it is very hard for a good young and honest police officer to stay that way – he is quickly taught bad ways, like new boys at schools or joining kids' gangs on the Flats. But I must not waste your time – you cost money! I want to tell you how hard I am finding the Solomons murder follow-up. I am being pressured by my superiors, the politicians and even criminals. As you know it was an assassination that was meant to frighten off the opposition. But the quarrel is about whether they were the drug gangs or rival competitors for Siyeza tenders. Or both?'

'I see. But how can I help with an official police case?'

'I have a fund to hire specialists. I want you to do your own clandestine enquiry for me alongside the official investigating team. Have you ever done that?'

'Well, not exactly. But I've often worked alongside uniform branches while I served in the Special Investigations Branch – the military plain clothes branch. Not a big problem as long as egos are kept reined in. But you're wanting me to do this confidentially?'

'Yes. If you get discovered, I'll cover you, so there's no professional reputation to worry about. I want you to present your evidence fit to stand up to legal interrogation in court, if it comes to that. Does that give you any ethical problems?'

'Don't see why. I will name you as my commercial sponsor. Nothing would need embellishing, let alone falsifying, once our cover is blown and you want to use our evidence in court.'

'Right. That sounds what I want. Because I rely on others to draw up contracts, please do this one for me and submit it to me for approval. Once we agree the terms and the fees, you can start. But please only report to me personally. I think you have no more than a month. Our detectives are finalising their work now but the political wrangling will take ages. I will let you know the findings and give you any advice you want. Maybe we should meet weekly, or at least talk?'

Maddox smiled and nodded. He had one thought that he ought to get off his chest.

'Tell me, does either your sister or Mr Jali know about this plan? It would not go down well for the public to learn that a police chief didn't trust her own force and preferred a private investigator instead, would it?' Maddox opened his eyes wide by way of emphasis.

'Of course not. But between you and me, I'm thinking of Number One. I think you'll uncover evidence against big name crooks who are running rings round us. If it takes a woman to break up crime and police syndicates, then so what – that's good news? And with a sister as Minister of Women and a brother-in-law as the next Deputy President, I think I might do myself a favour, don't you?' Khanyisile probably felt she'd overdone it but Maddox smiled reassuringly to let her know that her secrets were safe with him.

'Excellent then, General. I'll get back within forty-eight hours with a draft contract, including costs. It won't be cheap, because the stealth is going to be very tricky and needs manpower. But let's see. It was a ghastly murder and I'll be delighted to see those evil bastards behind bars.'

*****

As Maddox delighted in his emerging garden perennials, Bram De Vries listened to his CEO at the group's office in the Hofkwartior district of The Hague, overlooking the Noordeneinke Royal Palace. Although not a recognised business centre, this location had proved perfect for the evasive Dutchman. It was a smart Dutch address with an all-important central Den Haag telephone number, it provided a personal answering service, and there was an impressive meeting place. Above that, it attracted no attention and had no bad neighbours.

'Bram, the risk is acceptable, given the Rand's slide and the declining rating that South Africa has collected recently. We recommend non-competitive participation, letting our international weight and credibility do the work for you.

For this offer, we'd vote in US dollars, which will never be at a disadvantage to either the local offer or the Trustcore's Sterling pitch.

'Who's going to give a read-out of our chances after Solomons' death?'

'Look, we have to trust Ravi Chetty because he's doing the introductions but the sooner we dump him the better! How do we know what he's swindling on tender presentations or outsourced building and development programmes? Every local name mentioned is on his payroll effectively, so it's not too different to having a unique contact like Trustcore has with Cape Town Municipality.'

'What do you mean by that?'

'We're saying Bram, that Chetty has the President in the bag. But he's finding the Deputy and other younger bucks a bit more awkward to get on board. We've no choice but to get in quickly and make some noise, so we're lumbered with Ravi Chetty. But we've eyes wide open for other running mates, don't worry. Please remember that Chetty has big entertainment interests. He doesn't own them but he facilitates and owns properties. So when we begin our core offers, it'll begin a fight and Ravi Chetty won't be on our side. In other words, we're dealing with a bit of an impresario. He can call on the President, local finance and organised crime. This is not Egypt or Nigeria – there are four and a half million whites, lots paying taxes, and the press will beach us if we foul up through Chetty. He'll drop us if things go wrong and swear to fill the gap with his local good men and true!'

'And Trustcore that you mentioned?'

'The boss, Harry Reynolds, knows Richard Kirkside, the broker and financier. They were at university and began life together at Trustcore. Kirkside handles the personal finances of Jali, the likely future Deputy President and husband of the very central Minister of Women in the Presidency. Just to make you sit up, she's the ex-wife of today's Deputy President, Nhleko.'

'Sounds like she's worked hard for her appointment!' De Vries had broken the ice, with all assembled revelling in the boss' earthy humour. 'But what interests me most today Hennie, is the facts behind the share offer being made by Cape Town Municipality. What's it like, has it taken off and need we do something about it?'

'Well, boss, South Africa has just freed this area up. Directors have been given greater power to issue new shares. In the Municipality's case, the shareholders are largely voting Capetonians, so we would judge that the directors, led by Labuschagne, will be able to raise the capital they want – only a few billion Rand to get registered – without the normal time delays and statutory agreements. So they'll raise that capital quickly – probably before we can influence things with a better offer.'

'Then it's a three-horse race!' De Vries did not disguise his impatience and dissatisfaction. He slapped both hands on the table and fastened his eyes on his CEO. 'Okay, okay, no more talk – this is what you will do. One: investigate the fine detail of Chetty's involvement and what it means to go in with him. Two: see if we can match his appeal to the President and ANC. If not, how do we stop his? Our international collateral leaves small chaff like Chetty in the dust – let's look like we mean business, for Christ's sake. And three: get the full low-down on Trustcore, the Municipality's Share Issue – the whole works – and see how it looks when we're all lined up, waiting for the starter's pistol. It's impossible, in my view, to see how we can be side-lined? Look, we start the three-legged race with the local hero but having crippled him, we only have the outsider stranger to beat. So what's your problem? There's too much negative briefing around, do you hear?' De Vries tapped his notes together, told his secretary to have his car sent round, and exited the spartan premises, cursing quietly about his staff. At least there seemed to be no spillage between his various outsourced agencies, but he had to work fast now to benefit from Solomon's removal.

*****

Maddox had a full plate. Business was booming, with some lucrative contracts raising the company's profile in the city's commercial community. He had strained his back gardening and in keeping a doctor's appointment, had re-met Katie Rawlinson, looking very attractive and now the practice administrator. Her late husband, Cyril Rawlinson, had been the much-respected local GP before his sudden death three years before, when Maddox had known them from his occasional forays to the neighbourhood Anglican Church. She told Maddox how Annabelle, their only child, had recently gone to Brisbane, leaving Katie without immediate relatives. Somehow, Maddox had found himself agreeing to join Mowbray Tennis and Sports Club, where she was a member; he was finding it increasingly easy to cross little boundary fences these days, as he fronted up to the Curmudgeon dinosaur. Katie assured him that the club pro would bring him up to acceptable scratch before he braved the courts. He had undertaken to go weekly although his time was not his own these days.

He had contacted Ami Kirkside and without compromising his evidence over the telephone, had made an appointment for her to visit his offices. He wanted to present the evidence put together by Joost in the correct technical surroundings of his studio. He was not looking forward to the interview but it could not be delayed further. He wondered how it would affect his professional relationship with Richard and his handling of his investment portfolio. Indeed, he worried that it might spill over into the whole Siyeza project and reduce the worth of his large investment in the Municipality's Shares Issue. Maddox decided it was overt curmudgeon-ism to be so negative, although he would have to tip-toe carefully around any ethics sensitivities.

The Solomons affair was another pressing commitment which was well under way. He had assigned his three most senior investigators to the task whenever they could be committed together. The deadline was troublesome but the contract's motivation clear – the media had already decided that the Cape Flats drugs cartel was responsible and were accusing the police of collusion. Brigadier General Mthembu was being surprisingly patient and the investigating SAPS team were being co-operative. But the forensic trail was taking time.

*****

Richard Kirkside stared at Lesebo Bafokeng, leaning up against his office wall, arms crossed, and an uncharacteristic bandanna enfolding her hair.

'Look Lesebo, I don't know why you're behaving this way. We did what we did because I thought you wanted to as well. Why can't we go on and find out more about each other? I know it was a first time and I know about your wish to…' Lesebo pushed herself away from the door and came within a metre of Richard, her arms moving wildly.

'Shut up, Richard, you hypocritical creep! You as good as raped me, admit it! I didn't know what to do – maybe I should have stabbed you – but I didn't want to do it then and I certainly will never do it again with you. You face a big problem, Richard, you will not get away with this. What about my father, what about Ami, what about Tristan, what about the university, your clients? They will all get to know.' She was leaning forward to scream into his face, her eyes a flashing black, her grey full-length African dress hiding everything except hands and face. Richard swivelled his chair to follow her. He was feeling flushed and tried to moderate his voice. But he knew he would never win this discussion.

'They don't need to know, do they? We keep it quiet, Lesebo. Okay, if you don't want to go on with it…'

'Go on with what?' Lesebo was screaming louder still. 'I'm not in this game, it's just you, you smug bastard! You took me for instant gratification, you took me as a lonely girl in your home and you took me as an employee. I hate you, can't you see? If I loved you, I'd listen but you took me by force and I will never forgive you.' She turned away to sob uncontrollably, her back shuddering as she covered her face with her hands. Richard approached her quietly and tried to put his arms around but she spun sharply and hit his face hard with her hand.

'Fuck off, you bastard! I'll sacrifice everything about this. You'd better think what to tell Ami before I do! And then think about my father. Remember Richard Kirkside, I'm rich too and you didn't pick me up kerb-crawling! I'm going to bring you to your knees, you see!' She pushed past him and crashed the door behind her as she ran to her flat. Richard felt the walls reverberate as another door slammed shut. She had to leave him as fast as possible but under what terms and for what advantage to her? She had all the cards and unless he thought on his feet, he was indeed potentially ruined.

Chapter Four

Maddox asked Ami whether she objected to Joost, the investigating officer in her case, being in the studio when he debriefed her, alongside one of his older female employees. As an old school detective with twenty years carrying the Queen's Warrant, Maddox had continued to protect himself as a private operator. Ami had no objection, having been assured of the absolute confidentiality clauses that covered her contract.

'Mrs Kirkside, the purpose of this meeting is to debrief you on our investigation into your suspicions that your husband is conducting a close liaison with another woman. Our meeting will be recorded and one copy will be retained for our reference purposes or to use as an exhibit if required. You may ask for a personal copy should you so wish. Our investigation took less time than we estimated but was conclusive. In demonstrating this, we have to ask you to watch and listen to a video film. You are likely to find this an unpleasant experience, so I will first summarise our findings, giving you the option to decline viewing the video. Is that all right?' Maddox realised his official style was unavoidably curmudgeon-like and made an effort to lighten his style of delivery – the Kirksides were going to be important to him as their reactions to this debrief unfolded. Ami nodded, completely withdrawn and silent, looking as only a composed university lecturer could when receiving important original information.

'Right. Joost van der Merve here is a senior detective and completed the operational investigation into your case. I suggest you pass any questions or comments you might have to me and I can invite Mr van der Merve to comment further on the factual aspects if we need.' The formalities over and the scene set, Maddox proceeded to the meat of the discussion.

'I must admit that we felt the circumstances you described when you engaged us suggested that your husband had formed a close relationship with Miss Lesebo Bafokeng, whom you recently hired as a live-in tutor for your son Tristan. We wanted to clear that lead out of the equation before embarking on the more lengthy and expensive investigation into a relationship with one of the investment clients. In the event this proved a correct assumption. We obtained clear proof that your husband had sex with Miss Bafokeng at your home on the evening of Friday the third of February. You were at a braai at the UCT with Professor Ashwin Chetty, I believe, and spent the night at his residence.'

'Don't make it sound like we do wife-swapping for God's sake! I'd had one too many to drive home, so Professor Chetty kindly offered me a bed. He and I have a strictly professional relationship, I can assure you.' Ami put this across calmly, rather than in anger. Ambiguous insinuations could neutralise Richard's guilt. She quickly refocused. 'But you're absolutely certain about this are you? She's only been staying a few weeks.'

'Oh yes. As I say, you can view the video yourself. But having said that, as I'll explain further in my written report to you, there's an impression that this was a one-off or at least a first time. Indeed, there's fairly clear evidence that it wasn't consensual sex for Miss Bafokeng, with your husband making all the running and probably forcing himself on her at the end. It was a very brief encounter in your kitchen, probably lasting less than three minutes. Your ridgeback was alerted by Joost's presence outside, forcing him to vacate the premises a little earlier than intended but the evidence is very definite, nevertheless.'

'How disgusting. The conceited fool – God's gift to hot chicks! What worries me is that this could be entirely coincidental. I've had suspicions for two months or so, as I told you, ages before he even met Lesebo. So I'm sickened all right but not convinced you've got the whole story – I think there's someone else or maybe more.' Ami sat forward on her chair and quietly put her face in her hands. She didn't move and there were no visible signs of her weeping. Maddox and his colleagues remained silent. When she sat straight again, her face was pale against her chestnut hair and bright blue collar. She looked steadily at Maddox and did not falter.

'Anyway, thank you for being so quick and considerate. I do not want to see the video or take a copy. I suppose I might in the future. I think I have all I need to confront Richard now. If Lesebo was an unwilling party, she will confess, I'm sure, so Richard has no case to answer, other than adultery. But if Lesebo wants to testify that she was raped, that's another very public problem for him. Please give the full report to me personally as soon as you can, with your invoice.' Ami looked around their faces, betraying no emotion. She stood, putting her handbag under her arm as she turned towards the door. 'Well at least my feminine sixth senses are intact but my target practice was faulty. I'm sorry for snapping at you when you suggested that Lesebo might be the femme fatale, Maddox, but it seems nothing had been brewing until now, does it?' Ami shook Maddox's hand and left, leaving them raising eyebrows and silently gesturing with open palms. Maddox knew that Richard Kirkside was about to lose a broker's most precious asset – credibility. And at just the wrong time for all the great and the good who relied on him to deliver.

*****

'Kobus, can we talk – it's Richard Kirkside.' The Mayor was listening to his PA running through his diary for the next ten days. She was looking harassed and Kobus was wondering whether she was coping with all the increased pressures being brought by the ANC on the Municipality. He was convinced that the DA could do more to relieve some of this but knew that party factionalism was putting a brake on him to frustrate his own political ambitions. He nodded to his PA to leave the room.

'Sure Richard. Any time. I'm on my own now. How can I help you?'

'Well, it might be a back-scratch. I wanted to give you a heads-up about the Siyeza shares launch. It looks cut and dried that we can launch now, with half a billion banked and every hope of opening up more European punters. I know you want to handle the timing and advertising style yourselves, so as far as I'm concerned, you've got a copper bottom to float in!'

'That's great news Richard, thanks. We're getting flak from all sides – some quite nasty stuff locally – but it seems that a Dutch consortium are putting their shirt on an ANC fund that the Municipality regards as bogus and very dodgy. But we're getting there. I just hope we can keep all the balls in the air.'

'Well that's the other reason I phoned. Ami hired an amazingly bright Basotho girl who has just passed out top in the UCT Maths faculty finals. We've employed her to help Tristan really push for an early scholarship to Cambridge but it's not working. Intellectually it's a case of like poles repel and biologically, it's upsetting young Tristan's hormones something rotten. She doesn't know it but she's dynamite – a fabulous looker as well as genius! I was thinking: how about her handling the shares account for you and see whether you think she's fit to oversee the whole Siyeza shooting match for you – I tell you, this girl stops the Adderley Street rush hour traffic!' They both laughed spontaneously. Kobus had trusted Richard's judgement so far with his own, and now the Municipality's financial trading. There was plenty of work for dedicated professionals in the Municipality offices, provided they had no political baggage. The thought of Rita's reacting badly to news of a black hottie working in the next-door office crossed Kobus' mind but he dismissed it as irrelevant – she would have to be grown up about it.

'I cannot look a gift horse in the mouth, my friend. Send her along. We're beginning to get submerged and I'm considering restructuring the management lines here to make us more efficient. What sort of salary are you thinking about?'

'I think you'll be impressed. Make it a one-off job to handle the rights issue account and let her move it into an overall Siyeza bundle. Half a million bucks to kick off?'

'Jeez, she better be good. Anyway let's have a look at her. From what you say, nobody turns her down!'

'Funnily enough, she's not a party girl – strict rich Daddy in Lesotho. But she's lovely wallpaper!'

Richard rang off, breathing more evenly. If Lesebo did as she threatened and told Ami, he could at least move her on promptly to an impressive and central job, under circumstances that need not betray the Kirkside secret. But controlling Ami was another matter.

*****

45

Lesebo Bafokeng had cried inwardly for days, without a friend to share her grief. She had not realised how introverted she had become, setting herself such high goals and refusing to relax her social codes in a shockingly lax student environment with casual sex, intoxication and drug use. And now, feeling dirty and violated, she had no shoulder to cry on, including her father, whose confidence she had not dared to share. Kirkside had been back to her twice more, pleading for them to continue as secret lovers, keeping the truth from Ami. But for Lesebo that was unthinkable. She had tried so hard and for so long to keep personal control of her destiny and Kirkside had shattered that for a few minutes' brutal gratification on a cold kitchen floor. It had felt ugly, it had hurt her physically and she had not experienced a second of excitement or even fondness for him. Judging by the way she felt now, she would never change that view. Worse, she already knew, would be falling in love one day with a man with whom she wanted children in a family – how could that happen now?

Lesebo's mourning was interrupted by a sharp knock on her door. She had locked it but heard Ami's voice calling:

'Lesebo, please let me in. I want to talk to you immediately please.' Ami's tone terrified Lesebo. The cheated white wife and the young black seducer. Could God be on the side of the innocent? She walked softly to the door and gently turned the key. She stepped back and opened the door wide, seeing Ami looking prim and formal in a yellow silk shirt and loosely twined scarf over a straight black skirt worn above the knee, with flat sandals.

'Let's sit down Lesebo please.' Ami waved aside the offer of a proffered coffee as they pulled out chairs with padded seats and sat opposite each other across the small dining table in Lesebo's breakfast-kitchen room. Lesebo was dumbstruck. She could find no courage to pretend self-confidence but felt an inner anger at becoming a circumstantial victim, then accused.

'How long have you been fucking my husband, Lesebo?'

'Never. He fucked me once against my will.'

'Would you lie to me about this?'

'Ask him. I was a virgin. It was to all intents and purposes rape. I bled for two days. I have never liked him and now I hate him. You are wrong to ask such a horrid question and assume I wanted it to happen. Is it your turn now to violate me with words?' Lesebo's courage had swelled up from nowhere. She was suddenly at her imperious best, staring at Ami with haughty indignation. Ami was momentarily thrown off track.

'Well, what did this innocent little virgin wear on the evening in question, seizing your chance while I was out? If it was so sudden, you must have been accessible?'

'It was a hot evening. I went to the kitchen to make some cocoa before going to bed. I was wearing a light top and some running shorts.'

'So you looked pretty inviting and they came off in five seconds? Did you intend to start something?'

'Absolutely not. Richard took one look, ripped off my clothes and threw me on the floor.'

'Have you done it again? Has he tried to? What has he said to you? Does he want it to go on or is he paying you off?'

'Ami, you're letting yourself down. I was the victim, you are the abused. Richard has harmed us both. I must go, obviously, but I haven't decided whether to press charges of rape against him. Or at the very least, make it widely known – the power of social media and all that. No man should get away with treating a woman that way – is that all I worked for after beating every man fair and square at UCT?'

'Dead right you must go, Lesebo. I haven't spoken to Richard about this yet, so I'd wait until then. I don't think I can stay here either but let's see.' There was nothing superior about Ami as she strode out of Lesebo's quarter. The tall girl collapsed onto her sofa, her mind whirring. Would Ami leave Richard? Would that be just retribution? What would the Kirksides suggest to her? Would she co-operate and if not, where would she go?

It was Maddox's weekly rendezvous with Brigadier General Khanyisile Mthembu, this time in the picturesque Gardens district at a vegetarian restaurant specialising in Lebanese dishes. Like most moments in Maddox's day-to-day life, it was an adventurous occasion. Gone were the peremptory ten-minute exchanges in an anti-septic high-rise office or furtive encounters in experimental coffee shops. Having visited the General in her headquarters, it was agreed that it was unwise for him to be seen there regularly and he had selected an increasingly ambitious choice of lunchtime restaurants for their weekly meetings. The dying curmudgeon reminded him of the costs and time involved but he reflected on how his clientele were increasingly impressed by the swish outer-office frills – cynically, the customer paid for the relaxed experiences.

The open plan kitchen offered all manner of delicious shawarmas, a Levantine Arab meat preparation, either as a fast-food wrap or within a more elaborate combination. Khanyisile was generously proportioned and seemed to enjoy the weekly excursions conducted by Maddox. She had long ago settled into a ruthless routine of three cooked meals a day, of which at least two centred on meat.

'So some progress at last, Maddox?'

'Very much so, Khanyisile, yes. We have the ballistic read-out which confirms the SAPS analysis but we're suffering from their inaction from that point, I'm afraid. Our guess is that the weapon used to kill Solomons was the same one used in four other shootings in the nearby area within the last eighteen months – Ottery and Philippi. They were gangland shootings, defending or aggressive action within well-established drug manors. With a bit of energy, that could be found or the research narrowed through audit but your boys don't want to know. I regret to say that they won't go too far in naming names or even gangs, for fear of retribution. I've actually been astounded at how far the power of the drug barons extends, undoubtedly accelerated by a compliant police authority.' Maddox took a large bite of his mixed meats shawarma and sipped his Diet Coke while Khanyisile was unable to join in while she dealt with her double portion of accompanying French fries.

'We're almost at a point where we can link Sonny Chopra's little sideshow with the probable gang leader in Manenberg who carried out the job. From what we're finding out, it seems that Chetty is using Chopra as hatchet man around the Flats fringes, but that this is uncharacteristic of him. It coincided with all the sudden overseas interest in Siyeza, so we're doing our best to see how far the Dutch contingent might have been involved. We've got a reasonable history on them, which is revealing. They're extremely bad buggers who have connections to Belgian, French and even German crime syndicates. We suspect that there is a strong link between them and Ravi Chetty, but it's all a bit hazy because of the ANC-Dutch recent chummy stuff.' Maddox was under contractual remit to tell the General all he knew but there were limits to the prospective help that might be obtained from clandestine SAPS sources. There was a cross benefit that he hoped to cultivate from these weekly meetings too.

'Any interest being shown by your sister or brother-in-law in all this?' he said, smiling gently while sipping his Coke.

'Not directly to me. But I know all about the pressure Jali is bringing on my subordinates. The report's limitations and dead ends have been mapped out in advance by senior ANC attorneys. That's why you're here. But I'm hearing how difficult it is for you, depending to a large extent on unofficial and sometimes irregular access to privy information belonging to SAPS. I'll do what I can but if the word is coming out from the Presidency, we must all be sensible and realise we cannot resist it. Again, that's why you can play such an important part for us all, not just me. I think your findings will coincide with other statements and high-profile comments, that'll make everything easier for you!'

Maddox smiled and drifted off to thinking about his forthcoming evening session with Steady Eddie, the Mowbray tennis club pro. He had been told to move his feet more and in order to do so, to abandon his ginger hiking boots with long laces. The outlay amazed him, paying as much money for playing tennis on squashy platforms as he last did for a pair of London brogues. But for the first time, he had undertaken to hire a floodlit court to share with Mrs Katie Rawlinson, 'Just to see how he felt away from the coach.'

Ami had been devious in making strenuous love to Richard and complimenting him on his virility and versatility. There was a delicious deceit in doing this, with her selection of exactly the right moment uppermost in her mind. They took a languorous shower, with her mock encouragement to initiate an even bolder coupling while she dried one foot on the sunken oval bath. He couldn't match that but was encouraged to bring out a bottle of champagne to their bedroom balcony, with glorious views of the sea and its twinkling shoreline.

'You were marvellous sweetheart, better than ever. I'm so lucky to have such a potent husband. So many of my friends haven't had sex for months, you know – it really is unfashionable among the over-forties. Anyway, the intelligentsia debate it, not do it! They clinked glasses and sat in their puffy wicker chairs, their dressing gowns loose around them. After a glass, Ami provocatively pulled her gown apart and fingered her nipple, fixing Richard with a come-hither open-mouthed grin. She lifted a bare foot and began stroking Richard's thigh. She aroused him quickly and pulled her chair to face him, sliding down on her cushioned lining to lie wide legged, with her knees outside his legs. He put his glass to the side, opened his robe and knelt in front of her.

'Ah my young lover! Who says you can't go twice in an hour, like times of old my darling?' She giggled and helped him mount her, moaning deeply. He began to whisper deeply himself, now determined to prove his ability.

'It's just like Lesebo described it darling. When you see bare tits, up you come and in you go. She said it didn't last long and you were a bit rough with her?' Richard froze in his gliding thrusts.

'What the hell are you drivelling about?'

'Not drivelling darling. Please keep going. She was a virgin you see and it wasn't quite the romantic moment she expected with a fat lobola in a few years' time. You screwed it in more ways than one, it seems!' Richard pulled out and scrambled back to his chair, closing his robe and wiping himself dry. Ami didn't move from her prostitute's pose, everything in view, her face sharpened to an angry stare.

'What are you going to do? Deny it? Run off with your new black hottie? Pay her off? Swear to start a new life? Guard your millions with a pack of lies? Would you like me to give you the video for your birthday? Or would you like me to parade Lesebo in front of us to give us her view of what happened?' Ami sat up abruptly, pulling her gown together and tightening its cord. 'I loathe you Richard Kirkside. You are a depraved and pathetic creature, who fucks an innocent twenty-three-year-old black virgin because you fancy her and judge her available. A bit on the side. Well look. This is a problem you began and you must bloody well finish it. I'm off with Tristan very soon. Tell me what you plan, because the world wants to know: me, Tristan, Lesebo, her father, your investors, the UCT and the social media piranhas. You'll be picked clean and bloody good riddance. Go to her now if you like, because I'm locking you out from now on!' Ami swept away, kicking her champagne glass and shattering it as it crashed against the wall. It made a fitting sound and symbol for Richard Kirkside as he stared out at the sea, draining his champagne: glittering, jagged fragments lying worthless in a wasted pool of privilege.

Richard sent Lesebo an immediate SMS message, feeling a prisoner in his own house. *DISCUSSED WITH A. TAKEN FULL BLAME. SHE IS LEAVING WITH T. FOUND YOU A WELL PAID AND HIGH-PROFILE JOB STARTING TOMORROW IF YOU WISH. MUST TALK AFTER BREAKFAST.* He followed up with a second message to Kobus: *WILL SEND OR BRING L TOMORROW FOR JOB INTERVIEW. SORRY TO BOUNCE YOU BUT YOU WILL BE VERY HAPPY.*

As he did that, Aimi sat on her bed and sent a tearful message to Professor Ashwin Chetty: *ASHWIN DARLING. HOPE YOU TOOK MY THREAT SERIOUSLY: WILL BRING TRISTAN TOMORROW TO STAY GRANNY FLAT. WILL MOVE KIT TO STORAGE AT WEEKEND, MINIMUM TIME YOUR PLACE WHILE I FIND GOOD FLAT. WILL PAY IN ADVANCE. WANT MINIMUM PUBLICITY WHILE THINGS SORT OUT. DON'T REPLY – TOO*

DISTRAUGHT. TALK EARLY AT WORK. YOUR KINDNESS A GODSEND. BLESS YOU. AMI. X.

The two breakfast conversations were both strained and emotional, but at least concluded with both Kirksides being granted their desperate wishes. Ami left very early, slamming every door she passed through, ending with her powerful car that sprayed chips as it sped away down the drive. She left a scrawled message amid the crumbs under a toast rack on the breakfast room table. Her engagement ring rested on top. *'Will take Tristan away this afternoon. Make decision about Lesebo – I will get her short-term student accommodation if she is still here tomorrow. My possessions go into storage on Saturday. Might not be home tonight. We should meet tomorrow to agree about access/keys/payment of invoices etc.'*

Richard stuffed the paper and ring into his pocket as he heard Lesebo approaching. She was dressed as though she was departing somewhere.

'Do you want some coffee or tea?'

'Tea.'

'Toast?

'Nothing. Can we talk now, since I'm in a rush?' Lesebo sat, awaiting the kettle's whistle. She appeared composed in a light, zipped jacket and clinging culottes, a colourful rimmed bandanna striking the usual electrifying first impression.

'Sure.' Richard placed their coffees on the table and pressed down the toaster handle. He sat opposite Lesebo. 'Lesebo, I don't know how your thoughts have gone since we last met but as I said, Ami sprang a really underhand trick yesterday and trapped me into an absolutely open admission of guilt as far as she is concerned. I neither confirmed nor denied what we'd done but she was able to quote everything in intimate detail – either you told her or we were traced somehow.'

'She did the same with me – she screamed the full facts before I opened my mouth!'

'Then she hired a spook, but why? We hadn't touched each other before Friday?' He stared to elicit a confession. Lesebo did not move and Richard continued. 'Anyway, the truth will emerge somehow but the important thing is to look after you.' He winced as he heard those words but Lesebo made no objection to the sentiment, waiting with gently clasped hands on the table. 'I've got you a job in the Mayor's office, running the huge Siyeza Rights Issue Fund that's set to raise two hundred billion to underwrite the Siyeza project on the DA's behalf. Once you've stabilised that, you'll co-opt it within the central Siyeza administration focus and assume responsibility for the on-site operation, steered personally by the Mayor, Kobus Labuschagne. Kobus is one of my private investment clients and I've facilitated the Rights Issue Fund's launch sponsorship, so know that he is crying out for high quality help. Your salary will kick off at half a million but ask for more very quickly. I have a penthouse flat reserved for you that we can visit after we've seen Kobus – don't worry, no tricks, I've paid the first three month's rent in your name and you can make changes downstream. You can keep the Golf, so don't worry about transport. How does this sound?' Kirkside looked suitably concerned for Lesebo as he encircled his coffee mug with his hands, his wedding ring clicking against the porcelain.

'I'll go. But only to keep my mind occupied and to give my father the impression that it was an offer that couldn't be refused. But you must understand that this changes nothing! I am ruined because of you and I have still not worked out what to do about it. But I hope that you suffer the same amount of pain.' Lesebo tucked her bottom lip under her top teeth, holding on to her emotions as she stared blinking beyond Kirkside into the garden, a branch of pink bougainvillea swaying in and out of the window's frame. She jerked Kirkside back into focus. 'Okay, let's go, what are we waiting for? What lies have you told Labuschagne about me – an easy lay coming his way? I don't suppose I need ask whether he's married, since it seems that girls are safer with single men.'

'I've said you're a cerebral star and that you weren't cut out to be a teenager's tutor – that's not far off the truth, is it? Anyway, he's snowed under and needs some intellectual heavyweights to bolster up a lacklustre staff. All he hopes is that you're not an ANC plant! And he's not married, by the way.' Richard tried a polite smile but cut it off – Lesebo was at her most austere. He was skating on very thin ice and however disastrous his own position might seem, he had to settle the whole Lesebo involvement first. 'Fine, then I made an appointment for eight thirty, if that's all right? I'll move your stuff whenever you're ready. Do you know the way? If not, just follow me, it's only a fifteen-minute drive at this time of day.'

*****

'Ashwin, you really are a wonderful friend, you know that? I'm too old to be your girl, too young to be your mother, too bright to be your acolyte…' It broke the ice, with both of them laughing to release the tension caused by these new embarrassments in their ten years together. Ashwin feigned mock anger, Ami ran a few skittish paces as they made their way through the UCT lawns to the best view of the sea. 'No, you know I'm kidding. But believe you me, when you *really* need a friend and the nearest has gone so far away, then you plummet the depths. But you're always here, through thick and thin and I really love you for it. The terrible thing is that you bring no reciprocal baggage – you seem to lead a life without anxiety or controversy?' Ami was not being false. Despite her present anguish, Ashwin would have been her first thought of refuge if he'd been living in Jo'burg or Durban.

'Put it down to platonic love, Ami. I worship your brain and your intellectual integrity. In ten years, you've become a bench mark and sounding board for me. We've never noticed our racial differences, or our gender or age – we revel in each other's minds. So if you ask to stay with me for a while, it's a natural thing to welcome it. You would take me in tomorrow, so it's all about helping each other, end of story. I'm guarding my intellectual mate with a new ferocity!'

Ashwin laughed loudly this time. He reached for her hand and nestled into her shoulder briefly.

'I know. I know. Of course I know. But the outside world can bring acrimony and poison. Let's be sensible, by moving in with my head of department, we're not improving our respective images, are we? It has all the melodrama ingredients, from race to gender, age to power. I promise you this will not take long. To be truthful, I'm already staggered at my misjudgement of opting to move out when I'm guiltless! But I must stick with one plan. Lesebo was meant to be a solution for Tristan and he now returns as a problem, through no fault of his own. So I'll see that through, without Richard's involvement. When that's sorted out, I'll be much more confident to look after myself and begin again.' Ami nudged Ashwin as they neared the rough plank benches that overlooked the ocean. She had a clip-down plastic lunch box in her copious handbag, with a rapidly amassed menu of Woolworths buffet delights and a bottle of Sauvignon Blanc to share in their plastic cups. She'd selected one without a cork in the Tops outlet and was now wondering whether she appeared too cunning? She'd noticed students recognising them but felt defensive – had they anything to lose, whether their news stayed private or blew wide open on Face Book?

*****

Kobus couldn't believe his eyes. As a forty-eight-year-old Afrikaner from Bloemfontein, who still felt challenged on the verge of reaching the head of a political party his grandfather would have despised, he was never fully relaxed. As Rita, his cooling girlfriend reminded him a month before, the only thing that was slipping through his fingers was time. He had the power, the money, the backers and the will to move to the top, on the back of a spectacular term as Cape Town Mayor. But Kobus wondered whether Rita was writing her own lament; at 35, she had a last chance to have a child and a last chance to marry well.

Maybe that's why he couldn't believe his eyes as Richard Kirkside held his office doors apart for his Goddess-like companion. Tall and elegant, with a confident presence, her entry was an entirely pleasurable experience for Kobus. Was this the woman Richard was recommending as one of his pillar deputies, to safely entrench his precious Rights Issue Fund and so cement the DA position as rightful custodians of all things Siyeza? And if successful, would this head-hunting coup enhance his imagery for election as DA leader, eighteen months ahead of the next national general election? He stood up clumsily as a beaming Richard approached him alongside his unsmiling PA, wincing momentarily as his shins struck the ancient Voortrekker bureau.

'Kobus! *Hoe gaan dit met jou? Laat ek u voorstel. Mejuffrou Bafokeng, Meneer Labuschagne.*'

'*Goeiemiddag, Juffrou!*'

'Hi.' Lesebo was going to start as she intended to go on, from the safest and highest ground. She eyed up Kobus and felt no animosity. A big, affable man who was building his own personality cult at breakneck speed. 'Come and sit here please. We've some coffee and scones on the way. Richard, are you staying with us? It would be good to hear someone singing Lesebo's praises in case she's too modest?'

'I don't think so Kobus, thanks. Lesebo has her own car here. Let's stay in touch, heh? If Lesebo cannot launch the Rights Issue, then Siyeza is dead and buried! She'll tell you where her ambitions lie but I'm sure she'll straighten out a few minds when it comes to logic and the art of the possible!' It was dawning on Richard, perhaps a bit late that his platitudes and hyperboles were wearing thin. Lesebo was looking at him distastefully and he felt diminished. He excused himself from the Municipality Offices and hurried back home, thinking about Ami's activities at UCT and the effects of having an estranged wife living with a younger Indian.

*****

'So, Miss Bafokeng, you've never worked in a corporate or municipal workplace before?'

'No. UCT, the Kirksides, now here.' Lesebo allowed herself upturned lips. Her thoughts since breakfast were crowding in fast. Richard Kirkside had done wrong to her in all respects but without letting him know, he had also been a revolting sexual prospect. Lesebo had been brought up as a Brahmin Basotho but that involved a generous measure of racial judgement and measurement. Kirkside had been an anaemic factor until his act of violation. Thereafter, Lesebo found her judgement clouded by race, power, wealth, gender, age and intellect. A white plutocrat had violated her as his younger employee, which was nothing more than the history of existence in the Western Cape through the centuries. It followed, in her simple analysis, that this powerful and fiercely ambitious Afrikaner would be no different? In fact, to take it to extremes, was it an important event in the minds of these people? Historically, they had Khois, Malays or Hottentots, then Xhosas and Zulus for domestic sex. They still wanted to now, but social codes had adapted. This lonely Afrikaner looked vulnerable through his tough business façade.

'I'm told your academic achievements are exceptional. We'll ask for credentials obviously but it seems you need to occupy yourself with some appropriate challenges.' Kobus waved a vast pamphlet in his hand that they'd used to announce the forthcoming launch of the Rights Issue Fund. 'Bedtime reading before you start tomorrow, heh?'

'I think you ought to explain it to me in detail before I sleep tonight, Kobus.' Lesebo was smiling her most winning of expressions, straightening up in her chair to show her shape down the front from neck to hips. She got up from her chair and stepped nearer to Kobus, holding his shoulders as she kissed him fully, with full strong lips preventing him doing anything other than returning her warmth forcefully. Kobus had lived a life of education, rugby and family ambition. He had friends from farms who boasted about their secret black girlfriends but he had never got close to one before. He was overwhelmed by all her differences and immediately felt bound to prove he was more than capable and willing to match her excitement. During those inexplicable moments, he was no more able to justify nor explain his actions than Richard Kirkside had been ten days before. But for Lesebo, this was a deliberate reversal of roles; she was the calculating and irresistible predator, Kobus the powerless victim. It was the first step towards her revenge against Richard Kirkside, male domination, racial slavery, capitalist exploitation and a Eurocentric Africa. With no experience other than the brief horrors with Kirkside, she willed herself to appear the seductive lover, hoping that Labuschagne would be considerate and gentle.

Chapter Five

'No, but Maddox – that's just not true! Your backhand returns are so much stronger now that you're moving faster to the ball. I think it's amazing how Eddy has brought you on like that in just a few weeks.' Katie Rawlinson beamed across the net in their floodlit Mowbray tennis club court. 'I think you're ready for social doubles now – I'll happily partner you if you wish. Or maybe you'd like another couple of sessions with Eddy, concentrating on your serve and volleying at the net?' She oozed encouragement and sincerity and Maddox was disarmed.

Maddox had complained despairingly as another backhand had soared over the steel netting fence but had recovered composure as he realised he was more or less managing with the adorable Katie, bouncy and nimble in her short white tennis dress. More than anyone else, Katie was frightening off the curmudgeon dragon, making Maddox besotted. He loved the simple things they did together at least once a week – a latest film plus supper, a vineyard lunch, a jazz club evening. Somehow, 'social doubles' seemed irresistible.

They made their way to the clubhouse, where an "Honesty Bar" provided refreshments. Ever the social secretary, Katie had made sure another couple were playing under floodlight, making the surroundings more relaxed. But little did she know that her friend's partner was Travis Heggie, a seasoned columnist from the *Cape Times*, with whom Maddox used to while away an evening in the newly emerging Waterfront twenty years before. In the South African way, the quartet segregated by gender and Travis began grilling Maddox about Siyeza.

'I'm hearing you're involved on the Solomons' case? Is that right? It all sounds a bit grim?'

'There isn't a copper in Cape Town not involved, nor a security agency,' was Maddox's best effort at protecting his position.

Heggie stared hard. 'I haven't seen you for a while Maddox, but you haven't changed, mate!' Maddox smiled while reflecting equally hard. The evidence he'd collected was not going to improve and although the SAPS attitude to the Solomons case was stubbornly fixed, Maddox now realised that it was time for him to present his case, take the fee and run. There were bigger fish to fry. He caught Katie's eye.

'Are you making your way out, Katie? I'll follow you out to the Claremont roundabout and bid you farewell?' Katie smiled as she gathered her belongings slowly, making no fuss of leaving their friends. The relationship was developing so well that neither of them felt a need to accelerate nor slow down. Maddox was satisfied about this but was getting anti-curmudgeon urges – should he not force the pace with such an attractive woman with whom he had found friendship by accidental chance?

*****

Khanyisile Mthembu was more animated than usual during her next lunch date with Maddox at the Buitenverwachting fashionable outdoors restaurant on the edge of Constantia. Maddox intended it to be their final clandestine meeting and had risked splashing out with an above average setting, cuisine and wine. His business instincts reminded him that this would make it easier for them both as he passed Khanyisile a hefty invoice to dent her slush fund. They were sharing one of the vineyard's famous hamper lunches, alone at a small table tucked underneath a towering London oak tree, with a light breeze keeping down the warm afternoon temperature.

'So really, all you've done is complete the whole picture that we refused to finish?' Khanyisile crunched some croutons within her broccoli and anchovy salad as she watched Maddox sip his house Sauvignon Blanc. 'That's a perfect solution for me, you know that, don't you?'

'I think the detection was not too difficult but your boys are only telling three-quarters of the story. My guess is that they know everything that we do but are holding back under instructions, probably issued through bribery. You'll see in the dossier I've given you how the evidence linking Solly and therefore Ravi Chetty to the Manenberg drugs lord hit man is as plain as a pikestaff. Solomons was murdered by being shot through the head in his car as he arrived in the neighbourhood. The assassination paraphernalia was a Chetty embellishment, a bit of lurid criminal theatre to impress De Vries who was the banker throughout. So SAPS can arrest the Manenberg killers and can definitely get convictions, but they are being told that the background story is unclear and won't pass muster in court. It's my guess that Chetty put in the bribe as well on your boys – I've named the two officers who appear involved.'

'You've done really well Maddox. I wish you were my senior investigator. We'll put those killers away as fast as I can push things but the bent cops on my squad sickens me. I knew it was going on, which made me engage you anyway but where do I go now, with all the different pressures from my sister and brother-in-law?'

Maddox sympathised in part with Khanyisile. He was certain that the Nhleko position would cause further problems, with the growing magnitude of the Siyeza plan fostering irresistible temptations for government ministers, everyone in the development's tendering circus and the major sponsors. The agency's recent commercial successes had fallen in step with the renewed spirit of Maddox the buoyant entrepreneur, which he made apparent at that point to Khanyisile Mthembu.

'Khanyisile, I've been thinking. Maybe there's ongoing police advice I can give you until this Siyeza cloud passes over? I respect the fact that my contract over the Solomon murder ends here but as you say, your management difficulties are not going to go away as elections loom and big-time development begins on the Flats.' Maddox finished his glass of wine and placed it among the picnic hamper debris on their wrought iron table. He paused before using both hands to gently emphasise his spontaneous proposal. 'I'd appreciate settlement so we can draw a line under Solomon. But what about a retaining contract obliging me to give you information that will defend your position and decisions as political pressure increases? I have a strong suspicion that there will be further serious crimes related to Siyeza where your investigating teams are going to embarrass you unless you either clean out the team or go public on the corruption culprits? I would be a telephone call away to run an enquiry that would probably give you truthful information faster than it would take your team to cover the bush track with a bare twig?' He smiled and watched her stare at the distant paddock with grazing horses as she bit into a surviving radish.

'I have very much enjoyed our lunches Maddox. If we do as you say, I insist on elevating things to an evening dinner once a month!' They laughed loudly in unison. Maddox wondered whether he had made a suggestion that was to have far-reaching consequences or whether it would become a millstone round his neck. He decided there and then to keep the SAPS contact intact; the repercussions from the Kirkside scandal were about to filter through the financial dealing of several influential Siyeza players and as a modest punter, he needed all the advance intelligence he could obtain.

*****

Ravi Chetty sat with Sonny Chopra in the cocktail bar overlooking the Rondebosch golf course. The two call girls Ravi had ordered sat at an adjacent table sipping mixers, demure and in-place with their dinner plate shades and simple knee length dresses. The bar was thinly populated by golfers reliving their game and the odd couple enjoying aperitifs before dining.

'Sonny, we've got a job on, man. My informer tells me that they've fingered our Manenberg friend who has decided to squeal. We don't need that, brah. The case looks a given, he says, and they're offering the munt ten years off to talk in court.' Sonny stayed immobile, spoek'n diesel in hand, anticipating his boss' thoughts. 'So it's a no-brainer. We must rub him out Sonny. My cop will give him 24 hours compassionate parole when I tell him and I want you to arrange something nice and obvious in Manenberg again – nothing fancy heh? Just another Capie gang quarrel because they heard he was squealing on them – put the word out just beforehand. Simple stuff – bullet in the head, okay?' Sonny nodded. He worried about how close the police had got to his name if the munt had started singing already – maybe the sooner the better to rub him out. Some of these friendly cops made plenty of money playing the double.

'Sure, yeah OK. No probs. Let's do it quick – maybe Sunday for a parole heh?'

'Dead on. Set things up for then.' Ravi slammed his glass down and stared at the girls. 'We're going to have to watch that fucking Dutchman, by the way.

He won't want connections to gang wars. But we've got to wait until we know where his money's going – I reckon he's buying off Jali as well.' He stretched his joined palms behind his head and grinned. 'Okay Sonny, which one is yours? I'm saying you take the smaller one because I would hurt her, eh?' They sniggered together as they rose, the two girls gliding out behind them without a word nor glance exchanged.

*****

Malusi Jali looked overdressed in the Cape Town SABC studio. He was wearing one of the three new suits he had bought from his Constantia Village tailor and regretted it under the hot glare of the studio lights. An off-set assistant had mopped his brow twice with a pad and applied light powder but it had made no difference. He had convinced himself that the interview was a big moment for him and the party, a first moment to declare the ANC's hand officially regarding Siyeza, so a formal appearance was important. His interviewer, Hennie Strydom, sat beyond a low table between them, looking cool to the point of seeming disinterested. They had run through the first question and the broad drift that was likely to be followed. Strydom was the regular anchor for *Cape Trends* each Wednesday evening, and enjoyed a local reputation as a fair but thorough interviewer. The lights switched, a digital chime sounded and Strydom was into his stride.

'Welcome to *Cape Trends*. I'm Hennie Strydom and I'll be with you for the next twenty minutes, having a close look at something that Capetonians have begun to regard as the city's major talking point and prospect for development that has ever come our way – Siyeza. First mooted twenty years ago, it has emerged in the last few months as potentially the greatest chance of all time to rid us of the squalor and shame that has characterised the Cape Flats since 1950 as "Apartheid's Dumping Ground". The 2011 census told us that a 15 percent growth over ten years had propelled the population to five hundred and seventy-five thousand. Unofficial estimates now put the Cape Flats Planning District population at six hundred and twenty thousand, 60 percent coloured, 35 percent black. While close on 70 percent of the workforce are employed, less than 50 percent of the inhabitants live in formal dwellings.' Strydom paused as the camera switched to the perspiring Jali.

'With me this evening is the Minister of Trade and Industry, the Honourable Mr Malusi Jali, into whose political bailiwick Siyeza lies. His wife is Mrs Lindiwe Nhleko, currently Minister of Women in the Presidency. Both are Cape Town residents and have played a prominent part in the enormous political flurry caused by Siyeza's emergence as the Province's prime hot potato. Mr Jali, welcome and thanks for agreeing to appear on the show. May I begin by asking you to outline the Siyeza proposal in broad terms for the viewer's benefits?' As Jali began to talk, the camera showed a map of the Cape Flats area, accompanied by a succession of graphics and listed headlines.

'Thank you for inviting me and good evening. Maybe it is an overdue opportunity to explain this exciting project to your viewers. It is important that they understand the government's intentions to make Siyeza a permanent legacy, justifying its relentless efforts to uplift the poorer sections of our society. At present the development targets exclude Khayelitsha, some of south Mitchells Plain and the coastal strip running between Muizenberg and Mitchells Plain. So although your figures are not disputed, I would guess that we're looking at directly effecting around 60 percent of the households, albeit over a five to seven-year period – hopefully eventually effecting around one hundred thousand dwellings.' Jali shuffled in his chair and glanced at his notes. He put a hand up to stop Strydom's next question.

'I think it would help if I finish explaining the project's objectives. With substantial foreign aid and co-ordinated government and provincial common interest, it is intended to upgrade all informal housing within designated districts and suburbs, supported by fully upgraded structural public services. That's roads, water, sewage, electricity and rubbish disposal, as well as schools and clinics,' Jali glanced at the notes, 'and care hostels, creches, sporting facilities, rail, bus and taxi services. And given private sector enterprise, at least two supermalls, banks, fuel stations and entertainment centres.'

Strydom nodded and rather than tie the conversation up over the broad outline, introduced the first controversial area.

'Nobody would doubt that this is a grand benefit for 15 percent of the Greater Cape Town inhabitants, but for over ten years now, the Western Cape has been run by the Democratic Alliance with a firmly entrenched DA Mayor and DA-controlled Municipal Council. When I spoke to Mayor Labuschagne this morning, he was at pains to remind me that the revived modern Siyeza project is very much a DA baby, if you like, with a Shares Fund already standing at around half a billion bucks.' Strydon watched Jali lick his lips and wriggle in his seat. 'Indeed, this fund seems to be attracting overseas capital too. Are we looking at a mismatch here or an unhelpful political spat between ANC and DA? Surely it's a municipal responsibility to manage Siyeza, along the same lines that Cape Town remained in charge of building Green Point Stadium for the Football World Cup?' Jali was prepared for this obvious question and had been drilled twice before the programme on how to handle it by an ANC team from the Presidency.

'You know, there really is no problem here, although I think the media is perhaps being a little mischievous. You see, you cannot have something as large as this being managed outside senior government hands – the Treasury is automatically committed with such a vast inflow of foreign capital, for example. And of course, it's not just the funding but the overall strategic significance and experience that we need to bring to the undertaking. Such resources are only found at government level – it may involve some international skills for example. Above and beyond this of course is the need to dovetail a housing and development programme of this size into the national grid from a funding, resource and equity perspective. So we're lucky to have an efficient and motivated mayor and municipality on hand – it really doesn't matter that they're currently DA, because it might be the ANC once more next year after the elections, and we cannot threaten such an enterprise with petty party politics.' Jali hoped he had put across a convincing answer but was bounced by the sharp retort from Strydom.

'Where's the foreign money coming from? Why are government and Province operating independently over fund raising?'

'Well, as ever with ambitious projects such as this, international institutions, banks, financial houses and consortia are either invited or offer themselves as investment partners...' but Strydom interrupted, since his producer was telling him to force the pace, since Jali had produced nothing that was not already in the public domain and the programme's time was half spent.

'Forgive me Minister, but I think the public needs to know why the government called for international assistance three months after the DA and Cape Town Municipality had launched the original investment? As I said, they have a colossally successful shares fund in operation, over half due to foreign investment. In effect, South Africa stands a decent chance of private enterprise virtually entirely underwriting a mega-development venture, principally to benefit half a million citizens that the ANC and other parties ignored for over sixty years! Who are the secret donors – I'm told a Dutch consortium are already heavily involved?' Jali was now both angry as well as physically uncomfortable, beads of sweat glistening over his forehead, his shirt collar dampening.

'Please do not over-step your remit, Mr Strydom! I cannot tell you about any financial involvement yet. The SABC does not pay you to criticise the government when it is so clear to your viewers that this is all about just another ANC success story – an ongoing result of responsible government management at the macro level. Of course this is a national affair, with the Province helping manage a project of national significance. If they handle it sensitively and efficiently, it could become the vanguard of a whole train of similarly ANC-inspired schemes at several other carefully selected population hubs. Let me emphasise...'

'Can you tell us about the Dutch involvement?'

'I cannot comment on financial matters at this stage. It is improper to ask that anyway, since the legal and financial structures are not in place.'

'So you cannot explain why two funds exist, one run by the national ANC and another by the provincial DA?'

'You must be patient and not grasp straws in the wind Mr Strydom...'

'Sadly, Minister, the public patience has long run out. I'd like to be very fair to you now. If I told you that next Wednesday's guest will be Mr Kobus Labuschagne, the elected mayor of Cape Town and a DA member of parliament, would that encourage you to be a little more open about this whole question of control of Siyeza?' Strydom looked very calm as he rolled this grenade towards Jali who knew instinctively that he had been trapped. Rather than obfuscate or be angry, he remembered how Nhleko had been insistent that Jali promoted the ANC's national party line.

'Equally sadly, Mr Strydom, I have found your demeanour unprofessional and offensive. I have given you clear answers. If you continue to be fascinated by a supposed controversy that never existed, then I can only suggest you address your enquiry direct to the Deputy President, Mr Jabu Nhleko? His office has overall control of all Trade and Industry matters above certain financial ceilings.' Jali sat forward offensively, pointing at Strydom as he raised his voice loudly. 'Meanwhile, I look forward to hearing how Mr Labuschagne intends to transform thirteen thousand square hectares in five years without recourse to foreign funding and skills. Remember one important fact Mr Strydom: the only democratically elected government ever to operate in the New South Africa is the ANC and unless Mr Labuschagne drops that pathetic provincial wrangling fast, he seems set to lose both municipality and province. It is becoming obvious that the only party capable of managing such a heaven-sent gift in the international arena is the ANC. They will do it on behalf of the nation's poor, homeless, downtrodden and unemployed...'

Jali's spirited recovery ran over time, with microphones turned off and Strydom and Jali seen leaning across the coffee tables to shake hands. With viewing figures matching a Stormers home match at Newlands, the Siyeza issue had become the headline that would run and run in Cape Town. The ambiguity about its management coincided with some radical action among those already connected to the project. The evening news that followed *Cape Trends* led with Siyeza, ahead of a report of a gang leader shot dead in Manenberg. He was out on compassionate parole from prison, awaiting trial for the murder of Benny Solomons. The TV reporter was circumspect about locals saying he had turned state witness to reduce his sentence, leading to his killing by others responsible for Solomon's slaughter. A SAPS spokesman confirmed that the murdered gang leader had indeed been charged with the murder of Solomons but said that their enquiries regarding his accomplices were continuing. The identity and position of the deceased would be published once family associates had been consulted.

*****

Lesebo Bafokeng had surprised herself at how both Kobus and she settled into a hollow chamber relationship so naturally. She had appeared for work the morning after their frantic coupling on his office sofa. He had paused at her office doorway, with a half-quizzical, half-amused expression but lacked the boldness to counter her frozen exterior. She had stared intently at her desktop screen, not even glancing in his direction. For the first couple of days, they treated each other dutifully, as if they just had to observe normal civility and the awkward relationship would fade into oblivion. Then Kobus realised that the general office atmosphere had become tense, with fellow officials sensing an unnatural attitude between Lesebo and himself. He overcame this to an extent by inviting others to join him in discussing Siyeza topics with Lesebo. She limited herself to cogent comment, delivered in a quiet and formal way. He noticed how she dressed down in a slightly academic fashion, with long, dull dresses and stretched cardigans.

She toned down her hair and make-up and could be found with legs curled under her on her office easy chair during lunch-time, munching an apple and reading high-brow economics magazines.

In fact, Lesebo was being patient for her first post-coital period to arrive. There had been ten days between the Richard and Kobus encounters, leaving a week to elapse in her menstrual cycle. The moment came and passed. She had never been late before, but was uncertain how sex, and indeed first sex, might influence the cycle. She had been brought savagely into the adult female's world by it all. Being a confident and aloof student star, she had never taken any contraception measures. For all her intellectual gifts, she was unworldly about sexual relationships and all the posturing and deceit that seemed to accompany them among her university friends. Periods came and went with her but she listened with semi-disdain when a fellow student had passed an aside about being late with a period and mentioned testing and possible abortion. She had no moral objection to all this but lived a consistently ascetic life within which she hoped that abortion would never arise. Her eventual husband would want children and she would provide them. But now, a week after her period was due, she went to an upmarket Constantia clinic and asked about pregnancy testing.

After testing with a urine test, Lesebo became upset. She found the procedure sordid and confusing and did not trust her technical interpretation. She had entered the wicked world for which she was half-responsible as victim of Richard, seducer of Kobus. A blood test followed with an expensive private doctor, with an interminable five day's further waiting for a result. She found the consequent interview with the doctor intimidating but soul-searching. She returned home alone to think hard and long before deciding upon her next course of action. She was determined to restore her equilibrium by substituting the now shattered path of marriage virginity with an equally logical but much more complicated plan.

*****

Bram De Vries fumed as he flicked through his fourth thumbed car magazine in the ante room adjoining Jabu Nheko's office. An hour has passed the appointment timing and apart from a waddling and trussed PA assuring him that the Deputy President had not forgotten him but had been unexpectedly delayed by a Chinese trade mission, he had been ignored. De Vries was not well disposed to Africa nor Africans: he wanted Nhleko to grasp the enormity of the Dutch offer and the depth of implications that already enveloped the Presidency. At the other end of the Siyeza scale, he wanted to straighten out Ravi Chetty and impress on him and his cronies their ham-fisted and inconsequential contribution towards the whole story, plus the very real danger they confronted if they threatened his position again.

'The Deputy President will be delighted to meet you now sir! Please follow me.' De Vries followed the PA, marvelling at the profundity of her rump that switched to alternate sides as she teetered in her tight high heels. There were creases under her arms, creases across her back and creases above her hips as her shiny and loud dress struggled with flesh intended for a garment three sizes larger. Was this the African emerging middle class? Did the upper class feel attracted and the lower class jealous – what was going on the no longer "New" South Africa? She opened a heavy mahogany door with polished brass fittings and stood aside for De Vries to enter. After a hurried dismissal of a more slender and younger female aide, Jabu Nhleko rose to meet him, psychological preparation complete: with Chinese super-power treaties and snatched dictation to secretaries, De Vries was incredibly fortunate to obtain a few minutes with this African potentate! Well versed in chicanery and treachery, double-dealing and dishonesty, De Vries took it in his stride and played the preferred role to start with.

'Mr Deputy President, it's obvious how busy you are and I really appreciate you finding time to see me. I realise how we might have communicated another way but I felt that I needed to discuss a few things with you to avoid any misunderstanding.' De Vries let Nhleko hang on to his hand with both hands after the statutory African hand shake. It was not a masculinity squeezing exercise practised by Europeans but rather an ineffectual moment when pleasantries are exchanged at very close range, as vacuous as it appeared in an empty room.

'Never, Comrade! You are never off my lips or out of my mind. I have impressed your name and its importance throughout the Presidency staff and am proud to be part of what will become one of the most prestigious partnerships this government has enjoyed!' Nheko ushered De Vries to a sumptuous easy chair and sat in his own sequel, except that the back was conspicuously higher and monogrammed. 'Bram, if I may be personal – please call me Jabu – would you like some iced tea or maybe something a little more fortifying?' With De Vries declining, Nheko placed all his fingers together and beamed at De Vries. 'Well, my friend, it's your call – you asked to see me so you must tell me what's on your mind!'

'Thanks Jabu. Look, I'm not a great one for beating about the bush, so forgive me if I respect your time. Siyeza's caught the overseas market's eye as you know, since the whole thing is way too expensive for any third world country to handle. My guess is that you'll have to bend on your 51 percent investment to get going, let alone see things through. As you know, I'm involved in a wide range of activities, some of which I see as important as the housing deal, quite simply because they keep me going. I'm no philanthropist and as a fellow man of the world, we have to accommodate partners all the time in different ways in order to keep a common objective on track.' Nheko sat impassively, hands clasped across his bloated stomach. The air-conditioning unit blew a cool stream of air their way, reducing the vapid Pretoria climate. De Vries didn't want to spend long with this lightweight politician but wanted to make it clear that his advantages over Nhleko were very real. 'Okay, that being said, you're looking for quick and non-governmental cash inflow that will not just launch and sustain Siyeza but will put you on the pharaoh's throne for re-election or who knows, promotion to the highest position in the land? I can facilitate all that for you, you know.' De Vries waited for this to sink in, but Nhleko scarcely moved. 'But my conditions are straightforward too. First, you make me the prime overseas bidder for the structural project work, from services to housing and civic amenities. By that I mean entertainment and by that I mean big-time clubs and gambling. That's how I line your pockets to become President, okay? Nothing is public and everything is filtered through world-class financial lawyers and Swiss banks. We will look after your account and future 100 percent. We've done this with two other African Presidents as I think you'll have heard, so the system works fine.' De Vries smiled as far as he ever allowed. Nhleko had grown sufficiently hardened by habitual graft to prevent him being over-impressed or enthralled. He waited for any trace that might expose him before the election or in the fullness of his term, leave him to inherit corruption charges or even smears.

'No, Bram, that's all in order. It's good to take off the gloves when alone – this isn't being recorded.' Nhleko lied implausibly, bringing another faint smile from De Vries.

'I haven't quite finished though, Jabu.' De Vries sat forward, bringing his sinister face closer to Jabu, a hairless jagged scar showing clearly on his jaw. 'A few things have worried me recently. Firstly, that arsehole Jali was on your prime-time TV interrogation show, saying that you must front up about the funding and control of Siyeza. What the fuck's going on, man? Who's the Deputy President round here? Can we get things sorted? And then that lowlife shit Ravi Chetty kills off some drug gang hopeful because he's turned state witness for the cops! I'm telling you straight. If he'd sung, all deals with you would have been off and who knows, you might have had to answer up to a corruption charge. I don't want to debate this one Jabu, but you're dealing with a grown-up foreign firm. I want to close my bets and put everything on your number but I still need some reassurance that you're safe. Until then, I'm staying in Siyeza on two fronts. Do you follow me – I've got fingers in the local Cape Flats drawers and the people aren't very nice...' De Vries leant backwards, his delivery complete. He watched nervousness spread over Nhleko for the first time. The fat man was looking away and became fidgety.

'Bram, I guessed all this. I understand why you're backing two horses. But I think we can do something about Ravi Chetty. For us, the most important factor is Labuschagne and the DA. There's an election round the corner and they already have the Western Cape in the bag. Everything works in Cape Town and we'll never overturn them there unless we hit lucky with really dirty tricks. They've set up an alternative fund that's getting more inflow than ours so we look a bit stupid at the moment.'

'Do something about your image. You're all coming across as a bunch of greedy last-hope cronies. Get clever about the way you do things and stop the bickering – what have unions and communists got to do with inward investment, when you're 30 percent unemployed?' De Vries felt he'd said enough without making Nhleko feel impotent and resentful – there was no shortage of fellow travellers willing to come to the ANC's aid, whatever he said. The meeting ended amicably but neither participant either liked or trusted the other. Nhleko felt neutralised and De Vries was more dubious than ever. His later meeting with Chetty was hardly more rewarding.

*****

Ravi Chetty brought three henchmen, including Sonny Chopra, to the meeting at the Grand West Casino outside the city centre. They were all dressed for action in shining suits without ties, ubiquitous girls in tow playing blackjack. It was Ravi's choice of venue and a deliberate ploy, similar to the high office pitch made by Nhleko – it was a power game move to stand up to the anticipated bluster and threats from a foreign criminal. De Vries reflected on his own past and rake's progress. From small time insurance agent, then security company chancer and a bit of enforcement, he'd hit lucky with immigrant housing and labour deals before drifting into the tougher world of organised white-collar crime in Amsterdam. He now operated a two-tier existence, with an impressive legal development capability he deployed internationally and an underground network of online scamming, entertainment and immigrant labour employment that supplemented his overseas ventures. He had reached a stage where he could comfortably operate on a visible high plane, without being seen below. It was ironic that he was meeting Cape Town's biggest mobster at the kind of establishment he knew he could replicate, with different imagery, at Cape Flats.

'Good evening, Ravi. An evening out for the family? Any chance of a private chat, do you think?' De Vries was having trouble hiding his reaction to Chetty's response to meet up to discuss "things that weren't going quite right". There was no doubt that he needed Chetty to perform local dirty work but there were other ways of reaching a successful Siyeza conclusion.

'You well Bram? Where did we meet last? Was it Cape Town? Anyway, welcome. Look we come here now and again and play a bit. Don't you like my friends?' Ravi indicated the girls at the tables, one of whom was in a contrived provocative pose. Sonny and the others looked spare, drinking at a table without conversation. De Vries summed it up as an attempt at grandeur in a noisy and glittering lights setting and responded accordingly.

'Ravi, no flesh tonight, my friend! I must be getting old but I'm not finding them as good as they were, once-upon-a-time!' De Vries looked around and added, 'Nice place but not quite right for us tonight. Can we find a poker room without the razzmatazz?' He was shouting and losing patience. Ravi stood still, considering whether this either meant loss of face or diminished trade. He knew how De Vries was riled about the gangland killing and had hoped to avoid a one-on-one confrontation which the erudite De Vries, superbly bi-lingual, would win hands down.

'Pity you're a party pooper Bram. But I'm the host and Sonny must be there. Always helpful to carry a witness if you don't carry a gun, heh?'

'Not fussed Ravi but let's get going – I've had a heavy travel schedule and am not here to party.'

A flick of Ravi's fingers and a whisper to an Indian floor manager brought the three of them to a quiet corner, the folding green beige table placed against a wall, another low table spirited in, with a waiter on call for drinks. The hubbub of the gaming floors was subdued and the overhead fans made the room pleasant. De Vries was in no mood for another lengthy preamble.

'Ravi, it's important for us to meet. I want to talk about our size and importance.' Ravi and Sonny had wanted the first word but were uncertain about interrupting after such a provocative comment. Sonny swirled his whisky while Ravi pushed back his dark glasses on his nose, glancing at the fan. 'I've been all over but have run international partnerships for twenty years. I work both sides as you know and am well connected with the government here – probably at a higher level than you. So you have to understand that I'm an international trader, looking for deals. I like to keep the deals, but if they foul up, I take advice.' Sonny was deep into the "no white bastard is ever going to impress me" mode, immobile except for a shy sip of his brandy mixer. But Ravi was agitated, keen to keep his place in the rapidly expanding Cape Town development contracts field and his self-respect in the rewarding enforcement and contracts world. His close ANC connections promised an Indian in Cape Town favourable advantages, where ethnic balances ruled against him.

'Isn't this where we are? Have you come from Holland to say nothing?' Ravi knew this would provoke De Vries but not to the extent that resulted.

'Twenty years ago, you would not have got away with that, Ravi. Never mind. I've a lot to offer and very little to say, as opposed to you. Please listen carefully. I'm supporting both direct government intervention and provincial enterprise as far as Siyeza goes. So far, you've fucked up everything I paid you to avoid – half a million! You've used the wrong guy to kill Solomons and when he starts singing, you kill him. Meanwhile some ANC prat goes on TV to say that Nhleko must say whether Dutch money is involved. So what am I getting for that money, Ravi – answer, zilch! Let's get this clear: we'll dry you out, and I mean a drought man, if you ever fuck up anything else that carries my cash or Siyeza chances. You're not as big a crab in the Cape Flats sands as you imagine, my friend! Do you get it?' The message was unambiguous. Ravi Chetty never apologised. He pushed his chair back, nodding to Sonny, leaving himself a vestige of honour and chance with his major benefactor.

Chapter Six

'God, you look thin! Have you taken up Banting?' Ami Kirkside approached Richard through the attractively landscaped and manicured gardens at the Bistro 1682 café. He was in the shade of the tautly stretched table umbrella, seemingly in a reverie, a half-empty cup besides a coffee pot. There was an empty second cup opposite him and Ami slid into the seat, slim and tanned, behind her saucer sunglasses. Richard half rose, too slow to peck her cheek. He stood momentarily, glancing at his watch, realising with embarrassment his habitual irritation to his wife. He sat without speaking. 'I know, I know, I'm late but there we are! You haven't changed, except that you're definitely leaner – it suits you!' Ami waved to a waiter to fetch a fresh pot of coffee and produced a slim cigarette from her boat-shaped shoulder bag. She lit it and puffed amateurishly towards the garden spaces. ''Can I smoke here? Is someone going to throw me out?'

'No idea. Take a chance. Anyway, how long have you been doing that?' Ami had never smoked before, which further compounded Richard's unhappiness about their separation.

'Not long – since I left. It calms me down with morning coffee.' Ami turned to view the restaurant. 'They've sharpened this place up, haven't they? Very larny. Do you bring your clients here?' There was an edginess about Ami, spilling over into spite. She had difficulty relaxing and fiddled unnecessarily when the coffee arrived, spurning Richard's offer to percolate and pour.

'Actually I chose it because I wanted us to be alone and try to concentrate on some bad news I have for you.'

'Oh my God, what now? My little spies tell me you've become a recluse.'

'Just calm down for a few minutes Ami. This is important for us both.' Richard removed his sunglasses and sat forward, speaking in confidential tones. He drew a deep breath. 'Lesebo is pregnant.'

'Oh for Christ's sake, Richard! How do you know?'

'She came to see me – the first time we've met since she started work at the Municipality, by the way. She produced a registered blood test result. It showed with virtual certainty that she conceived six weeks ago, which was when, you know, we...'

'Fucked on my kitchen floor, you bloody lunatic!' Ami pummelled her cigarette into her saucer, with no ashtrays in sight in the clearly No Smoking area. 'So what are you going to do – adopt it and send it to Michaelhouse?'

'Ami, I told you to stay calm and hear me out!' Richard raised his voice but there were no adjacent tables occupied. 'She told me it was my child and asked what I wanted to do. Her options were a paternity suit or a rape charge. I told her I did not want it to go viral and that I would pay to terminate it. She said she would only do that if I paid her half a million bucks!' He waited to see how Ami responded.

'I told you she was smart. But what about me Richard? I'm still deliberating divorce proceedings. If it wasn't for dear Ashwin, I'd have filed already. My first reaction is to say you pay her what you bloody well want but it strengthens my resolve to get rid of you altogether!' Richard stared at her for some time, trying to read from her eyes and mouth.

'Look, I don't know about you but I'll never be able to tell you how much I regret what I have done to us and how much I miss you every minute of every day Ami.' He reached across for her wrist and noticed the engagement ring in place, without the wedding ring she had returned. He was surprised she did not pull away but rather left her arm limp in his hold. 'Whatever happens to us, she cannot have the child. She must have an abortion and be paid what she demands. I think the rape thing will go away because she does not want publicity either. And anyway, she was much more flirty that evening than she's letting on, by the way. So in a macabre sense, it closes an unfortunate chapter, doesn't it? Let's come together again now – I'll hire a visiting bearded male professor to tutor Tristan.' Richard risked a smile at his exaggerated suggestion but Ami was not warming.

'Richard, do as you wish. By all means close the curtains on this whole ghastly mess. I didn't go for a knee-jerk divorce but that doesn't mean that I can ever forgive you for what you've done or stop worrying about you doing it again, does it? You want your cake and to eat it, as ever, don't you? Well, you're going to have to sweat it out a bit longer Richard – let's see how your bored rich housewives behave when they hear we're living apart, shall we?' Ami smiled artificially, put her cigarettes and lighter back into her bag and pushed her chair back, smoothing her dress over her flat stomach. She stood up, slung her bag under her shoulder and kissed him lightly on the cheek without them touching. Richard watch her stride to the door as the waiter appeared to scowl and point melodramatically at the stubbed cigarette.

*****

Lesebo had applied her active mind to map out a new life. Being defiled by Richard Kirkside had fragmented her life. There had been no sacrificial discomfort in losing virginity; indeed as a beautiful girl, it was reassuring to know how love was to be found everywhere. The heart and mind were there to find one person above all others whom had come before or would follow. The artificial imposition of a prize by her father for retaining virginity until twenty-five years of age was helpful but not the main achievement. He adored her and wanted to demonstrate how he accepted the pressures that she would face in the decadent environment of UCT and a famous seaside city. But now that had been shattered and something else had to be built.

Kirkside must repent for what he had done. As a precocious philosopher and mathematician, Lesebo felt his sin embodied all that was wrong in the African woman's lot. He was male, he was rich, he was white, he was married, he was an employer and he was a pillar of ex-colonial society. He had abused all these advantages and rendered her powerless, discarded, self-critical and biased. His arrogance in brutalising her body was against ancient mores and cultures and he must now confront anything that modern society did to prevent or punish such sin. A charge of rape was a definite option, despite its certain personal degradation and its chances of being rejected. Public humiliation was possible but carried not only personal loss of pride but also risks of backfiring and exploding very publicly in her face. Causing the Kirksides to divorce was an option but brought heartache and loss of pride to Ami, whom Lesebo saw as blameless.

Lesebo's reasoning had been a prelude to her anxieties about pregnancy. When the specialist told her that she was pregnant, he had been very sympathetic about her choices. If she did not want the child, she could abort it medically before the seven-to-nine-week point or if she delayed, it could be aborted surgically within the first three months. Lesebo was immediately convinced to have a medical abortion but she knew there were other factors crowding in, not least her wild seduction of Kobus Labuschagne just ten days after the Kirkside horrors. But she had to consider that Kobus was the father too.

Being as responsible for what happened with Kobus as Richard had been at deflowering her, Lesebo thought deeply about the most beneficial but appropriate retribution against Richard. She had done what she had with Kobus as premeditated revenge against the accumulated sins committed by Richard and his forebears and perhaps as statement of self-esteem. She had restored her pride, used her beauty and feminism, discovered about sexual attraction and its power, had strengthened her career and become an adult. She was well aware how these motives compromised her former tenets and cultural beliefs but her mind told her to act in her newly changed circumstances. In other words, she must move on fast and use all her natural advantages in a totally different way. So although Kobus was a victim too, there was a strong chance that it had not caused him personal harm.

Her conclusions became clear. She would tell Richard that she was pregnant and present him with certain proof. She knew he would not dispute paternity because of the video that Ami had mentioned. He would want her to abort. She would agree but only if half a million Rands were paid into an Investec account in the Channel Islands that Kirkside would establish anonymously. As far as Kobus went, she would never divulge the Kirkside moment but instead provide proof of her pregnancy along exactly the same lines as Richard. Although single, she knew that Kobus would want her to abort and once more, she would agree. But in this case, without wishing to harm Kobus, she would insist on accelerating her career with Siyeza. Lesebo hardened her heart. For five minutes' sex with two middle-aged white men, she would end up with an offshore Sterling account and a job that would soon carry benefits of over a million Rands a year – all before her twenty fifth birthday. And damage to her fellow man? Maybe they weren't adjusting fast enough to Africa's new drum beats?

*****

Kobus Labuschagne took his white hard hat, with its engraved municipality motif, from the back shelf of his Toyota Fortuna. It was a dull day with the dust hanging sullenly in the Hanover Park atmosphere. He gathered his rolled worksite planning map and made his way towards the diggers and cranes on the local horizon. He called Moses Sithole on his cell phone and made his way to an agreed meeting point. The lively site manager greeted him warmly and suggested they move away from the main centre of noise and dust.

'Big progress here Mo, since I last visited! Well done. I see they've begun the ring road already, which is great – we'll have some amenities in before we demolish the Zone Delta maisonettes.' The orange dust covered Moses' face, cleared only where he'd wiped his mouth or eyes. His blue overalls were coated with grime and even his yellow safety waistcoat showed trails of equipment spray and drips of sweat amid the dust coating. 'You're working your balls off Mo! Good for overtime but not so good for following the Urban Warriors, neh?' The foreman shook his head slowly – words failed him to describe the continual effort. 'But help is at hand. I tell you what: I'm going to put in a Project Manager to oversee the big expansion here, leaving you to concentrate better on the construction side. There's too much here for anyone to handle and it's going to get much worse quickly!' Kobus knew it wasn't the right place or time to mention Lesebo Bafokeng but felt happier just to have laid the seeds in readiness for her promotion. Relationships had improved slightly with her, since she had laid out her terms for staying with the Municipality without letting anyone know about their crazy few minutes together. He suspected it was as much a lunacy on both behalves but intended to check with Richard Kirkside about any known details on her private life. Meanwhile it made sense to satisfy her and protect his own reputation and political future. It seemed curious that neither of them had shown any signs of developing an intimate relationship further.

*****

Lesebo held her nerve. She made it quite clear to Richard that there would be no abortion, or medical documentation to certify it, until she received proof of payment into her new Investec offshore account. Her specialist's deadline for initiating medical action was easily met and four days after her course of treatment began, she experienced everything that he had predicted. Subsequent examination showed no internal damage or after-effects for later pregnancies. She showed the certification to both Richard and Kobus who reacted similarly: relief tinged with gratitude. Meanwhile Kobus had begun her lengthy induction as Overseeing Project Manager of Siyeza Pioneer Enterprise, firstly with designers, architects and development experts. A series of government briefings and an impressive Open Day and media briefing were held in the new, custom-built headquarters installed near the Hanover Park-Ottery borders. Considerable surprise was expressed in the media and Cape Town chattering classes about her relative youth and inexperience but the grasp and intelligence she displayed in interviews and discussions reduced criticism. The Siyeza spotlight slowly swung back to illuminate the government's involvement and the in-fighting at provincial level between political parties.

*****

Kobus Labuschagne had fared well on *Cape Trends*. Strydom's opening gambit was an uncompromising probe into the control and funding question which he had answered thoroughly and fully.

'Cape Town municipality, supported by the Provincial government, has clarified Siyeza's objectives and time lines – the expertise and funding to take us through the first two years are now in place. The essential services are being installed now and an arterial road and major social and civic amenities will follow. Then the housing project will begin, moving as fast as we can in the sequence I've told you.' Labuschagne made reassuring smoothing movements with his hands and allowed himself a smile. 'A first phase has started but because of its infrastructure, the public won't see the accommodation benefits yet. This is way beyond any local budget capability, so we have to protect management continuity.'

Labuschagne sat back and folded his hands together as in prayer. 'Now, who holds the whip hand in all this? The answer is every Capetonian and to an extent, every Western Province citizen and tax payer! We've designed a budget programme to reduce extra burdens on everyone. That said, taxation rates might rise between 3 and 5 percent for the first two years, before tapering away. Our Rights Shares Fund is performing strongly, with almost one hundred billion invested – I expect it to double in the next twelve months. Naturally, expenditure forecasts will bob a bit until tendering is finalised, but they'll stabilise after the contracts are finalised.'

Kobus considered pausing but was frightened of Strydom's ability to throw presentations off track. 'There has been lots of discussion, quite understandably, about the potential conflict between government and province. The fact is that I am in regular touch with Mr Jali, the Minister of Trade and Industry and indeed with the Deputy President. I'm always talking to the provincial government and cabinet, who are multi-party, and of course with my own party and its shadow ministers. I'm not aware of any criticism concerning the Municipality's place in the Siyeza driving seat. It's our natural function, relying on provincial and national governments, professional institutions, labour unions and some specialist quangos. As far as the National government fund goes, sadly, I think it's been seriously misrepresented. The reason why Siyeza has been dormant for twenty years is lack of central funding. When it woke up a couple of years ago, it was first and foremost based on Cape Town Municipality. We used private enterprise muscle to kick-start the project – hence our runaway investment fund. But even that won't cover the full expenditure – the government accepts that. So there's no "rival" fund. It's nothing more than government ring-fenced funding maintained for later distribution. So let's drop this aggravation for once and for all: we have funds for two years, with prospects of a further two to three years. So yes, government has a hand on the Siyeza tiller, which pleases me no end, but in my view, the forthcoming elections will have no serious detrimental effect on the enterprise. I'm still looking at five years for completion but we'll confirm this when contracts are publicised.'

Kobus' confident and clear account reassured the critics and Cape Town community. Journalists described him conspicuously out-manoeuvring Jali, which fanned the controversial flames. There was consensus that he had cut away most of the brushwood under which any corrupt political agenda might have hidden. His heart leapt when Lesebo phoned him out of the blue.

'Well done, Kobus. You were brilliant. You've made me feel much more confident!'

'Ah well, thanks Lesebo. That's really kind. I didn't expect you to call.'

'Praise where praise is due! But tell me, are you still filtering my visitors or can I keep my own diary?' This was put across in a half-jocular way but made Labuschagne remember what a formidable character she was.

'Let's talk it through. I think the symposiums run by us are going well? We need to keep the focus high locally, with critics saying we're not giving it sufficient the political and diplomatic clout? But let's appear together on some future profile or interview? By the way, I liked the features on you I saw in *Elle* and *Woman's Domain* – you're the talk of the town!'

'Thanks. Yeah, they weren't bad, a bit superficial maybe.' There was a pause as the conversation flagged. Kobus risked a personal note.

'How're you keeping, Lesebo?'

'Fine. And you?' As ever, Lesebo floored him.

'Ag you know, not too bad. Can't complain. I'll pop over and see you on site later in the week.'

'See you then.'

*****

'Brrr, I'm freezing! Just our luck. I thought we'd beat the wind and now it looks like its bringing rain. Let's go back to the restaurant for some tea and scones, to see if this blows over!' Katie was hugging herself, with only a thin jersey over her blouse. The cable car ride up Table Mountain was the latest amusement item to tick off their impressive list of things to do in the Cape Town area but the untrustworthy weather had changed sharply.

'I will, providing you'll let me have Cornish cream and raspberry jam on my scone!' Maddox put his arm round her shoulders. 'Do you want my jacket or can you make it to the tea room?'

Most of the cable car's passengers were huddled inside the restaurant, reluctant to walk the length of the Table Mountain ridge. The weather was closing down fast, with a lower temperature and a damp wind setting in. It brought a salt sea smell that didn't neutralise the kitchen aroma that escaped each time the door was opened. The mist obscured the view along the cliffs from their window seat but Maddox's thoughts lay with Cornish cream.

'Maddox, you're maddening! Here you are, Senior Wimbledon beckoning, tightening your belt by two inches and all you want are cream teas!' Katie's face glowed around her twinkling blue eyes as she pulled his leg, her hand on his arm. 'But I want to talk to you about your African lover, darling!'

'Which one, Mrs Rawlinson? You remain a noble ambition!'

'Oh Maddox, who knows? Since Cyril died, you've filled my thoughts. But stick to the point. I want to talk about this black lady that you're escorting around the city's romantic high spots. Who is she and don't you think you should tell me about her? Am I already a cuckolded widow?' Katie's mocking expression carried a trace of uncertainty.

'Katie, you're mad! Anyway, I thought I was the one running an investigation company? Your spies are excellent – are they moonlighting from Maddox Private Investigators?' Maddox was laughing now, nudging Katie as gently as he could while she lifted her coffee cup to her lips. 'But they're spot on! Since you asked, I'm the black lady's toy boy! She pays me a fortune from public funds to check on her SAPS subordinates! It's dodgy but I think I might be the only ex-policeman to be spying on BEE cops on behalf of a politically appointed chief!' Maddox adopted a mock seriousness, staring fixedly at Katie. 'She's Brigadier General Khanyisile Mthembu, nogal, Cape Town's deputy police boss. Her sister is Lindiwe Nhleko, Minister of Women in the Presidency, discarded wife of the Deputy President. She's married to Malusi Jali, Minister of Trade and Industry. Now how's that for connections? Anyway, we meet monthly so I can tell her all about her missing bits and pieces that she would know already if she ran half a decent set-up!' Maddox was so uninhibited that Katie was nodding vigorously before he finished.

'But why are you seeing her so regularly and at such prestigious places?' Katie's smile was still there but her voice was a little more enquiring.

'It sounds ridiculous, I know, but we decided to meet weekly while I completed an investigation into the Benny Solomons murder but then we agreed to meet monthly by way of retainer – I'm looking at the drug lord murder at Manenberg right now. It's all about her being straight but affirmative, while all around her are being crooked and lucky. It's a big departure from the way we began but one way and another, my modest business has exploded tenfold in the last two years.'

'I'm so pleased for you darling but I'm worried that lots of your new work centres around Siyeza, and let's face it, that's where Cape Town's nasty crimes are happening!' Katie finished her coffee, eyeing Maddox in a matronly way as the solitary scone lay untouched between them. He knew an unequal force when he met it and beckoned the waitress.

'You're right but it's changed everything around us. It would be madness to turn down the extra work. I think Khanyisile Mthembu is a rare beast, relatively impervious to bribery and dare I say it, to men in power? I think there's a push-pull relationship with her sister but she's not an easy prospect for either Nhleko or Jali, whatever the relationship. They put her there but she rather likes being the Mother Superior and uses me as her confidential vigilante.' Maddox didn't mind bouncing thoughts off Katie, who had become his confidante and partner. She was looking understanding as he mustered up courage. 'Anyway, that's one thing. I've confided in you about my ebony mistress. Now then, what do you think about a weekend in the bush for us? How about Addo Elephant Park?' Katie's face seemed to light up momentarily before she set it in mock headmistress mode.

'That sounds wonderful Maddox. Thank you.' They both laughed as they gathered their belongings to go to the cable car entrance, hands swinging in happy unison.

*****

'Lesebo? It's Kobus.' He heard an unenthusiastic response but continued. 'You grumbled about me governing your diary, so how about Harry Reynolds, Trustcore Development Corporation boss calling on you this afternoon? He's actually an old mate of Richard from university days in UK. He's a nice guy and deserves to be where he is. He's been married but separated for years, I think. As you know, there's a real nonsense about the government announcing the results of the tendering bids but the whole world knows that TDC are head and shoulders winners. That'll be confirmed soon, since frankly, it's become an embarrassment. I think we should treat Harry nicely.' Kobus waited and was about to enquire whether Lesebo has received his message.

'Fine. But it's getting familiar, Kobus.'

'What do you mean?'

'I mean an influential white man handing me on to another influential white man, having had sex along the way! Do I perform for Harry, give him the contract and wait for an intro to Prince Harry?' Kobus shuddered and kept quiet. His incoming calls were recorded and he had begun this one in the hope that it would be another small step towards healing their personal wound and increasing her exposure as a symbol of Siyeza's importance and success.

'Get real Lesebo, for Christ's sake! You asked for more freedom and influence and I'm giving it to you. Are you making yourself into a black Madonna or something, getting favours through abuse? Remember Lesebo, I met you full on, but boy, did you come at me! Have I handed you off or handed you on? All I know is that I've helped someone with whom I've had a lightning fling – are you with me?' Kobus was as angry as he was surprised about Lesebo's cynicism. He had to get in touch with Richard Kirkside about this girl – she was destructive dynamite.

'Okay Kobus. I look forward to meeting Richard's old university and business partner, Harry Reynolds. We will discuss his multi-billion Rand bid for the main construction contract. Sounds fairly easy to avoid cronyism, doesn't it? Probably best that the media aren't informed or invited...'

*****

Harry Reynolds had been warned that things were not quite right with Richard Kirkside. They had drifted in and out of contact over the years after they began their careers together with Trustcore. They had met more frequently in the last few years as Richard's fortunes soared and Harry was appointed TDC's CEO. There were significant investments to monitor in South Africa and adjoining countries and Harry invariably managed an overnight stay with the Kirksides in Hout Bay. As TDC's potentially largest participation in South Africa began with Siyeza, the Kirkside relationship had become disjointed, leaving Harry to ask his moles what was going on. The story emerged about Ami moving out of Hout Bay to live with an Indian professor, who was head of her political studies faculty. The gossip did not mention an affair by any party, but Harry was watchful when he arrived for his overnight stay with Richard. There were all the customary courtesies and privileges on offer but without Ami's presence, it seemed strained. Richard had invited the Mayor of Cape Town and the British Consul General to dinner, so Harry wondered if he would have a chance to hear about Richard's personal difficulties.

'Ami and I have had a bit of a fall-out,' Richard began, rearranging his jacket to prevent it creasing in the easy chair. He watched Harry's face carefully before going on. 'Yes, we're cooling off a bit but it will blow over. I've been a bit of a silly bugger and she's gone off in a huff to shack up with her university professor, which is not very sensible. It's got all the tongues wagging, but I don't think there's any nonsense going on – he's some Indian sage, who's always on the telly, waffling about high-flown geopolitics. So I'm sorry she's not here to see you. Next time maybe?' Kirkside injected a smile to change the subject. 'Anyway Harry, how's it all going? The stupid bloody clowns are sitting on the tendering decisions over Siyeza but I haven't heard anything to suggest you're not going to get the cut, have you?'

Harry Reynolds was a calm character who was a good listener and ran a very tight ship at TDC, now the third largest UK construction conglomerate. The group had prospered due partly to his management skills and sophisticated recruitment and in-house training policies. A TDC sponsorship for an engineering graduate left the brightest candidates with PhDs and early meritocratic opportunities in an international construction and development environment. Harry had managed this despite living apart from his wife by mutual choice. She had opted to live alone in London to pursue her publishing career. Their son and only child worked in Dubai. The bachelor existence seemed to suit them both, without third parties being involved; they had decided that it could remain that way until one or other wanted to remarry. Meanwhile, his business reputation was one of firm but fair leadership with an emphasis on delivery rather than promises.

'Well, it's South Africa Richard, so you never know. We've had to be very tough this time, painstakingly thorough. You know, it's terrifying to experience the graft and cronyism that's overtaken the trading and diplomatic world here. And it's not getting better, with more dependency on foreign aid and skills. There used to be a political level to work at, using a fair price at 5 percent more than your competitors to undercut them once they added their 20 percent bung. But nowadays, the graft reaches to the top, real dog-eat-dog stuff, with BEE appointees selected from school onwards. Loyalty to the party binds in the cronyism. So do you know what we do now?' Reynolds put down his whisky and placed his hands on his knees, nodding emphatically to emphasis his point. 'We put 10 percent of the overall figure into TDC academy training. If we get the Siyeza bid, for example, there will be over twenty initial engineering scholarships in UK on offer – hopefully for black students – and another twenty integrated internships for suitably qualified and experienced local engineers and technicians. The secret is to convince the young ones that theirs is the kingdom of heaven if they've got the grey matter and healthy ambition. This will cost us around five hundred million bucks a year but it'll be money well spent for those involved, let alone South African expertise and of course TDC.'

'It's the only way,' agreed Richard. 'Are you seeing Kobus Labuschagne tomorrow?'

'Yes, first thing. Then there's an on-site symposium with the new director and principles there – Lesebo Bofokeng, or some such name. What can you tell me about her?'

The doorbell rang as Richard's guests arrived. 'Not much. We employed her here briefly. Very clever and well connected within the Lesotho hierarchy – a chief's daughter. She's making a good impression, I think, and Kobus Labuschagne is a safe pair of hands. I think you'll like him. I'm handling quite a bit of capital belonging to all manner of interested parties but Kobus doesn't trust the opposition. There's a parallel path being followed by the Deputy President and all his henchmen, including the Trade and Industry directorate. Obviously, there's confidentiality to consider but let's meet before you leave and compare notes. Anyway, let's go and be civil to the stuffed shirts, shall we?' They walked into the ante-room to greet the Consul General and Mayor.

*****

Harry couldn't believe his eyes when he was introduced to Lesebo Bafokeng by Kobus Labuschagne. There are some women who can kill conversation stone dead when they enter a crowded room. Harry mused over why the cranes, drills and trucks did not grind to a halt with Lesebo on site. Her rainbow nation patterned safety helmet, her tailored yellow fluorescent waistcoat and her tight-fitting all-weather trousers made her ready for the catwalk, rather than a construction site. Harry was introduced to key personalities, visited the arterial road site and was briefed on large maps. The municipality's site headquarters was virtually completed, allowing them to have discussions in an insulated board room. Lesebo seemed "to the manor born", addressing Kobus in a friendly professional manner and handing Harry an impressive and personalised portfolio. They brought their coffee to the board room table, where Lesebo was formally invited by Kobus to begin discussions.

'Mr Reynolds, we hoped to welcome you to Siyeza as the official main contractor, complete with formal government pledge. But it was not to be. The government is promising to release the bidding results shortly but all we can say from a Municipality viewpoint is that we have regarded you not only as our preferred bid but as the only one that approached the capacity and credentials required for such a challenging undertaking. So that is your position with us and this discussion will reflect that.' Lesebo gave Harry a soft and slow smile that carried a genuine reassurance.

'Thank you, Lesebo, that's very kind. I'm delighted to meet you! We too hoped for something conclusive by now but your Deputy President has said this might be possible before I leave in a week's time.' Harry was interrupted by Kobus hurriedly leaving the room to answer his cell phone. 'That said, we have an enormous army – am I allowed to describe it this way – stood by to invade?'

Kobus had returned, whispering to Lesebo's acolyte. He stood next to Lesebo now, talking to her intently as Harry was distracted, wondering whether to continue. Harry decided that unless he spoke now, all would be lost.

'Look, this project has signs of going stale. We've watched it from afar and worried about who would walk the talk. There's nothing substantial coming from national government and…' Harry broke off, distracted by a voluminous Malusi Jali filling a doorway, while his scurrying ensemble were ushered in at the back of the hall.

'Mr Reynolds, er Harry, forgive me, just a moment please.…' Lesebo strode away from the party towards Jali, whom she embraced in a well-meaning African way. While Kobus and Harry stood watching, completely sidelined as onlookers, Jali wandered round the party, shaking hands and exuding bonhomie. After a few minutes spent whipping up yet more tea and coffee and miraculously, unopened packets of biscuits, Lesebo's voice was heard, motioning everyone back to the table, where Jali's party overwhelmed the chairs and space. It was only at this point that everyone noticed a television camera duet at the back of the room, facing Jali at the centre of the table that he had usurped.

'Well my friends, comrades, brothers in African progress. It is wonderful to be here at a momentous moment at the dawn of this great government project called Siyeza!' For gall and for bombast, Jali was winning high points. He showed no awkwardness or theatre as he beamed at the camera. 'Yes, my friends, because this is the moment when as your Minister for Trade and Industry, I am personally empowered by His Excellency the Deputy President the Right Honourable Jabu Nhleko to announce the award of the major construction contracts for the undertaking.' Glancing around, it was clear that neither Labuschagne, Bafokeng nor Reynolds had any part in this dramatic upstaging ploy by the government. Jali was literally taking their breath away and stealing thunder. 'There has been due deliberation, comrades, as your elected leaders in the government considered the offers made by a host of bidders, both international, regional and domestic. In the fullness of time, as the huge Siyeza story unfolds, there is hope that all of them will be remembered and included – this is a grand African episode where we hold hands in advancing together away from the agonies and obscenities of poverty and unemployment that was Apartheid's legacy.' Labuschagne winced as Jali slipped into the fall-back diatribe, glancing anxiously at Reynolds who looked uncomfortable as he stretched his legs out and stared down at his shoes. Jali noticed the shuffling and discontentment and opted to finish abruptly. 'So with no further ado, my friends, I am delighted to announce the selection of Trustcore Development Corporation as the prime focus for construction and technology in the ongoing Siyeza Enterprise! There are many aspects that need considering and agreeing as co-operative ventures but that is why it is appropriate that we make this announcement during the visit to our shores by TDC's group CEO, Mr Harry Reynolds, who will be signing this historic agreement with the Deputy President in Pretoria next week.'

The gathering was not an occasion for American-style whooping and euphoria but nevertheless, there was energetic hugging and hand-shaking, with Harry Reynolds looking every inch the self-effacing Englishman as he expressed thanks modestly and made solemn undertakings to bring the highest professional standards to the scheme. As Harry gently embraced Lesebo, Kobus caught her eye and winked; things were moving at breakneck speed for this Basotho beauty.

Chapter Seven

Gary Bennett, Maddox's deputy, and Joost van der Merve were under no illusions about the importance of the connections they had made in the aftermath of the Solomons murder investigation. Reaction to the low-life gang leader's subsequent killing had been subdued around the Manenberg district and the contacts they had made had renewed meetings at their urgent request. Maddox was sanguine about any further investigation or involvement in SAPS business but because of his retention with Khanyisile Mthembu, he agreed that they stayed abreast of news from reliable sources. In so doing, Maddox's two leading investigators were told the identity and circumstances of the gang leader's death. There appeared to be firm evidence against Sonny Chopra's payment to a rival drugs gang, alongside his loan of a pistol and half a dozen rounds with which to carry out the killing. Predictably, the pistol had disappeared under the pretext of inter-gang fighting, but Gary had been promised its return on production of further payment.

Maddox listened to their story with disquiet, knowing that they could not keep this evidence in their private possession. He suspected that they were about to open up a can of worms, either at the same time or just before the SAPS murder squad reached the same conclusion.

'Look you two, I'd like you to treat this as need-to-know around the office. After Benny's murder, I've had some privileged access to SAPS intelligence about their activities among Cape Flats criminals. I've a hot line to their Deputy Commissioner, who now pays us a retainer from SAPS slush funds to update her on main events. Amazingly, she's conducting a one-woman purge against corruption in her force and particularly the detective bureau. It's all regular and going through the books with full documentation, so don't start thinking that I'm doing double deals!' Maddox chuckled and saw their relief at being able to joke about this unusual development.

'So what do you want us to do with this information, boss?' asked the pragmatic Joost. 'We could get the weapon, put it through forensic and nail Chopra, couldn't we? Or do we hand the lot to SAPS and wash our hands of it?'

'We must keep the sources alive, there's no doubt about that. If we can pin down the ID and whereabouts of the murderers and get some pre-emptive stuff about gang warfare, without getting embroiled and gobbling up time, it would help me to update Deputy Commissioner Mthembu. We don't want that weapon used again. The forensic traces might have worn thin but I think it's worth our while paying the tout – SAPS will pay in the long run of course! Having gone that far, I think we should pause and wait for her advice. I think I'll recommend that she puts the suspect and his mates into a safe house this time, probably way out of Cape Town!'

*****

Richard Kirkside had followed the unfolding Siyeza saga with mixed feelings. He did not recognise Lesebo as the young girl who had left a year before. Her performances on television had been outstanding and easily matched conservative critics who derided her inexperience, youth and in scarcely concealed language, her colour. She struck a reassuring picture alongside Kobus Labuschagne, which did the Municipality's and DA's imagery no harm around the city. Having set up an offshore account in her name, into which half a million Rands had been deposited, Richard wondered about her long-term plans. Would she see through Siyeza to its bitter end or would she use her charms to be head-hunted elsewhere?

Malusi Jali's antics were unclear. Richard had a million Rands of his money riding in an investment consortium which made no secret of its heavy investment within the Municipality's Rights Issue Fund, now in access of a hundred billion. Yet Jali had insisted during a recent TV interview that he had no personal interests in Siyeza and that there was no requirement for government funding in the scheme in the immediate future. But the most puzzling aspect of Jali's stance over Sizela – and therefore Jabu Nhleko's and the ANC's – was his ambiguous remarks about the conditions governing the selection of Trustcore as the principal construction group. Before departing for UK, Harry Reynolds had expressed similar misgivings but felt that unless they placed themselves above the law and manipulated the Constitution, the South African government had committed itself to a binding contract that was defensible in British and South African High Courts. There was an increasing amount of "supernumerary" contracts appearing that assumed that TDC was party to anonymous alliances working within, and therefore drawing from, their contract fund, which smacked of deliberate duplicity and cronyism. Again, Reynolds felt that his contract's terms were sufficiently watertight to either nullify their existence or else force the government to pay the multitude of small companies, some of whom were formed en masse and in haste in Pretoria, as separate entities. Reynolds prepared a review with his accountants and lawyers, to be deployed whenever necessary, outlining wasteful government spending.

Another troubling matter for Kirkside was his brokerage for opposing interests, with investments made on behalf of Labuschagne and a mysterious Ukahlamba account. When asked to withdraw a hundred thousand Rands from there the previous week, he had checked the account's ID with his Pretoria colleagues. It appeared that Ukahlamba was some type of holding account belonging to Hlabisa Brabazon, an overseas company which in turn had links to Ravi Chetty's Amalgamated Holdings. Kirkside smelled a rat but was loathe to invite comment from Maddox, whom he was certain had produced the evidence on his involvement with Lesebo. He pondered for some time, until convincing himself that he could act as if he was unaware of Maddox's investigation on behalf of Ami. He invited Maddox to visit to discuss his holdings and for preliminary comment on the ESOP, which Maddox had successfully launched some months before.

Maddox was equally circumspect about meeting Richard alone but judged that his growing investments with Kirkside justified the meeting – there was no certainty that Ami had named him as the agency involved in the Lesebo affair. Richard Kirkside was more formal than usual but certainly had an ulterior motive for seeing him privately. 'Having dealt with your own accounts here, there's one other thing that I wish to discuss and ask your advice about, please. As you know, I'm doing a lot of trade for the Municipality's Rights Issues holdings and by and large, confidentiality and ethics can be observed without difficulty. It's quite busy – I handled a huge sum from Holland the other week and international interest is definitely picking up. But last week, I was instructed by an anonymous European with all the FICA whistles and stops, to take a hundred thousand out of an obscure account called Ukahlamba and put it in a foreign account called Hlabisa Brabazon. This was a bit unusual. When something seems a bit fishy, I run a check with my company and account registration sources up in Pretoria. It turns out that Brabazon is within the business grouping of Amalgamated Holdings, which is Ravi Chetty's catch-all umbrella account. This got me thinking: should I be happy broking for a politician who denies having money invested in Siyeza and laundering stuff for the city's leading mobster who denies having any business interests in Siyeza?' Richard kept a serious expression as Maddox remained attentive and immobile.

'When did you say the withdrawal was requested and made?' Richard tapped his laptop a few times and scribbled with a pencil on a notepad.

'It was the fifteenth, last Monday, which I transferred the same day. I have a fast brokerage facility so it would reflect in Brabazon by last Thursday, perhaps even Wednesday.'

'Interesting, very interesting indeed, Richard.' Maddox jotted in his own notebook. 'Well, for what it's worth, I'd be very interested if this happens again.'

'Well, that's the thing. I delved around these unknown portfolios and saw that there's a Phalaborwa account that was opened at the same time as Ukahlamba, again tracing back through Brabazon to Amalgamated Holdings. A hundred thousand was withdrawn from that one too, about six months ago – let me give you the dates.' Kirkside searched his computer again, writing on and tearing off from a jot pad to pass to Maddox. This time Maddox stared at the note in deep concentration. He lifted his head to smile at Kirkside, waving the notepaper to make his point.

'As I said, this is most interesting Richard. I think there are connections to be made. Would it be too much to drop me a hand-written short summary of these two instructions please? And if anything similar occurs, I'd love to hear straight away – many thanks!' Maddox stood and walked ahead of Kirkside to the front door, where he turned to say farewell.

'I hear things aren't quite right with Ami?'

'No, we've had a bit of a tiff. She's not here at the moment but I hope it'll all blow over quite soon. Anyway, thanks for coming. All's well with your investments at least. And let me know if I can help further with that Chetty business.'

Maddox drove away from the Hout Bay luxurious suburb, with its steep descent to the city, the ocean sparkling in the thin autumn sunlight. It seemed the Kirksides were weathering their storm and that Maddox was not being fingered as the snooping pariah. More immediately though, he had the strongest of hunches over the mysterious withdrawals completed by Kirkside for Ravi Chetty or his acolytes. He hurried back to the office to check his facts.

*****

The Eighth African Construction Convention was being held at Sun City in Bophuthatswana. The monstrous symbol to entrepreneurial tourism had been engineered in the dying throes of Apartheid. Following democratisation in 1993/4, the four "TVBC states" were subsumed into neighbouring provinces. Nothing was too loud, too brash or too outlandish there, with its modern reputation as a premier international golf, theatre and entertainment centre. None of the delegates attending could confirm whether there had been seven Convention predecessors but it didn't matter, since it gave the gathering some ballast and respectability. The programme was undemanding, with a golf day, a "revue bar" entertainment evening and helicopter taxi rides to a giant picnic and braai site set up in a neighbouring tribal village, with local choirs, dancers and artists providing background entertainment.

Bram De Vries had not attended before but was drawn for three reasons. Firstly to investigate with his small Dutch entourage the lessons to be learned in reproducing a reduced scale version of Sun City's mass entertainment within the Siyeza rebuild. Secondly, he wanted to explore the possibilities of co-operation with Harry Reynolds' TDC, recently named as the leading construction conglomerate in the overall enterprise. Lastly, De Vries wanted to network and parade his interest and existing commitment to Siyeza, hopefully to annex the more gullible of the freshly appointed minnow companies established for the relatives and families of senior politicians and favoured entrepreneurs. He arranged to meet Reynolds and TDC's leading design engineer for lunch while the majority of delegates were playing golf. He was accompanied by his own Group Administration Chief. The four were given a veranda table overlooking sweeping meadows and golf estate, away from the view over cluttered hotels and theme parks.

De Vries' pitch concentrated on inward investment and state of the art technical support equipment and workforce. He delivered his interest in a relaxed manner, mindful of the size and credibility of TDC. In essence, he could act as guarantor for TDC if South African funding froze or was denied. He offered to produce a digitalised compendium of all Siyeza activities and a cost analysis with time lines measured against programming. He could co-opt a raft of skilled scientists and specialist engineers in land reclamation, underground tunnelling, water courses and geological survey. If necessary, he would consider a formal technical partnership with TDC.

Reynolds had obtained current intelligence about De Vries. He knew of his bi-polar funding approaches to Labuschagne and Jali and he was aware of business tittle-tattle associating him with some unsavoury entertainment industry personalities in Hong Kong, Thailand and Singapore. He had heard how De Vries had taken a team around the gambling palaces and fairground facilities at Sun City for two days – so much for his "technical partnership"!

'Bram, before I overlook it, could you help us find your current listings, please? We searched in the stock exchanges and registered company's files, so obviously we were looking under the wrong accreditation details. What does your parent group trade under – is it all under your "Bee de Vee Bee Vee", which was the only link we could find in the Dutch Company Registrar?' Harry was asking in a subdued but earnest way that scarcely disguised his disdain, hand poised over his cell phone.

'Yes, that's us too. But we're listed in London under Old Royal Hollander Banking, where we're the major shareholder and as De Vries Entertainment in Antwerp and The Hague. We have a deliberately low profile because we don't have major shareholdings in huge construction companies like yours. So we operate with tiny overheads and no glossy marketing, because we pull together all the global names at an add-on price. Our reach and speed provide the business.'

'How much are you involved in the entertainment world?'

'Look, we find that no modern new build of consequence can exist without entertainment these days, so we've specialised in this field, from sports stadia in Olympic cities to betting shops in downtown suburbs.'

'And in Siyeza?'

'It's not on the start-up blueprint but I'm in negotiation with the government to see if there's a market or a return. There's plenty of space in the Cape Flats and once the community infrastructure begins to take shape, I think you'll find your designers fitting something in at government request. Why do you ask?'

'Well, because it goes against the altruistic spirit that I'm picking up during my visits to Cape Town. You don't fill bellies by taking the breadwinner's earnings at black jack do you? Are you thinking about clubs and bars too?'

'Maybe but let us take one step at a time? Forgive me, but I think that you're starting with an old-fashioned attitude: once such large projects take shape, they adopt a new life and shape of their own. There are six hundred thousand souls out there who've known nothing but street crime for fifty years. Just you wait to see how they take control once the schools and shops are in place.'

De Vries and Reynolds parted with a shared loathing of each other. It was as clear to Reynolds how De Vries was a syndicated entrepreneur operating by his own rules as it was to De Vries that Reynolds was a traditional British businessman who read the small print and weighed risks before weighing them again. To their accompanying partners, it seemed that the referee had briefed them both, they had touched gloves and gone to their corners to await the first bell...

*****

Katie had embarrassed Maddox with her jibe about entertaining Khanyisile Mthembu so regularly. He had stretched the frequency to every six weeks or so but this time he had something important to offer and wanted some in-house favours. He chose the Buckhara on Victoria Wharf – in for a penny, in for a pound, since the world knew about their assignations – where they both enjoyed some excellent North Indian tandoori dishes. The honey and yoghourt sauce over the skinned chicken, with heavy ginger and garlic tastes, smelt wonderful as it was roasted on nearby grills and tasted excellent. Khanyisile was no slimmer but was well corseted in a mauve dress with a light lime wrap. She told Maddox excitedly how she was making progress on unearthing her corrupt police constables and officers – one had been caught red-handed on camera in an interview room, accepting cash for omitting evidence, leading to a dismissed case.

'Well done. Keep it up. And guess what? I'm the bearer of good news too! Here's a brief on the ID of the gangland leader's killers – you know, the ones who got inside information from your boys about his bogus compassionate parole and shot him in the head? Well, you'll read who pulled the trigger, who were the accomplices and much more importantly from a Big Fish viewpoint, who set it up with the cash and the weapon.'

'Hauw, you're way ahead of us again, Maddox! Or is it my detectives not telling me what's going on?' She forked hungrily into her delicious chicken. 'Please go on, I can listen and eat!'

'I'm not surprised – it's delicious isn't it? Well, I hit lucky with a circulating snippet about one hundred thousand Rands in cash being handed over. It was done by Chetty's sidekick, Sonny Chopra, to the killers of both Solomons and his murderer, who was on parole. The dates, events and bank transfers all fit neatly and are corroborated in part by local touts. But better still Khanyisile, I've got the weapon they used. It cost us a couple of bob but it's yours for forensic testing. We'll have to go very carefully on the continuity of evidence, because our covert relationship is only multiplying the witnesses and forensic trail. If you can get Chopra's prints, we might be in business – there's no hope of Ravi Chetty handling it but we're getting too close for comfort, don't you think?'

'That's wonderful Maddox – please come and work for me!' Khanyisile leaned over the table, frightening Maddox that she was being serious. 'We must do that – it would be dereliction to ignore it. But this time we will get an outside force to arrest and detain. We cannot have crooked cops and drugs barons running Cape Town.' She waved her fork at Maddox. 'Absolutely no way, Maddox!'

'Great minds think alike Khanyisile! Let's do that. But there's one small favour, as always?'

'Go on, trying to catch me when my defences are down!'

'I'd like you to tell me anything you find out about a Dutchman called Bram De Vries. He's in the thick of all the Siyeza news – his name keeps cropping up but nobody knows anything about him. It seems he's paid two-way bets – a wonga to your brother-in-law to reinforce the bogus Government's Siyeza account and another whack into the Municipality's Rights Issue Fund. One way or another, he wants to be noticed. I think we all need to know more about him, since with Trustcore now the publicly elected main contractor, De Vries might be one of the dangerous sharks swimming off False Bay! Can you do that, without upsetting or alarming your sister?' Maddox closed his knife and fork on his plate and smiled enquiringly at her.

'Let me see what I can do. Our exchanges are working well, don't you think? The trouble is that we're not meeting so often, which makes me appear much fatter each time I meet!' Khanyisile gave a wobbly laugh as she wiped her mouth on her napkin. Now then, what's for pudding, Maddox – look at that lovely chocolate that girl's having over there!'

*****

It was a week later that Ravi Chetty met Sonny Chopra at the Diwali Festival at the Eco Park in Green Point. It was a suitably crowded and natural place to meet, with every Indian in the city gathered for the noisy and colourful festivities. There were clothes to be bought, music to hear and every imaginable curried dish to sample. Dancing, traditional Indian songs and a non-stop cinema of Indian films showing. Chetty and Chopra, with a coterie of female relatives providing unremarkable cover, leant on a rail watching a female dance routine. They carried a bottle of beer each and as ever, Sonny was smoking.

'Sonny that was a nice clean job, no doubts. But you know what man? There was a big klopjag on Manenberg touts last week and they hit lucky. They've fingered your man and his mates from the Americans street gang – not too difficult heh? But this time they've disappeared – my tame cop has no idea who took them, or where. But they've been hunting around for cash, because they seem to know how much you gave them. Any ideas about that?'

Sonny threw his cigarette butt into the dirt and screwed it under his pointed shoe. He exhaled from his last puff and looked at Ravi while he thought. 'Nah. He got the lot in new hundreds, same as the dead feller got. He counted them out, nobody watching or in sight. Put them in a shirt pocket under a jacket. Where d'you get the notes, anyway?'

'Never you mind – what's it to you anyway? You've picked two munts now that get fingered in five minutes – what about the weapon?' Ravi looked angrily at Sonny as he asked, watching him answer.

'It's fine. Got it back a couple of days later. Wiped clean and hidden away.' Sonny was a good liar, not showing any flicker on his face. 'But look, don't get mad, I'm asking where you got the cash – twice, do you see what I'm saying?' Sonny knew that Ravi was sensitive about this and used it to help cover his lie about the missing weapon. Ravi stared back for a few seconds. He looked over Sonny's shoulder at the monotonously swaying girls.

'Yeah, okay. Maybe. Worth looking at. There's a stockbroker in the middle of all the Siyeza cash, making a bloody pile. I've got accounts which are indirectly linked to a big central one run by a financier. If he got suspicious, I suppose he could pin something together. Come to think of it, I withdrew twice, both for a hundred grand, soon after the jobs were done. Mmm, maybe, maybe not. Let me look at that. But I'm getting nervous man, for the first time, know what I mean?' Sonny nodded, feeling for another cigarette. 'Look we can't fix the tout this time – they're hiding him. Maybe they're linking payments to my business. And they've picked a fucking Pom to do the building work. It's not looking good. And to make it worse, I'm not sure I trust that Dutchman either. So what are we doing, paying skellums good money to kill munts that put the knife in on us? I tell you, I don't like the way things are going, I'm nervous!' Sonny was more nervous though, haunted by his lie about the gun, the likelihoods of it being discovered and Ravi's calculating and violent reaction.

*****

Harry Reynolds decided that he needed to debrief Kobus Labuschagne in a video conversation, which they set up in their respective offices. After the usual pleasantries about the competing stair rod rain of London and the howling winds of Cape Town, they had a professional exchange, without other assistants present. Harry's short haircut showed his London pallor, with a bright blue tie silhouetted against a pale pink shirt. Kobus looked his usual ruddy complexioned self, more relaxed in an open necked white golfer under a grey suit. They joked about their respective coffees as they exchanged mock toasts.

'Kobus, I want to fill you in on something about Siyeza that came up when I was last in South Africa. I don't want to keep it until I see you there in ten days.' Kobus nodded, sipping his coffee. They had established a good working relationship and now that TDC had been given the official government nod, Kobus frequently exchanged Siyeza information with Harry. 'When I was at the Construction Convention at Sun City, Bram De Vries nobbled me over lunch. He put on a laid-back, super-plutocrat manner with his Oxford English, laying out his table for Siyeza – foreign capital injection, technical know-how, specific engineering expertise, digital programming and the like. I wasn't impressed because we'd done our homework on him and felt he was as slippery as an eel. When he eventually shut up, I try to pin him down on the formal registration and listing of his companies, but the evasive bugger trotted out where I'd find him on the bourses, including a sizeable entertainments industry group operating in the Hong Kong, Thailand and Singapore marketplaces. We looked into that and it peeled our eyes back – he's a notable impresario in the gambling and club scene, including state sanctioned prostitution, casinos, mass karaoke dens, pornography shops, strip and pole clubs, betting shops, you name it...' Harry and Kobus laughed at each other, while realising the implications.

'Well, well, well, the slimy sleazeball!' exploded Kobus. 'This explains a lot Harry. My financial friends say he's got funds in both camps – with our renamed Siyeza Future Fund and some undisclosed government fund which doesn't really exist. It's not registered! It's a ghost fund in other words, probably being used by the government to move stuff around where required, including back pockets.'

'Yes, that rings true. His business hardcore, in more ways than one, is clearly entertainment. All the rest is facilitation – probably drugs, sweeteners, bribery. He can put muscle on the ground but none of it is his capital. Those who own it are skating on thin ice in terms of international licensing and registration. Look, I'm biased as a rival businessman but we have to recognise that some global conglomerates are pretty tarnished – look at the South Africans caught out with their football stadia shenanigans!'

'Harry, I'll tell you what I'll do. I'll get together with your stockbroker mate who's become pretty central in all – and Lesebo Bafokeng. There's also a private investigator I trust who's following some of the recent gang warfare nonsense. We've got to straighten things out, because there's some sophisticated syndication that's already embedded, which will make us look like arseholes in a year or so. So thanks for all this, Harry. Let's meet up when you're over again, because I'll hopefully have my finger on it all by then!' They parted amicably, both feeling that they'd made useful progress. Kobus was beginning to feel that the government hierarchy was orchestrating the likes of De Vries, rather than being manipulated by foreign crime syndicates.

*****

Lesebo Bafokeng felt a vicarious thrill as they assembled in her site headquarters, or "Infinity House" as its impressively carved sandstone logo now read over the pillared porch entrance. About two years ago, she was a virginal innocent at university. But today, she presided over a gathering of Wise Men to agree a strategy for the funding and control of Cape Town's largest-ever construction undertaking. And two of those three were her ex-lovers, neither of them anything other than a sudden and solitary act of sexual gratification. In that short space of time, she had rediscovered her self-esteem to become the focus of the most important factor in local lives. She was a young and beautiful black girl in charge of all their destinies. And she was the only one present who knew the whole sex triangle story.

For Maddox, it promised to be an interesting meeting. He felt slightly out of place rather than out of depth. His potential embarrassment about dealing with Kirkside had evaporated but he wondered about the ethical considerations that would surface. Through his inside knowledge with Khanyisile Mthembu, he realised that he would have to be sparing with information in order to guard police confidentiality.

Richard Kirkside was more concerned about his increasingly precarious position as a witness in the Chetty investigations than he was about Lesebo's presence and position. He was genuinely pleased to see how well she had fitted into the Municipality machinery, obviously hitting it off with Kobus. Apart from his Lesebo secret, Richard had a unique knowledge of their respective investments in Siyeza Future Fund or SFF as it was being coined. He had carefully researched the De Vries investments and designed a way to inform the meeting without breaking confidences.

'All right, all of us. Thanks for coming along at short notice. We all know each other and there won't be any minutes or recording. Kobus has called this special meeting because he has become concerned about aspects of Siyeza funding and administration that have come to light following a long conversation he shared with Harry Reynolds yesterday. It's best for Kobus to lead on this.' Lesebo smiled sweetly at Kobus, totally at ease in her high-profile role. Both Maddox and Kirkside wondered where her relationship lay with Labuschagne – she was a real fatal attraction.

'Thanks Lesebo. Yes, sorry to grab you like this but Harry got me worried when he described a meeting he'd had with Bram De Vries at the Construction Convention. When De Vries couldn't satisfy Harry's curiosity about the nuts and bolts registration, listing and audited capital worth of his group, Harry dug around. It seems that virtually all De Vries' wealth and assets lie in the entertainments industry, which flourishes in Hong Kong, Thailand and Singapore, from betting shops with sports and turf, brothels, porn shops and discos, casino, online pornography syndication, the works. A really nasty piece of work. He runs a slick international network without any upfront ego image and has facilitated contracts and laundering for a number of mega-projects, including Kampala and Mauritius. Harry said De Vries spent two days with a team putting a toothcomb over Sun City during the Convention. Now your guess is as good as mine, but there seems to be a strong chance that he aims to include this sort of super-emporium within the Siyeza plan. I wondered whether this rang any bells? If so, I think we need to make unambiguous decisions about how to deal with it.' Kobus leaned back, slightly flushed after his uncompromising revelation. He nodded towards Richard to encourage a view.

'Well, that's interesting isn't it? Like us all, I'm bound by a few confidentiality caveats but that needn't stop me putting in my five pen'orth. I know Harry well, so I don't think there's any hyperbole or misconstrued stuff here – if anything, Harry veers to fact, rather than fiction!' Richard was playing himself in carefully, slightly edgy. When heads nodded assent, he opened up. 'To get to the point. De Vries, through different foreign sources, injected a substantial early investment in SFF – probably around 20 percent of the fund at the time, which has dropped to nearer ten percent as other investments flowed in. Around the same time, and we're talking of well over a year ago now, he made a similar investment into a ghost government fund to which Messrs Nhleko and Jali, our respective Deputy President and Minister of Trade and Industry, had access.' Richard leaned forward and lowered his voice. 'Here I must ask for your confidentiality assurances. Mr Jali deposited a million Rands into SFF through my services. The transaction came from his personal account. It's reasonable to assume that this emerged from the De Vries investment – or was it a donation, I don't know? So as things stand, we have a De Vries investment plus a Jali investment, made with or without De Vries' knowledge, or indeed cash!' Kirkside sat back in his chair, watching their faces. There were muttered exchanges, none of them offered for general consumption. Lesebo tapped her pencil on the oak table.

'The plot thickens, I think we can say? Kobus, do you want to comment on that or shall I ask for Maddox's contribution?' Kobus pointed at Maddox, who was looking his implacable self.

'Thanks. As you might imagine, I didn't expect to be included. Before I say anything, I must declare that I have an SFF investment, or at least its forebear, made through Richard. I have been party to some investigations into the recent murders in the Cape Flats, where my investigation agency has assisted the police.' He glanced at each face, where a nodded understanding was expressed. 'Without divulging sources or police confidentiality on live cases, I can say that evidence, including information from those present, has come to light incriminating Mr Ravi Chetty and associates as accessories to the murders. Subsequent investigation shows that they, or their holding interests, were funded by payments made by Mr De Vries or associates, through an extremely circuitous laundering arrangement. So to add to Richard's news, it is possible, perhaps likely, that the government and De Vries, maybe as a formal syndicated unit, plan to create a large entertainment entity – there's a euphemism – in the midst of our beloved Siyeza!' Maddox ended by holding Richard Kirkside's gaze a little nervously but saw no sign that he had divulged client confidence.

'Phew! Well let's talk this through. We're sworn to secrecy so must decide about our collective future action – what do we do, and how?' Lesebo turned to Kobus. 'Is this a business enterprise thing or is it political? Both perhaps?'

'I think it's definitely political. It seems that there are government answers to hear and international interests to address. What is coming out is that there is a syndicated attempt with either complicity or invention at Presidential level. It involves a Dutch consortium linked to local mobsters. Vast bribe payments are in place and sponsored murders have taken place.'

'It looks every bit as bad as that, I agree,' said Kirkside. 'It doesn't fall out of a Ruth Rendell thriller, does it? We need to make crystal clear to everyone that the SFF is the only Siyeza fund. Nhleko is on record to the nation in saying that there is no ring-fenced government fund at any level that is dedicated to Siyeza. This should force some hands; De Vries will want to know where his investment to Nhleko and Jali went and he will be unhappy about his absorption within SFF. The next thing, I would suggest Kobus, is to create a public company out of SFF with board and opaque shareholder interests. I don't want anything to do with this, but it must be done now, possibly by an overseas accountancy if you think the big South African firms are tainted?' Richard was animated now, feeling much less cornered.

'All that sounds sensible to me,' added Maddox, smiling at last. 'We must be subtle though, because it'll come to naught unless we get charges to stick. There's all sorts of forensic, financial and witness trails to tie up, and SAPS are vulnerable. I think Richard is right about flushing out something when De Vries realises he's been shrunken down to small fish status. So, absolute confidentiality please.'

'Agreed.' Kobus took the floor with refreshed authority, seemingly with Lesebo's agreement. 'Thank you and congratulations on some great work so far. SFF has topped two billion and once we restructure its management, I think government will resent the private ownership and will have come to the party. But let's cross that bridge when we get to it, heh? This will move fast and we'll need to get together again – maybe we should all adopt the four musketeer's names as pseudonyms? I'll take Arimis!' They all laughed as the meeting broke up. The stage was set for some rumbustious repercussions.

*****

'How much longer are we going to potter about like Derby and Joan, love?' Maddox asked mischievously as he brought a tea tray with cups and crunchy cake to the garden seat at his home. Katie had arrived with several seed trays full of plants and flowers from a nursery and they had spent an energetic couple of hours planting and watering, trimming back branches and bushes and edging the overgrown lawn. It was not a large space but had been transformed in the last six months through Katie's green-fingered enthusiasm and skill.

'If this is pottering, maybe we ought to call it a day, darling!' Katie held her hand over her eyes as she gazed up at Maddox against the sharp noon light. She giggled, gripping his arm. 'Let things take their course Maddox. Not much has gone wrong so far, has it? We've given each other acres of space and both look forward to the next meeting. I suppose we're a bit set in our ways but frankly, I didn't realise how busy you would be!' She giggled again and looked coyly at him, untidy even by his standards in his baggy old flannels and frayed long sleeved shirt, cuffs rolled on his forearms. 'Not to mention so rich and important either!'

Maddox looked across at her, taking her hand. 'Well my dear, all the better to look after you in our dotage. I didn't anticipate all this Siyeza stuff either, nobody did, but I must admit I feel young and active and because of you, just plain happy! One of these days, in the not too distant future, I'm going to make an honest woman of you!' He stared at her ageless eyes, face pink from her gardening exertions.

'Aren't you getting it arse about face darling? First of all you have to make a dishonest woman of me!' They laughed loudly, Maddox waving an admonishing finger at her.

Chapter Eight

Tristan Kirkside had grown used to learning and working alone with his mother or specialised tutor. At first, he had accepted their word that he was advanced, needing a higher challenge. Later, he wanted to prove for himself by completing tests for adult scholars or solving mathematical problems during occasional visits to evening classes. He had embarked on a senior distance learning course with UNISA, which he found easy. His parents' recent quarrel had unsettled him badly, since he found it impossible to divide his love and thoughts; he was seeing too little of his father. His mother had become ultra-literal about everything and he felt out-of-place sharing her company with Professor Chetty, although he found him friendly enough.

His weekly visit with the Cape Dolphins water polo team to the Gardens Centre Swimmable Swim Pool was an enjoyable highlight. His mother rightly felt that home tuition without any peer company was damaging, particularly with sport. The club was well known among several of the city's bigger schools and UTC. Every Wednesday afternoon, around fifty teenagers gathered there, divided into competitive polo teams, defending their places in a well organised league. Tristan had learned to swim early in their pools and was a good player. Although the teams were single sex, girls' teams competed as well and Tristan, like all his team mates, was beginning to respond to the urges of a fifteen-year-old. If at all possible, depending on the arrival of parents to drive them home, they lingered informally in the pool, playing the games and talking the talk of adolescents, boys showing off, girls emphasising their attractions.

Such it was that afternoon, with Ami late at picking up Tristan. He was among the last to get out of the pool and upon reaching his changing room, he found his locker empty. The changing room was desolate and there were no clothes in sight. After searching frantically and having no access to his cell phone in his shorts pocket, he made his way to the reception area, dripping in his swimming trunks, to enquire about his clothes. A middle-aged man was sweeping the floor nearby and shouted across the hall.

'Are you Tristan Kirkside? Okay, no probs, your mom rang to say she'd had a blow out and I offered to take you home. She's fine but wanted to make sure the right garage turned up to attend to her larny motor!' He laughed, putting brush against the wall. 'My car's out here. I'm Charlie, nice to meet you, man.' He shook Tristan's hand and led him out of the building.

Now shivering and a little self-conscious, Tristan was glad to find help so quickly, although the theft of his clothes – probably for the cell phone – would take some explaining. Charlie opened the front passenger door and let him in before reversing the car from the parking spot into a secluded edge of the swimming pool surroundings. Tristan's only recollection thereafter was a strong arm suffocating his throat from behind and a damp, medicinal smelling cloth being pressed against his face.

Tristan's experience had been preceded by Ami being pushed against the shelves in the empty kitchen equipment section in the Spar Supermarket in Constantia Village and having her handbag ripped from around her arm. She was bruised on the forehead and arm but otherwise unharmed. The two assailants were small Indian boys of about twelve years old, each with ubiquitous gel-spiked hair. They wore dark clothes and ran like the wind, vanishing through the garden section before Ami could think about shouting. She was due to collect Tristan from water polo but by the time she had reported the theft to the store detective and made a statement, the best she could do was ring the Garden Centre where a helpful man said he would find Tristan and bring him home. But that was two hours ago and as Ami obtained a substitute car key from the dealer's garage to return home to Ashwin, she felt out of control and feared for Tristan's safety.

She threw herself into Ashwin's arms, realising that no warning had been sent anywhere, losing precious time to start a search. Ashwin was calm but a bit dithery, not used to handling such events. He rang the police, the swimming pool and the local radio station. He then mustered half a dozen friends and dispatched them to public places along the Gardens Centre and Hout Bay route. By six o'clock it seemed the trail was cold and she watched the local TV news which mentioned Tristan's disappearance without any film. Only then did she suddenly link her mugging and Tristan's disappearance.

'Ashwin, I'm being so stupid! They're linked, don't you see? There's a gang that set the kids up to steal my phone and keys, while they abducted Tristan from the pool. The police say that Tristan went out with a man who worked there but the general manager says there's no such person! Don't you see?' Ami was weeping, her voice screaming at the quiet Indian professor. 'The police are useless, can't you see? I've got to call Maddox – he knows me and all my family secrets and is an honest cop!' Ami took time to trace Maddox's number without her handbag or cell phone but eventually managed.

'Maddox? Maddox, hello, its Ami Kirkside. Have you heard about Tristan? I think he's been kidnapped. I was mugged in a shop just beforehand and lost my bag and everything in it, including cell phone. Can you help please? The police know but I trust you more after all the horrors with Richard. About an hour? That's wonderful. What? *Don't* place a stop on my bank cards – are you serious? All right, anything you say. Maybe we could do something about that when you come? Remember I'm not in Hout Bay. I'm at 27 Ednam in Rondebosch Village – it's a block of luxury flats where I'm staying temporarily with Professor Ashwin Chetty. Thanks so much Maddox – I'll see you soon!'

Maddox was there within the hour, accompanied by Joost van der Merve, whom Ami had met at Maddox's office. Ashwin left them alone as Maddox conducted a fast but sympathetic enquiry, with Joost making phone calls as the evidence emerged.

'Ami, we must be patient, since if it's a kidnap, they are invariably accompanied by threats or extortion. I didn't want you to cancel your bank cards just yet because a thief usually rushes somewhere familiar to make purchases. Obviously you'll get any stolen amount back later from Standard Bank. So cancel them all at midday tomorrow please. Actually, there are grounds to believe that some criminals might want to threaten your husband, which could be the background. Strictly between you and me, he has incriminating evidence – through his professional business connections – connected to an ongoing series of large crimes.' Maddox's mind was working overtime.

'Please forgive this question, because I've no wish to offend you, but is there any possibility of you moving back to your Hout Bay address please? That will be the focus for communication and it will be much easier to set up an ops room with telephone detection kit and the like.' Ami scowled at first but nodded.

'Of course, I'll phone Richard. I'm sure he'll understand. He's as distraught as me.' What Ami did not guess was that Maddox wanted her as far away from the Chetty family influence as possible. There were no reasons to regard Ashwin Chetty as anything other than an honourable academic but he remained an inviting pressure point for his evil brother to apply merciless pain.

'That will make things easier. Could you manage this evening please? I'll be along later, possibly with some SAPS assistance if you've no objection?' Maddox glanced around the flat to thank Ashwin Chetty for accommodating them but he had vanished.

*****

Professor Ashwin Chetty was rarely invited to his brother's grand home in Parklands, on the edge of the fast-developing Blaauberg on the Atlantic Coast. There was an increasing number of well-to-do Indian families living in the district, often distinctive through their mock temple turrets and ornately scalloped terraces. Ravi Chetty had chosen a well-appointed place that was high enough to have its own sea view but set back from the road with impressive walls and fencing with elaborate security alarms. Clearly Ravi did not welcome unannounced visitors. Ashwin had not warned Ravi of his visit, coming impetuously when Maddox had arrived to interview Ami. He waited at the gate for five minutes while approval was given to the staff to open the huge wrought iron gates. Irritably, Ashwin drove up the drive through spacious gardens, devoid of flower borders and shrubs. Ravi had never found time for charm or human graces and had slipped into the real-life persona of an Indian mafia boss in recent years. Ashwin shuddered when he heard some of the behaviour and crimes with which he was said to be involved, from child pornography to underage drugs and prostitution. At school, Ravi had been two years ahead of him, which had made life difficult for an earnest and brilliant scholar like Ashwin. He blamed his father, a prosperous jeweller, for doting on Ravi as a first son, allowing him to develop lawlessly as a spoiled rich kid. Now Ashwin cursed himself for becoming so obsessed with academic study, missing the boat with girlfriends and a family of his own. Ami's presence had stimulated this regret powerfully, suggesting he should change his life by his mid-forties.

He was ushered into a bare entrance hall with a towering marble staircase leading to an equally soulless first floor. He first heard and then saw Ravi, clip-clopping in boots studded with metal motifs along an uncarpeted floor, skin-tight designer jeans and a collarless shirt with ballooning sleeves and pinched cuffs. Ashwin thought about an old version of *Gone with the Wind* he had seen, with Clark Gable as the swashbuckling hero. 'Howzit bro? How many birthdays since we met heh? Come on up man, the wife is away with her mother but I've got some friends staying. I wasn't expecting my famous brother to visit! Come to think of it, I haven't seen you on telly for a while?' Ravi wore sunglasses inside the house, accompanied by a glittering gold medallion and bracelet, never relaxing the image.

Ashwin joined the group upstairs, all Indians lounging around on sofas in a large room with a clear Atlantic view, white rollers crashing on the foreshore in the fading evening light. There were some young girls in the adjoining kitchen, crammed with stainless steel gadgetry. Two drooping chandeliers, with cut glass trails and expandable gold sheaths from the ceiling were the eye-catching items in the room which again had no wall pictures. There were thin tables along most of the walls, festooned with ornately framed pictures of family and special gatherings. Traditional Indian music played softly in the background and there was a distinctive smell of curry. Nobody moved or acknowledged Ashwin as he entered with his brother, despite Ravi asking them whether they knew him. Ashwin was not in a retiring or forgiving mood though.

'Ravi, can I have a word alone please? I'm sorry for interrupting but I won't keep you long.' Ravi looked visibly annoyed, raising his eyebrows in a sarcastic gesture to his friends, but pointed towards the rear of the house, where several rooms could be seen leading off the empty corridor. He overtook Ashwin to lead the way as there was some light muttering and jeering from the friends about Ashwin wanting some advice about government politics. Ravi turned into a windowless study that was lined with chocolate brown mahogany furniture and fittings, with a permanently lit table lamp providing the only pink illumination. Ravi sat behind his leather lined desk in a swivel club chair and motioned his brother to choose one of the plump easy chairs.

'Coffee?' Ravi poured two cups from a warming pot behind him without waiting for a reply. He put Ashwin's cup on a table beside him and returned to his chair. 'What's up? You never come here, so something's biting you? Word is you're shacking up with a fancy married piece?' Ravi gave Ashwin an unkind smile, knowing his remark would wound his gentle brother.

'Ravi, you're as rough in your language and tastes as you are in your behaviour! Is that the best I can expect as a brotherly welcome after six months?'

'No offence, brah, but that's the word on the streets. Some fat cat's chick – a stylish looker apparently? Didn't think you had it in you, Ash!' Ravi was not letting go, deliberately muzzling Ashwin's purpose and explanation for this unexpected visit.

'Just relax Ravi, okay? You live in the gutter, not even the streets! There is indeed a lady living in my flat – there's plenty of room. She's staying there for a short period while some personal problems are sorted out at her home. I don't have to explain further, but just to disappoint your dirty mind, we're professional friends, not lovers. I'm doing her a favour. Anyway, that's not why I'm here!' Ashwin was still angry and did not want to lose any momentum.

'Sure, sure, go on man.'

'Well, funnily enough, I'm not here to criticise but to ask for help. It's all about this woman that you seem to know something about already. In fact, she's Ami Kirkside, a UCT lecturer in my department. She's married to Richard Kirkside, who's an affluent Hout Bay stockbroker and financier. They've quarrelled and she's moved out while they mend the fences. That's all there is to it, except that they have a fifteen-year-old boy who is home-schooled as a bright kid. He was staying with her until earlier today when he went missing after playing some water polo at Gardens Centre. He left the pool with an oke who offered to drive him home because Ami had been mugged and lost her car keys. So it's looking like an organised kidnapping – did you hear about it on the news?'

'Nope. Nothing. So why are you here?'

'Look Ravi, you and I don't mix or talk. But we know enough about each other from family and friends to be adult about this. I know you cut a few corners with the law and have some funny friends – all of Cape Town knows that! I'm here to see if you can find out about this boy, help the police, and get him back unharmed – or whatever!' Ashwin was impassioned, appealing with outstretched arms while on the edge of his chair. Ravi didn't move though, sizing up his brother's motives.

'The way you're talking bro, it seems that you really are a bit sweet on this chick. Or is there some blackmailing going on?' Ashwin was infuriated that Ravi continued to wear his sunglasses in such a dimly lit room.

'I'm very fond of her, yes! We've worked together for ten years. But I'm not like you Ravi – I don't sleep with other men's wives. I feel responsible for her, and because of her problems, I'm the one she's turning to. Can't you see this? Come on Ravi, stop playing games – can you help me for once in your life?'

'I can put out feelers. I don't know enough to ask the right questions to the right people, if you know what I mean? He might be with friends playing tricks, he may have gone mad, he could have run off with a girl, he might be on drugs – who knows? If he's been kidnapped, there will be a demand, won't there? That might give a clue. Tell me, did she go to the police?'

'Of course. Store detective, police and then a private investigator she's used before.'

'Who's that?'

'Known as Maddox – I don't know anything about him.' Ravi sat back and folded his hands on his lap. He nodded his head slowly.

'Okay Ashwin, I'll do what I can. No promises because it's all so vague and it's a bit early. But something should come up. If it does, I'll let you know straight away, okay?' He stood up to end the meeting and walked with Ashwin down the broad staircase, with more chandeliers providing bright light. He opened the heavy door with its carved grapevine scenery on its central panel. 'Do you see much of our Mam these days…?' Ashwin passed by without a word, pausing to pick up a dropped set of house keys in front of his car. He considered taking them to Ravi but didn't see why he owed him any favours.

*****

Maddox was sitting with the Kirksides in the Hout Bay manor the morning after Tristan's disappearance. Joost was in Richard's study, using phones and laptop. Ami had received two calls from Standard Bank internet banking centre, revealing purchases made from her stolen credit cards in the last few hours. Joost had been tireless in his follow-up calls to bank and business centres and approached them with notepaper in his hand.

'Okay, boss. There's a bit of a pattern starting up. They're going for some hefty hits, I'm afraid Mrs Kirkside, but there we go! The first one was for sixteen thousand odd at Makros at Kenilworth – a huge, double opening wine and beer cooler – very larny and the biggest in stock, they say! The second purchase was an hour later at Sammy's Liquor Store in Gugulethu, where they spent six thousand on assorted booze and soft drinks. So it looks like they're on a mission for an existing or prospective shebeen, doesn't it? They're about fifteen minutes apart and right in the heart of gangland, as you know.' Maddox looked at Joost's pocket town map and stroked his chin. The areas satisfied his early guesswork. The Indian boys who stole the bag had obviously handed it on to adults as instructed, who in turn rushed out to buy something fast before stop orders were placed on the cards. If hurrying, people would not go across town to buy a heavy piece of kit like an industrial-sized beer and wine cooler. And having put it on a bakkie, they'd have gone to another convenient outlet to fill it up with booze. Firstly, it showed promise, being on the northern fringes of Cape Flats and secondly, it pointed towards an Indian trader in the district. He looked up at the Kirksides.

'Sorry that your card has been dented for so much, but as I said, we'll help you get the cash back. May I ask another favour please? Please stick it out it for just one more purchase. A pound to a penny, it'll be for a blow-out at Nando's or KFC in the Northern Cape Flats region for a dozen hungry crooks wolfing down chickens and steaks – it's the usual pattern! Please let us know, and anyway, when it happens, cancel all cards, whatever the purchase. The police are following up too and should be able to fast-track your replacement ID. We'll get them on the trail of local shebeens. Needless to say, we need to know about any messages about Tristan – check post boxes at your gate and the post office too. We'll come back later today, if that's all right?' Richard was looking gaunt and restless, while Ami's red eyes betrayed her anxiety.

96

After they'd left, the Kirksides sat together on the veranda, staring mindlessly at the garden and the swooping birds. Richard was remembering the magnificent Verreaux's Eagle Owl they'd seen some months before, looking for prey away from the cliffs beneath Hout Bay. The huge owl, Africa's largest, had made the tell-tale deep grunting call before they saw it in their tree lights, with creamy bill and brown barred feathers. He wanted such moments to return. Ami startled him by sudden conversation.

'What have you done Richard? Why are horrible people after you? Are you determined to destroy what's left of our lives, or what?' Ami looked more accusatory than enquiring, forward in her seat, clasped hands between her trouser thighs.

'We mustn't jump the gun, Ami – we don't know enough yet! But if it turns out to be a kidnap, it can only have something to do with the SFF account, which is being restructured right now into a colossal private holding, with accessible details concerning donors and investors. I've pretty well handled its accountancy as well as its brokerage since it began but at last the accountancy will now go elsewhere. Not before time – you're talking about ten billion plus washing around, making buckets of profit already. Everyone who's anyone in Cape Town and across the country – all the main JSE investment engines – have put their money in, inevitably including some dodgy bastards from abroad and here.' Richard described the story slowly and in a friendly way, pausing to smile as he explored the likelihoods.

'But that doesn't explain why you're linked to criminals?'

'I'm not, per se. But as I'm saying, and it's only a theory, I have provided information on SFF investments to a very small and trustworthy group investigating the recent serious crimes in the Cape Flats. It's possible, and no more than that, that someone's put two and two together and worked out that I might be the most likely person to know about deposits and withdrawals, including those made by criminals. So this might turn out to be someone putting the frighteners on me.'

'Oh my God.' Ami put her face in her hands and sobbed gently. Richard went to her and put his arms around her shoulders, holding her gently, reflecting that the last time that he had done so, he had received a heavy slap on his face.

*****

When Tristan woke, he felt dozy and had a light headache. He blinked and was frightened as his eyes looked around the large and still room. He was lying nude on a bed covered by a white blanket which looked freshly laundered. There were two other empty beds in a row, similarly covered by clean blankets. An old-fashioned ceiling fan whirred overhead and there was a long double tubed fluorescent light overhead which was switched on. Some tidy blue curtains covered an extensive window on one wall and there was a small table and two comfortable looking chairs. There was a small built-in wardrobe. The floor was fawn carpeted and clean. A small hand basin was in one corner with a large cabinet above it and a full-length mirror alongside. A confined shower with plain glass panels filled a corner, with a pair of large fluffy bath towels draped over a towel rail. There was a lavatory nearby. A row of three spotlights on a rail at the far side of the room looked incongruous. The only door had no handle. As far as Tristan could imagine, he was in a stranger's house but had no idea why. He got out of bed and pulled back the curtains, revealing a giant screen – a half-wall TV monitor without controls. His memory was not helping him as a voice terrified him by filling the room with sound.

'Hello Tristan. You've had a good sleep! You must be hungry. Have a shower and you'll find clothes hanging in the wardrobe. You're quite safe so do not worry or do anything silly. When you're ready, you can have a cooked breakfast. Do you mind saying "Yes sir" to me to show you understand everything please?' Blessed with a hyper-active brain, Tristan made a hundred constructions on all this but was interrupted.

'I didn't hear the "Yes sir", Tristan?' Tristan knew he looked frightened, not knowing where to look. He guessed that the screen was a one-way window and that the voice was in a room next door, since it was next to the handle-less door.

'Yes, sir.' His voice wobbled, neither child nor man. There was no further sound and glancing everywhere nervously, Tristan had a shower. He was amazed to find his stolen clothes from the swimming pool changing room in the wardrobe, which helped restore his kidnapping memory. There were other new clothes that looked his size hanging there. He heard a lock turning in the door and a young African girl of about his age entered the room carrying a tray with a plate full of bacon, eggs, sausage, tomato and mushroom, with knife and fork. Another girl of about the same age followed her with a mug of tea, a full toast rack, butter and jam. The door closed quietly behind them. They kept their eyes on their tasks and did not talk. One tapped on the door which was opened into darkness and they both disappeared, the door closing softly behind them. Tristan looked at the food and fantasised about being poisoned. This time a female voice filled the room again.

'Sit down and eat your breakfast, Tristan. We will feed you well. Use the lavatory whenever you want. We will show you some films after you've fed. Later, you will have someone to talk to and take some exercise. Please acknowledge.' Tristan was ravenous and decided to think about nothing else until he had finished the meal. He looked at the screen falteringly.

'Yes, sir.'

'It's "Yes ma'am" for a lady, Tristan. We must teach you the difference between boys and girls!' Tristan nodded, not knowing what to do. 'Let me hear it please, Tristan: "Yes ma'am".'

'Yes, ma'am.' He sat down and began to devour his food, which tasted excellent.

*****

'Ashwin? It's Ravi. I just wanted to say that your girlfriend's boy is safe. Please tell her that. I don't know anything else, so don't ring or pester me please. And Ashwin, please don't tell anyone else – I mean anyone, man – that I gave you this news. No computers nor telephones, heh? It's a personal favour from your brother and I'm taking a big risk for you. I might call you in a couple of days. Ciao'

*****

Ashwin marvelled at the opulence of the Hout Bay houses as he drove there to give Ami the news. He was touched that she had chosen to stay with him as a preference to all her rich friends or neighbours. He knew that Ami did not wear her liberalism too firmly stitched on her sleeve; when they engaged in politicised debate, it was invariably Ashwin who took the middle to left ground. She was the champion of self-determination, of gender and racial equality. But her eyes blazed when confronted with government welfare subscriptions and bloated state-fed bureaucracies reducing ambition and encouraging dependency. Ashwin had to be at his most eloquent and diplomatic to gently disabuse her of such bias; not many women were born into such privilege of race, wealth, beauty and intellect. He had not dared to warn her of his visit and wondered whether her quizzical expression when he arrived at her door was partly resentful.

'Ami, are we alone, just for two minutes, my love?'

'Yes, Richard's in his study. Are you going to ask me to be a bigamist, Ashwin?' This relieved the tension, as she pushed him by the elbow towards the rear croquet lawn. 'What's up?'

'Ami, I had to go to Ravi. I know we both think he is a brutal and cruel man, probably wicked through-and-through but that's why I went. It's the same as you, grabbing Maddox straight away because you thought he would get the first answers. In my case, I ran to my sinful brother because I thought he'd hear the low-life dirt before anyone else! Well, sure enough, he has. He rang me to say that Tristan's unharmed. He couldn't elaborate and that on pain of death – and Ravi means that when he says it – I wasn't to get in touch with him nor tell anybody other than you. So I'm happy for you but shit-scared too. It looks like there's some horrid stuff happening to your family!'

'Oh Ashwin, bless you my darling, bless you! We're all frightened but to hear, even from a villain, that Tristan's alive, means so much! Thanks for finding out and being brave with Ravi. I'm sworn to secrecy and won't even tell Richard but I wonder whether Maddox should know. What do you think?'

'I'm not sure. I trust him somehow too. But how about telling him in strictest confidence once you receive a demand for Tristan? That way, it's reasonable to assume Tristan is safe and Ravi's secret will be public knowledge.'

'Yet again darling, I know why you're my professor and I'm your lowly lecturer, your fawning acolyte!' Ami flung her arms around Ashwin, disturbing his glasses. She whispered in his ear. 'Do you know you're sometimes irresistibly sexy too? I've got a guilty feeling this is one of those moments.' They hugged and laughed, before Ashwin planted a chaste kiss on her forehead.

'I must fly. But let's pray it's true and that the news gets better?' Ashwin drove slowly round the hairpin bends back to the city. He was forty and unmarried, with delectable women like Ami enticing him. Maybe he ought to look around seriously? What about one of those discreet dating agencies?

*****

De Vries was controlling his anger with difficulty. He had re-assessed his Siyeza options and decided there was one more opportunity to get his message through to Jabu Nhleko. With just three months to go the general election, that was where every politician's mind lay in South Africa. The ANC's hammering in the local elections, losing them three provinces and reducing their popularity to 53 percent, meant that they were frantic to regain Gauteng and Eastern Province. The Western Cape was a lost cause but Siyeza had made this considerably more important for the DA – a force multiplier in voter appeal terms. De Vries judged that Nhleko was more interested in saving his own skin as Deputy President or even advance to the Presidency, provided a 20 percent lead was maintained in the overall vote. Although they would not be able to summon a two-thirds majority any more, Nhleko still judged the presidency a prize worth winning. In De Vries' cynical logic, Nhleko would do almost anything to protect his own image and popularity in his party caucus.

De Vries' Golden Boy image was fading. The restructuring of the SFF had exposed his donations and investments into ephemeral government funds. Nhleko and Jali had clearly cheated on him. Chetty had become increasingly random and unfocussed with his targets, sanctioned by the politicians. Where was the tripartite alliance he'd formed of ANC, organised crime and Dutch philanthropy? Before departing from Holland he planned a short, sharp lesson for Nhleko with two enforcers he used in Hong Kong – a very painful stick but a final fat carrot…

Jabu Nhleko's PA had told the Deputy President that De Vries had invited him to cocktails in a hired hospitality suite of the Sandton Sun at six o'clock. He had brought his senior banker and lawyer to make a new proposal concerning Siyeza, designed to dovetail in with the Deputy President's election programme. It was recommended that his bodyguards were excluded from the conversation and suite for the sake of discretion. Nhleko was both apprehensive but impressed. He felt he could weather one more tirade from the arrogant Dutchman and backpedal concerning the investments which were unaccountable. Of the five million Rand 'memorandum of business understanding' made by De Vries, Nhleko had placed three million in a presidential "holding account", moved a million into his private account as a "faciliatory charge" and had passed a million to Jali to set up an initial "Trade and Industry Siyeza Stand-By account" to be used, and increased, if private enterprise faltered. If De Vries insisted on knowing the full facts, he was willing to tell him, provided it did not adversely affect whatever new investment proposal De Vries had in mind.

Nhleko arrived at the base of the prestigious hotel in the middle of three sleek black Mercedes. The doorman, in purple suit and black top hat, said to be imitative of London's Hyde Park doormen, attempted to open the rear door with his white-gloved hand but was waved aside by a bodyguard already out of the lead car. Nhleko, ever more corpulent and less mobile, extracted himself from the car with just the slightest of a discreet pull by the elbow by the bodyguard. The general manager met him in the foyer while three bodyguards slid around the walls, one going straight to hold the lift in position. Once the Deputy had wheezed his way past sycophantic staff and chatted briefly to some prominent personalities he recognised, he gained the lift, where two bodyguards accompanied him. The lift rose swiftly, uninterrupted to the sixteenth floor, where De Vries met him to guide him across the thick carpet to their hospitality suite.

'Mr President, how wonderful to see you again! As I said to your PA, I suggest your men come inside and have a look round and then wait outside if that's suitable?' De Vries was confident that flattery was the best course. Nhleko nodded affably. He did not want to upset the prickly Dutchman further. All four of them made their way inside the suite, with its internet cubicles, kitchenette, refrigerators, video links, cash dispenser, huge satellite TVs, sumptuous sofas and assorted chairs, tables, poufs, shower room and lavatory. There was an extending screen raised into the ceiling and projection equipment. A waiter poured them champagne and placed delicious looking small canapes around the tables and took his leave, promising to return when a bell was pressed. De Vries's thugs, looking every inch an international banking executive and lawyer in their well-tailored lounge suits and quiet ties, rose to greet Nhleko before returning attentively to their chairs and attaché case contents, to studiously check their briefs. Nhleko nodded to his bodyguards, who left the room; one would stay outside and the other would stand by the lift station.

'Mr President, your very good health.' De Vries raised his glass politely as toasts were exchanged. He sat down and put a card on the table. 'That is my wish list, which you know about. But you're not delivering as agreed and I've run out of patience. I see there is now two billion invested into Siyeza, so I've facilitated about 2 percent, which is not bad for a private individual is it? And yet the five million I gave you has gone into thin air! Why's that Jabu?' De Vries was keeping his voice subdued as he sat close to Nhleko. I want to leave two messages for you. First, you get my little San City at the top of the programme, completed within the first three years. Just so you remember this, my accountant and lawyer will explain to you.' Faster than the obese little politician could move or think, one moved behind him and pinned his throat to the back of the chair with a bungee, and stuffed foam in his mouth, while the other lassoed his legs together with plastic ties. De Vries loomed over him and hammered his right palm into his groin, grabbing and twisting his testicles in a single excruciating movement. He held on and squeezed and twisted more as Nhleko writhed, contorted with pain. 'So my friend, please remember me next time and don't try to cheat. All right?' De Vries released his hold as the others took off their ties as fast as they had applied them, resuming their places in their chairs. The whole episode was over in thirty seconds. Nhleko tried to muffle his groaning, eventually staggering to the washroom to vomit. He had difficulty walking back and propped himself up on a chair back, rather than sit. De Vries had not finished.

'So before you go, please remember who you are and what you want to be in three months' time. You're no longer the most popular boy on the block and will need all the help and money you can get to be re-elected as Deputy or even convince the Executive that you're a prospect for President. Siyeza can change that for you, my friend, and I'm here to help too. If you do as I ask this time, there's twenty million going into the election account of your choice tomorrow – just ask. Are you hearing me, my friend? Bruised but not on the canvas?' Nhleko raised his eyes, watering black pools, full of hatred but defeated. He nodded, as if in answer to whether he would survive or whether he would never tell of tonight's incident. De Vries held his arm to judge whether he'd pass muster with his bodyguards. He was unsteady and gasped as his right leg moved forward. De Vries could not resist a parting shot. 'You'll have to hold back from that fancy piece masquerading as your PA. No class. We've got several videos and we think you should trade her in – she's not Presidential material, my friend!' De Vries reached the door, opened it sharply to wake the guard and patted the Deputy on the back. 'I think the champagne disagreed with the Deputy President – we all thought it was a bit odd. I'll complain to the management. A very good evening to you all and thank you so much for coming!'

De Vries slipped back into their room. 'Okay, let's make tracks – as quick as you can! We're booked on the nine thirty-five to Antwerp and have plenty of time if we don't dawdle.' He chuckled as completed their hurried departure. 'Wasn't that good, seeing that fat bugger scream? He won't forget us in a hurry!'

Chapter Nine

As Opposition Leader for the previous four years, Robin Phillips was judged a mediocre performer by the DA's opinion formers. More particularly, it wasn't the caricature moaning white voters that scored him that way but the decisive Coloured bulk of the Western Cape, where their vote was influential. Similarly, the straggling Eastern Cape with the high employment "automotive" towns of East London and Port Elizabeth were critical. This was an important factor, since Phillips was the first coloured leader of the Democratic Alliance, at a time when Siyeza was supposed to steal the domestic political limelight. He was seen as an honest exponent of liberalism and racial equality and outclassed Nhleko when allowed air time by the biased SABC. But the blatant corruption and professional incompetence of the ANC leadership had continued unchanged. Some party chiefs blamed this on Phillips' lack of combative spirit and his unwillingness to challenge the street-fighting and denialism of the national government. They suggested that the institutional fibre of government had been progressively undermined through factionalism and by manipulation of both the Constitution and the Parliamentary rule book. There was a general belief that the government should have discouraged populism in order to justify a co-operative private sector.

Nobody was more aware of the political conflict than Kobus Labuschagne. Now three-quarters through his mayoral term of office, he assessed his chances of either mayoral re-election or consideration to succeed Phillips as above average. If Siyeza continued to promote hope to the city poor and if the DA managed to avoid ANC suffocation, his star would rise. But in the irony that always underlines political manoeuvrings, Siyeza made Labuschagne an enigma. He could be judged an essential component to see the Siyeza story through to completion or represent a chance to invigorate the lacklustre DA leadership. The party had to choose quickly, to allow him a year before the local elections, unless he was judged sufficiently formidable to stay on as mayor while leading his party – a not unknown phenomena.

It was with these undercurrents flowing around Cape Town that Kobus Labuschagne received a peremptory bidding from the Presidency to present a "Pre-Election Progress Report on the Siyeza Enterprise" that would be overseen by Malusi Jali. It would be funded entirely by government as a two-day inter-party forum to examine its progress and participation, agree its handling and determine its next five years. It would be introduced by the President, with the Chinese Minister for African Affairs as its keynote speaker. A draft programme indicated that Labuschagne and Bofokeng would be allotted ten minutes' speaking each on the second day. Harry Reynolds would be invited to sit on a panel chaired by Jali, which would include De Vries, the Communist Party leader and the trade unions executive national chairman. With three months to run for the General Election, it appeared to be a cavalier hijacking attempt by the government and ANC, intent on distorting facts and wresting the project's control from Labuschagne and the DA's grasp.

'Did you know I got a call from the President's DA this morning?' Lesebo asked Kobus as he arrived for their weekly conference. He's organising a huge Siyeza fundraising pageant at Sun City and wants me there as his "Miss Siyeza" partner. Are you invited too?'

'First I've heard of it. They are pulling out all the stops, aren't they? All of a sudden, Siyeza is showered with confetti and taxpayer's cash. How do you rebut someone like Nhleko? He's hammered senseless everywhere he goes but he won't lie down. You know, despite all the glitter, I sometimes wonder whether Siyeza is the Number One horse in the national stable. There are artificial pressures that are keeping it pumped up, aren't there?' Labuschagne paused to enjoy this private conversation with Lesebo before they entered the building. Every time he came to the site, there had been further exciting progress, with major roads in place, the benchmark civic buildings begun and the first few estates cleared in readiness to begin construction. There was land clearance stretching from Ottery, Hanover Park and Manenberg across to Philippi and Rocklands. The level of concurrent industrial activity was prodigious, with TDC entering the frame in full force as the perimeter was made ready. He smiled approvingly at Lesebo. 'Anyway, did you accept?'

'I said I would if you could come as Mr Siyeza!' She laughed and touched his arm. 'No I'm lying Kobus! But I accepted. They will fly me there and back first class, with all expenses paid at Sun City for two nights. But don't worry Kobus. I haven't changed. I'm not a celebrity. My little black feet are firmly on the ground – in the dirt, in fact! If they invite me to say anything on the record, they will be severely embarrassed!'

*****

Harry Reynolds had been invited to Parliament for an informal discussion with Malusi Jali on "industrial co-operation". He was in the middle of site management meetings in Cape Town but accepted that the TDC contract would experience perpetual ministerial interference. As always, the consummate businessman had gone through the drills before flying, by debriefing Labuschagne, Bafokeng and Kirkside, besides examining recent government co-operative partnerships with constitutional and government small print. Upon arrival, he was met by a departmental functionary who showed him into an empty room. After fifteen minutes, a secretary fetched him and led him along a long corridor to the largest assembly room on site, designed as a university-style lecture amphitheatre. At first sight, Reynolds guessed at fifty members being scattered around the ascending seats, all equipped with desk microphones. Jali sat at a small table with two chairs in the small, semi-circular stage. He saw Reynolds arrive but finished his discussion before greeting him.

'Ah, Mr Reynolds, welcome! This hot seat next to me is for you, my friend!' Jali rose, indicating the pine sit-up-and-beg school chair he was offering. He waited for Harry to sit down, before introducing him. 'Honourable comrades, guests, ladies and gentlemen of the construction industry! It is my pleasure to welcome Mr Harry Reynolds, CEO of Trustcore Developments Corporation, the British construction company that was selected as an overseas partner in the impressive collection of interested parties that we've assembled here today.' He turned to Harry. 'Mr Reynolds, we've been deep in discussion for a couple of hours discussing our unique South African skills and experience in such undertakings and are keen to hear how you will dovetail in. We thought it best that selected individuals introduce themselves and invite you to say how you can accommodate them through co-operative agreements, partnerships, tenders and the like?' Jali did not wait for anything from Harry, promptly ducking into an armchair in the front row, an expectant grin on his face. Like all influential businessmen, Harry Reynolds had been exposed to attempts to "bounce" him into decisions or to deliberately misinterpret his action or words. This one was an extreme example however and he knew there were no neutral witnesses.

'Thank you Minister, and good morning to all of you. May I begin by asking whether this is an on-or-off-the-record discussion, or whether it is being recorded in any way please?' Harry stared at Jali who looked flustered.

'I think we have to say that it will get into the public domain, Mr Reynolds, because of our many different representatives here.'

'Fine but in that case, to protect my contract obligations, I must ask for it to be recorded and to be given a transcript on departing please.' Harry sat absolutely still, looking at Jali who squirmed in his seat and muttered instructions to an official who entered a booth and activated the recording equipment. This took two minutes, during which a hubbub of conversation rose among the delegates.

'Okay Mr Reynolds, we are live now. Please proceed.'

'Thanks. I have flown up from Cape Town in order to have an informal discussion with the Minister about industrial co-operation, so this assembly needs some explanation please? As the CEO of the main contractor appointed by the government to deliver the entire Siyeza enterprise, I am bound by the text signed by the Deputy President. The document is both complex and definitive, running into two hundred and fifty pages. There is nothing to be found in that document that requires me to issue tenders per se, although the legal aspects of sub-contracting are clearly described. We have already signed off several sub-contracts to both foreign and domestic companies and anticipate many more in the full course of the project's completion.'

'Sipho Ndebele, General Secretary COSATU. Why are you giving jobs to your friends? Nobody here was invited to bid for your sub-contracts. Do you know about Black Economic Empowerment, my friend?' Mr Ndebele looked full of menace, shouting into his microphone at close range.

'You interrupted me before I got going, Mr Ndebele! You might not know that bidders for the main government contract had to submit a full list of anticipated sub-contractors in the initial bid – from memory we submitted twenty-seven annexures, of which twelve covered indigenous choices. Our bid was scrutinised thoroughly by the government. In its notice of acceptance, the sub-contracts were seen as a persuasive element that helped secure the contract. So these sub-contracts were written into the bid and fully costed. We will enforce these sub-contracts at the quoted rates – obviously we achieved agreement in all cases before we submitted the bid. So I'm not sure what you're getting at, to be frank?'

'I'm not meaning these sub-contracts you refer to. I'm talking about the offset benefits for South African industry and labour that must come with contracts of this size. I'm not talking about companies that are going to do your work at a lower price to maximise your profit! I'm talking about wholescale benefits for the community at large in the Cape Flats, carried out exclusively by local labour. There has been no mention of TDC offering anything!'

'Mr Ndebele, it is always helpful if debate is free of insults or provocation and if all stated facts are based on truth. The sub-contractors have been engaged using every South African political and labour relations contingency, following the advice and drafting carried out by government-contracts experts. Secondly, your offset worries are misplaced. There is absolutely no obligation to introduce offset clauses within contract bids. However, however...' Reynolds raised his voice above the jeering that had erupted, '...however, since it has become commonplace in South Africa and elsewhere, TDC went to considerable trouble in setting up a comprehensive training scheme to benefit South African engineering students through UK university scholarships and bursaries. The first twenty students will begin civil engineering degrees next October at four British universities. In parallel, TDC will fund and establish preparatory science colleges in Cape Town, Johannesburg and Durban, aimed at promoting science, engineering and technology, from whom twenty students per year will be selected competitively. Subject to performance, they are all guaranteed employment within the greater TDC group working at Siyeza. This will continue for five years.' Reynolds paused, to allow random interruptions to be formed as questions.

The delegates maintained their glowering and dismissive gestures but offered no comment as Reynolds continued. 'So eventually a hundred South African engineering graduates will be deployed, with transfer arrangements facilitated between TDC and South African companies or institutions requiring such professional skills. They will remain under personal binding contracts themselves to continue working in South Africa until the government pronounces Siyeza complete. Now, overall, this will cost sixty million Rands to launch the teaching institutions, superannuated by the government, while the bursaries will cost over a hundred million Rand annually, found by TDC. This was TDC's "offset" contribution, if you like, agreed with the government, who presumably share our view that extra-mural expenditure is best directed towards the academic and skilled employment shortfalls experienced here.' Harry scarcely moved or gestured as he explained this to a fidgeting and muttering Ndebele. The body of the delegates were similarly restless but became silent. This was no ordinary boss who shouted and dug his heels in, but Ndebele decided to change tack.

'Okay, okay. But nobody told us this before. How can South African small businesses and labour unions have a part in all this? Before you arrived, we decided with the minister that we needed more say in Siyeza and he will tell you about the council he will establish to protect our interests. We are very concerned that things are being done that are harmful to our interests and we need to look at all the contract details. Maybe we need to re-negotiate some things? We would be able to register objections through the council, which would have a day-to-day control of the Siyeza operation?' Ndebele had come to the main point behind Reynolds being summoned to meet them. It was an instrument to undermine and challenge TDC, perhaps to split it into digestible parts which the ANC and the unions could more effectively understand and control. Reynolds stared at Jali as the portly minister took the floor.

'Maybe we should have asked you along earlier to share our thoughts Mr Reynolds, but the government shares the concern of the small businesses and unions that your contract was perhaps too all-embracing, neglecting the needs of the urban masses? Maybe even your training scheme needs re-thinking? You see, my comrades, Mr Reynolds will say that additional tasks and employment must be part of fresh government contracts, because he has already accounted for some companies with his own sub-contracts. But two years downstream, we're worried about what we agreed and feel that it deserves a re-think. Maybe Cape Town Municipality must be asked to reconsider some of the elements of the overall plan? Is there sufficient large-scale enterprise in the planning, is there a huge attraction to magnetise trade and business to the Cape Flats once everything is complete? We must decide soon about all this and approach the Presidency to set up a high-level Council immediately. Mr Reynolds, we thank you for your contribution and time. You have given us much food for thought. We intended breaking for lunch now, where you are welcome but after that, we don't think you need stay. We will be itemising the list of companies and structural objectives that we will inform you about in due course.' Jali had never been so emboldened and decisive. The threats delivered personally by Jabu Nhleko had left Jali in no doubt. Not only was his political future at stake but also his personal safety.

*****

Tristan was lying on his bed, not knowing what to do or what would happen. He was in permanent daylight, in neither hot nor cold temperature, and had been fed another delicious meal by the same two girls. They had collected his tray afterwards and he had been told he would have visitors. The door opened and the two girls re-entered. They were both dressed in skimpy T-shirt night dresses and carried rolled-up towels. They sat on the edge of a neighbouring bed, swinging their legs and for the first time, smiled nervously at Tristan. One of them spoke.

'Hello Tristan. I'm Thandiswa and this is Mashu. We've come to wash and go to bed.' She stood up and pulled her nightdress over her head in one movement, dropping it on the bed. She sat on the lavatory and smiled at him as she urinated, before opening the shower door and adjusting the spray's temperature. She beckoned to her friend who copied her actions, joining her under the shower. They washed each other, giggling and shouting. Tristan was transfixed. He'd never seen girls so intimately before and could not ignore them in this small prison cell. Because there were two of them, both about his age, he felt intimidated. If he spoke, he was worried about taunting or recriminations. They seemed so natural in their nudity, scarcely paying attention to him as they dried each other with the same gentle attention. They put their nightdresses back on and clambered into a bed together. Thandiswa noticed his stare and spoke again.

'Why don't you have a shower too, Tristan? It's late and we must go to sleep. They turn the lights off quite soon.'

'I'm fine thanks.' Tristan found his voice, which he wished would stay deeper. He heard a stifled snigger from the girls. 'I had a shower earlier.' He removed his shoes and got under a blanket in his bed. He heard the girls talking and laughing softly and heard them shuffling in the bed. His loneliness surfaced and he felt frightened. He dare not cry in case the girls heard him. He stared at the ceiling wishing the light would be switched off. He couldn't remember when he went to sleep or when the light was doused, waking the next morning with the light still on and the girls vanished. The disorientation was increasing his anxiety and he yearned for something to do or read, somebody to talk to. He missed his mother and father acutely.

*****

When Richard Kirkside cleared his post office box one Saturday morning, he found a recorded delivery slip among his post. He presented it at the post office counter and was handed a sealed bubble-wrapped parcel. Upon arrival home he deposited the mail, which was still plentiful, despite the era of digital communication in the investment world, on his office desk. It was lunchtime before he recalled leaving it there. Having poured a glass of wine for Ami, who had returned home after shopping, he plundered the pile in a random fashion. He slit open the bubble wrap envelope and drew out a vellum note placed between two pieces of stiff cardboard. Unfolding it, he knew in advance that it concerned Tristan.

Mr Kirkside.

We know you are worried about Tristan. He is safe with us and will not be harmed if you follow these instructions carefully.

1. *Send the Text Message 'Received' to 987123654*
2. *Do not inform anyone about this message*
3. *Wait for our next instruction, when we will ask a big favour from you*
4. *If you tell the police or media, Ami will disappear and not return*

Richard's hand trembled as he read the message again. It had a childish but chilling style to it. He heard Ami moving around in the kitchen, preparing a light lunch. It was not a question of whether he should tell her, but how. And Maddox must be told too.

*****

Noting that Harry Reynolds was in country again, Kobus Labuschagne called an emergency meeting of the 'Three Wise Men' in Lesebo's office and asked Harry to attend. It was a wet, grey day which seemed an appropriate backdrop to their overall morale. With very few pleasantries, Kobus opened the discussions.

'When we last met, we said we'd only meet again if things went very well or very badly. We all have a different story to share but I'm pretty certain that we all feel there's been a genuinely dangerous and irrational attempt by the government to hijack Siyeza wholesale. I know Harry Reynolds has been deliberately picked out and targeted so I'm making a unilateral decision to include him in this crisis meeting. I know it breaks business and contract Ts and Cs but unless he's involved now, we are powerless to prevent state intervention and control. Does anyone have exception to that please?' Kobus glanced around before adding ironically, 'After all, this assembly already breaks every ethical rule in the game, as is invariably the case when covert discussions take place, but we all agreed that no alternatives exist?' There were a few heads shaken but no comments, allowing Kobus to carry on. 'It seems that this surge to usurp Siyeza – its contracts, funding, the municipality's management, the DA connection – are coming from the Presidency, probably Nhleko himself. As far as I can see, there is some extraneous backing for him, centred on the forthcoming election. Nhleko wants to tell the country that the state has every aspect under control and that the union's misgivings will be addressed. There will be an injection of high-profile development as a core attraction, not just to Cape Town, but the provincial hinterland.' Labuschagne threw his hands upwards. 'Am I getting this right, Harry?'

'Oh yes, you are but it gets worse! I much appreciate being included today because the very basis of TDC participation is being politically undermined. I was summoned to an informal discussion with Jali a few days ago which turned out to be a carefully orchestrated ambush, with fifty BEE candidate firms and major unions represented. I was more or less told that the TDC contract would be re-examined and probably redrafted and broken down to match personalised tendering, with overseas bidding excluded. I've approached the UK government and a junior Foreign Office Minister is seeing the Deputy President with the British High Commissioner next week. Meanwhile, as Lesebo will tell us, we've had our first labour troubles on site, with supply vehicles being prevented entering construction sites at Hanover Park and Manenberg. Probably a thousand protesters blocked the routes, heavily reinforced by rent-a-mob, objecting to foreign companies employing South African nationals without union agreement. Now, this is hardly a unique experience to TDC but this time, there is no point of arbitration to defuse the conflict, since government is a scarcely veiled agitator.' Harry was not his buoyant self, which had a disheartening effect on the others. They were not used to him ending any account without ending on a positive 'look forward' solution or recommendation. Lesebo decided to confirm his story.

'I was blatantly targeted by the Deputy President when he asked me to appear as Miss Siyeza fund raising pageant in Sun City. I went along, having spoken to Kobus but refused to speak in a contrived back-slapping evening show. All the government and quite a few Joeys' high society were there and there was a general understanding that I was a bought item in the ANC arsenal, there to ensure that their will was imposed at Siyeza! The government PR machine is working overtime, as we're all experiencing, with spin doctors on all the news channels, phone-in radio and broadsheet and online columnists. The DA and Cape Town Municipality never feature in any of the handouts or discussions.' Lesebo let this sink in before she turned to the site management. 'On site here meanwhile, things are tense and the atmosphere's unpleasant. Some cars have been stoned in the mornings and there's no extra police presence. I was visited by a Department of Trade and Industry 'management investigation' team and some of the labour force are being waylaid by union representatives, accompanied by Department of Labour officials. They're definitely slowing the game down, as if ordered to do so by high level edict.' Both Richard and Maddox were listening intently as these first-hand accounts emerged. Richard did not want to divulge any detail about Tristan and while Maddox was in a privy position in the information loop, he was bound by confidences to the Kirksides and Khanyisile Mthembu. But both felt it necessary to fill in some gaps between the commentaries for their collective good. Labuschagne looked at Kirkside, whom he admired for attending during such harrowing times for him and his wife.

'Richard, it's really good of you to come. Our prayers are still with you and your wife as we all await a peaceful outcome. But there's no doubt that you continue to occupy a central position in the whole story through your control and knowledge of the funding that underwrites the whole concept. So anything you can add will be much appreciated.' He smiled reassuringly at Richard, who although pale and thinner, managed a smile and looked in full control.

'Thanks Kobus, and everyone else here, for your kind remarks and prayers. Like you, we can only wait and hope that we're dealing with realistic criminals and not deranged lunatics. Since we last met, Tristan's abduction has not only preoccupied me personally but has also overflowed into the general Siyeza picture. We are advised to say nothing about any developments regarding Tristan but I can say that there is a proposal to rename and restructure the entire SFF holding, following the unexpected resignation of several board members and their replacement by government appointees, including Sipho Ndebele, COSATU General Secretary. There is an implicit warning that the funds might be frozen by government if private enterprise decides to withdraw support. So my personal position on the board has become tenuous, with further proposals to reposition the professional brokerage arrangements that currently exist. That cannot be done overnight and we can appeal for preventative court orders if need be, but in the long run, it seems that Nhleko has extended presidential control over financial management matters. It seems that the likely intention is to redistribute assets to match the rewritten contract that Harry has just warned us about. In other words, cancel a considerable proportion of TDC's existing contractual remit in order to divert funds towards alternative schemes which have not yet materialised.' Kirkside was being as frank as he dare but his story completely corroborated that of Harry Reynolds; the government had moved fast on a wide front, ignoring any legal or constitutional restraints. By forcing the resignation of a neutral chairman from the private sector and replacing him with Malusi Jali, the government was challenging private enterprise head-on and demonstrating the rapid arrival of populism on the national stage. The inevitable court orders, court hearings, appeals and counter-appeals would follow but in their present mood, it seemed that the cabinet was not only prepared to try, but was insistent upon, this course of action. The options for compromise appeared few. It was a time for cool-headed decisions. Maddox judged it the right moment to dispel the overall pessimism.

'I have a couple of points. The investigations into serious crime in the Cape Flats are making progress. As you know, Solomons' murderer became a murder victim himself during his parole and police enquiries have gone well in tracing those responsible. We're told to expect arrests shortly. There is firm evidence incriminating an overseas element who are funding and to some extent orchestrating Nhleko's actions, certainly timed for maximum election appeal. Intervention there is proving very sensitive and complicated, so it might be that we try to keep the boat steady until beyond the Election. Negotiation, legal appeal, even litigation, with clever news releases might be necessary. Obviously TDC have right on their side and can raise an enormous international firestorm whenever they choose.' Maddox raised both arms in the air, appealing for support but unsure of his position. 'Maybe we can de-stabilise Nhleko's bid for either Presidency seat? Right now, all the politicians are pounding the beat, chasing the vote, so I think there might be a short breathing space when we can get in the right position to strike back? I'm out of my depth here, Kobus, so forgive me! Maybe you'd better guide us all to beyond the Election, when the ANC will go into a coven to hand out the spoils? That said, you've got your own hands full for your mayoral race and DA hustings, I assume?' Maddox broke off with a grin, forcing a wry acknowledgment from the robust Afrikaner.

'*Luister na die Engelsman*!' Kobus waved cheerily at Maddox and stood, his mind whirring overtime as he deliberated on a middle course to retain control of Siyeza, while confronting the government and ANC's audacity in attempting a political and business coup. He pulled up his slipping trousers waistband and leant forward, knuckles on the table. 'Maddox is right. We're all ensnared by the Election. I'm spending a lot of time around the constituencies in the next few weeks, although Siyeza is obviously my main preoccupation! But Lesebo will be a wonderful anchor for us all, I'm certain. Let's agree a line then. Harry will follow his business instinct and take whatever legal advice he thinks necessary to protect his contract, even if it includes UK litigation. Richard may be forced to place injunctions on the SFF board if the ethics and legally binding contracts with clients are contested or manipulated. Lesebo might have to invoke municipality and police co-operation if construction activity is further delayed or wilfully obstructed. As for Maddox, well I think you must keep us all commonly informed from now on, regarding any blow-by-blow occurrences regarding criminal arrests or formal charges being preferred? Concurrently, we must expect more pressure in the next month, as the ANC tries to brainwash the public and play the denial game regarding Harry's contract and the SFF board. I think that all is far from lost, because Nhleko has shot his bolt by being so naïve in the political arena a couple of months before his supposed re-election!'

*****

Khanyisile Mthembu grinned at Maddox as she sipped her Nespresso coffee. Her brilliant green and gold turban matched to perfection her amber dress with cuffed three-quarter sleeves. It was fair to say that nobody would guess she was a senior policewoman, but then she had not had sufficient time in the force to adapt to the standard behaviour and appearance. They had enjoyed a light lunch at a Fish Hoek seafood café at her request; like Maddox, she had accepted that over-eating was spoiling other things. She was in a good frame of mind, full of her successes in gradually cleaning out the rotten apples in her police headquarters barrel: three of the target list of seven had either resigned, been posted or accepted early retirement terms. Her sister, Lindiwe Nhleko, ex-wife of Jabu, was proving helpful in her Minister of Women in the Presidency capacity, largely because most of the dismissed police had committed crimes against female witnesses. The gangland murderer, still in custody with another force, could stand trial now but partly due to Maddox's advice, it was being delayed to be twinned with arrests and charges against Sonny Chopra and Ravi Chetty. Maddox had elaborated on this for her.

'Khanyisile, I think a little patience will pay big dividends. We're waiting for a trigger concerning the Kirkside boy kidnapping, having heard nothing from those involved, except an anonymous message that he was unharmed. When we get that, I think you can nail them, if your lawyers are fully confident about convictions.' Maddox privately worried about the eventual conditions that the criminals would impose on Richard Kirkside, who filled the critical key witness role against Chetty and Chopra. Maddox remained convinced that they would pressure Kirkside into refusing to appear or even give false evidence.

*****

'Hi, Pedro Salamisa, isn't it? Good to meet you!' Richard Kirkside greeted the small but portly client on his doorstep. The swarthy Portuguese had telephoned a few days before to make an appointment with a view to making investments into the SFF. Richard was receiving half a dozen new clients each week and despite his invidious position and family danger, felt that as many commissions as possible was a sensible venture, in readiness for a possibly absurdly high extortion figure he would receive any day for the return of Tristan. 'Nice place you have here, Mr Kirkside. Is business going well for you?' Kirkside was leading him through to his study. Ami was out shopping briefly, both of them hugging the house as they waited for news. They both sat down in chairs either side of the solidly carved table. Richard was doing his usual first impressions analysis of Salamisa, who had turned up in a locally registered Hyundai hatchback. He was drably dressed, wearing heavy glasses, no showy signs of wealth, middle aged, and mild Portuguese accent – not a typical Kirkside punter.

'Well Mr Salamisa, you are looking to invest in Siyeza, you said?'

'Listen carefully and don't say anything or do anything stupid – remember we've got Tristan. No recording, photos, telephone calls, okay?' The portly visitor looked casually menacing, as if he did this sort of thing for a living. He sat forward and spoke with authority. 'The oke in hiding with the police is moving back to Cape Town on Monday. He will be charged along with Chetty and Chopra. You are the key witness. You will not give evidence or make any statement, do you understand? Maybe they will go ahead without you – it doesn't matter. When the trial's over, Tristan will be released. That's that, but of course there's a service charge. Details are in your PO Box. Follow the instructions and wait for the trial to finish but like I said, don't do anything silly. You won't see me again.' Richard heard the stranger's car drive away on the gravel, before he realised he had not noted the number plate apart from the Cape Town letters. He waited for Ami impatiently, since one of them had always stayed in the house since Tristan disappeared. He had to empty his post box.

*****

Maddox read the note again, before looking at Ami and Richard.

Make the following transfer via EFT from your Kirkside Wealth Management Holdings account to the following destination:

Pacific Horizons Bank
Chiang Mai Branch, Thailand, 38673
Account No: 75038812043
Account Name: Save the Children Fund
Amount: One million Rand [R1,000,000]
Once completed, send the Text Message 'Dispatched' to 987123654
Allow 5 days for the transaction to clear
Do not communicate with either police or media during the trial and do not go to the court

Do not give evidence against anyone – you know what this means
If you make any mistakes, Ami will disappear and never return

*****

'Well this is about what we expected, isn't it? Certainly a nasty sting in the tail. My contact tells me they've pulled in Chetty and Chopra and several other Cape Flats mafia. My guess is that Tristan is safe somewhere quite close. It's a cynical game, making a million bucks seem incidental to your non-appearance as a witness. I'll get my girl to get Interpol working on that Thai account's ID. When I get advice back, I think you should pay up. Not many people can kiss that much goodbye Richard, but forgive me for thinking you might be one of them? And in your game, you've probably got indemnity against bogus investments?' Maddox had a bit of a glint in his eye as he spoke, with Kirkside remaining imperturbable. Ami just kept staring wide-eyed at Maddox, holding Richard's arm tightly. 'I think they'll go ahead with the trial – the government need credibility over Siyeza and a successful prosecution would help. They should nail Chopra, since your evidence didn't affect him. But Chetty will get off without your proof of international transfers. So De Vries will live to fight another day too. But there we are – it's a big start and with luck, we'll have Tristan back quite soon.' Maddox was speaking his mind, since there was nothing to hide or withhold between the Kirksides and himself. Ami dissolved into tears however, turning her head into Richard's shoulder.

'You hear the most ghastly things about lengthy kidnapping of rich victims – the villains are sadistic and drugged, as well as violent and greedy. They're perverts, who don't like innocent people to feel they've won a single point!' Richard held her head gently, stroking her hair.

*****

'Wake up Tristan, we've been told to wash you this morning. We all get clean clothes on a Monday! And then we're going swimming!' Tristan stretched and opened his eyes at Thandiswa and Mashu who were half-kneeling on his bed, unabashed in their short cotton nightdresses. He had gained sufficient confidence to talk openly to them and not be so self-conscious. Thandiswa pulled back his duvet and gently tugged his arm. 'Come on, you'll get us into trouble.' She pulled her nightdress over her head and stepped into the shower. 'Come on, there's just room for the three of us!' Tristan moved in shyly alongside Thandiswa but was surprised by Mashu's hands as she wet the soap and began to wash him, beginning where he hoped she would never go. The fast-flowing water drowned some of their excited laughter and chatter but Tristan had begun to enjoy it as much as the girls. 'Now me Tristan, you haven't washed me down there yet, have you?' Tristan did as the girls told him and was embarrassed about his excitement as the girls dried him. A booming woman's voice broke their chatter.

'Did you enjoy that, Tristan?' The hollow voices were part of his life now and he had stopped objecting to their simple questions or instructions.

'Yes ma'am,' he replied in a matter-of-fact tone, bending to dry his feet. This time, he almost meant it.

Chapter Ten

Harry Reynolds was demonstrating the terrain adjustments within the Land Rover Sports he used on site during his frequent visits to South Africa. Lesebo Bafokeng was moderately impressed but preferred something smaller and practical that went as quickly and was easier to park.

'What you must remember is the power of advertising. If you're conditioned by petrol head mythology – like "all Land Rovers break down" – then you're unlikely to judge it against peers, variants or even predecessors. Land Rover began as a military vehicle during the Second World War, like the American Jeep, and kept its no messing military image because that's what sold it around the world. Here, look at this now!' He interrupted his lecture to demonstrate an abrupt descent down an embankment being excavated by earth moving equipment, with his hands and feet off all control levers. 'Isn't that something? And yet Land Rover critics don't believe because they don't know. They did break down but then nothing else went off road! They did everything in Africa – military, farming, game viewing, hunting, trekking. But smart motor mechanic skills dried up in Africa – no servicing garages, no dealers. Along came Toyota – cheaper, plentiful, quality improving. Plus, of course, militant unionism struck British industry in the '60s and '70s and Land Rover went through American, German and Indian hands – that's the strength of a big brand!' Harry seemed in his element as an engineer playing with a perfect toy. 'And then the roaring SUV race started, with every brand wading in. But now, the Landy is back at the top, but a bit technical because of the competition. Here, have a drive!' Reynolds stopped the vehicle and jumped out, moving swiftly around the bonnet to open Lesebo's door. 'Mark my words, you'll be getting one before the year's out!'

'It hasn't got a front passenger mirror for God's sake! And how do I adjust the seat?' Lesebo looked at home, in laced leather boots, light khaki trousers and a tailored green shirt with breast pockets and epaulettes. A fawn bandanna accentuated her rounded forehead. She pressed the button indicated by Harry. She set off confidently, switching between terrain modes, unfazed by steep gradients or recently disturbed construction surfaces. 'Yes, it's fun, but too expensive just for looking pretty and being the best off-roader, don't you think? It's a status for young rich mums in the city but too big for a parking space to pick up the kids at school!'

'Well, that's not your worry, is it Lesebo, as CEO of a multi-billion project in Africa?' Harry laughed and pointed to a vantage point from where they would be able to view the latest areas that were being graded for housing. Lesebo took them there as if she'd owned a Land Rover all her life, and once there, opened the front windows and switched off. Harry shuffled in his seat to face her and disconnected his iPad. 'While we're here, let's talk about the "what ifs" of adjusting the contract serials. Have you looked at my proposed options yet?'

'Of course. It looks like replacing about 15 percent of the contract serials, with a start value of about seven and a half billion Rands?'

'About that – something like three hundred million Sterling. It'll fluctuate with forex and inflation but it's a hefty chunk. Look, it's not the end of the world. It seems that the government are after land in certain areas, rather than awarding sub-contracts to competitors or their cronies.' Harry was subdued. For all his experience and powerful support staff, he was talking realistically to an African woman whom he already respected and trusted. 'My guess is that they'll turn to us for a fresh construction contract but nobody knows, because the SFF, or SPF or *Siyeza People's Fund,* as they're now calling it, is being run by left wing populists.'

'So how are you going to stage things, to stay on side if things reverse themselves after the Election?'

'Well, I'm saying we ring-fence a thousand-hectare block in the northern edges of Schaap Kraal, between the Ottery and Phillippi Industrial boundaries. That's a big space but not too much hardship for architects and planners. There's that arterial road already skirting it to the north – look there,' indicated Harry by pointing. 'But until we know exactly what they've got up their sleeve, we can't have a tidy plan. I don't think we'll know until after the Election – if it was a vote winner, we'd have heard about it by now.' Harry smiled at Lesebo. 'I bet you want to drive us back to your office to give me a cup of your very best coffee?'

'Great minds think alike, Mr Reynolds! I might borrow this wagon when you go back to UK next week! How does your wife take to all this separation, by the way?' Lesebo flashed Harry a look as she began to trundle across broken terrain and littered construction debris.

'We've been apart for over ten years. But we're still married. She lives and works in Clerkenwell as a publishing editor and loves the life. We don't agree over much but never quarrel, if you know what I mean? We meet up now and again.' He paused before adding, 'There's a grown-up son who's a futures trader in Dubai.'

Lesebo resisted asking more personal questions. Harry had shown no sensitivities and appeared to regard his family life as normal. Be he didn't want to dwell on it.

'If you want to use this, regard it as yours, Miss Bafokeng. But I'll check the mileage when I come back. I don't want you impressing the folks, running a taxi business to and from Lesotho!' Lesebo gave a huge smile and held out her left palm for a high five smack. Harry obliged but held it for some time as his beautiful chauffeuse steered them, effortlessly one-handed, to her headquarters.

'Better still, you drive me to the airport and I'll buy you lunch!' Harry said as they slammed doors and made their way inside the building.

*****

Jabu Nhleko sounded uncompromising on the phone to Malusi Jali. Having been threatened with his life, besides his ministerial post, Jali had led a blindly obedient existence to enforce several irregular decisions. He had reminded the Chief Justice where his loyalty lay and to whom he owed his appointment when the question of changing presidential contractual obligations arose. The TDC contract was potentially in shreds although it would probably take some union support to force the changes. He had virtually emasculated the Siyeza funding by forcing resignations on the board and replacing incumbents with committed presidential appointees. He had invested ten million Rands from the deputy president into the renamed SPF and removed Kirkside to an advisory brokerage role. Perhaps more decisively, he had prepared the ground for a prime area of development that lay within the TDC remit to be set aside for undisclosed purposes that would be made known after the Election. What more could Nhleko want? It transpired that he wanted as much political capital making out of the Cape Flats murder trial, with Jali deploying family and tribal leverage.

'I want you to talk to your wife's sister, that large policewoman. What is she doing in that job, because I never hear about any prosecutions of the enemies of the state my friend? I hear about squabbling and the DA scoring points. Well, now they have the gang leaders and puppet masters on trial for murder, I want it to move quickly! The President says, "Speed it up", man. A successful prosecution of a big crook looks good in your conviction figures for your election manifesto. So get her to take the gloves off – she's supported at the top.'

'What about the foreigners and local underworld?'

'That's what I'm talking about, you poephol! Just get it done fast!' Nhleko slammed the phone down on Jali, who now loathed him above all others; one day Nhleko would pay a heavy debt for his arrogance and cruelty, which Jali prayed would come about in the Election and subsequent ANC selection Indaba.

*****

Maddox sent Gary to sit through the trials of Tito Buthelezi, the Manenberg gang leader accused of murdering Solomons' killer. Two of his gang associates and Sonny Chora and Ravi Chetty were also on trial. On the first day, the case against Chetty as accomplice to the murder was dropped by the State, unable to prove the connection between Chetty and the passage of money between either external sources or Chopra. The other cases went ahead at uncharacteristically fast speed, with the female judge granting a minimum of delays or adjournments. Chopra changed his plea to guilty. Within ten days, a verdict of life imprisonment with pleas for remission at the ten-year point was handed down on Chopra, with Buthelezi getting a life sentence without remission. The two accomplices received ten years each. The case was given an unusually high exposure on all TV channels and sustained online, phone-in and broadsheet coverage.

Maddox was quick to inform the Kirksides who had kept a low profile during the hearings. Having paid the financial bribe, they were uncertain how the dismissal of the case against Chetty would influence Tristan's abduction, if at all. Maddox did not know either. He emphasised to Khanyisile Mthembu how all the Cape Flats regular informants should be worked day and night to obtain local gossip and report unusual activity. Ami's anxiety became uncontrollable, now wondering whether her contact with Ashwin Chetty would harm Tristan's position.

'Ami, what can I do? I appealed to him, as you know, which at least got us news that Tristan's unharmed, if we're to believe it – we both do, don't we? But further than that? I don't know if he's involved or picking up gutter gossip. We might be blood brothers but I sometimes feel we had different fathers – nothing in our character is the same. Now he's a free man again, he'll be settling scores.' Ashwin turned to pace behind him, before facing Ami again with a sad smile. 'But if Richard is not linked at all and the case collapsed because of that, then it seems possible that there is no further fear about his evidence? I think that Chopra oke is just another Chetty fall guy and nobody will be too interested in getting him pardoned. You've seen how cock-a-hoop the government is over the conviction, because it strengthens its "strong on crime-and-violence" card.'

'So what will happen to Tristan, now the local mafia chief is free again?'

'Darling, I really don't know. If they don't need more levers on Richard, they'll let Tristan free. But let's be positive: we're in a better position than we were before the trial started. None of us know who's driving Chetty – local politicians, foreign businessmen? Please try to be patient for a few more days. Do you want to stay here?' Ashwin smiled at Ami and held her hand. 'Who knows, one of those sexually irresistible moments might come to pass?'

'Not while this is going on! You're so kind Ashwin, but I must stay with Richard to keep lines intact. Maddox is being his marvellous self but even he's a bit lost at the moment.'

*****

'Tristan, we're going to take some exercise – the girls are getting too excited about you and we're not quite ready to start your training yet. Put on shorts, shirt and flops and wrap your swimming shorts in a towel. The girls will put a beanie on your head and lead you out to a car. Get in and do not move the beanie until you are told. Is that quite clear Tristan?'

'Yes, sir.'

Thandiswa came in immediately, smiling and happy, telling him they were going swimming. She placed a black woollen beanie over his head. He held her hand as she led him out of his prison. He was led up some stairs and along a passage to a car and guided gently into the back seat with Thandiswa and Mashu sitting on either side. After what seemed to be a twenty-minute ride, including stopping, starting and turning, fast and slow, smooth and finally rough, one of the girls pulled the beanie off his head. He blinked at the fierce sunlight and had no idea where they were. There were two men in front, one being Charlie, his original captor at the Swimmable Swimming Pool. The other man, aged about thirty and a Virgin Active muscular type with tattooed forearms, got out of the car to open a padlocked farm gate, which he fastened again before returning to the car. They wobbled down an untarred road, turning to dirt as they came to a clearing by a large greyish quarry lake. The driver switched off the engine and turned to face him behind large sunglasses.

'Okay you three. Do exactly as I say please. You need some exercise so I want you to swim ten widths across the lake. It's quite deep in the middle. I know you girls aren't as good at swimming as Tristan but do your best. We want you to make yourselves tired, because you're all getting too horny shut in your little room heh?' He gave an unpleasant snigger and Tristan guessed he watched them all through the darkened window. 'Oh and one last thing, don't try to run away, because Milo runs very fast and really hurts with that bullwhip he's got, okay? Let's go!' He opened his door and released the rear door fastenings. 'Come on, come on, who's first across the lake?' The three youngsters alighted uncertainly, creeping to the lake's edge in their flops. Tristan went in first and winced at the cold temperature, despite the warmth of the sun. He dived forward and began a vigorous crawl. The girls were more timid, easing themselves in with shrieks and setting off with a gentle breast stroke. The lake was about thirty metres across, with the far side rearing jaggedly up a hewn rock face. Milo wandered along the side, flicking his bull whip. Tristan enjoyed the release of energy and re-familiarisation with his favourite sport. The girls had learned to swim at school it seemed, but waited for Tristan to lap them at the sixth width. With Tristan tiring at the end of the eighth crossing, Charlie called them to dry off and return to the car. As they were driving out, reversing the routine with the farm gate, Charlie suddenly yelled at the girls.

'Quick, put that beanie on his head, they're some frigging okes coming to fish!' Tristan was certain he was seen before Thandiswa managed to get the beanie in place. There was a stilted conversation between Charlie and some strangers before the car moved off. They eventually got out of the car where Tristan was led along corridors and down some stone stairs. He heard a door close behind him, and then the inevitable voice, which he now felt sure belonged to Charlie, the dirty-minded driver – "a perve", as his mother would call him.

'Take off the beanie Tristan. We hope you enjoyed your exercise. The girls are doing some work but will be with you later. You will find some books to read on the table and later on, you will see a video film. Do you understand?'

'Yes sir!' Tristan's mind was spinning fast. Although he was not certain, he thought that one of the men going to fish in the quarry pool was Chappie, the handyman-caretaker at Ashwin Chetty's block of flats in Rondebosch Village.

*****

Katie and Maddox had just won their first doubles match together. Maddox was under no illusions though; providing he managed to get his serves in, the bouncy Katie did the rest, volleying and smashing and generally flat-footing their arthritic opponents. Both were as thrilled as children but had to restrain themselves as they shared some tea and scones with their vanquished opponents, who departed early to collect their pills from the chemist. Katie was unrestrained.

'Maddox, you were so good – my own Andy Murray! Power serves, getting your return in, banging in those low backhands – I'm so proud of you!' She leant across the table and kissed him several times. A few months before, Grumpy Maddox would have objected, but now he revelled in her affection and company, oblivious to other club members muttering into their teacups.

'Katie, you're blind my dear! You were catlike at the net. I didn't see you miss one. The poor old Goodhews, I don't think they'll want to play us again!'

'Well, it's made my mind up: we're entering the club championship this year. If you won't give me a ring, I might as well bag a trophy!' Maddox was noticing a fairly regular banter about their relationship which made him want to share more time with Katie. He knew she was naturally retiring but was summoning up courage in case he retired back into his curmudgeon cave.

'You must be mad! You got to the semis with Henry last year and were unlucky not to go through! If you settle for me, we'll be out in the first round, darling!'

'Henry's an exhibitionist. You're like old wine or Stilton – you get better and better!'

'Remember we're Southern Hemisphere darling! Wine and cheese don't hold up so well! But if you're prepared to squander your chances to play with an old duffer like me, I'll do my very best not to embarrass you – how's that? Where would you like to go to supper tonight?' Maddox kept enquiring eyes on Katie as he reached for his tinkling cell phone in his jacket draped around his chair.

'Hello Ami! Good to hear you. I'm at the Mowbray Club, just finishing tennis. What's going on?' Katie watched Maddox as he spoke to Ami Kirkside with his eyes on her. When the conversation ended, Maddox put his phone away abruptly.

'That was Ami Kirkside, who says there's been a possible breakthrough with Tristan. Some sort of witness might have spotted him. These sort of trails fade fast, so I'd better see her now. Look, you can come too – she's at a Rondebosch Village address. Her companion there is a good tennis player incidentally, although you wouldn't believe that he's the brother of our villain number one, Ravi Chetty! Anyway, you'll meet Ami, which is no bad thing. It's high time I paraded my girlfriend to the world, isn't it? You keep nagging about it! So let's see what needs doing. Then we can change at my place and find somewhere to murmur sweet nothings at each other! Can you beat it?' Katie mumbled about wearing short tennis dresses in other people's houses in the evening but nodded reluctantly.

They were at Professor Chetty's flat in quick time. It was sumptuously furnished inside, not at all a bachelor pad. There was the slightest whiff of curry but Maddox convinced himself that he was unfairly pre-conditioning his senses. Subdued classical music was playing, which Ashwin reduced further. He had a sober and reserved manner, as if apprehensive about the improving outlook over Tristan. Ami seemed surprised but delighted to meet Katie, who somehow fitted the image of a perfect partner for Maddox. She brought Ashwin into the group by encircling his arm.

'Look Maddox, this might be nothing. But you told me to get hold of you if anything happened. I'll let Ashwin tell you, because it's all to do with his contacts.' Ami threw back her hair from her forehead with one jerk of the neck, in an attractive gesture. Ashwin smiled gently. He was never shy or nervous to speak about anything, anywhere but had a subtle sense of place and priority.

'We're sorry to call you here and are always grateful when you come to help us. My handyman, Chappie Basarwa, takes Saturday afternoons off to fish and drink with his friends, often in the Lafarge quarry on the old Pinelands road. It's private property, owned by a quarrying company. When he went yesterday, he saw a vehicle leaving – he noted the number and type – which was unusual. Apparently, the occupants used a key to open the track gate. He saw three teenagers in the back of the car with two white men in front. There was a white boy in the back in between two black girls. When it drew near, the girls put a black wool balaclava over the boy's head. Chappie was convinced it was Tristan.' Ashwin paused to give Maddox a chance to comment.

'Have you got the number please? We need to put that out over the police network immediately. And where is this quarry – can you show me on a city map? All of this is good news by the way. It falls into a rough plan I've had for a while. Ami, if I was you, I'd let Richard know, if you haven't already, but not by telephone. It might mean something to him. Ashwin, can I use your study for a few minutes? I need to get some people working on this.' Maddox was moving purposefully as he threw a cheerful comment over his shoulder. 'By the way, Katie plays a mean game of tennis and has coached me to championship status!' He moved to the next-door room and shut the door, before opening it again to shout another request. 'And Ashwin, can you get hold of your man Chappie please? Tell him to come here to talk to the police.' His muffled voice could be heard, activating both SAPS and his own personnel. Being dressed as she was, Katie felt there was little option to do as Maddox suggested and began discussing the way modern racquets do not need their strings tightening, as was common twenty years before, while Ami rustled up some tea and biscuits.

Maddox galvanised Gary and Joost into action, checking facts and reconnoitring the suburbs of Claremont, Athlone, Rondebosch and Kenilworth. He sent another investigator back to the Swimmable Swimming Pool. It was when he rang Khanyisile Mthembu that he received a welcome surprise.

'We're under big pressure to finalise the Cape Flats trials successfully. The order has come from the very top, via my sister, needless to say! They didn't say anything about the missing boy but that doesn't stop me doing so, because it's obviously directly linked. They've sent me four top detectives from the Raptors, would you believe, so they think it's important. I'll put them onto this now – they can start with interviewing the handyman witness. We'll get the car details out and let you know its history. Anything else, do you think, Maddox?'

'Yes. Do a check on prostitution and child racketeering crime fringes in the white/Indian suburbs around the north-western fringes of the Flats, probably centred round Rondebosch, Claremont, Kenilworth. I've a hunch about this – online child pornography and the like? You might reinforce the car park and garage searches in those areas too. But go steady, because it'll point us to the hideaway – we'll only get one chance for a raid, remember!'

Maddox waited with Katie until both Chappie and two of the Captors team arrived. Time was running out to keep his promise of a tete-a-tete supper. Maddox beckoned Ami to one side.

'What size are your feet, Ami?'

'Six, why?'

'Good. I want a big favour. Can you find Katie a simple dress and some sandals please? We've run out of time!'

'God, Maddox, you've got a brass neck! I'll do it, but only for you! You're lucky I've left some of my clothes here.' Ami smiled broadly, giving him a mock punch. She then clasped Katie's hand and led her towards her bedroom wardrobe.

*****

De Vries found himself among some South African household names at the ANC Beneficiary Dinner at the Mala Mala game reserve. He was there at Nhleko's invitation but this seemed irrelevant, among the floating glitterati and raft of black society who owed the party their loyalty. It was a last super-human heave to get the party and its leaders over the election line amid vast donations and laudatory speeches. He had enjoyed the game viewing before dinner, although even that was overdone, with yawning lions staring slit-eyed and impassively in their appointed favourite bush haunts as expensive zoom cameras were pointed down at them by hordes of gawking visitors in outlandishly stretched and polished Land Rovers. Forget the glorious Greater Kudo bull or the impish Meerkat; instead, they were thrust in front of an easily located "Big Seven", including Cheetah and Hippo, within the first half hour. For all this, De Vries noticed how Jali registered more on the audial "clapometer" than Nhleko – maybe the surge of activity surrounding Siyeza had promoted his popularity?

After the dinner, De Vries found a chance for a quick word with Nhleko. It was bound to be an awkward encounter, after the violent punishment meted out on the overweight Deputy President during their last meeting.

'This is more comfortable than last time, Deputy President! I know you've no time to spare now, but it's always useful to take stock, yeah?' De Vries sipped his port and gave Nhleko no time to consider an answer. 'I must congratulate you on the way you're putting things right quickly. You and Malusi are controlling your own mega-city funding, you've opened up the contracts nicely to keep your unions and black business sweet and you're cleaning up crime in time for the Election.'

'Well, not quite – the Cape Flats gets more income from drugs than it does from light industry! I exaggerate, but at least we've got those blocking the Siyeza idea. But Ravi Chetty wriggled free because the evidence collapsed.' Nhleko chose his words carefully. 'The key witness was discouraged, shall we say?'

'Yes, I know. But there's no point in persisting with him now, is there? You've got the desired effect and we're both in the clear, aren't we? You've got a clear run for the Presidency and I can get my little Siyeza plan going. Are we singing off the same song sheet?'

Nhleko nodded quickly. 'I think so, yes. I have put the top cops into the city to hurry the trial along but what about Chetty now? We can freeze him out of business maybe, because we have all the Siyeza levers now, but that won't stop his syndication and mobsters. He'll find a dozen new Sonny Chopra's.'

'Well, okay, maybe. But then you have an Election in ten days. Do yourself a favour and get that Kirkside kid freed and then start sticking it on Chetty? Once I'm half up-and-running here, I'll get the drugs side moving on a better business footing. They call it symbiosis – living off and needing each other, like those red-billed oxpeckers feeding off buffalo ticks! So he's served his purpose Mr President?' De Vries finished his port and placed his glass on the table. They both stood and parted with an African handshake. De Vries held his grip a little longer to pat Nhleko on the shoulder with his left hand. 'And best of luck with the Election and your own selection! My little donation goes into your account tomorrow!'

Ravi Chetty had summoned his principal bosses to his palatial home for what he termed a "council of war". He was much more indignant about his arrest than he was relieved about his release. Much of his Cape Town reputation depended on his public image being distanced from local crime. He had grown sufficiently large to separate the white-collar insurance, motor dealerships, fuel stations, DIY stores and maintenance teams from his seedier interests in gambling, prostitution, enforcement, taxi services and the drugs trade. When his very public arrest and charging as an accomplice during a gangland murder sank in around Cape Town, his credibility evaporated overnight. To make things worse, the assured political support from Jali and the heavyweight overseas backing from De Vries was cooling fast. Compounding this was an over-active police presence around all his key interests or areas, with his reliable SAPS go-betweens being either dismissed, prematurely retired or given a golden handshake. His survival instincts told him to draw breath and consolidate, perhaps find partners, but although he was expendable, he sorely missed Sonny Chopra on the streets.

He stood facing the semi-circle of seated henchmen. They were a mixture of Indian, coloured and black. Only one was an ex-convict, which demonstrated the truth behind gang networks – the bosses kept their distances and left the legwork and action to the otherwise unemployed and often drug-dependant foot soldiers.

'We've got to think straight now. We lost two strikers and we're running out of friends. There's stinking cops everywhere – they'll get bored and move in on shebeens, whores and peddlers, just to be spiteful. Now I'm off the rap, they want to hang me out to dry. So I'm after ideas guys!' He didn't smile, always keen to maintain his tough exterior to his subordinates.

'What's happening about that kid they've got? Isn't his Dad the one who didn't want to testify against you? But you're out now! What are they going to do?' It was the diminutive Khoisan, Herbie Baartie, who ran a successful taxi business around Mitchells Plain.

'How do I know? There's some freaky gang in Kenilworth that's got him, you know, the kinky sorts with kids and that? They owed a friend of a friend a favour so I don't know the small print. But look, just wait!' He advanced in front of Herbie and wagged his finger close to his face, although scarcely raising his voice.

'Herbie, I'm telling you! That poephol Kirkside backed off because of the boy, right? But he's still got the evidence, heh? And he's sore now, because he had to put in cash and he's lost his grip on the whole Siyeza thing. And he's got a fucking lunatic of a wife being fucked by my brother, who's a Jehovah's Witness anyway – man, that's bad for family reputation! So what do I owe this guy, heh?' Chetty broke off amid ribald laughter and hand clapping. 'No my friend, I tell you what! I'm going to ask for another Christmas tip from Kirkside. Look, if the politicians and foreigners are getting cold turkey, I've got to look after my businesses, haven't I? If he gets funny, we'll take that bitch who's screwing my bro. You've got to understand Herbie, old scout: Siyeza's in new hands now but we don't know if they'll look after us properly, do we? A little bit of leverage goes a long way, do you follow?'

'But what about the kid?'

'Well, what about the fucking kid? Who cares, you Kaffir freak? We're all businessmen, aren't we? From all accounts, those kids start earning a living while very young, I tell you! A short and happy life, dead by their mid-twenties! But that's the way it goes, heh?' There was more uproarious laughter; depravity that made cash was fair game, provided rent and protection money kept coming in and nothing upset their own activities.

*****

Maddox always had to clench his teeth when among SAPS policemen wearing military clothing and badges of rank. Brigadier General Sizwe Dlamini, the Raptors team leader, was cuboid, at least a hundred and twenty kilogrammes, with a broad leather belt slung under his hanging stomach. Insignia hung from both his shirt pockets and epaulettes and he wore a brigadier's stars and crown on the front of his blue kepi to supplement those on his shoulder slides. His dark glasses and bushy moustache completed what he hoped was an impressive appearance. Khanyisile Mthembu, although his equal in rank, deferred on this occasion, it being considered a high security and organised crime syndicate case. It was two o'clock in the morning and they were crowded in the briefing room in the Cape Town police headquarters – the full Raptors team, twenty or so SAPS officers and constables – some as large as Dlamini – Maddox and four investigators, a police doctor and nurse and three women, dressed like prison warders with insignia, from a government social services Quango. Khanyisile clapped her hands and brought them to order.

'Good morning all of you. We all know the importance of this operation so please listen carefully and do not leave the group without permission – we cannot afford to be compromised. Before Brigadier Dlamini, commander of Task Force Hotel from the Raptors, takes over, I want you all to hear the background from Mr Maddox Illingworth, owner/director of Maddox Private Investigators in Cape Town. He does a great deal of co-operative work with Cape Town SAPS and is an ex-officer in the British Army's police. Maddox?' Khanyisile was positively beaming as she introduced her secret hero and confidant, almost giggling as she gestured to him to take the floor. Joost and Gary nudged each other mischievously.

'Thanks General. I'll be quick. The Kirksides asked me to assist when their son Tristan was kidnapped, after playing water polo at the Swimmable Swimming Pool in the Gardens Centre about two months ago. It transpired that Mrs Kirkside was mugged in a Constantia supermarket by three children, preventing her from picking up Tristan from the pool or contacting anyone quickly. We knew a middle-aged man who was masquerading as a pool official took Tristan away in his car, no further details. Mrs Kirkside's bank cards were used for three purchases before we froze the account, indicating that the children, or more likely adults who directed them, lived or worked in the North Western Cape Flats district. We obtained unsubstantiated information that Tristan was unharmed. After ten days, the Kirksides received instructions confirming this but telling them to await further directions, depending on the outcome and progress of the Solomons murder case. We knew there was a strong political and international connection to much wider organised crime.' Maddox paused, not inviting questions but ascertaining whether his information was sinking in, so early in the morning. It appeared to be, so he continued.

'Further instructions were sent to the Kirksides, telling them to transfer cash and warning Mr Kirkside not to give evidence in any forthcoming trial connected to the two Cape Flats murders. They followed these instructions and the trial was completed, convicting Sonny Chopra and others of murder. Ravi Chetty was released because the State could not bring charges of being an accomplice to murder. Last week, we received information that Tristan and two black girls were seen in a car with two white men. The girls pulled a balaclava over Tristan's head to avoid recognition. The witness was able to pinpoint the quarry from where the car was driving and provide the car number and description. Using digital analysis and SAPS records, we decided to concentrate on any known paedophile or child prostitution rings suspected to exist in five or so principally white suburbs to the north-west of Cape Flats. We believe we've hit lucky, thanks to some excellent work by Cape Town SAPS and the Raptors. Three possible child prostitution rings were investigated, with one in Kenilworth being possibly linked to a national paedophilia network. By scrutinising some video coverage with the government social services, using Deeds Office, estate agency and Vodacom information, we believe that a vice ring exists in the cellars of two adjacent semi-detached houses. Census information is thin but there are at least four middle aged occupants listed, none with previous form. A car in a nearby kerbside park has been confirmed as similar to the one seen leaving the quarry. That takes us up to where Brigadier Dlamini will give us our orders for this morning. Just one word of warning – today's targets are sub-contractors, so there are bigger fish to follow!' Maddox managed a cheery grin as the waddling Dlamini took the stage.

To be fair, Maddox and his colleagues were impressed by the Raptors. They were all high-grade quick thinkers, giving the SAPS body some confidence. They anticipated no violent resistance and there was a very high emphasis on preservation of evidence. The Raptors had conducted a thorough nocturnal reconnaissance. While the double storey buildings and garages were surrounded, the SAPS would gain forceful entry via a thin kitchen door to allow two Raptors to immediately secure all electronic equipment including the nine cell phones and three iPad/tablets from bedsides and communal areas that they had identified. The cellar's control room would be searched concurrently by two Raptors policemen. The majority of the SAPS force would only then enter, and directed by the Raptors, identify and arrest all occupants and search the premises. The social service women would then accompany the SAPS commander to the children's cell. The teenagers would be evacuated direct to a pre-arranged safe house for care and de-briefing. The forensic squad would be on standby to begin work throughout the early morning. After a professional de-briefing at police headquarters, municipality and government officials would be briefed, prior to a national announcement during the evening TV news.

Maddox knew there was nothing worse than being an unemployed nuisance presence, so chose not to take part. With his second gratuity from Kirkside denied, and his bargaining card confiscated, Maddox knew that Chetty would be in a dangerous frame of mind.

Chapter Eleven

The television coverage was excruciating but Maddox conceded that this always the case. Unlike older democracies, the eventual outcome did not seem in doubt – the ANC would win, but by how much? Bussed in ANC voters weren't offered the luxury of being undecided. They were guided to the point of almost having their voter's pen held, awarded with food parcels, baseball hats, tee-shirts and party flags to wave. They were confronted at polling station entrances and interrogated – there was an element of interrogation by gaggles of aggressive, noisy youths. But although such party strategy may have recovered some votes, it did not correct the slide away from a previously unassailable majority. As the results were announced with agonising formality and hype, it was soon clear that two of the nine provinces would be lost, joining the Western Cape to form a thirty-five percent opposition. The era of absolutism seemed over or at least in suspension for another four years. After spending half his adult life in Cape Town, Maddox now understood the despotism and lack of constituency responsibility in South Africa's MPs, but it didn't make it more palatable.

'If it goes on this way, and they lose three provinces, what will happen to our friends in government, darling?' Katie was cooking them supper at his Newlands home, glancing at the television, while wiping her eyes after peeling onions. 'Will some of the heat be taken off poor Richard?'

'Sadly not, unless the government resume patronage of Chetty – it's straightforward Cape Flats mobsters he's up against, not corrupt politicians. We won't know about appointments for a while, until they've cooked the books at their scout jamboree near Harrismith. They get into a giant huddle and draw up a batting order from one to maybe three hundred. They then draw a line under the number of seats they've won and those below it are told to shove off. Those above become MPs and the top fifty get the juicy jobs. They're able to look after their disappointed mates by appointing them to quangos, tribunals, standing committees, new contracts, and bogus companies and so on. It's all very reminiscent of the British Trade Unions in the sixties, with the massive membership union bosses having puppet power over wannabee socialist MPs. I'm not sure how the DA do it but I'm dying to know how Kobus got on!'

*****

The unwieldy spread of the ANC caucus gathering on the banks of Sterkfontein Dam, a gigantic series of Arabesque marquees, completely monopolising the nature reserve setting, was a curious combination of secrecy and mob rule, with a thin veil of establishmentarian spin for the media. The President had made known at the last moment his preparedness to stand for a second term, which had concentrated Nhleko's mind and those of his advisers. The entire gathering, mindful of their worst election results in the twenty-five years of New Democracy, drifted into two boisterous halves, opposing each other with increasingly drunken and extreme action. Jabu Nhleko, like all the government's great and good, waddled among the tents with his posse of acolytes, soaking up the feeling of being important and powerful. But it was clear that his fortunes were fading, with his old allies and trade union roots avoiding him. He watched a white girl journalist on a TV screen, suggesting that his support had drifted away recently, which enraged him: hadn't he orchestrated the Siyeza "revisionism" single-handed, hadn't he restored the union's faith in the project, hadn't he encouraged inward investment, despite serving a President without character or energy?

Malusi Jali, on the other hand, was feeling buoyant. He sensed the stalemate nature of the Presidency issue and judged, as did the majority of party officials and supporters, that the President would be returned for another term. If so, it seemed unlikely that the caucus would stick with the same presidency running mate for another full term? He strutted pompously among the groups gathered talking and inevitably wolfing refreshments from perpetually replenished tables. He too had his posse but earned extra credits by trailing a tame television cameraman in his wake. His latest girlfriend was in attendance, signed on the payroll as an "auxiliary office administrator", having trouble with her stiletto heels on the hessian and carpet flooring throughout the tents.

If the voting antics had a Western trade unionist flavour, the control aspects were decidedly Soviet. A myriad of overlapping committees, boards and councils, most with obtuse titles and superfluous purpose, somehow wrung out decisions that were inviolate. After a long lunch break, the caucus sub-divided into many factions and management layers, which took an hour to settle as delegates wandered lost, trying to find their designated body and venue. The executive council, comprising existing cabinet ministers and some deputies, plus senior personalities and life members who somehow clung to positions of power, had the ultimate authority. It was they who approved the final critical appointments before the patronage set in with family and friends. This was an old political party, well versed in patronage.

The existing President was unanimously returned for another term by an exuberant caucus, with any deviants having been muscled into oblivion over lunch. But there was an even greater turmoil over the selection of a Deputy. Instead of a similar cut-and-dried announcement, the delegates swarmed and shouted, with several melees around the central hall where the executive were seated. Some candidates were dragged hither and thither, as vote bargaining became crude and direct, with provinces and unions, communists and women, the Youth and the breakaway factions all flaunting their power. The succeeding candidate would never be allowed to forget or manipulate any promised patronage, with vast contracts and grants, loans and priorities being in the balance.

Jali found himself in a surging sea of supporters chanting his name and dancing outside the central hall, where he had been asked to congregate. He would normally be with them, but as the opinion of the caucus swung to and fro, the money settled around Jali and one other candidate, a woman who had done reasonably as Minister of Health. Both of them were anxious to capture media attention and had been surrounded by their supporters. When he reached the executive, all of whom were friends and colleagues from the outgoing administration, he was greeted warmly, with some rising to shake his hand. The Chairman was an elderly "struggle" veteran who asked him to join them and explain why he felt Siyeza was so important to the ANC and to the appointment of senior members of the cabinet. Jali composed himself, holding back excitement as well as tinges of revenge, with Nhleko removed from power.

'My dear comrades and wise heads above our exultant assembly!' He felt that theatre would play its part, throwing his arms skywards. 'With great pleasure! Siyeza? Siyeza is the saviour, the life-blood, the force-multiplier that will transform our fortunes! We as an executive, we as the party and we as the country! Through Siyeza, we will become what we have been trying to be for a quarter of a century, after throwing off the shackles of Apartheid. Siyeza will be the magnet that draws trade, banking, tourism and industry to not only South Africa but the African continent! When we announce tomorrow the project's most closely guarded secret, there will be universal approval and inward investment like we have never seen! Clever people are talking of the amoeba, which absorbs its neighbour, either for the benefit or detriment of the whole. But in our case, there will be expansion that will dwarf some of the most prestigious achievements of the United States, Europe and Asia in recent times. When Britain closed its mines and factories, it was rescued by Japanese and German investment. Look at it now, without a single coal mine but turning out millions of foreign cars! It is the fifth biggest economy in the world! So will we be, the furnace and engine room of Africa, attracting investment to export our products. And it will be Siyeza that sows the seed, mark my word!' Jali was elated, never doubting himself as the lucky chosen individual of the moment. He jigged happily by the table.

Two hours later, all the TV and radio programmes covered the Harrismith story, with the same President shown clasping high the hand of Malusi Jali. Siyeza was linked to the selections, as was the announcement that the DA would leave its leadership unchanged, with Kobus Labuschagne continuing as Cape Town Mayor to see Siyeza through to a successful conclusion. It took several days before all the cabinet appointments were finalised – eventually twenty-nine of them, an all-time record. Each had a deputy, a civil service department, an office block headquarters, grace and favour quarters, a fleet of limousines, a platoon of bodyguards and limitless employees, which collectively consumed half its bloated budget. The new Minister of Trade and Industry, replacing Jali, was the Reverend Nicholas Mahlambi, an elderly but much respected Christians

United Party leader, who had swung their vote behind the ANC after the election results were announced. As such, it was a brotherly sop but Mahlambi had a history of taking his evangelism into the streets, which promised friction in the Cape Flats and Siyeza situation.

*****

Kobus Labuschagne was reviewing his position. Much water had passed under his bridge during his previous term of office, some deeply disturbing. The shocking incident with Lesebo Bafokeng, her bribed elevation to the top Siyeza appointment, his on-off personal relationship with Rita, the hijacking of the TDC contract terms, the two Cape Flats murders and subsequent trial, the manipulation of the Siyeza Peoples Fund, the presence of international crime and to cap it all, his re-election as Mayor with a doubled salary but denial of the DA party leadership. As a successful politician in his late forties, Kobus needed to adjust sights. If he was going to marry, now was the time, at the height of popularity in Cape Town, with political advancement postponed, rather than denied. Similarly, he was holding out hopes for the Reverend Mahlambi having a balancing influence on the chaotic politics and crime of the Cape Flats. Added to that, he had been told that Brigadier General Khanyisile Mthembu had been promoted to head up the entire Cape Town SAPS force. The well-informed DA bush telegraph told him that this was a parting gesture from her sister as she left for the presidential life in Pretoria. As the wife of the ex-Deputy and his successor, Lindiwe could rightfully claim to be a king-maker, with Khanyisile's appointment causing no embarrassments to any ANC faction. It was with these thoughts in mind that Kobus called the third meeting of what he now jokingly referred to as the "Four Wise Men plus a Woman Council".

As ever, the meeting's timing was governed by Harry Reynolds's availability in-country, but it was managed within a fortnight of the Harrismith Indaba. He arrived with Lesebo, both having completed an updating reconnaissance of some recent Siyeza construction. Maddox in turn had visited Khanyisile to offer congratulations and to exchange intelligence on Ravi Chetty. Richard Kirkside was his usual gaunt self but was making private assurances that his private life was taking a turn for the better. The atmosphere was less downhearted than that of their second meeting but without the informality and urgency of the first. Kobus had anticipated this and decided to open with an impact suggestion.

'Hello everyone! This is our third meeting and to be fair to ourselves, we have only come together when things are either going badly or are marooned! But actually, I'm optimistic and if you'll forgive me, I'll tell you why.'

Kobus looked comfortable and relaxed, very much in charge. 'Firstly the election and politics. Nhleko is consigned to history and my sources tell me, so is Jali. He could always interfere but to be frank, Mahlambi would make ten of him, with a strong anti-crime ticket. He's a churchman, who's always carried weight in Cape Town politics. I'll tell you in a second how I aim to use this advantage. Secondly, SAPS support. As you know Khanyisile Mthembu's been promoted to head up the city police force. She's led a crusade against police corruption in the last few years and almost by chance, has become an ally. We've relied so heavily on Maddox, who has done somersaults around the ethics committees, but it's time to beef up SAPS as a proper community service agency – I'm acutely aware of this shortcoming as Mayor. Thirdly there's crime. I think it will get worse quite soon but in a way that we can deal with and eventually defeat. All the indicators I've seen suggest that the politicians are backing away from Siyeza's control levers – the management, the finances and the intimidation through public disorder. I look forward to hear what Harry and Maddox say about that.' Labuschagne searched them out and stared pointedly before continuing.

'Fourth is the finances. The all-party tribunal investigating the irrational disqualification of the fund's board condemned the action as illegal and have proposed to the President that SPF should be restored to its intended government and private sector partnership. Better still, and I'm sure he's too shy to tell us, they're recommended that Richard Kirkside re-joins the board as a permanent member in the capacity of Director of Investments. You can't get better news than that, and I suspect the President will sign it off in double-quick time to clear the way for Mahlambi. Richard, you'll want to fill us in on that. Lastly there's me. I'm here for another four years! I make no secret that I wanted the party leadership but it seems that I must wait until we put Siyeza to bed. So I feel really focussed, without those stressful early distractions. So much so that I've decided to get married a week before I'm fifty, in two months' time!' Kobus couldn't avoid a glance at Lesebo as there was a round of polite applause. Her look was steady, composed but friendly.

Every member had their news. Harry Reynolds described how the British government had registered a formal protest to Pretoria concerning both SFF and the TDC contract interference. If the issue went to international tribunal, South Africa would be held liable for losses of two billion Sterling, including five hundred million that would have been invested through wages and support services and equipment here. Harry welcomed the new-broom-sweeps-clean potential offered by a new minister and an elevated police chief. Lesebo welcomed them too, still plagued by labour disturbances and disruption of services. Richard Kirkside seemed humble, thanking them all for the support they had given his family during the last year. He confirmed his re-instatement to the SFF board, hoping to restore its reputation in the foreign market and stock exchanges. Maddox as ever, ended with sober reminders.

'It's good news about Khanyisile, excellent. She's had quite a successful purge of her own kith and kin, which has greatly improved investigation and crime prevention. So if she can up the ante against gangland, so much the better for a properly directed community-minded Siyeza. But let's remember that Chetty and his cronies are alive and well and want to fill the gap left by withdrawal of government favours and decades of police complicity. And the international crime involvement is alive and well, stirring the pot, offering the bungs, sweet-talking the politicians, remember. Needless to say Kobus, as the senior citizen here, I'd like to offer you many congratulations on your engagement and give both Rita and you our best wishes for a wonderful, long and happy marriage. I'm sure it will take Harry two minutes to rustle up some champagne from his Land Rover fridge!' There was laughter and applause as Kobus quietened them one more time.

'I wouldn't put you lot past anything! But before we go, I'd like to make a proposal that may surprise, disappoint or delight you. I suggest that we too have a coup d'état regarding membership. Having exchanged the views we have, it seems critical that we move the perceptions about Siyeza management. We are unofficial of course and can meet again whenever we want but I'm suggesting that we raise a formal board to oversee progress. It should be chaired by the Reverend Nicholas Mahlambi, with myself, Lesebo, Khanyisile Mthembu and Harry as fixed members? Being an open oversight board, it can co-opt Maddox and Richard – or anyone else – when it sees fit. Do I have your support in this please?' There was a united raising of hands in approval and murmurs of congratulations. Kobus grinned happily as Harry and Lesebo disappeared in search of chilled champagne.

*****

'So how did that go today?' asked Ami. They were sitting on the side of their heated pool, drinking chilled spritzers. Tristan was ploughing up and down with three of his polo club friends, before watching a video Ami had hired. Since he had returned to them, Ami had felt she should be near him and more by circumstance than decision, she had moved back into the Kirkside family home.

'Very good. The on-side woman cop has been made the city chief, an evangelist preacher has replaced Jali, Harry Reynolds has all guns firing and Kobus is getting married!' Richard smiled at Ami, raising his glass. 'We've agreed that Maddox and I stand down, replaced by the Holy Man and Honest Cop. It makes sense to bring it into the open and oversee the management and money.'

'Who's Kobus marrying?'

'Dunno. Some bird who's been chasing him for years. It'll do his image good.' Richard splashed his feet in the pool as he added quietly, 'The only worry now is Chetty. He's an unpredictable psychopath really, isn't he? I worry for all three of us to be fair, but I'm hesitant to keep Maddox on a string. It looks like things could get nasty on the Flats again, with a vacuum left after the police 'no-go' policy was lifted. Hopefully the bastard will have his hands full defending his manor.'

*****

'How the hell did Maddox know I carry champagne in my Landy?' quipped Harry. 'I was taken aback – is Lesebo betraying confidences, I wondered?' They were waiting their turn at a noisy bowling alley, sipping fruit juices and laughing about their "gender free" footwear. They liked to break away from usual places and habits to spend time together.

'Not me guv! Doesn't he realise that every British sophisticate carries Moet or Bollinger in his vehicle? I'd say sixth sense.' Lesebo adopted a childish coquettish pose.

'News to me that you're a wine buff as well? What else have you got to tell me?'

'Dear Harold Reynolds, Companion of the British Empire! To be fair, I think Moet and Clicquot are rather ordinary. My father swears by Taittinger.'

'Does he by Jove? I must visit your old man's pad whenever I can grab the Landy back from you! You're a bit of a rare species, you know that?' Harry was keeping an eye on their bowling lane, where an inebriated large lady had twisted her ankle by veering off the lane as she hurled her ball in the wrong direction.

'I'd love you to come. Did I ever tell you that my father promised me a fortune if I waited until twenty-five until I married?'

'How old are you now?'

'Nineteen.'

'Seriously?'

'No, you silly man! But things change, Harry! I was meant to get a doctorate before then and instead, look, I've got a big job! My father accepts it.'

'Why don't you get fast-tracked on our engineering or specialised sciences course? You'd pick up an MSc in a flash. You could be back here in a couple of years, running continental projects for us or anyone else you preferred?' Harry stood up as their number flashed on the scoreboard.

'Because I want to stay in charge of myself until I'm ready. In every respect. I'm not doing badly, am I, Harry? Are we off? Okay, but I want you to tell me what we're going to do with these sixty South African companies or wannabee companies or Nhleko's girls' companies that reckon they're owed a big slice each of the TDC action!' She sprang up and Harry was proud and excited to follow her swaying form towards their lane. Lesebo picked up the nearest ball. 'You take this one Harry. It's snow-white, medium-sized and well-used!'

*****

It was the Reverend Nicholas Mahlambi's turn for interrogation by fire on the *Cape Trends* show with the formidable Hennie Strydom. Mahlambi was no stranger to the Cape Town audience, more usually leading Christian crusades against crime and corruption, discrimination against the Khoisan people or any increase in the price of food staples.

'It is my pleasure today to welcome the Reverend Nicholas Mahlambi, leader of the Christian's United party and recently elected Minister for Trade and Industry in the new administration. Pastor, my principal purpose in inviting you here is to learn about the new governing arrangements that have been put in place at the Siyeza undertaking. How can a priest who is not in the ANC hope to contribute in an issue with such a turbulent political history?'

'A priest can often pour oil on troubled waters, Hennie! But I welcome the chance to explain to the public what we've got in mind. We have a precious chance, during the short honeymoon phase of the new administration, to set the wheelbarrow back on its legs and pick up the bruised apples. Two things have gone badly wrong. Firstly the blatant and totally irregular meddling with the now renamed Siyeza Peoples Fund, which is the banker and focus for all Siyeza funding and handling of huge foreign investments. There is no doubt that this was a government error, which the recent tribunal underlined, recommending that the board's appointments should follow standard legal and business practice. There is every hope that our re-elected President will address this.'

Mahlambi put on a dazzling smile for the cameras. 'The other issue is the disqualification of the terms used in awarding the major contract to Trustcore Development Corporation, the British construction conglomerate. Without any legal or constitutional authority, the government are supporting the cancellation of 20 percent of the contract, worked out on a geographical rather than funding basis, which of course, threatens to lame the whole project. I want to examine this carefully, seeing whether there are grounds to believe that the contract was awarded to the detriment of the South African construction industry and workforce – I'm inclined to feel that government and trade union axis has acted prematurely, using faulty information and analysis.' The cleric beamed engagingly at Strydom, the studio lights reflecting unhelpfully off his darkened glasses.

'But even if you manage to straighten this out through compromise and debate, what about the raging crime in the area? The Cape Flats have been nigh-ungovernable for two decades, with a drugs regime holding more power and influence that civic authorities?'

'Well, I think you're over-stating the case but nevertheless the very real criminal element within the Siyeza heartlands must be brought under control, both prior to some delicate stages of development and also in tandem with it, as its benefits begin to flow. That is the main reason why we have decided to totally reorganise the project's management'

'Can you tell us something about that?'

'Yes, of course. I aim to show that government has a hands-on part to play in this partnership. Although there had been ongoing consultation by the main role players, there had been no central focus or open communication on a fixed, regular basis. My committee will change this. There will be a small official composition representing the Municipality, the Siyeza Directorate, the main contractor and most welcome and important of all, the SAPS – all at the very highest level. Being small, it will be efficient, but I anticipate constant attendance from financial advisors, the trade unions, non-political public bodies, perhaps some of them becoming ex-officio members.'

'Are we meeting deadlines and can we still afford it?'

'Well, as you can imagine, you cannot have the sort of disruption caused in the lead-up to the Election without some sort of delay. There is some ongoing intimidation and unlawful behaviour at several sites, which the trade unions are roundly condemning. I think we'll see improvement in the workplace as the key issues I mentioned take effect – especially an uncompromising approach to law and order. As far as funding goes, there's no denying that probably 20 percent of investments were withdrawn, mostly from overseas sources. Given restored equilibrium in the construction arena and continued diplomatic negotiation between Britain and South Africa in particular, I foresee funds returning. If you look at Siyeza's JSE figures, they are rising again after a disappointing patch. There are strong indicators of normality and serious industrial headway being made in the next six months.'

'The Reverend Nicholas Mahlambi, our new Minister of Trade and Industry, very many thanks for appearing on the show. We wish you luck in your new appointments.'

*****

Grannies with small charges on tricycles, inveterate horticulturalists, pensioners on shaded benches and groups of foreign tourists didn't take any notice of the two small groups of young men of mixed racial composition who hung around intersections on the winding pathways. They were far too intent on savouring the beauties of Kirstenbosch National Botanical Garden on a perfect viewing day, with a light breeze keeping the heat down. If they had bothered, they would have seen the incongruity of the men, hands stuffed in windcheater jackets, paying no interest at all to the floribunda surroundings. Instead they sauntered around the fringes of lawns and shrubberies as separate groups, keeping their targets in sight. They knew the setting was deliberately bizarre with overtones of melodrama but that was the way their bosses chose to behave. When it came to rare meetings like this, with possibilities of showdowns over turf and business, they were nervous and jumpy.

The contrasting figures of Ravi Chetty and Bram De Vries were equally unsuited for the tranquil natural surroundings of the world-renowned botanical garden. Chetty, short, slim and sleek in black from head to foot, including a baseball cap and dark glasses. De Vries, towering, bulky and overdressed in the "safari" garb favoured by German and Dutch visitors to Africa, khaki, multi-pocketed, detachable leggings, bush walking boots and a wide-brimmed Australian sun hat. They had agreed to meet, at De Vries' request. He was anxious to ensure that his undisclosed personal project within the Siyeza was on track, despite the unexpected aftermath of the South African general election. He had run out of political backers and worse still, was confronted by a religious zealot and a police force under new management. Last time he and Chetty had met, he had promised the little Indian that he would meet fire with fire. He was uncertain now and wanted to explore trade-off options with Chetty. Maybe leave Chetty's turf alone in exchange for support in suppressing critics of his scheme?

For Chetty, his attitudes were always coloured by fear when De Vries was in the frame. He was confident that the Dutchman couldn't edge him out territorially, although his drugs network would eventually outmatch him. But if

De Vries got the go-ahead to put up some Caesars Palace-type of place, backed by all manner of offset promises to the government, municipality or labour barons, then he might quickly build up a base that drained his manor dry. How could he highlight De Vries as the bad guy and somehow restore his image as the Robin Hood of the Cape Flats? Like De Vries, the change in the political set-up had upset him badly and the aggressive police posture was making business hard. Four brothels and a bookie had been closed and half a dozen shebeens, making the gangs fractious and unreliable. He had kept his powder dry about that snake in the grass, Kirkside, but Chetty had been told how he was still active with SPF, which might need sorting out again – the police were too close to him these days, so a proxy might have to do the job.

'You know, when we met last, the knives were out, weren't they? But who'd have guessed that things would change after that little shit Nhleko was kicked out? I cannot believe about this priest being the overlord here, or that the fat bitch cop would get a leg-up from her sister.' De Vries glanced around at their bodyguards and indicated a bench alongside some Cape chestnuts, with their ribbon clusters of rose-pink blooms crowding the branch ends, well clear of the spotted pale green leaf clusters. Chetty brushed the gnarled old seat clear of fallen tree debris and sat down gingerly. De Vries joined him, a body width between them. 'So how are we going to work together then, Ravi? How much of the gangs do you control?' De Vries was leaning forward, elbows on knees, staring seaward.

'You never know, you know that. When you find someone putting up their protection in your patch, you know you've got problems, don't you? Unless you're on the streets with contacts in all the gangs, anything can happen. I miss Sonny, I must admit. But you know, there's not much problem this side of Mitchells Plain but a different sort of nonsense is causing trouble now, with all this rent-a-mob stuff at the building sites and truck entrances. If it gets worse, there will be major ructions man, because the gangs will want to take that over too. At the end of the day, if you've got roaming rights for your pushers and donkeys, you've got the gangs by the balls.' This was what De Vries wanted to hear, since Chetty would be blown away when San City was creaming off the trade. But it was all about getting to that point, while the Municipality and police were getting headstrong.

'Tell me about Kirkside – what were they going to do with the kid if they hadn't bust the place?' De Vries was searching for any remaining levers to prevent the Siyeza directorate getting back into full swing.

'Not sure. It was just a back scratch – we helped those wierdos before. They owed us. Suited us nicely – safe house nearby, dealing with kids. They were about to put him to work with those two black chicks you know – that's their main line of business.' Chetty suddenly glanced at De Vries. 'Hang on, are you thinking what I'm thinking – find someone friendly in the Court archives to slip us a video?' Chetty allowed himself a rare chuckle, fishing his worry beads out of his shirt pocket. 'Come to think of it, it could get better. I've got a proposal for you. You know Kirkside's wife stayed with my kid brother because they'd quarrelled? What about, I ask? Did you know that the Lesebo chick at Siyeza was hired to teach that kid at home? And then, boom, she's gone and the Kirksides split. She gets that top job from nowhere – why?' Chetty sensed a brief ascendency over De Vries, who shook his head casually?

'So what? What's it worth if you can't prove it? It'll be rubbished as dirty tricks and bounce back at you?'

'I thought you were the big brains, heh, Bram? I'm saying, there must be evidence. And you know who's been cosying up to that fat cop for the last year, don't you? He's a private dick called Maddox, quite a big private investigator in the city. He's the guy who's done all the Kirksides snooping. Am I getting there, Bram? What I'm saying is that there's probably evidence in his offices downtown. We can get some boys to pay them a visit?' De Vries was visibly more alert, straightening his back and turning to face his Indian companion.

'But who will it belong to, Ravi, you or me? If I leave all the dope trade to you until after San City is up and running, and then we'll renegotiate – that's probably three years, isn't it? In which case it's mine. It's more use to me to negotiate with that chick, done and dusted, don't you think? You can only blackmail or sell it and you'll be better keeping me out of your nice smelling hair?' Ravi took his statutory time to decide but slowly turned to Bram, with his right palm raised.

'Okay, brah, put it there! I've enjoyed the stroll. We'll call you on that funny number within the week.' They broke off, their minders trailing them in different directions. As they made their way to the gate, both had misgivings about the other's intentions and on the course of action to take if they were cheated.

*****

It was Katie's idea to ask the Kirksides to join them in a friendly mixed doubles at the Mowbray Club. She thought it would prepare them nicely for the following week's mixed doubles club championship, which was unnerving Maddox slightly. It also provided a chance for the Kirksides to be seen again as a couple, enjoying themselves. To Maddox's surprise, the Kirksides accepted; Katie guessed that they felt indebted to Maddox and had reached a self-confident stage in public together. Katie's mild bossiness continued on the courts.

'Look, we need to compensate for Maddox's brilliance so I suggest you partner him Ami and I'll team up with Richard?' This pairing started well enough but both men were not up to their partner's standards. Maddox was amazed at the gymnastic versatility of Katie and her ruthless dispatch of his weak returns at the net. Ami was lissom too and although out of touch, was very reliable on the base line. Maddox and Ami found themselves trailing six-three after the first set. The Kirksides seemed relaxed and despite Richard's lack of fitness, they obviously enjoyed themselves. After one endless game with ten deuces and as many rallies, Katie and Richard edged ahead, playing off Maddox at the net and over-pressurising Ami on the base line. They ran out six-two winners, but nobody felt outclassed. Katie poured effusive praise over Maddox, assuring him of certain progress with her at the championship.

As they sat on the clubhouse veranda, watching the sun drop sharply over the treeline and drinking tea, Maddox received a phone call. He apologised but answered. Katie watched his face as his eyes and mouth widened.

'Just now – in broad daylight? Didn't we set the alarms? Oh God, why didn't she tell anyone? The studio safe? What old files and archives? Oh those! Hell's teeth, I'm coming straight away. Where are you? I'll see you there!' Maddox walked back towards the table. 'The offices have been broken into. No equipment gone or much damage but they've taken a small safe in the studio by drilling the wall around the screws. I'll have to go now darling, I'm so sorry everyone. May I ask you to take my lovely partner home please Richard?' He laughed as he kissed Katie. 'I'm making too much a habit of this, aren't I darling? Our tennis in jinxed!' He hurried from the club, his car engine racing.

'Have we an inventory Gary?' Maddox asked. There were portfolios, court hearings and current evidence envelopes strewn on the studio floor and Maddox wondered what was missing.

'Yes, it's here, boss. You know what I notice missing straight away? The box of evidential DVDs – in fact, I cannot see anything else that's gone!' Gary crouched, sifting through the files and envelopes with an extending pocket probe, mindful of preserving evidence.

'Oh no, are you thinking what I'm thinking? Joost's DVD of Kirkside! You wouldn't believe it, I've just left him at the tennis club. Get the SAPS forensic gang here quickly Gary, while I have a word with Khanyisile Mthembu. I'll have to tell both Richard and Lesebo. It'll be bad news for both of them, rebuilding their lives, but it will be worse if it goes viral in the criminal underworld or gets splashed on Facebook or Instagram! And we won't come out of this smelling of roses, either...'

Chapter Twelve

Jabu Nhleko had been nursing a grievance against Malusi Jali since the ill-fated day when the Harrismith caucus had unceremoniously bounced him out of power. Although Jali had implemented most of the Siyeza corrective steps before the Election, it was nevertheless Nhleko's enforcing authority that had transformed the troubled Cape Flats operation. Above that, it was he, Nhleko, who had suffered the indignity and pain of De Vries' coercion and violence. And now, despite being thrown out of office, the menacing Dutchman was reminding him that he had kept his half of the deal with the pre-Election sponsorship money. Nhleko had failed him by losing office, with nothing to show for De Vries' generosity. He had made renewed threats concerning Nhleko's future safety. Nhleko listened to his advice, by being reminded that it was customary for political casualties to be rewarded in the spirit of *Ubuntu* – the quangos, tribunals and state institutions were littered with yesterday's great men and women who had been passed over for further headline-earning political appointments. And so Jabu Nhleko decided to appeal to Malusi Jali's better nature. He knew how there had always been bad blood between them, probably exaggerated through recent disagreements by their clan chiefs, but the party loyalty should hold firm.

'What I'm saying, my comrade, is that there is still room for more oversight at Siyeza. Think about it: a preacher-man refereeing for the party, a woman cop huffing and puffing, a Basotho schoolgirl sitting on top of the pile – what can they do about all the people who want a slice of the cake, my friend, heh? Nothing! The President doesn't want trouble but he's frightened of the unions and the left wing.'

'But what are you saying? They've dismantled all the changes we made to the control and financing. Old Mahlambi goes down well with the white trouble-makers and makes us all feel that we're back in the Siyeza driving seat without them realising it! I think it was a good move by me, not you, I must remind you!' Jali was a changed character these days, self-confident and prepared to keep his independence as the Deputy President for as long as he need – with the President set to serve a full second term, juicy options would surely come his way.

'I must congratulate you about that – a masterly stroke! But I even have a name for my door, my brother!' Nhleko grinned with massive teeth to help persuade his former subordinate. 'How about 'Ombudsman Siyeza Contract Equity'? I could oversee contracts as elements within the overall budget and the project's template without interfering in the individual bidding and selection?' Nhleko had done some mental rehearsal and was satisfied with his use of impressive phrases. 'I've kept a few clever and loyal members with me who can get a convincing Terms of Reference and contract to the Presidency office by the end of this week. Are you happy for me to do this, Deputy President?' Nhleko was digging deep, sounding fawning as he restrained his dislike of Jali.

Jali felt a wave of self-satisfaction wash over him. It was fitting that his bullying and greedy former master was eating humble pie. He tapped the table, looking out of the Union Buildings window over the vast sloping lawns, deliberately taking his time.

'I can let my successor at the DTI glance at it. We cannot have more delays but I concede that it's important to let the left wing and unions believe that we are popularising the company inventory and workforce issues. Let me at least try that since we all owe you a debt of gratitude for what you did for the party over so many years. I'll let you know what they think.'

Nhleko left Jali feeling reasonably confident. If Nhleko made known that the party had cut him adrift for several months and turned down his own proposal to help them out, it would backfire on Jali as unwarranted resentment. He had a few days to keep De Vries at arm's length while his cohorts drafted a Terms of Reference and contract for Jali. Although it was largely at De Vries' urging that he had designed the appointment, he judged it could be an effective move. Once in the chair with hand-picked party minions to hand, he could see ways to ensure that De Vries' dramatic proposition was successfully adopted by Mahlambi's Council.

Maddox found it embarrassing and harrowing to tell both the Kirksides and Lesebo Bafokeng about the theft of the incriminating DVD. Professionally, he was bound to use Ami as the recipient of bad news, since she had engaged him originally to spy on her husband. Since then, through the twists and turns of the Siyeza story, he had developed a personal relationship with Richard too, which had become much firmer during Maddox's part in obtaining the release of Tristan. He asked Ami to visit his offices to ensure confidentiality.

'Bad news, I'm afraid Ami, which I have to tell you, rather than Richard, for all the obvious reasons. There was a robbery on these premises last Friday and all our DVDs were stolen, I suspect in order to obtain the one that you declined to see concerning Richard and Lesebo Bafokeng. We made no copies, I'm afraid, so someone has the incriminating evidence for blackmail. Naturally, I'm honour-bound to tell you because it was part of a professional contract but I must also tell Lesebo Bafokeng. She knows of its existence but nothing more.' Maddox pursed his lips, awaiting a hysterical response. Instead none came. The razor-sharp mind was slicing in another direction.

'Oh my God, what next? I've got a thought. I'm hearing that Lesebo's getting pretty thick with multi-millionaire Harry Reynolds. Is it too bizarre to include her as a suspect, intent on assembling any incriminatory evidence of her past before she repairs to her mansion in the Shires?' Ami's waspish character and high intellect made a formidable combination. She crossed her legs distractingly as Maddox considered her unexpected reaction.

'Highly improbable, I'd say Ami. I'm inclined to feel that Chetty or a crooked financier is trying it on again. First against Richard, with the trial evidence, Tristan's abduction and threat to kidnap you. Now this one, I'd guess aimed at Lesebo, rather than Richard, although you can't keep him out of the frame. In other words, it's either the same person or group who dearly want their way over Siyeza. It'll all be linked to the reversals they've had since the Election, when the government laid out a new set of rules for keeping their grip on the project. So as with the kidnapping, we might be able to put a cold towel on and narrow it down?'

Maddox became enthused, happy to challenge Ami's powerful intellect for a few moments. 'There are only a handful who lost out badly and very few of those have the know-how to back a hunch and do a cheeky robbery on a Saturday afternoon. None of that helps you I know, and I'm sorry that this means a "Return to Start" for Richard, back to when you were making your mind up about divorcing him or not. So once again, he stands to lose all his credibility and business following. At the moment, just as happened waiting for the bribe over Tristan, we have no choice but to wait. Meanwhile, since I'm very involved in this one, I'll go all out to find the culprits before they go public.' Maddox had run out of assurances and ended the interview with Ami, who kept her composure throughout. She was becoming hardened to repeated family tragedies.

It was harder still with Lesebo. Maddox decided to meet her in the Reference Section of the city public library, scratching his head to retain confidentiality without a casual café setting. Maddox found Lesebo poring over the Constitution, elbows on table, fists supporting her temples, reading glasses on, looking every inch her former bluestocking persona. They greeted each other softly but warmly. Lesebo knew there was something ominous afoot. She trusted the disciplined mind that Maddox brought to the most muddled of Siyeza problems.

'Lesebo, this is a sensitive issue. Forgive me, but I come as a legally-bound confidant, rather than inquisitor!' Lesebo's warm smile changed to a worried expression. She took off her glasses and put them gently on the small print smothering the tissue-thin pages of the leather-bound tome.

'I don't want you to frighten or disappoint me, Maddox – you never have!' A trace of a smile as the deep pool eyes came and left him.

'It will not make you happy I'm afraid, but let's think it through. Last Saturday, there was a robbery at my offices and all the DVDs we keep in a safe were stolen. As you know, we were engaged by Ami who suspected that Richard was having an affair with one or several of his professional clients. You'll have to forgive us, but when we saw the existing circumstances, we suspected that you were the femme fatale. So we investigated and filmed Richard Kirkside assaulting you as professional evidence for Ami. She declined to watch the video but reserved the right to see or take it later, so we stored in the safe. Well now it's gone!' Maddox looked plaintively at Lesebo, who kept staring at him, her hands clasped together on the table. 'So this joins the list of bribes – Richard's evidence at the trial, Tristan's kidnap, the threat about Ami. It's highly likely to be the same person or group, firstly trying to nobble Richard, and now you, although Richard has everything to lose as a businessman, rather than husband this time.'

'If this had happened earlier, it would have caught me psychologically disturbed. It was my lost virginity, my abandoned doctorate, my promise to my father, my loss of the will to live – what for, when I had worked so hard to come top of a white class?' She underlined some words with sudden nods of the head, as if she was recalling a beautiful view. She went on in a subdued hiss. 'But now, I've started again. A top job instead of doctorate, maybe a love life to replace the indignity of rape and cover girl for Siyeza! You could ask, 'which was the worse to lose'?' She looked steadily at Maddox. 'Maybe because the last two years have flashed by in a whirl, with unreal things happening, this would be the greatest damage. What a terrible irony: being pilloried, and losing everything, because you didn't go on Facebook to say, 'I've been raped!' Lesebo let a despondent look appear. 'What now, Maddox?'

'Well it hasn't happened yet. The thieves don't have to issue bribes to either you or Richard, or both, of course. They might think they can inflict as much damage by just releasing the video to the social media. So you have to shore up your life in anticipation. Maybe tell your father? If you have a close friend, perhaps share the dilemma?' As Maddox spoke, the enormity of her most dreaded consequence settled in her mind. Neither Richard nor Kobus Labuschagne knew of each other's brief encounter with her. With half a million given by one and the most prestigious of jobs by the other, she would seem a scheming harlot. The biological fatherhood debate would flare up, impossible to end amicably, and her callous resort to abortion would lose her all public respectability. Lesebo was on the edge of screaming out this predicament to Maddox when he continued. 'Have you a shoulder to cry on or a wise head to consult? You're quite friendly with Harry Reynolds – could you talk to him?' Lesebo looked wildly at Maddox, lowering her voice from the high whispering tones.

'Are you mad? He's my future love and happiness. Anyway, it's worse Maddox. There are other complications.' She lowered her eyes and began to cry quietly, turning to spasmodic sobs as tears dripped onto the Constitution. Maddox put his hand on her shoulder and said nothing, waiting a full minute. Lesebo wiped her eyes and tears with a tissue. She blew her nose and blinked her large eyes several times. 'Maddox. I lost my senses after Richard raped me. I became irrational. I had almost a blood lust against white bosses, white money, colonialism, female subjugation, racist arrogance, bigotry – I lost control, can't you see?' Lesebo was desperate to tell Maddox the full story that only she knew but her courage left her. She fought back more tears. 'Maddox, let me digest this please? May I talk to you again when I'm a bit calmer?'

'Of course, Lesebo, whenever you wish.' Maddox noted the incomplete comments and her unwillingness to divulge a fuller account. But as it stood now, she might win sympathy – a young black girl raped two years ago by her white employer, too afraid to report the experience, but since landed the city's top job.

Why should she be penalised further by a criminal attempting to defame her and collapse Siyeza by publishing the video? But it was the wrong time to build up her hopes too far.

*****

They called it the "Noon Day Gun", with their video talk going live at twelve noon Cape Town time. The ritual bordered on ludicrous. De Vries always wore sunglasses and a low brimmed hat with window light behind him, making him unrecognisable. Ravi Chetty always went into the back of The Sound Connection TV and electrical goods outlet in Rylands, where skinny youths with half-shaved heads did the technical stuff. He sat there, also with glasses and hat but better illuminated than his Dutch conversationalist. Such communications were unusual, normally reflecting a deterioration in relationships or a co-operative proposal. This time, De Vries wanted to talk about the robbery at Maddox Private Investigators. They always used veiled speech and never mentioned real persons, place names or dates.

'Did you get what you were looking for, shopping?'

'Yeah, no probs.'

'Happy about that. So what?'

'Dunno really. Waiting for right moment – you know, gotta be seen to mess up.'

'No, no, no! That's not what we said. I want to use it for trading, okay? That's the whole point!''

'Look, it's my baby, so it's my neck, okay? You put new management in the shop so let's have some badly pissed-off shoppers, right?'

'I said no, smartass. How many more times? I want it when I'm over next time – two weeks okay? Then I'll give the gift personally. All nice and quiet, but things will happen. Your way won't work. You'll get burned. Like we said...' Ravi had glanced across the courtyard to give the sliced throat cut-off signal to the shaved heads. Let that Dutchman stew in oil.

De Vries watched the picture vanish and did not bother to re-connect. He rang a Cape Town number.

'Jannie? It's Bram. Okay, time to get the mail out. You have the first five addresses, don't you? Post your parcels now. Talk to those two postmen now, okay – could be tomorrow?'

*****

'Look darling, I've spoken to George today, on a no-names-no-pack-drill basis and he's adamant that any sender of moving sex piccies can be hammered there and then for storing and peddling obscene material. Character defamation is a no-hoper in litigation but then all the thief has are the DVD pictures. He has to prove identity, without any text or independent live commentary. Voice-over and print-over texts are inadmissible. Depending on the quality, which I suppose one or both of us is entitled to check with Maddox, the defendant can always resort to consensual intercourse, in that Lesebo did not register intent to sue, with well over two years dues spent. So it seems that the sender is on very thin ice. All that said, he can send an anonymous DVD or Instagram at any time.' The Kirksides were ambling along Franschoek's main thoroughfare, hunting for a promising light lunch at a French street restaurant. They made their choice, a fairly cosmopolitan affair with blue and white checked table cloths and table water carafes encased in raffia jackets. Richard ordered two Chenin Blancs.

'All right, but Maddox insists that this one is aimed at Lesebo Bofokeng.' Ami always did her utmost to de-personalise Lesebo in Richard's company. 'And as far as I can judge, she's fairly fire-proof too? So she had a fling with you? What the hell? She's over sixteen and told nobody about it. Your wife knows about it already. So it all depends on the crook's spin-doctor, doesn't it? If it contradicts something particularly commendable she's achieving on the tax-payer's behalves, I suppose she could be made vulnerable, in which case, an uncompromising rebuttal might save the day. I think it's been stolen to give to her personally, to get her to cave in or co-operate with gangland mafia on the Flats.' Ami sipped her wine carefully, nodding appreciation. 'In which case, we may never hear any more about it unless idiots start pushing copies around the underground shops and clubs.'

'I'll drink to that sweetheart. I have to. I haven't got that amount of self-confidence about it, I must admit. But someone went to a great deal of trouble, taking considerable risk, to steal the DVD. We must go and see it, because I'm damned if the film can be technically acceptable quality? After all, you've never seen it and we're going on Maddox's word that it would stand up in court!' Richard signalled for the menu and refilled glasses.

*****

The fires gutted the poorly constructed bookmaker's shop and the adjacent shebeen and pool table dive within an hour. The fire services, police and key holders were impeded by the rocks and cast-out fridges, beds and cookers that blocked the main approaches leading into Hanover Park and Manenberg. The pall of smoke hung low in the windless night, with stubborn wooden frames resisting the water canon hosing with exploding red and yellow sparks. The early investigation suggested an old-fashioned incendiary cassette with an ignition timer, hidden under a bench cushion, as the cause of the fire, beginning around midnight. While the police and firemen were still sifting through the remains and dousing the last of the glowing ashes, news came over their radios of a second fire in the Manenberg-Gugulethu border area, again another betting shop and its attached neighbour, the Rub-a-dub Indian Curry Takeaway. This time the fire engines were able to reach the premises quicker and managed to douse the flames before they engulfed the entire properties. As the first signs of dawn appeared, the drifting smuts and acrid smoke made a melancholy haze in the poorly lit district. There were more onlookers in streets that never completely emptied during the night, as rival gangs wandered either protecting their patches or "travelling intent on crime", as the law enforcement agencies described it. Stray dogs gathered close by, knowing how people always leave behind something to sustain them, vultures trailing predators at the kill.

'Same owners. Coloureds. They've got a string of betting shops on this side of the Flats. Talk to that key holder there and send a van to his other addresses until it gets light. Looks like some gang war stuff to me.' The police captain stood giving orders in a gaggle of police and onlookers, some curious, some media, no doubt some street gang scouts. As firemen always pointed out, probably the arsonist himself was there, drawn to gaze at the exciting flames and enormous damage he could cause undetected with a child's watch with its tiny battery and simple ignition circuit, packed into a cassette with a dose of match heads or thimble of petrol. Some larger cars were arriving now, bringing back seat passengers.

The local onlookers muttered noisily as they parted to allow them to the front of the police cordon, taped off with red and white plastic streamers. Again the police radios began to chatter. This time a tank had exploded in a taxi as the driver went to collect it for the first early morning fares to town. Loudly wailing ambulances now joined the fire engines and police vans as dawn broke, a pall of smoke and lingering stench of burning fuel, rubber and paint enshrouding Manenberg's dismal and rock-strewn, neglected streets. Some new and smarter dwellings that had sprung up rapidly as the Siyeza venture took root were vividly silhouetted. The two large Mercedes cars slid away together, their own short-wave radios busy, the sinister figures in the back snarling into cell phones.

'So what are we looking at Mannie? Three of Krishna's shops and one of his taxis and Darsh's clothes place off Vanguard? Any money in the betting shops? No? Good. And a shoot-out you say? They thought they were going to Arnav's superstore? Anyone hurt? Pranav gone to hospital – is he bad? Okay, and the guy with burns looks serious? Right, let's all meet up at Pelli's Place at nine – get the street chiefs there. Looks like we've got a war on our hands!' Ravi Chetty was thinking fast as he was raced back to his plush home to shower and eat. All tonight's targets were properties within his known area of responsibility. It seemed certain that De Vries had broken their uneasy and unofficial truce, angry at Chetty reneging on the Kirkside video deal. Chetty would have to show muscle to keep his trade and position going. If the districts broke out in all-out gang warfare, it might be the right time to play the DVD card with Lesebo Bafokeng.

Khanyisile Mthembu was disturbed to hear the news during her early morning briefing in police headquarters. During the night, a dozen premises had been destroyed by fire in five separate arson incidents. A taxi driver had died from acute burns and a man suffered "very serious injury" gunshot wounds, allegedly during further arson attempts. Four people had been hospitalised for serious smoke inhalation treatment and one street beggar was reported missing. It seemed that the attacks resulted from opposing groups of Flats street gangs fighting for turf, with four of the main gangs taking on the remaining three for territory. Intelligence suggested that the arson attacks had taken place in the more western half of prime gangland, generally assumed to be under the overlord watch of Ravi Chetty. It was agreed that he should be interrogated for information to prevent any escalation of the trouble. Khanyisile demurred at calling for military reinforcements but asked the colonel in attendance to stand by to provide a street presence in twenty-four hours' time if the situation deteriorated further tonight. As ever, she rang Maddox for reassurance.

'For what it's worth Khanyisile, my bet is that this has been incited by a combination of political and foreign influences disputing the new Siyeza dispensation, as they say here. There are less than ten really vicious gangs who kill as part of their drugs war *raison d'etre*. Because they sub-divide geographically, they are easy to mobilise against each other. Someone is orchestrating internecine Flats violence which can pass off as nasty gang warfare, which it is on one level. But the other and more important purpose is something much more profound, much more defining for future years. I think we're right back to where we all came in, with this being the Battle of Siyeza, not Cape Flat gangland – do you see the difference?'

'Mahlambi has called an emergency council meeting for this afternoon. The only change since you were last there is that there is a new oversight group headed by our friend Jabu Nhleko. They're supposed to oversee the balance of foreign to domestic companies within the overall TDC contract but anyone can see that they've been put there to give the nod to all the wannabee companies. Apparently, they're queuing up for BEE, VAT and Compensation Commissioner Certification – the government departments will strike for overtime to stamp their papers!'

'Interesting. How's Lesebo holding up to all that?'

'Fine. Very well in fact. Everyone is whispering about her and Harry but if you're as beautiful as her, people always gossip, don't they Maddox?' Khanyisile sounded uncharacteristically arch.

'What are you trying to say Khanyisile? Are you saying I'm a gossip?' Maddox retorted jocularly.

'Not at all, no. But keeping my ear to the ground, as you and I are paid to do, I'm hearing funny stories about why Lesebo was propelled to stardom overnight – through the bedroom! Are you hearing this too, or is it just an example of the tittle-tattle we're talking about? Maybe you're sworn to confidence?' Khanyisile had returned to her professional friendship manner.

'It might ring a distant bell. Do you think it could embarrass her – if it's true, it sounds like private business to me?' Maddox was boxing cleverly, since he wanted a second opinion confirming that Lesebo had nothing to fear from the missing DVD video.

'Well, the story is that it involved a prominent white gentleman. Cronyism for sexual partners is universal, Maddox, isn't it? But we seem to be in the same Super League as the French and Italians, don't we?' Khanyisile was in a strange mood, Maddox decided, switching now to that of the coquette.

'If I didn't admire your professional discretion General, it sounds like you're propositioning an innocent subordinate!'

147

'Oh no Maddox, you know me! I'm old fashioned. I always insist on first refusal, not the other way round!' They both roared with laughter before ringing off. Maddox was satisfied on two counts: firstly Lesebo had no personal worries but secondly, De Vries and Nhleko were stirring up an ant's nest for some ill-gotten gain nobody knew about yet.

The following night saw increased violence around Athlone, Manenberg and Hanover Park, with fires and minor shooting skirmishes erupting throughout the night. Pelli's Place, a renowned underworld drinking haunt was torched beyond recognition, a plastics factory was badly burned in Philippi's light industrial estate and five shebeens and pool combos were either ransacked or burned by roving gangs. By dawn, there had been seven deaths, five from gunshot wounds. The fire service and police were deployed in substantial numbers, reducing the violence levels and keeping the gangland factions apart with water cannon and plastic baton rounds. Twenty-seven arrests were made, mostly comprising rival gang members. One ominous development was the theft and vandalism within a large storage depot that housed TDC and subsidiary contractor's equipment and construction materials. Two diggers were stolen but recovered.

General Mthembu invoked constitutional rights by requesting military assistance, leading to the deployment of two companies of infantry in armoured vehicles. Chetty refused to accompany a police officer to police HQ, so was arrested and brought under protest to confront Khanyisile and her police subordinates.

'Mr Chetty, you're under arrest purely as a way to bring you here – you can go the moment our discussion has finished.' Chetty had not physically resisted arrest and appeared calm.

'We can talk about damages and wrongful arrest later but the conversation is over before it starts okay? I've got nothing to say. Talk to those gang bosses, not me lady.' Chetty stood up, ready to leave, gesturing to a policeman to open the door.

'Sit down, Mr Chetty. You will be arrested the moment you leave the barracks. We want you to help us to restore law and order on the Flats. Without incriminating yourself – you can have a lawyer if you want – we know that you have authority as a community leader, shall we say? If you're happy with that, we'd like you to quieten down any citizens who might respect your authority – happy so far, Mr Chetty?' Khanyisile had made great strides as a police leader in recent years, which was making an impression on professional criminals such as Chetty.

'Go on.'

'But it takes two to tango, doesn't it, so it would be really helpful if you could point us towards your opposite number who could similarly persuade his citizens to quieten down so we can discuss the problems round the table?' Khanyisile was speaking in a bright and light-hearted way, a nursery school teacher getting her class motivated, first thing in the morning.

'Look, let's not play games, heh? As a community leader, you start by saying these folk were slammed in tin shacks by the whites and had to build their own lives and neighbourhoods, okay? They get fussy and a bit protective. You're not welcome in Manenberg if you're from Constantia, you know what I mean? So this neighbourhood vigilante game started. No jobs, houses, shops, amenities but plenty of time and kids. Guess what? Crime!' Chetty was now preaching to Mthembu to teach her a lesson.

'Okay Mr Chetty, as a policewoman, I know the history of the Cape Flats gangs. I'm asking who the other big community leader is – we've got to sort out this fighting straight away!'

'Work it out for yourself. It got nasty when they gave the big construction job to the Poms, so it's someone who reckons he should have got it instead, isn't it? So where does that leave you? Trade Unions fat cat, foreign muscle man or a noisy politician? Don't look further, madam – maybe they're hand-in-glove, heh? Now can I go please?' Chetty stood up and placed his chair under the interviewing table. He was confident that he'd sown sufficient seeds of suspicion under De Vries and Nhleko.

'Why not? Just one last thing. Have you got a grudge against Lesebo Bafokeng?' Khanyisile was standing opposite Chetty, her hands resting on the back of her chair.

'Long legs for a black. Not short of boyfriends, I'm told. Newspapers say she's a child prodigy – what the Germans call a wunderkind? But she's messing up badly now, isn't she?' Chetty paused to stare theatrically at Khanyisile. 'Grudge, you say? What the hell for? She needs our pity working for that clown Labuschagne!' Chetty smiled and waved, turning on his heel to be escorted downstairs. He had not mentioned his worries about the arson attack on Pelli's Place, which he used as a meeting place with the gang leaders.

*****

The Reverend Nicholas Mahlambi screwed his eyes tight shut as he said an introductory prayer, bellowing 'Amen' in the traditional black churchman's fashion. His smooth, unlined face belied both his age and a reputation for fiery outbursts. The emergency council meeting was held in the police headquarters for security precautions. With the public disorder raging in the Cape Flats, the mood was chastened, with Khanyisile opening with an updated account of the Manenberg disorder.

'Half an hour ago, things were at last quietening down with no reported arson or gunshots. But there is still sporadic shoplifting and stoning of site vehicles, taxis and busses. Arrests are being made and there is a public community gathering in the Zionist Gospel Hall at Ottery this evening with Municipality and church leaders. There is no declared cause for the violence, other than turf war flames being fanned. There was definitely a Third Force involved in the initial attacks, which is under investigation. The Army will stay another forty-eight hours, providing the level of violence continues to decline.'

'We owe the public services our heartfelt thanks General. The fire services, the police, the ambulances and paramedics and the military have all been wonderful. Thank you all. Now then. I gather our byword is normally specialised commentary, governed by confidentiality? Maybe as the government's representative, I should say that this whole episode is seen as a tragedy. The ambiguous posture by the government before the Election was regrettable, there is no doubt, but with this group reassembled and the SPF re-established on a firm business foundation, there was every reason to feel Siyeza was going to roar ahead successfully, benefitting the neglected thousands of the Cape Flats suburbs. And then, without warning or reason, this mayhem erupts, threatening to destroy any community stability that the region might have, aimed at disrupting, maybe even overturning, the project's progress.'

Mahlambi cut himself short to remove his dark glasses and rub his eyes. He looked blind, his eyes screwed tight shut, before replacing the spectacles carefully. 'We are not going to sanction this, ladies and gentlemen, have no fear. As the leader of a small but independent political party that is supporting the ANC in the Parliamentary lobby, I hope I can convince you that I abhor violence and destruction of anything – and particularly of a fine ideology, like the Siyeza initiative. We must hold hands to deliver this twenty-year dream, my friends.' The clergyman paused, nodding benignly at everyone seated, detecting a marginal impatience in some of their expressions. 'I see that some of you are frightened that I'm in my pulpit, so let's hear your views too please! Lesebo?' The attractive Siyeza director, resplendent in a clinging dress in the Rainbow Nation colours, looked tired but determined.

'Yes, I don't want to seem melodramatic but I wondered whether there is a case for engaging National Intelligence? Because I endorse the General's convictions about a Third Force: there seems no motive for the gangs to behave this way without prior warning and without a justifying slogan or spokesperson making demands or protests. It's been like a natural combustion fire on Table Mountain – totally spontaneous. I'm well aware that the gangs are able to mobilise fast but never before without a war cry. Those that aren't under the Chetty umbrella were sent to war against those that are – it was as simple as that! But who is this Hannibal? The best intelligence seems to be a maverick faction within the ANC acting in tandem with an exterior force, or the other way round, of course?' She paused as the chairman held up his hand.

'My dear, there are more maverick factions within the ANC than there are in the Anglican Church!' The resulting laughter relaxed everybody usefully. Lesebo continued with a smile.

'Be that as it may, we'll get no further until we expose the mysterious puppet master. If there is tacit government support or acceptance, the only hope is to resurrect the DA and Municipality flag but that's just another forlorn step that will backfire again.' Lesebo looked devoid of inspiration as she smiled shyly at Harry, shrugging her shoulders slightly in a girlish and apologetic gesture. Harry looked at the chairman to get his nod to speak. He stood, his face reflecting their common mood: a moderately expressed but undeviating intention to bring out the whole truth.

'As you can imagine, I'm in touch with the Foreign Office as much as I am with Lesebo and Kobus concerning Siyeza. It's TDC's biggest overseas current project – by far – and the FO are taking a keen interest in its progress. There are two British banking groups with heavy investments and several other household-name companies involved too. The intelligence I'm receiving, obviously to be treated with discretion, is that there is a South African government individual who is acting in conjunction with a foreign national operating in a private, not national, capacity. The foreigner's intention is to coerce agreement for his alternative Siyeza proposal through domestic criminal violence. This is what we're experiencing now, it being the foreigner's aim to have his idea accepted as a peace-keeping compromise to end the trouble and reinforce the holistic Siyeza undertaking.' Harry's stare went round the table, seeing immobile faces and widened eyes. 'I haven't the slightest doubt that the two government intelligence and diplomatic authorities are completely at one about this and that this will be out in the public domain very shortly. In fact, I've delayed my UK return, since it's that imminent. Until then, needless to say, stay silent and on our toes, ready to move fast!' There were quiet exclamations but no exchanges as Harry sat down, receiving an adoring smile from Lesebo. Kobus had little to add, so summarised on the pastor's behalf.

'Phew! Okay, well at least we were all on the right lines! So keep it under your hats and let's get through this nasty business first. The army and police will be giving mobile coverage to the whole of the Flats, from Ottery to Khayelitsha, with on-call reserves throughout tonight. The other emergency services will all be at immediate notice to move. Let's continue the construction plan where we can, although watch out – remember Harry's mention of "domestic criminal violence" which means Chetty and his gang leader opponents under foreign pay! How will they feel when they find they've been domestic mercenaries, heh? We'll take advice, but it seems that the conflict resolution could be taken out of our hands. I've got a feeling we'll be meeting again soon though, so keep your sleeping bags rolled up!' Lesebo put her hand on Harry's thigh and whispered.

'I've got a really big one for freezing Lesotho nights.' Harry grinned back. But Lesebo's courage was wearing thin as she agonised about the dreadful warning of blackmail or defamation given to her by Maddox. She knew that she and Harry would soon be lovers. He was as honourable and considerate as she had been before working for the Kirksides, but they were now both in love. They both felt that their respective positions would be compromised if they consummated their love affair. Meanwhile, Harry had confided that he and his estranged wife had filed for an uncontested divorce on grounds of unbroken separation for eleven years. But for Lesebo that wasn't the worry. Instead, she knew she could not become Harry's lover without telling him of the Richard Kirkside and Kobus Labuschagne incidents. Just as necessary was the requirement to tell both Richard and Kobus about each other and attempt to justify her double blackmail. She lay awake at night, tortured by the likely sequence of managing this and the jumbled variety of lurid consequences.

Perhaps dear old Maddox, that rock of a father figure, was her only answer? She decided to call him the next morning.

Chapter Thirteen

'Good morning everyone and welcome to SAFM, South Africa's News and Information Leader. This is the Six o'clock News and I am Nophumelela Sibiya. Top Story today: the Deputy President, the Right Honourable Malusi Jali, attended a Gala Dinner at Sun City last night. He welcomed a Dutch trading delegation who unveiled plans for a vast entertainment community to showcase Cape Town's Siyeza development project. The Cape Flats area, which has been the focus of gang violence in the last few weeks, has been undergoing a massive face-lift construction and civic restoration programme. The project could eventually cost ten billion Rands, the bulk of which it is hoped to raise through private investment, including 30 percent from abroad. The latest addition to Siyeza was described by Mr Bram De Vries, the Dutch entrepreneur who heads up the exciting enterprise as a "once-in-a-nation's-lifetime".' The coverage switched from the news room to De Vries' announcement.

'It is appropriate tonight that we stand in Sun City, South Africa's iconic entertainment city that captured the world's attention when it hit the stage – bold, imaginative, multi-purpose and on its day, very naughty! Well, our Siyeza dream goes further still: San City will fill fifteen hundred hectares of the down-at-heel Cape Flats with twenty four-hour sizzling entertainment, with something for everyone. You can see a movie or watch live shows, play golf or fly microlights, club it up or take the kids on adventure rides. And you can definitely find a partner!'

De Vries drew breath, winking at his own innuendo, mimicking a Republican candidate promising the earth in the American Primaries. 'There will be a theme park, pubs galore, an underground canyon, shooting galleries, a nature farm, a botanical garden, a rugby stadium and cricket field, an Olympic pool, clay pigeon, an ice rink and an aeronautical school to get you flying. You can ride a horse, you can cash a card, you can watch a film, dump your kids in nurseries and summer schools and you can spend all your money in ritzy arcades. You've got it! There's everything for everyone, including a projected workforce of five thousand, probably doubling over five years. We've blueprints for an over-and-under rail connection to the city and there will be round-the-clock Uber taxi and corporate bus services. So forget the bad grey images you've been getting with Siyeza – of course the people are fed up with waiting and are throwing rocks! We are so proud, so pleased, so excited, to bring this first San City to Africa. We have three others creating legends in Asia, all booming regional business and employment hubs. Mark my word, you truly have not seen anything yet. Get down to San City in about three years from now. Follow the frenzy on all social media, starting with *San City for all.com.'*

*****

'Don't talk shit, Darsh! Where's that fucking video?' Ravi was confronting one of the leading gang leaders under his care, who had owned Pelli's Place, since incinerated by the opposition. 'I need it now and sharpish, okay?' he said, pushing his head towards the young and nervous street crook, whom he had talent-spotted as a schoolboy pusher ten years before. Ravi never travelled alone and his two accompanying minders surrounded Darsh, shoving him gently around the circle they'd formed in the pool room in Athlone. There was no way out.

'Ravi, it got burned, along with everything else! It was in the cupboard at Pelli's because I thought you'd take it after that meeting, but you never said nothing and...' Darsh collapsed with a deep moan as the first knee and kick went in. Ravi watched as they thudded in kicks to his head and body for two minutes, quickly unconscious as his temples were struck. Ravi raised his hand to call a halt, with Darsh motionless and bleeding from the ear and mouth, the two thugs satisfied that there were no marks or stains on their hands or clothes. Now it was a question of facing up to De Vries. Probably like the Afrikaners a hundred and more years before in the Anglo-Boer War, he would have to judge when he couldn't beat him up front but resort to guerrilla tactics. From then on, he would have to pick him off piecemeal.

*****

Lesebo met Maddox on the Waterfront in a main thoroughfare café. She looked her cover girl best, in a fine wool jumper with black and white stripes and slim cotton skirt above scarlet semi-heeled grey sandals that matched her necklace and bandanna. Maddox was not normally careful about meeting young women alone but now found himself looking around defensively as eyes analysed what he was doing with such an eye-catching girl. They ordered a dry white wine and a small plate of tapas. Lesebo was smiling and composed as they both leant close across the circular table to speak softly.

'Maddox, I almost told you last time what I'm going to tell you now.'

'I could tell there was something else that you wanted to say.'

'It's about the video, obviously. If that goes public, there's more to it than just Richard and myself.' She waited, not wanting to blurt it out as a confession.

'You mean you don't want your father or Harry to know?'

'Well no, but there's others.' Lesebo drew a deep breath and stared hard at Maddox. 'I was a virgin when Richard raped me. I was ready for bed and we were alone when Ami was out for the evening but I didn't mean to seduce him. I wandered into the kitchen for coffee and that was that. My plan for a vast lobola bonus of five million when I was twenty-five or older was holding good. Richard

154

was terrified afterwards and found me the first job with Kobus. That's my downfall, because I deliberately seduced him upon arrival, ten days after the Richard incident. I was completely messed up, wild with rage, with a racist lunacy about white men, subjugation, and all the mixed race lies of South Africa, you name it. I wanted to get my own back, I wanted to be in control again and I wanted to strike a blow for black feminism!' Lesebo's voice rose, a shrill whisper, as Maddox leant closer.

'So how long did that last?'

'Being crude, three minutes! Sorry, I know you don't mean that – we never went near each other again, and by the way, there has not been anyone else since, despite the rumours about Harry!' Maddox nodded understandingly, fascinated by the way the story was going. 'Anyway, I missed my first period and took some tests which said I was pregnant. I went to a gynaecologist who confirmed it and gave advice about abortions. I decided to have the quick medical abortion as the only real chance of revenge on rich, white men. I told Richard and Kobus separately and they both offered to pay for the operation. I told Richard to pay me half a million into an offshore account and I told Kobus to appoint me Director Siyeza Enterprise. They did that without a murmur and life has gone on, reputations untarnished!' Lesebo sat back, raising both hands in front, in mock surprise. 'You are the only outsider that knows this, so you can see how I trust and respect you Maddox? It's advice I want now, for future action, not moral counselling!' Lesebo smiled as she gripped Maddox's hands over the table.

'Of course, don't worry. But just to get this straight. Neither of them knows about each other or the payoffs, do they, so it's the recrimination about unproven paternity and the abortion blackmail that's terrifying you?'

'That's it, hole in one. What do I do?' They both sipped their wine and waited in silence as the tapas were put in front of them, with an inviting display of chorizo, smoky cheese, tiny shrimps and cauliflower cubes, gently washed in garlic and oil.

Maddox took his time as he assessed the lunch display. 'I've well-weathered, you know Lesebo – two broken marriages and life laid bare as a copper for forty years. So you'll get no criticism from me. But you're in a pickle, I can see that.' He stared at Lesebo, nodding slowly. 'Richard is easier to handle inasmuch as he knows about the video, his marriage has survived and you've prospered. All he'll fret about is a shattered reputation and loss of a flourishing finance business. You'll put his nose out of joint about Kobus and he'll be sore about the bribe he paid. Ami will want to gouge your eyes out of course, since she always blames you. But then, paternity couldn't be proved anyway, could it, so how else were you to apportion responsibility?' Maddox was worried that Lesebo was taking more than her fair share of his beloved chorizo and paused to spike some slices with his fork. Lesebo chewed rapidly, looking away at neighbouring diners in the pleasant midday Waterfront sun, a light breeze moving the parasol panels and tablecloths.

'Yes, he'll feel as bad losing his name now as he would have done had he been discovered then. Also, he knows about the video going missing, so he has time to prepare. There's little chance of Kobus making a public fuss, is there? He won't be kind to me privately, will he? He'll say he didn't know I'd had sex with Richard just before and will feel duped about paternity, which could make him very angry.'

'That's right. Kobus will feel worse cheated, and let's face it, he was, by your own admission. That's really the only thing that need worry you. What you do with your body is your own business but if you sue or blackmail an oke over paternity and he thinks he's closing the relationship with an abortion and a generous hand-out, then he's bound to feel badly wronged.' Maddox raised his eyebrows and leaned back from the table, crossing his arms to show there was no negotiation. Lesebo's eyes went down as she toyed with the shrimp and cauliflower remnants islanded in the oil. Maddox broke the silence.

'But hope might be at hand. Look, Kobus is marrying Rita Marais next week and probably won't want to start off his marriage with a sex scandal confession. His resentment might linger about paternity but since he won't want to rake over the coals, his mind might settle on it passing into history as an unknown factor, perhaps confessed on his death bed!'

'So when you break it down – and you are astonishingly good at this sort of thing Maddox, you know – Richard will be the main loser, provided I'm prepared to appear unscathed, adopting a haughty attitude about intrusion into my private affairs when the journalists show up?'

'Well, I think so, yes. My advice would be to lie low and make a superb job of sorting out this Siyeza chaos, so your reputation stays high in the public eye. If the story comes out, Richard loses out badly but might have got his ducks in order regarding his responses. Kobus doesn't need to know in advance because we judge that he'll have no angry axe to grind. Can you live with the tension?'

Lesebo looked up from catching the final salad remnants and smiled. 'I can Maddox, I can now. And to end with an evil thought, if Richard suffers, so be it, since he committed the first horrid act that started all this. He paid half a million for a minute's gratification, I know, but I'm not sure that's ample punishment for a multi-millionaire!' Maddox didn't ponder on that as he left cash under his plate before they departed together, Lesebo drawing stares among the grazing lunch hour Capetonians.

To accommodate the public outcry that followed the unveiling of De Vries' San City plans, Hennie Strydom chaired a panel on an extended edition of his *Cape Trends* show. He had gathered Kobus Labuschagne, the Reverend Nicholas Mahlambi, Jabu Nhleko and Lesebo Bafokeng. The morning's news had featured sporadic civil disturbance in scattered Flats townships and an interview at the site where De Fries intended to develop. Internecine gang violence continued at a lower key but there seemed to be a breathing space during which opposing factions were doing their sums before they committed firmly one way or the other.

'The Reverend Nicholas Mahlambi, it's probably fair to start with you as the government appointee and chairman of the Siyeza Council. I realise that Miss Bafokeng and Mr Labuschagne sit on that Council with you but I'd like to hear your personal opinion, but not so much on the greater Siyeza question. I'd rather concentrate on the Dutch proposal to erect the continent's most comprehensive entertainments centre within the existing Siyeza boundaries, where contractual agreement already exists on use of the land?'

'Well, it might be difficult to believe but neither I, as a political party leader and government official, nor my council members, including as you say the Mayor of Cape Town and the Siyeza Director, knew anything of this proposal's detail until that television launch at the so-called San City. Since the Election, there has been talk of an additional element being included within the overall package as a catalyst for a more ambitious and embracing Siyeza. Now, I suppose the idea has been launched this way for greater impact, but after two and more years, we're still negotiating within the TDC contract for example, even though construction is well under way. All arterial routes are in place, two civic centres are built, five sewerage farms are functioning, the electricity power lines are almost completed and more than a dozen starts have been made to housing programmes. The new railway station preparations are being made as I speak. The upgrading of roads to the airport has begun. The money is in the bank, the skills and equipment are on site and the labour issues are being processed as fast as the government and Municipality can handle them. Even with the public disorders of the last month, the overall programme remains on track, which is a considerable achievement by the Directorate and Municipality. So the addition of a lookalike Sun City within the Siyeza metropole is going to be very hard to handle. Although the Directorate earmarked an appropriately sized area, none of the infrastructural basics have included such a plan, and it is certain that deadlines will slip and costs will rise if it is accommodated.'

'Mr Nhleko, you are the recent Deputy President, now chairing the newly formed tender oversight committee. You were prominent during the volte farce when the government derailed the Siyeza management with an irregular coup d'état on the project's funding? But now, just as previous arrangements were restored after the Election, we have yet another body overseeing yet another body doing the same thing! This deliberately sensational announcement of the Dutch deal seems incoherent, inconsistent? What's going on? Why has this been done as the Cape Flats are burning?' Strydom looked as incredulous as his question implied, his hands and papers waving vigorously. Both Labuschagne and Bafokeng were interjecting with supportive adverbs as Nhleko waited, an aggressive appearance on his face.

'Mr Strydom, you're dropping below your own low standards of impartiality, if I may say so! You have posed a ridiculously loaded question, which…'

'Can you explain the irrational changes though, Mr Nhleko?'

'Please don't interrupt me when I'm trying to give you a responsible answer. Which changes?'

'The status quo pre-Election, the changes post-Election and now the lurch back to an authoritarian diktat with a spontaneous foreign scheme! I say again, Mr Nhleko, what's going on?'

'My impetuous friend, hear me out. Siyeza has been neglected by the DA since they formed a provincial government in the Western Cape…'

'The ANC ignored it for twenty years. The DA got it going immediately,' interjected Labuschagne.

'As I was saying…'

'You've said nothing! What's going on and why have you crept back? The public don't share your views, Mr Nhleko.'

'That is a defaming comment my friend! Are you saying I'm not welcome because I blow the whistle on your British chums?'

'Gentlemen, gentlemen, we cannot bicker this way please! Please stop obfuscating Mr Nhleko and answer the question, 'what is going on?' Strydom felt in control, since he anticipated Nhleko's unpopularity and weak position.

'I'm being interrupted continually. I'll tell you what is going on. We're breathing life into a corpse that failed to catch the public imagination nor deal with the chronic unemployment and crime in Cape Town!'

It was Mahlambi's turn to spit venom. 'But what am I doing here as the government's gesture of compromise between the two wings of the ANC administration? You're wrong to describe Siyeza as a corpse into which life must be breathed. If that was the case, it is for me to judge and pronounce and not you! As I understand it, you're appointed to prevent tokenism and monitor the division of domestic and foreign contracts in the overall Treasury budget for Siyeza? If that is correct, please stick to your remit and don't cause political enmity when there is no cause.' The pastor was incensed as viewers saw, his voice soaring from the pulpit as he glowered at Nhleko. Mahlambi was a force to be reckoned with, mused Strydom.

'Thank you for telling me how to do my job, pastor! I didn't hear much from your church when I was Deputy President! My friend, by rationing the contract quotas, we prevent corruption and embezzlement, as you know. We cannot have six hundred thousand people watch their new houses being built by foreigners taking gigantic profits out of the country. What are your congregations telling you?'

'They are chanting at me, never fear. They sing, 'When is our day oh Lord, when do we share our rewards?' And now I am closely involved, they also pray loudly, 'Why do they dash our dreams oh Lord, why is blood spilt on the family floor?' The dream is Siyeza and I will instil fair play. The family is the ANC which has long been a house divided. Half knows there is bread for us all but the other half steals it and tells the neighbours to go to the next village to find bread. My congregation knows which half I stand in. You must decide for yourself, but do not be so ignorant as to hope that the family does not notice and judge you too!'

'Gentlemen, these are matters for the next ANC lekgotla, not a national TV programme! So it seems we have no clear answers other than a divided ruling party living with compromises and concessions that cause confusion and dismay to the country's body corporate – including the three quarters of a million Capetonians who await a better life. Miss Bafokeng, you have been patient listening to some unproductive and even destructive commentaries. Maybe you can end the programme by telling us how you feel this will eventually map out?' Hennie Strydom had a soft spot for Lesebo and usually supported her when criticism arose.

'Thanks Hennie, yes that was a little disappointing but I think some of the rancour is there because we're not being candid with each other. I'm apolitical as it happens, although I tread a sensitive path between provincial and national masters. In Cape Town and the Western Cape, the ruling DA antagonises a broad ANC rump that assumes no opposition exists in any shape or form in the country. So historical fact, constitutionality and legally bound conclusions resurface continually as a squabble, requiring a didactic, or lesson plan if you like, to teach opposing parties moral principles.'

Strydom marvelled at the grasp now shown by Lesebo. She really did seem to be a neutral and intelligent voice to take the huge project forward, perhaps to see it through. Lesebo continued. 'This wastes months, not days, drawn out as much by materialism as ignorance. So when a government awards the major contract to a foreign conglomerate with multiple first world experience of vast and complicated schemes that cross several international borders, you're entitled to think "job done". And when that same government agrees to private funding to accelerate the project and reduce public spending, that again reinforces optimism. But instead, for approaching three years, this same government has done its utmost to frustrate at best, or at worst destroy, the progress that responsible managers, engineers, craftsmen and skilled workforce are attempting to perfect. We have tried to find out why, but as Mr Nhleko has demonstrated, there is a limit to the credibility of a plan that is either ill-informed or dishonest, or perhaps both. So no explanation can emerge. As the Director of Siyeza, I can see no corporate or downstream social upliftment advantages in supplanting clinics, schools, community centres, shopping malls or indigenous skills factories with a cesspit of filth!'

'All right Miss Bafokeng, we must end.'

'No, Mr Strydom, let this be the last word for your viewers! A cesspit of filth, a cesspit of filth, whose main income will rely on prostitution, drug trafficking, gambling dens, money lenders and enforcement agencies, non-stop live sex shows and cinemas, clubs and pubs, online paedophilia sales and porn shops! Don't be fooled by all that talk of children's playgrounds and swimming pools – have a look at what Mr De Vries and his business colleagues do in Malaysia, Singapore and Hong Kong – all of them proudly under the uncompromising banner of perversion and coercion of the penniless – "San City" is in fact "Sin City"!'

There was no time for a resigned Strydom to round off the show as the programme's footnotes scrolled silently, with Mahlambi and Labuschagne still applauding Lesebo enthusiastically. Nhleko slouched in a defeated pose, with a look of undisguised hatred, his corpulent stomach creased like a folded party balloon.

*****

The opposition parties, headed by an exuberant Christians United following, wasted no time in obtaining legal clearance to mobilise several thousand marchers as an immediate protest against the controversial Dutch proposal. The young student placard factory were not lost for words, with eye-catching slogans such as "No Dutch Caps", "Sex at Home, not in the City!" and "Baby Clinics Before Brothels" adorning a colourful and peaceful gathering in Adderley Street. Forming up around the memorial, they processed slowly up towards Parliament, ending in the Company Gardens where several speeches and media interviews were held. Traffic was diverted and the message was clear on the evening TV channels: Lesebo's impassioned performance on *Cape Trends* had fired the public's imagination and awareness of the full Siyeza story, where the sporadic violence was withering their sympathy.

At long last, battle lines had been drawn within the ANC's divided politburo, making both political alignment and rejection an easier choice. The demonstration was enough to force the party's heavyweight composite parts – the national executive, trade unions, Communist Party, Youth and Women's Leagues – to hop off one fence and land on another, with predictable controversy and ambiguity. Calls for a full government tribunal were mooted by ex-gravy train officials within the judiciary, reading statements planted by the Presidential office to test the water. The media antipathy to the San City proposal approached crescendo levels, with De Vries as the central villain. The Deputy President, bobbing and weaving like a top in meetings with the media, eventually chose a safe ANC party rally as a secure and uninterrupted opportunity to make what he hoped to be a calming statement.

'You know, it is extraordinary how some sections of the media distort and plagiarise government statements and intentions. Take this Siyeza disturbance over the foreign investment proposal, for example. I defy anyone to find where the government said that the proposal is cast in stone and is the very pillar of the government's objectives for rebuilding the shameful townships around the Cape Flats. You will not find it, comrades! Where did the Director of the Siyeza project get those slanderous ideas about San City, I ask? Maybe it's a figment of a deranged imagination – perhaps top of her own little secret wish list?' Roars of male laughter greeted this, with rough retorts and insults filling the air.

The tubby Nhleko dripped sweat off his chin as he took encouragement from the noise. 'I would ask her to take her friends who are saying these things – I know she comes from Lesotho where life is still quite primitive – to visit our magnificent Sun City, the pride and joy of the sporting, cultural and family fun world. Now then. Did the visionary Sol Kerzner worry that there was no immediate market for what he built in a bare and unknown Bathutaswana? Or did he know that the busses and cars would never stop flooding in from Jo'burg and Pretoria? Did he not predict that it would become a global destination, a shining beacon for the continent of Africa? Of course he did! Because he was a real genius, not a clever schoolgirl with a rich daddy!'

Nhleko was into his stride in front of a home crowd, keen to demolish the new-won accolades won by Lesebo. 'So why doesn't Miss Bafokeng realise that a San City rising like a Phoenix from the rubble and filth of Cape Flats will be flooded by Cape Town punters? What is her problem? Let me tell you comrades, it's not difficult. Her problem is that she is an African Barbie Doll, dressed up and taught words to say by her capitalist masters!' The ululating women, with wobbling ANC tee-shirts and their bearded, stick-waving male partners refused to stand still for some time as Nhleko milked the crowd further with some stiff-hipped dancing antics. He felt the job had been done. 'So let us be forcible comrades and support our Cape Town brothers. Do not listen to the lies of the capitalist but know, like the great Sol Kerzner, that the government's imagination and enterprise will soon succeed in Siyeza, with San City as its flagship, making Cape Town the equal of Las Vegas!' He ended to rapturous applause and dancing, with his full speech being shown on prime-time TV that evening. Only time would tell whether such naked class and racial lines in the sand would have a beneficial outcome for the Cape Flats citizens.

Nhleko's address had an inflammatory effect on the Siyeza disturbances. The military were re-deployed to reinforce the police in dispelling lawless crowds across an area that had spread into neighbouring suburbs around Manenberg and Hanover Park. The De Wet road district in Ottery became a trouble spot, as did the Lansdowne and Weltevreden Roads on the eastern side of Philippi. The random rabble-rousing deteriorated into Black versus Coloured conflict where there were neighbouring ghettoes. Although over 60 percent of the Cape Flats Planning District's population was coloured, far more blacks were unemployed, with a resulting disparity in standards of living and housing. It wasn't difficult to throw the torch and fan the flames.

*****

The British Minister for Africa, the Right Honourable Jeffrey Felbridge looked younger than Harry Reynolds had expected. He was a pallid, balding forty-year old with an unsmiling face and carefully composed conversation. He had summoned Harry to the FCO to discuss the growing crisis in Cape Town. Harry had met his predecessor when TDC was awarded the Siyeza contract, since it amounted to the largest British investment and structural development in South Africa for twenty years. But increasingly, the High Commissioner in Pretoria, spending more time in Cape Town for reasons only known to diplomats who have two grace and favour mansions, was pointing out to London how British interests were at increasing risk because of the divisive government policy. TDC was suffering from the deteriorating community structure and causing him concern. His own diplomatic round was drawing a blank. He had advised the Foreign Secretary's staff in London to offer a negotiating position in as neutral a way as possible. Maybe the Minister of State at the FCO might intervene, using a Commonwealth card, or the Minister of Africa with a broader territorial remit?

'Well Mr Reynolds, I have to say how much we admire the way you've kept an unprovocative but effective TDC presence in the Cape Flats – it cannot be easy?'

'Far from it, Minister. The High Commissioner will have updated you but the political message is vacillating and undelivered. It's no surprise that advantage is being taken of this, or why the general public are at a genuine loss. The Municipality and the project Directorate are stymied, despite their talent and energy. Frankly, I'm concerned too. I'm stoic about large overseas contracts – they're bound to be erratic now and again – but the local adult male population worry me most. The informal trading rump, mostly illegal, is being blocked by a permanent security force presence. So it's a tinderbox existence. There have been several lukewarm efforts to negotiate, with oversight councils and the like. But recently inflammatory statements have sharply divided the greater community, not just Cape Flats. If it gets really hairy, we'll have to draw stumps'

'Hope not – take an early tea perhaps?' The Minister managed to smile at his analogy, while Harry cursed himself for using favourite diplomatic metaphors. 'Well you've confirmed what we've heard. We're thinking that some sort of loose initiative might be suggested by London. Perhaps myself and a couple of African hands, maybe one from the Minister FCO's staff, to come out and stay a couple of days with the High Commissioner? We're not suggesting we burden the South African government with a formally hosted conference with all the Cape Town garden party frills!' He smiled, hoping he wasn't treading on toes. 'Maybe a multi-party gathering of properly appointed officials charged with the security, trade and development and perhaps international co-operation portfolios? What do you think?' Mr Felbridge looked a little more sincere than he sounded and Harry gave him the benefit of the doubt.

'As far as TDC goes, I'd be very grateful. It would be no bad thing for South Africans to realise how highly the British regard the project. I don't know whether there's been any diplomatic exchanges with the Dutch over their wretched San City?'

'Oh goodness, yes, very much so. I think there's room for movement there, quite frankly. If all goes well when we come out, we have a few thoughts on how to incorporate their outlandish proposal – a very unfortunate presentation, I have to say!' He rose, extending a handshake and accompanying Harry to the lift. 'When are you flying back?' He paused as Harry wondered whether he was going to offer to bring out some Marmite or Branston Pickle. On hearing that Harry was leaving the next day, he nodded vigorously. 'Jolly good. Well, we'll be in touch within the next couple of days. I look forward to meeting you out there. Quite warm I gather, this time of year? Well done, keep up the good work, old chap!' Felbridge, ten years his junior, clapped him on the shoulder. Harry descended slowly in the asthmatic lift, reading a framed statement asserting the gender and racial equality tenets of Her Majesty's Government. As he entered Whitehall, he smiled inwardly about briefing Lesebo personally before she bumped into the old-before-his-time Jeffrey.

Maddox and Katie reached the second round of the Mowbray Tennis Club's Veterans Championship. Maddox teased Katie about expecting some silverware to prove the point. Their opponents, five years their seniors, with the man playing with his left hand ['usually right handed but the arthritis is giving me gip'] and his partner tripping over her laces in the first set, didn't exude congratulations, any more than their vanquishers in the second round. But they took three games per set off them, which placated the competitive Katie.

'She was an ex-county player before they emigrated. And he got to the Men's Doubles Semis last year. So we did jolly well darling!'

In thinking of a suitable way to celebrate Katie's important birthday, Maddox finalised his Exorcism of the Curmudgeon. He booked two tickets for the forthcoming tour by Rodriquez at the Grand Arena. This had personal memories for himself, since he had gone to the singer's first South African concert shortly after his own arrival in 1998. He had been overwhelmed by the local frenzy for Rodriquez and the amazing folk singer's legendary existence. Unaware of the strong South African following for his songs from releases like *Cold Fact* and *Coming from Reality*, which they treated as anti-Apartheid anthems, he had disappeared into obscurity. But in 1997, the year before Maddox emigrated, the South African public rediscovered him in Detroit, leading eventually to the Oscar-winning film *Searching for Sugarman*. Katie had been an adoring Rodriquez fan too as a doctor's wife, attending the same concert as Maddox. It was an inspired gift by Maddox who realised cheerily that he had become an unabashed and nostalgic romantic.

They tried to remember some of the words to the more famous of Rodriquez songs, without much luck, as they drove along the straight R102 Voortrekker Road among many Grand Arena-bound concert-goers. The arena was packed, with all ages and colours on parade – much had been made in the local press of how Steve Biko had been inspired by Rodriguez lyrics and his messages for life's underdogs. Katie and Maddox were deafened by the sound, even though Rodriguez was now in his mid-70s and sang folk ballads rather than crashing rock music. They were spellbound, as were the whole crowd, by what they claimed to be their very own, specially re-invented Bob Dylan. It was a magical evening with a wonderful sky and early stars as they tip-toed away, hemmed in by the happy thousands, edging their way back to their cars and taxi ranks. It was then that Maddox's greatest moment of courage dawned as he drove to a favourite bar for a nightcap.

'Jumpers, coke, sweet MaryJane
Sugarman
You're the answer
That makes my questions disappear'

'Maddox, that was lovely! You've learned the words too!' Katie giggled and put her arm on his shoulder.

'But it's not finished darling: "that makes my questions disappear" it went. But I've still got one for you!'

'Whatever it is, the answer's "yes", my sweetheart.'

'But I haven't asked it yet!' said Maddox squealing late to a halt at the lights as they approached the city.

'Well go on then darling, ask it!'

'Will you marry me, sweet MaryJane!' Maddox looked across to her, his face pink in the red traffic lights.

'Of course I will, Maddox. I love you to distraction and want to marry you too.' They each leaned across the bulky compartment towards each other and slowly kissed. They did not see their faces turn green as the driver behind beeped his horn in irritation. They pulled apart gently, Maddox glancing in his rear-view mirror as he gave him a friendly wave and pulled away. Katie gripped his left hand and quietly cried and laughed, wiping her eyes with her left hand, as Maddox blessed his automatic gears and did his best to remember and navigate them to their popular destination. When they reached the car park, Maddox parked in a dark corner and took his new fiancée in his arms.

'Was it titanium or copper that you preferred, darling?' He felt in the glove compartment and fetched a small box. He opened it carefully and took out a ring. He held her left hand and put it on, hoping furiously it would fit. It did but in choosing a darkened corner to kiss, there was no light for her to see it. 'It's a sapphire surrounded by diamonds, my sweetheart, to remind you forever that your eyes captured me!' They kissed again and Katie hugged him tightly. Ever the practical operator, Maddox felt deeper into the glove compartment and produced a pen torch, which he shone on her fingers. Katie gasped and held her hand closer to her eyes.

'This is the most beautiful thing in my life, Maddox. My birthday, Rodriquez, this ring and only you to look forward to. I do so love you Maddox. You're a wonderful, beautiful and good man. I will treasure this as much as I treasure you, forever, my darling!' They held each other silently, Katie still fighting back tears, Maddox elated but dazed – a third wife, a last lover, a lifelong friend and companion. He had banished the Curmudgeon into oblivion for evermore...

Chapter Fourteen

The political limbo made ripe picking for continued lawless behaviour in the Cape Flats. The police reported a surge in street gang violence, claiming three more murders and several gunshot wound injuries. The recent east versus west gang warfare gave way to a more traditional pattern, albeit of heightened intensity, of drug turf war disturbances. The army kept a permanent presence, now at battalion strength, reinforcing a tiring police force who confronted rioters on most nights, firing plastic baton rounds and using coloured water in their cannons to facilitate arrests. A special court dealt with a hundred and fifty youths committing riotous behaviour crimes.

With such public disorder as a backdrop, the more directed and sinister disturbances proceeded virtually unchecked, with the army reacting only when the violence amounted to a general collapse of law and order. The Siyeza Directorate building was cordoned with razor wire and mobile concrete bollards, with access checked through a single entrance. The main routes into the Flats via both Muizenberg, south Peninsula and Table Bay had permanent police check points and the Lansdowne Road via Mitchells Plain was closed to all traffic. The TDC depot became a regular target for torch and brick attacks and there was an exchange of fire between some attackers and an armed security guard, with police recovering the gunman's dead body and his AK47 automatic rifle.

The workforce level had reached four thousand before the scale of violence saw it dwindle to under a thousand. The TDC directly contracted labour force continued its work, running the gauntlet with intermittent picketing, as did the contracted pipe laying and electricity pylon erection specialists. The trade union officials were at loggerheads with each other, with no clear COSATU guidance. Harry Reynolds monitored programme performance, reporting a 60 percent drop in productive activity, with the overall programme now a median three weeks behind deadlines. There were prohibitive penalties for missing completion deadlines; using a long-distance calculation by his staff, he mentioned to Lesebo and Kobus the likelihood of invoking the contract's Civil Disturbance clause. If programme continuation became financially counter-productive, he would cease activity, pending a return to normal circumstances. Kobus shuddered at the thought of such adverse imagery; as a Mayor, it was important to present a resolute front to lawlessness.

For Lesebo, these were troubling times. She had become the centre of media attention since Nhleko's "hate speech", which was being scrutinised by a rapidly assembled tribunal. She realised that she had to tread with extra care to preserve her hard-won praise following her *Cape Trends* appearance. She held faith with both Harry Reynolds and Kobus Labuschagne, showing them both undeviating loyalty as the enterprise's Director. All the while, the Damocles Sword seemed poised over her head as she followed Maddox's advice with bravery rather than conviction.

'Lesebo? Hello, it's Khanyisile Mthembu. I can't get hold of Kobus at the moment but things are getting nasty at the southern approaches through Ottery to the so-called Dutch site. They've burnt a forty-ton transporter hired by TDC and are blocking all site entrances from the Victoria and Retreat Roads in the south. The army have deployed but a rent-a-mob crowd of about three hundred are attacking them with what the soldiers call "dockyard confetti" – bolts and shackles stolen around the building sites – but the colonel is more worried about firearms being used. It's definitely organised, not impromptu. I'm being asked to shut down all site vehicles and house them safely and stop activity until further notice. So let's do this please in the interests of public safety – can you talk to Kobus and Harry about this as well, Lesebo?'

Lesebo dreaded a shut-down as much as Kobus but there was no choice. She pinned him down in a meeting and spread the word. Harry was in UK but had made known his discomfort at redeploying specialist labour to the so-called Dutch site, when his overall plan was to either substitute or abandon the De Vries proposal altogether. Kobus implemented the police request immediately, not wanting to appear at odds with any of the security forces. Harry Reynolds was informed accordingly and sent a copy of a formal request to the Department of Trade and Industry, invoking the contract's civil disturbance clause. The area designated as the San City site was completely closed, with armed security guards manning the entrance and patrolling within the sprawling compound. TDC equipment and labour was diverted towards other sites where work continued at a lower rate of output, inevitably decreasing as the disturbances and armed vigilante presence on picket lines became an institutional feature of Siyeza on the nation's TVs every evening.

*****

The word was out that Ravi Chetty was running scared of Bram De Vries. Whenever his scouts told him that the burly Dutchman was in town, or even country, Chetty went underground. But eventually De Vries caught him on a cell phone and Chetty decided to come clean about the burned DVD. He anticipated De Vries' incandescent rage, which was why he was keeping him at arm's length.

'I'm going to cut you up and feed you to township goats, you filthy little coward! You're going to lose everything you own before then, from your grand mansion to your fat wife and your diseased harem. All of you will suffer slowly and this time, the videos will go viral.'

'Go suck yourself, Dutch pig! You sent your boys to burn Pilli's, playing the tough boy, heh? Well, you burned your fucking evidence and any chance we had of turning the screws on the bitch at Siyeza. You, not me, do you hear, you! So

166

I'm getting on with my business. Stay out of here, man. Can't you see there's no room? Your scheme is fucked, there's no take-up by local Joes for that sort of dirty stuff, don't you know? Me? I do the girls, the bets and a couple of clubs. A bit of muscle and drugs, period, pure and simple, okay? This is Shitsville man, always was, always will be. They're all saying you're a head case with laundry money to burn, so go do it where there's a pay-off, not in fucking Africa!' The line went dead on De Vries. He would rub out Chetty when he wasn't busy – he'd had enough of the inflated little fool – but there was still a job to do with Miss Bafokeng.

*****

Lesebo Bafokeng was full of excitement as her small Mango aircraft landed with a bounce at Maseru airport. She was about to enjoy a well-earned week's break from the hectic pressures of Siyeza, which she'd left in a state of flux as the site work ground to a halt. She would be back in time to greet the British Foreign Office mission on its last-ditch attempt at playing honest broker within the warring factions of the ANC, trade unions, DA and Municipality. Harry Reynolds was coming over for that too but only after a detour to her Lesotho homeland to meet her family and see some of the beauties of the Semonkong mountain district. He was flying in by helicopter tomorrow, which was bound to impress the locals. Her father had told her he was very proud of what she was doing but wondered whether she could resume academic studies shortly! She had not seen him for many months and had brought copious presents for him and the family which she now loaded into her off-road hire car – sadly no Land Rover available to impress Harry, she discovered!

Lesebo never failed to be awe-struck by the haunting scenery of her homeland. She picked up the Old Main Road South out of the airport and set off for Roma and turned south for Mantsa. The journey from Maseru to her father's lodge at Maletsunyane Falls took an easy two hours along the much-improved one hundred and twenty kilometres road. She passed a few farmers on horseback, with short white miner's gumboots, with their drab blankets across their shoulders and their floppy beanies on their heads, herding straggling cows and the occasional sheep and goats, astride their squat, chestnut ponies. Every stretch, every turn of the gradient, every close country scene kept the huge fluffy white clouds in sight, banked against a faded blue sky, the temperature a defiant warm chill.

Halfway between Mantra and home, she drew up by a sheep shedding station on a raised promontory to attempt to call her father – it was an unlikely chance but she'd heard you could sometimes get a connection from this spot. As she stared at the horizon, two vehicles lurched from behind the sheep yard and blocked her front and rear. Her door was wrenched open by someone behind and her cell phone was snatched from her. Lesebo screamed but remembered the instinctive drills of a woman on her own who is mugged in South Africa – don't fight or scream but surrender all your valuables immediately. She saw four men, three black and one white, who leant in to take her car keys. Two of them manoeuvred the cars into a typical tourist's convoy and returned to her vehicle as the white man spoke.

'Apologies for interrupting your journey home, Miss Bafokeng. We won't keep you. We'll disable your phone and give it back. You won't be hurt, OK? We're going to do a short YouTube interview. It's your big chance to get things off your chest. Please help me – these boys are never satisfied, heh?' He was middle-aged, balding and authoritarian – maybe ex-military. He had an Afrikaner's accent and clean finger nails. Lesebo was too shocked to speak. 'Okay? But we won't send out the video if you agree to complete the San City build straight away – now, now! We'll tell you what to do, and when.' Lesebo knew the intention behind this shock attempt to blackmail her but could not fathom this bizarre ambush.

The man adopted an interviewer personality. 'It is widely known how you had sex with the finance millionaire, Mr Richard Kirkside, on his kitchen floor when his wife was out for the evening. In order to keep you quiet, Mr Kirkside, who was the Siyeza finance boss, found you a job as the Cape Town's Mayor's aide. He then promoted you to be the Director of the Siyeza enterprise, aged twenty-five, just three weeks after being the Kirkside's nanny. So you traded sex with first Mr Kirkside and then Mr Labuschagne in the space of ten days to land the Siyeza job. Can you tell us about this please?' The man signalled to the two men with cell phones to pause. 'All right Miss Bafokeng. No hysterics or lies. Keep it short. Admit what happened and we'll tell you what to do when you get back to Cape Town. Okay, here we go.' It was the worst moment of Lesebo's short but eventful life. What would they do physically if she refused? Did this worsen her desperate position? As she drew breath, she felt Maddox's hand on hers.

'I knew both Mr Kirkside and Mr Labuschagne professionally and separately for a very short time before I began my present appointment. We have never been lovers and never will be. In fact, I've never had a lover – my father promised me a generous reward if I completed my tertiary education without having a boyfriend. I have just found my first boyfriend who is also not my lover. I think you will find that questions such as yours are a violation of the national Constitution and the United Nations Bill of Rights regarding human dignity and intrusion into personal lives. So charges of slander and libel will apply. Any publication attracts heavy penalties through litigation. Does that help you, anonymous white man?' Lesebo had saved her imperious theatre for the right moment. Her manner told her interrogator that further questions would be worthless. He too made up his mind fast, silently busying himself with her cell phone before giving it back to her. He asked the cameramen to play back their video coverage. He signalled for the vehicles to be pointed back towards Mantra. The three others mounted inside, engines turning, waiting for him.

It had been De Vries' long shot to back a hunch by supposing that all the gutter gossip about the young Basotho girl was factual. He was practically certain about Lesebo with Kirkside but not with Labuschagne, which was a "no smoke without fire" line heard in bars and clubs. De Vries had told the team that if they hit lucky, she would cave in when confronted alone, in front of three menacing strangers. But it seemed to have backfired.

'Okay, Miss Bafokeng. I don't think you've passed the test, so the media will give you a hard time. If you do pass, stand by for those instructions.' He dangled the keys in front of her. 'You'll get these in this plastic shopping bag one kilometre back down the road, okay?' He gave no farewell gesture, swinging himself into the rear vehicle which chased its partner at full throttle, throwing up a cloud of dust that took a minute to settle. Lesebo threw back her head on the seat rest to think things through. She felt that she had done the right thing but only Maddox could be that judge. She walked down the road for the discarded car keys. Her morale felt low as she recovered her composure and made her way to her father's estate. Again, there were fresh agonies over whether she should share her experience with Harry Reynolds; somehow, the less men that knew about the Kirkside and Labuschagne horror stories, the better.

*****

On the whole, it seemed that Lesebo's judgement was right, in Maddox's view. Either the DVD was lost or damaged, had fallen into other hands or had been judged useless. Why go through a rigmarole that lacked impact and was open to a hundred opinions? While it was unlikely that YouTube would compromise obscenity laws, the possibility of private passage through texting still existed, but was there any benefit in handing around a slanderous statement, clearly asked under duress? Maddox suspected it was a last gasp effort, effectively bodged and the wrong choice, made by either Chetty or someone for De Vries. His money was on De Vries, since Chetty's gutter criminality didn't stretch to that basic sophistication. Lesebo's statement had admitted nothing, gave no recriminatory evidence and technically at least – she had not had lovers – told sufficient truth to see her through the courts if litigation arose. As a belt and braces measure, Maddox persuaded Lesebo to accompany him to see Richard Kirkside. He felt more confident on this occasion, since the DVD would not be mentioned by either of them, thereby clearing Maddox of the haunting ethical embarrassment he continued to experience in Kirkside's company.

*****

Kirkside had no objection to discuss the matter, with Maddox acting in his security advisor capacity. As a goodwill gesture, Richard suggested they meet at the Jonkershuis restaurant in Constantia for a sundowner wine, with Cape Malay crudités. With its sweeping views over the old vineyards and startling glimpses of False Bay, their alfresco gathering around a bench table on the lawn made a relaxing setting. Lesebo described her experiences, which clearly alarmed Richard. Although the Kirksides had lived with the threat delivered by Maddox a while ago, this new occurrence seemed confusing and ominous. He talked himself through the possibilities aloud, inviting Maddox's comments, ending up with a similar conviction that it was the work of De Vries.

'You know, we've all had dreadful ethical hurdles to clear since I did this awful thing to Lesebo. But I've tried hard to protect the personal financial aspects. Given where we are, and how we need each other at every twist and turn, I've got to share an idea that might cross a few lines here and there.' Kirkside nibbled from a chicken skewer as the others dipped their cucumber fingers and stuffed peppers into a rich hummus mixture.

'Maddox, you're an SPF investor. So too though, are Messrs Nhleko and Jali, as, embarrassingly, is Mr Chetty! But more interestingly, Nhleko invested a vast amount as a secondary investment as a result of a De Vries handout. The account title was overseas but I've done homework and am fairly satisfied that it emanates from a series of De Vries offshore accounts.' He returned to his seasoned chicken.

'How much?'

'Between them, combining several Far Eastern accounts, some rogue Dutch and Swiss titles and unreasonably large amounts from the politicians' personal accounts, it would add up to about five percent of SPF holdings. Anyway, my feeling is that there is sufficient evidence to do a fairly surgical exposure and freeze their assets until this settles down? More clinically, I'll suggest to Lesebo and Kobus that the withheld De Vries investments would probably cover the bulk of the San City budget forecast. I haven't seen it, but Kobus is entitled to ask for it, isn't he, and so is Harry Reynolds?' Richard had finished his chicken skewer and was fishing among the peppers and vegetables.

'Would that be difficult, legal and quick?' asked Maddox. 'Wouldn't you be watching your back all over again? Do you want the spotlight on the Kirksides once again?' Maddox could see all sorts of useful advantages but the operation was technically beyond him.

'Look, I'd get lots of help – the very best of accountancy and financial management lawyers. I've sounded out an old chum on the bench who agrees there's a case. You know, South Africa has become a hotbed of sequestration and frozen private accounts, so the experience is there. We'd have to use the honest Joes at SARS and a couple of government departments, but it needn't take too long? I reckon it could be done in a month, but of course the counter-accusations, appeals and court orders would fly like bees around a honey pot for a while. The point is, we'd nail De Vries' freakish project to get some breathing space for a compromise and for Harry to get going again?'

Neither Lesebo nor Maddox could fault it. Not so Mrs Kirkside however, who threw a professional tantrum when Richard told her his latest bright idea. This was the fourth attempt by him to commit suicide, she screamed – did he want her to follow on by committing suttee like a Hindu widow?

Kobus Labuschagne, Lesebo Bafokeng and Harry Reynolds met before the Siyeza Mediation conference that was to be held at the gentrified Cellars-Hohenort hotel in Constantia. Harry had agreed that they accompany Jeffrey Felbridge in a drive-through tour of the district immediately before the conference to give him a better impression of the area. The Land Rover entered through a narrow gap across rubble and rubbish in the northern fringes on Manenberg, around Kalksteenfontein. A police cordon was in position, but Harry's vehicle was recognised and allowed through. Jeffrey Felbridge sat in the front passenger seat, noticeably discomforted, holding his armrests like an inexperienced flyer during take-off. Harry took up the commentary.

'This area is where all the violence began and it's still pretty nasty. As you can see over there, we've put up a community centre on the left and that's a fairly state-of-the-art clinic up there on the right but until the trouble dies down, there's little point in starting on the shopping malls and housing estates.' Harry pointed to some figures hugging the shaded passages. 'See them? There are rival gangs around all the time and unless one invades the other's manor, the pond life carries on. They stick to their own turf, intimidating, extorting, running the shebeens and brothels or pushing drugs. The recent extremism has been whipped up by splitting the ten or so gangs down the middle and setting them at each other's throats. We'll try to get through to the area over there that they want for their San City area... watch out Minister!' Harry wrenched the wheel across but not in time to avoid a half brick that struck the minister's door, with a gang of ten or so youths hurling stones their way. Two more hit the vehicle as Harry accelerated through the poorly constructed barrier of burning tyres and wooden fencing.

'Oh my God, this is worse than Beirut!' said Felbridge in a high voice. 'How long has it been going on?' He was ashen and clearly wanted to leave the area.

'Not quite the weapon arsenal that they have, Minister!' said Labuschagne jokingly, from behind the politician. 'But the point is that the Siyeza objective is to complete a massive build with thousands of well-meaning workmen. A single stone thrown at them leads to a walk-out and the bus drivers are too intimidated to break the pickets. Now we have the police and army patrolling everywhere to protect property, so it has become a bit an internal security nightmare. Watch that gang up there Harry!' More stones fell short as Harry put his foot down to clear the rock-strewn no-man's land of southern Manenberg to enter the police control point going towards Ottery and the San City site.

'Well that's it, Minister, it's all sealed off but you can get an idea of its size and position' indicated Harry as they skirted a perimeter wire of a cleared open area, with piles of rubble and earth alongside new roads and paving and a couple of new buildings.

'What are they?' asked Felbridge.

'Actually you can take your pick' chuckled Harry. 'We put a template of our plan over the Dutch sketch and identified common structures that our boys said would not compromise their work. So one's a multi-purpose community centre and the other's a government one-stop, with several departments offering their services that would otherwise involve a whole day in taxis and queues. We're quite happy with those but we cannot keep up the subterfuge much longer.' Harry turned away from the perimeter and accelerated towards a rebuilt thoroughfare between abandoned housing. 'Okay Minister, we'll try our luck along the Khyber Pass and head back to Constantia – quite a contrast!'

The Land Rover bumped and jumped a few times as it crossed projectiles and debris to reach a group of fifty or so youths, barracking rather than violent. An equally sullen-looking platoon of Infantry soldiers prevented contact with adversaries four hundred metres away, similarly accompanied by soldiers. Harry's brain was as alive behind a wheel as it was when chairing a board. 'In fact, Minister, you won't get another opportunity like this to experience a local view first-hand. There's the Army and us three to look after you so how about staying in the vehicle and having a word with that lad there with the scaffolding pole? Harry waved at the police sergeant and made a curving halt alongside a group of picketers on his left, lowering Felbridge's window as he did so. 'Be careful though, it's a bit like backing off before a cobra spits!'

'Good morning! I'm being given a tour of this very troubled area. Obviously, you're expressing your concerns. Can you tell me what they are?' Felbridge had summoned up a strange falsetto voice, delivered at full volume, to further accentuate his perfectly clear diction. The scowling group were momentarily taken aback: people like this only appeared in films and TV, but within ten seconds, they'd made up their minds that this was some condescending foreigner protecting his own interests.

'Hello Soutie! You a big gadgie, neh? You got five Rands for each of us, baas?' Two or three stepped forward to crowd out Felbridge's window space. While two pulled downwards on the glass, the middle one snatched away his sun glasses before Harry could raise the window and drive through the youths who had gathered round the front. A brick thundered on the Land Rover's roof and a projectile struck the windscreen, leaving a tell-tale star. Felbridge put a best face on it. It could be regarded as corroborating evidence of Whitehall diplomats encountering physically threatening moments; on return, he would talk to the Department Finance Officer about travel danger compensations.

'Well, jolly well done, Harry! Not over-friendly were they? I can see how life is becoming intolerable around here.' He turned to Lesebo in the back seat. 'You all right, old thing? You're a tough girl working here, I must say! Does your mother worry about you?'

They arrived otherwise unscathed at Cellars-Hohenort. The renowned gardens were calming, with flowers and shrubs a riotous white, yellow and red. They enjoyed constant professional care amid the tailored lawns and mature and grand trees. They made a fine setting for what many saw as a last-ditch gathering to preserve the original Siyeza plan. Cellars-Hohenort had survived and prospered, almost without faltering, but with the declining Rand, it came at a price. Although it had been difficult to justify more than twenty hard-core negotiators, the hotel's fifty rooms were instantly oversubscribed. The British High Commission had negotiated the pecking order for their rooms, hammered out with not only hotel staff, but with government departments and even Minister's shrill PAs. The British had held back to allow Nhleko the courtesy of the Madiba Suite with his latest young assistant, costing a mere twenty-two thousand Rands a night. The FCO, in bidding for their two Ministers, Felbridge and his colleague Sydney Thwaites, the Commonwealth Secretary, could only manage a couple of Premier Suites at eight thousand seven hundred a night; at an exchange rate of twenty five to the pound, Felbridge was heard to be a bit sniffy at sleeping in rooms valued at three hundred and fifty pounds – 'I couldn't get a Third Secretary bag-carrier in on the basement at the Ritz or Savoy at that price.'

But the comparison was unfair, with a three-to-one cost-of-living index to consider. When Khanyisile had put in an innocent enquiry to Maddox about his prospective attendance as an observer, he had pointed out that his employee ownership of Maddox Private Investigators prevented him incurring such ludicrous overheads. Kobus and Lesebo felt they had little choice but to attend throughout, given the High Commissioner's and Felbridge's urging. The diplomatic trading had settled on Jali chairing the conference but with only four main speakers during the two day's main sessions – Nhleko, Mahlambi, Labuschagne and Felbridge. In the manner of diplomacy, the outward appearance was disappointingly low-key but behind the scenes, the lobbying and impromptu meetings proceeded at a hectic rate.

'Deputy President, forgive me but the main sticking point in negotiations is that we have no undisputed South African government spokesman for the Dutch solution. We'll get no further until that's resolved.' Felbridge looked at Jali and judged him a political nonentity, the very worst model for African leadership. 'Am I to take it that Mr Nhleko, as your predecessor Deputy and personally appointed by you as Ombudsman over contractual matters fairly recently, can be seen in that capacity? It would be helpful if a summary existed of where the inter-government disagreements lie over Siyeza. Otherwise, our progress is meaningless and our jointly drafted statement after the conference will not survive. The outside world detects a deep schism in the ANC, Mr Deputy, but there is no admission to hand. At the moment, I'm not saying you can heal your differences but I am insisting, if you'll forgive me, on an admission that there is a strong ANC factional objection to the Siyeza plan going ahead, without inclusion of the Dutch addition.'

Felbridge was wallowing in his warm Whitehall bath of delicate semantics, his hands joined by his thin finger tips touching, as in prayer. 'But all the unrest has featured either rival drugs gangs or an undisclosed pressure group that appears to link itself between the Dutch group and local organised crime? In other words, there's no formally stated populist or left-wing breakaway faction that's either declaring itself or attracting government opprobrium. Are we to expect a hat to be thrown in the ring before we conclude this evening?' Jeffrey Felbridge was on familiar ground, ironing out the precursors at the end of an African assembly, rather than use them at the outset. His trip around the Cape Flats had convinced him that a great deal of British credit stood to be squandered unless the government admitted to its unreliable and divided personality. Jali realised that he had to shed yet another skin to survive. To do so, it was now clear to him that the Dutch option had to be dropped by the Presidency and party. This could be done, albeit slowly, to make it appear that outside influences were the cause.

'Honourable Minister Felbridge, we must draw up a compromise draft now. We look to you to find a diplomatic way through this mess.' Jali smiled as broadly as he could manage. He wrongly judged Felbridge a powerful patrician, capable and willing to dispense favours. He was running out of friends at every turn and had begun to admit that the future looked grim without an unambiguous party line that everybody obeyed. He was not a communist but felt that the party leaders, like himself, had to back one horse, rather than feather their own nests competitively. He was not getting younger, richer or happier. And neither was he coping too well with the bevy of new girls they'd continually pushed his way since he became Deputy President. They would all cost money in the years ahead.

*****

The British mediation party agreed to stay a further two days in Cape Town. The magnificent conference stewardship by the Cellars-Hohenort staff made this a simpler decision, allowing Felbridge to organise a surrogate tennis lunch party to which he invited the Kirksides, Maddox and Katie. With Lesebo and himself providing the third pair, they were able to enjoy ninety minutes tennis followed by immediate discussion over drinks and lunch laid on by the hotel. Harry Reynolds and Kobus Labuschagne joined them after the tennis. Felbridge unfolded a compromise solution, principally aimed at Harry for comment, wherein De Vries' city was emasculated but kept recognisable along the lines already begun by Harry and Kobus. While the lurid entertainment items would disappear, sports and community sites would multiply. The revolutionary idea was for light industrial enterprises to be opened, serviced by Hong Kong, Singaporean and Thai export giants. Harry saw the sugared pill being offered De Vries by this tempting compromise option. At a stroke, the Dutch initiative would dissolve, to be replaced by competitive and rewarding alternatives. He supported the idea, while evaluating the overall worth of Jeffrey Felbridge and his type, with their huge inventory of ideas and brass neck. Unlike engineers, diplomats needed to prove nothing before ideas were applauded as astoundingly brilliant but in this instance, he was prepared to give it a laboratory test.

The "Felbridge Initiative" was named and adopted unanimously by the conference. Mahlambi was quick to point out how this would diminish the importance – even role – of Nhleko's ombudsman functions, while strengthening his own hand. De Vries was not present personally but had several confidantes in the discussion and was told how the British proposal was worth examining with a slide rule. Lesebo and Kobus thought it sustainable, providing the technical detail could be shared and the construction co-managed by TDC and some Dutch expertise. Nhleko felt abandoned again – his own party, the Dutch, the trade unions and communists. Nobody turned up to an emergency meeting he called, which convinced him to put it in suspension, pending the progress of the Dutch city project. As always, he feared for his own security.

As Harry embarked on full scale operations again, albeit with police escorts and plentiful High Commission advice, Kobus and Lesebo worked hard to publish an acceptable public statement for the media. There was no sign of internecine gang warfare lessening but it seemed that the mass organised crime was reducing – the directly targeted San City compound, the TDC headquarters and depots and the critical entry and exit points returned to virtually normal activity.

Maddox heard the news quicker than most and decided to call Richard Kirkside immediately. 'Richard, forgive the late call but I've just heard that Ravi Chetty's been shot dead. I thought you should know now because of Ami's connection with his brother.' Kirkside was calm enough taking the news in the early morning hours and undertook to tell Ami straight away. He woke Ami and broke the news. She focussed quickly.

'My God, it was bound to happen. I don't think Ashwin will lose too much sleep. That skellum caused us all so much grief, Richard' she said, punching Ashwin's number on her cell phone keyboard. The number rang out, ending with Ashwin's recorded voice telling the caller he was not available. At three o'clock, this seemed a reasonable answer and Ami gave up, lapsing back to sleep.

*****

Kobus and Lesebo finished their morning briefing. 'Let's see how big the funeral will be. The family are talking about a private one but it's customary for the criminal fraternity to put on a show when one of their top honchos dies, especially violently like this.' Kobus had rung Khanyisile who had no news of the killing other than to say it happened in his bedroom at his home, with several bullet wounds to his head. He was alone, since his wife was with her mother. No witnesses, no forensic evidence so far. 'Party headquarters were on the phone, by the way. They're convinced we've turned some sort of corner with the violence by following the Felbridge Initiative. They want news conferences and releases to say we're still in business and that the recent damaging government edict is being reconsidered.'

'Too good to be true,' said Lesebo. Her mind was racing around the blackmail opportunities that remained. With De Vries absorbed with coercing Far Eastern partners to put together attractive light industries for his watered-down city project and now Chetty murdered, would she be left alone?

*****

'Richard, I am worried about Ashwin' murmured Ami. 'There was no sign of him at work and none of his friends have seen him. He's probably deep into traditional Hindu burial arrangements but it seems odd that he's left his cell phone turned off.'

'He's probably in hiding. It was probably De Vries that killed his brother and he thinks he's next.'

'It's just that he's never been out of total touch before. He hasn't got a thousand friends, you know.' Ami rang Maddox for advice but got none: like Richard, Maddox thought Ashwin was frightened.

*****

Khanyisile had more useful information for Maddox. 'They're saying it was an unusual Chinese pistol, called the JS-2. It uses a 5.56 mil calibre round, which is apparently a fraction bigger than the NATO round, so it's imported from China. It uses a silencer. Chetty was hit four times, firstly in the forehead from blank range, then successively in the head as it presented a target to the assassin. There would have been no loud gunshot sounds from a small round using a silencer.'

'Has it been used before?'

'Not this one. But the weapon's model been used by gang thugs for assassination like this before. It's probably De Vries giving him the pay-off through a street gunman.'

*****

The Reverend Nicholas Mahlambi called the council to order. There was a full house, with Maddox and Richard Kirkside co-opted to attend. It was raining heavily outside of the Directorate which prompted the chairman to say that their security was guaranteed in their first return to the Directorate as a venue. 'We have a hectic time since we met but on balance, I think the changes are mostly in our favour. I'd like to ask Maddox and Richard to offer contributions in order that we can release them when we get on with our in-house business, so Richard, can you update us please?'

'Certainly Chairman. I've examined some accounts within the SPF funds. In short, there are around two billion Rands invested by De Vries and Chinese and Dutch associates, a large part of which was invested by Messrs Jali and Nhleko, occasionally in their names. Yesterday, after a colossal bureaucratic wrangle, our lawyers at last obtained authority from the National Director of Public Prosecution to issue an urgent provisional order, allowing the Asset-Forfeiture Unit to seize assets worth two billion Rands from a variety of accounts linked to De Vries that have invested in SPF – it's taken a month! This means that the funds are frozen but of course we require reimbursement. I have the Chairman's authority to tell you that he has secured assurance from the Treasury that this sum will be replaced by government subsidy – the first of its type in Siyeza history! So our lawyers are currently negotiating a 5 percent ownership bid by the government, which we can anticipate being increased if our private investments begin to run dry.' He looked around the table at the surprised faces.

'That's a turn-up! What amazing work, Richard. Quite incredible! But do we want this?' said Harry.

176

'Not really. But it's the first safeguard we've had from the government, which will embarrass them if disorder continues. Our funds are doing well, gaining 8 percent last year but the real expenditure is just beginning, as you know.'

'You bet. We're up to 85 percent production this week.'

'And I'm happy to announce that the ombudsman quietly slid away,' said Mahlambi with a shy smile. I am the sole government representative – and a shareholder, as we've heard!' They all laughed sympathetically.

'Before we go, a word on security,' said Maddox. 'Chetty was murdered in a way that gangland assassins use, with a small calibre pistol held close to his head as he slept. So please bear in mind that some of us have been threatened before, probably by those who have instigated this latest attack. If the government and foreign criminals are backing off Siyeza, remember the horrible legacy they've left the Cape Flat gangs, who were bad enough before this all began.'

Chapter Fifteen

Maddox had always suspected that the South African building labourer did not deserve the comedian's image of lying prone on the grass. The speed at which shopping malls, motorway bridges and new freeways appeared was astoundingly quick. When he returned to England occasionally, he wondered whether they managed to do things as fast. In questioning Harry Reynolds about this, he was told that African labour's chief virtue was its mass; he always factored in three times as many men for a month rather than imagine he was cost-saving by reducing the workforce to a third over three months – a howling false economy, he had learned long ago. This was levelling out however, with mechanisation replacing a rising wage bill factor. Maddox was reminded of this when he took Katie on an exploratory trip around the Siyeza site – an increasingly popular Sunday afternoon activity for the curious Capetonian, emboldened since the violence subsided. The serried ranks of custom-built factories and office blocks looked impressive, even from behind the perimeter wire. TDC and its subsidiaries had more than made up for lost time by agreeing a ten days on-two days off work cycle with the trade unions and had instituted a night shift in some areas.

'I heard that our Pacific Rim partners are hoping to start production before Christmas! Quite frankly, I can't see why not, can you? Amazing progress! You know, when I was a young Peeler in the British Army, there was always demographic change going on in West Belfast, some mischievous, some unavoidable and some high-minded, I suppose. The Catholics were hard done by, up to a point, being rehoused through Andy Town to Lenadoon, which began as Protestant. But they gobbled it up, and eventually spilt over into some mighty smart new estates on the western fringe, called Twinbrook and Poleglass, I remember. The flare-ups stayed in the older, bigger estates.' Maddox turned to smile at Katie. 'Now why am I telling you this? Well, I see it all happening again in front of our eyes. It won't be religion this time, but race – Coloureds, Indian and Black – squabbling for the larny stuff going up all over Ottery and Athlone, but not in dear old Manenberg. Look – there's nothing here! Maybe I could frighten our friend Harry Reynolds with some social, not civil engineering advice?' They both laughed but not too loud, as they absorbed the startling transformation from the shanty town shacks to the new two- and three-bedroom houses.

As they drove back to play croquet and enjoy tea and scones in a large shady garden belonging to some old friends of Katie, she stroked his hand, leaning back in her seat. 'Have you still got any jobs on hand for your unrequited black lover, Maddox?' There was a feminine mind at work, not driven by jealousy so much as tying loose ends before they married. Katie still enjoyed managing the medical practice which kept her occupied and paid reasonably well. But with combined pensions and savings, it seemed they could look forward to a prosperous retirement and marriage.

'Actually, George Washington cannot tell a lie!' replied Maddox immediately. It had irked him slightly to be asked a favour by Khanyisile Mthembu yet again and he had not told Katie. 'She rang me two days ago and said they're getting nowhere with the Chetty shooting. She's weeded out her bent coppers but is plagued by BEE replacements like the rest of us – kids with no training, apparently. So I don't know what to do really – we've got plenty of work on our hands and I was thinking of easing back a bit.'

'You've done enough for her now darling, surely?' Katie wanted to be supportive if Maddox decided not to help Khanyisile, but she knew it wouldn't be the case.

'I have, yes I have,' said Maddox, straightening his arms and hands on top of the car wheel, 'but you know, she could make life awkward. I like the way she's weeded out the bad apples and stood up to the political nonsense from her horrible family. Considering she's come from nowhere, she's a good manager, even if she's a lousy cop, so we must be thankful for small mercies.' He smiled, smacking the wheel for emphasis. 'Besides, Chetty's death has left a big gap which must be plugged before another oligarch steps in.'

'All right darling, I knew it would be a waste of time asking!' Katie smiled as she raised an open hand. She shuffled sideways to change the subject. 'Now then, the Arbuthnots. He's as deaf as a post, remember, and she's Number Two, much younger. Alice is my friend from way back, ages before she married Cecil. She's divorced from a ghastly little creep we all hated and is blissfully happy with Cecil, whose wife died about three years ago.' Katie paused as they approached the grand old house, set back from the road in Bishopscourt. 'And don't cause ructions with Cecil about the double roquet rule darling – remember house rules apply, so he's always right!'

'Yes dear,' murmured Maddox as the giant and ornately patterned wrought iron gates creaked open ponderously.

*****

Mahlambi, Labuschagne and Kirkside faced a battery of advocates in their cool Sandton offices, with Oregon pine panelling, whispering fans and mellow lighting setting an atmosphere of wisdom and authority. They had decided to follow a legal trail against De Vries, due to Jeffrey Felbridge's concerns that were relayed through the British High Commissioner. The original understanding was that De Vries would facilitate the introduction of the Hong Kong, Thai and Singaporean companies and presumably derive a handsome commission. But evidence had since emerged that he had bought influential shareholdings in the companies. On investigation by Kirkside and his financier friends, it seemed that the shares were funded directly from accounts that were fed from his sex industry earnings – prostitution, child enslavement and live sex shows. This placed the South African government in a dilemma, since it threatened the development of Siyeza's most promising early employment source. But as Kirkside reminded them, when he first exposed De Vries's funding of both Chetty's and the opposing gang leader's crimes, the funding came from identical sources. So, Kirkside argued, an international aspect of exploitation and crimes against humanity might exist against De Vries – murder, torture, arson, rape and extortion.

'Before we form an opinion on whether a robust case exists against Mr De Vries, we must be certain of our sequence.' Lennie Steinhoff was the senior partner in Christies, Boschoff and Buthelezi, the leading international law team in South Africa. He had an unemotional appearance, keeping his head and face immobile as he spoke quietly in a refined northern Johannesburg accent. 'First, we must prepare a justification and probably a defensive statement to explain our Provisional Restraint Order against Mr De Vries.' He shuffled papers to find facts before going on. 'This involved a very considerable sum of monies deposited in Siyeza Peoples Fund by persons or agencies connected to him. Sadly, as our earlier advice intimated, we feel the existing banking edict is rudimentary and will not hold up to international scrutiny. Can that be done by your associates or do you wish us to advise further upon this?' Kirkside noticed the slightest swivelling of small eyes behind the rimless, rectangular frames. The other two lawyers sat back in their tan leather chairs, hands relaxed on laps, awaiting their call for amplification or dredging up some esoteric expertise.

'We can manage that, thanks. It was just a marker to accompany the technical action. It's fairly standard so should be done quickly.' Richard wasn't to be overawed by these lawyers and their astronomic fees.

'Oh well, that's helpful. Thank you. Moving on, I would like to draw your attention to the main matter in hand, which is the available avenues, which in our judgement present opportunities for litigation within the international court arena – the International Criminal Court and so forth. Please understand that actions of this sort are immensely complicated, laborious and expensive. The European Union took seven years and several miles of paper to rule that future condoms would come in two sizes, the larger one available in North Europe, the smaller one in the south – an absolute fact, gentlemen!' This was a surprising but welcome indication that Steinhoff was the consummate advocate, attracting laughter around the table without changing his dry voice or implacable stare. As with many professions, theatre was a prime attribute.

'Having spent four years between drafting and enacting their proceedings, you can surmise the methodology. The Prosecutor initiates an investigation referred by a state or the United Nations Security Council. Please note that this is invariably the case, although the option exists for him to initiate an investigation on information on crimes from individuals or organisations. To date, just four states who are parties to the Rome Statute – there are now one hundred and sixty of them – and the Security Council have referred twenty three cases involving nine situations to the ICC. Once that has occurred, an independent and comprehensive preliminary examination with respect to crimes allegedly committed takes place and is presented to the court for confirmation to hear the case. If declined, the accused is released. If confirmed, he is held in ICC custody before committal to trial. I believe of the twelve who've appeared, only four are being held. Opening statements are compiled by the Prosecutor, victims and their defence and legal representatives are assembled and the wagon rolls. This takes years, gentlemen' intoned Steinhoff, flicking his eyes towards Mahlambi. 'The Reverend Doctor Mahlambi, may I ask whether the South African government would lend its authority as a Rome Statute signatory to arraigning Mr De Vries at The Hague?' Steinhoff's face never changed, convincing Kirkside that he could make a holiday living at the Las Vegas poker tables.

'I've ceased to be amazed by my government in the last few years. The President has somehow stayed out of sight throughout Siyeza's torrid existence, letting either Mr Nhleko or Mr Jali take front-of-stage. They are subdued now, while the caucus sorts the party out, but I don't detect any energy or initiative to makes matters worse for De Vries, as they see it. I suspect we'll see a finely spread veneer of respectability for a short while, maybe causing another reshuffle. I really don't see them getting involved, with so much back-stabbing going on. Their lawyers and spin doctors will deny that it ever constituted anything substantial. They will say it was an overseas investment in a project that was mismanaged by a DA provincial government, who failed to acknowledge the deeply ingrained criminal fraternity in the Cape Flats region.'

'Mmm. As I thought. And Mr Kirkside, even you lack the philanthropic will to pursue a private case?' Again the masked mischief and humour, with relaxed laughter among everyone.

'Not really. I agree with Nicholas. Absolutely no hope. In which case, we're reducing sights to money laundering? Maybe incitement and sponsoring of violence and public disorder?' Kirkside never felt that a crime against humanity existed unless it was introduced as a corollary to the laundering of funds from several overseas pariah businesses.

'Yes, we've looked at this, as instructed. Preliminary investigation tends to support such a case being raised. The seemingly inescapable evidence of Messrs Nhleko's and Jali's complicity is promising, I must say, but again, are we confident of the government standing behind or distancing itself from them? We could sound out the Presidency on this in the quietest of ways and I strongly suspect, with Mr Jali serving as Deputy President, that they will be islanded, albeit through a lengthy disassociation. That will make it more difficult to get at a serving Deputy, needless to say. But that's another battle; I'm saying we feel there is a case.' Labuschagne had been listening carefully throughout, his political antennae bristling.

'So firstly the case defending our Provisional Restraint Order. That can't wait, can it? So when can we hope to begin a formal investigation against laundering and sponsoring violence in a foreign state?'

'I really can't be quoted on that one. There are three foreign governments and several more banks, some of whom are not renowned for their compliance. There are international statutory bodies that have to be consulted and authorities are required all along the way. Constant linguistic translation is required. I can't see government sending those hasteners, sadly. So it would be unreasonable to hope for a hearing to begin within the next two years. If there is no orchestrated obfuscation and tortuous appealing, it might begin three years from now?' Steinhoff looked to left and right for confirmation, which was received with swift nodding of heads – they were still awake. Kirkside interjected sharply.

'Well let's be realistic. If we can uphold the Restraint, how does De Vries get back in the game, or indeed recover his assets?'

'Gentlemen, we are of the opinion that the Restraining Order will be upheld, but of course, the courts will not want to stop there. The question of forfeiture of such a vast amount could only be supported in a criminal trial against De Vries in this country. He would be charged with fraud and contravention of the Prevention of Organised Crime Act, including, presumably, racketeering. So he must appear here to contest Restraint, and having failed, must face criminal charges. His lawyers might well advise him not to set foot in South Africa to contest the Restraint of course, which will mean than forfeiture will automatically result, but only agreed after a long-drawn-out international legal wrangle.'

As they sat on the Gautrain bound for their Cape Town flight, Labuschagne spoke noisily in the empty compartment to his colleagues. 'Well at least we'll catch Jali out of office in three years, away from diplomatic immunity – he won't last another year. It'll be interesting to see which way the Restraining Order case goes – I think it will bring so much blame on De Vries that it might hurry things along. But it looks like we'll get a clear run to complete three-quarters of Siyeza uninterrupted, barring ordinary decent strikes, district jealousies and what have you!' He laughed as he told them a recent twist. 'Do you know what? Maddox, of all fine people, lectured me on how I was running the gauntlet of racial disharmony between Blacks, Coloureds and Indians by re-housing them according to their present township groupings? Who needs friends, heh?' He kept laughing until interrupted by Mahlambi.

'As always, old Maddox might have a point, my brother in Christ! You know the Coloured story better than me. They have an aversion to school and a propensity for alcohol. The Indians have a passion for schooling, business, gambling and houses and an aversion to Coloureds and Blacks. The Blacks don't care about schools or houses but want everyone else's land to keep goats, while they drink the White's alcohol! Can't you see how the Coloureds will always feel stitched?' They chuckled good-naturedly as they gathered their laptops and bags to dismount at the gleaming OR Tambo station.

*****

Joost van der Merve and Gary Hutchins, Maddox's faithful duo, were looking as smug as they dared as they updated their boss.

'Come on then, out with it. You both look like the cat who's got the cream. Have I overpaid everyone with the Ownership shares?' Maddox pushed back the folder he was reading and motioned them both to sit.

'Not far off, we hope, boss – I tell you, these SAPS 'special tasks' beat advising grannies about their security sirens! Boss, we've been sitting on an oke who runs a dodgy gun shop downtown, just behind the Shell garage on the corner of the Strand and Railway Station. Name of Winston Trudeau, a Mauritian. Slimy bugger but happy to talk. Got some form for illegal importation of firearms and tax evasion, but way back and got off with a smart lawyer. Small time but sophisticated hardware. Anyway, I took the liberty of asking your top cop girlfriend whether he featured and she said he had association links with Chetty in the past, probably supplying and moving shorts and ammunition around.' Gary was amazed he hadn't been interrupted, so thought he needed to pause.

'I'm listening. You were hunting any JS-2 info?'

'Yup. Bit more than that. I'm feeling guilty now, boss, but Khanyisile said she was able to give me a bit of help if we turned something up.' He smiled engagingly at Maddox.

'Don't know why you're being prissy about this Gary – we've been together a while, so I suppose that extends to sharing girlfriends?'

'Fair do's, boss.' Gary laughed loudly, giving him confidence to complete his story. 'Khanyi thought you'd done your bit for SAPS and had other things to think about, like your forthcoming marriage and all sorts!' The three of them grinned at each other and Gary carried on. 'Anyway, we encouraged Winston to talk about guns. He knows a lot. We wanted to look sideways, like you taught me in Rheindahlen – do you remember those Turks and Jocks?' Maddox sat immobile, remembering clearly but not wishing to interrupt the flow. 'Well, we began to learn that there was a big protection system, probably started by Ravi Chetty, that was alive and well after he was chiselled. Our man Winston was their tame provider, if you like, kept on a retainer, for all purposes selling rifles to hunters. We dug around and got an inventory of his armoury, which was scary – AKs and all sorts. We saw that he'd moved some JS-2's about, mostly to the Flats but a couple to funny folk in the posh suburbs. We eventually got him to show us his grotty little issues book and saw a Chetty invoice.' Gary looked at Maddox to get a reaction.

'Which Chetty are you talking about?'

There was no doubting the disappointment in Gary's face. 'It was just another Chetty, boss, you know, no signature or address.' He thought Maddox deserved better. 'It was a JS-2 given to Professor Ashwin Chetty – simple as that! Ravi's brother, Ashwin, you know, the one that Ami Kirkside shacked up with! No experience in handling guns, no previous business with Winston, but just connected by some Indian funny mob that meant no harm to anyone – probably spiritual? Bit weird, really.''

'So what went on with Khanyisile and forensic?'

'Brilliant! They got his prints and matched them up – it looked like Ashwin killed his brother – he'd had enough!' Gary had a strained look on his face. 'We've waited until we could go further, boss. Obviously, the forensic mob have done their stuff but we weren't sure when to draw the line with the SAPS investigation.' Gary looked at Joost. 'For our part, boss, we think that it's a family murder. A law abiding oke with a crazy schizophrenic brother cannot bottle up his anger anymore, so he tops him!' Gary had been in South Africa long enough to click his fingers in a backhand throwing gesture to demonstrate an end, a finality, done for.

'Any forced entry?'

'Nothing apparently. SAPS say he must have let himself in through an open door or with a key. Probably kept each other's keys?' Gary and Joost clearly felt it was a job well done and waited for Maddox's guidance.

'Well, you've excelled yourselves, lads! Well done. Let me do a bit of background checking on Ashwin through Ami – she might confirm movements, recent moods and the like.' He smiled at them both. 'Not sure who we're doing a favour to though, are you? But there we are – we all took the oath!'

*****

The Kirksides had invited Maddox and Katie to their Hout Bay residence for evening drinks. Maddox was glad to have the opportunity to kill two birds with one stone, but first had to endure the overwhelming enthusiasm of Ami as she unloaded her good news.

'We've had the most wonderful news and wanted to tell you ahead of the crowd. Tristan's won an Exhibition to Balliol! And he'll be just seventeen! Isn't that marvellous?'

'Well of course it is! Well done him. I only managed a Grammar School in Reigate which I left at sixteen to join the Army. I remember my parents were unhappy about me not staying on for sixth form and university entry. What does it all mean?'

'Well it's a little complicated. He's actually been awarded the only mathematics scholarship. It's the Hakeem Belo-Osagie Scholarship, awarded to any African student to read any subject that is taught at Balliol. Added to it, and we haven't got the final confirmation, is another award from the Clarendon Fund, which is some huge lump that covers the whole of Oxford scholarship applications. It actually isn't very much in cash on its own but if we get the Clarendon hand-out as well, it could be about twelve thousand pounds, or not far off three hundred thousand bucks over here. The Hakeem Belo-Osagie family are Nigerian fat cats and big philanthropists. He's a lawyer with Cambridge and Harvard degrees and has dominated Nigerian business for years. We think, but are not sure, that Tristan will be the youngest they've chosen...'

Katie decided the torrent had to be staunched. 'Truly exciting! And what an appropriate reward for you too Ami, with all your home schooling and for Tristan too, with all the horrible experiences last year. Is there any family in UK to look after him during the vacs?'

'Yes, there's Richard's brother who has children about Tristan's age. You know, another exciting thing is that I bet he will get a Half Blue for swimming – his backstroke times are amazing. He's been unofficially timed under thirty seconds for the fifty metres backstroke and the world record, I'm saying the world record, is only twenty four seconds, done years ago. Now you're not telling me, with another year and more muscle and top competition, he couldn't get beyond provincial level? We'll have to have a word with...' This time Maddox interrupted, finding Ami's monologue tiresome.

'Well, jolly good for young Tristan! We look forward to hearing how he finds the place. There's about a year to go, you say?' Maddox was doing his best to look keenly involved as he sipped the excellent Cabernet Sauvignon. 'Can I change subjects while we have the opportunity to talk in private please?' He sensed even a loyal Richard was happy to talk about something other than Tristan for a moment.

'Yes of course, sorry I went into overdrive there, I'm afraid – we're so excited!' Ami leant forward with a nervous laugh. She was well aware how she could become off-putting when on a hobbyhorse she rode so well.

'It's about Ravi Chetty. We've been loosely involved in helping SAPS and are looking for any faint leads. I suddenly remembered how you work with his brother, Professor Ashwin Chetty, and thought you might be able to say how the Chetty family seem to be taking their tragedy, or indeed how Ashwin is behaving?' Maddox continued sipping his wine, an off-duty investigator using a social opportunity to clear up a small point. Katie glanced at him, hoping he was not going to say anything insensitive.

'Yes, well I haven't seen an awful lot of him recently. I've visited Tristan when we were sorting out where we would go but that apart, haven't been to see him at home. He disappeared for two days to start with, switching off his phone and not talking to anyone. He's taken compassionate leave. I phoned his sister but she hadn't heard anything of him either – they all piled in for the usual massive Indian get-together but he wasn't there at any time. They put it down to Ashwin having no respect for Ravi. He criticised him for bringing down the Chetty name, because he's always found it embarrassing when interviewed in public.' Maddox listened and watched Ami carefully, assessing whether she was telling the full story.

'So you don't know whom Ashwin thinks killed Ravi?'

'Oh, just another gang warfare killing. So many were expecting one thing, promised another, but got nothing, with all the chopping and changing with government and Ashwin feels...' Maddox interrupted softly.

'But you said you hadn't spoken to him since the murder?'

'Well not quite. I said I hadn't seen him at home or work.'

'But you said he'd cut his phones off?'

'Maddox! What's come over you? We invited you to join us celebrating Tristan's achievement and you start grilling me about bloody Ravi Chetty's murder!' Ami blushed and stood up, drink in hand, gesticulating angrily towards Maddox. 'If you must know, I did go to see him, but on neutral territory in Simon's Town. I thought it easier to tell you a white lie because I'm extremely sensitive about Richard's attitude to my friendship with Ashwin. I know what you might think, but it's not like that. Richard is paranoiac about the whole Chetty thing and hates to think I've got any connection to the family.' Ami went behind Richard's chair and bent over to kiss him from behind. Richard took her arm and held her there.

'This is news to me Maddox, but it's as Ami says – its small beer, but we're both treading carefully, trying not to upset each other over anything. Ravi Chetty was indeed a red rag to a bull to me but I can understand why Ami wanted to find out why Ashwin is behaving so irrationally.' He looked upwards at Ami and patted her arm.

'I'm sorry, I don't want to tread on corns and it was inconsiderate of me to press you about Ashwin's views. Forget it Ami, it's definitely not that important – the answers will come from elsewhere.' Maddox was noticing Katie, who was building up to a fiancées retort – he had promised not to become inquisitive.

'No, Maddox, let's go on please. I've told you that I saw Ashwin to find out about his strange behaviour. So what do you want to know?' Ami had recovered herself and was smiling politely, seated on the arm of Richard's chair, a slim crossed leg swinging gently, her sandals kicked off.

'Ami, look, we're having fun and really don't want to mix business and pleasure, don't worry! I merely thought you might be able to tell me how you thought Ashwin was taking Ravi's death, that's all. I respect the sensitivities but now you say you've seen him recently. So forgive me again, but did he say anything about his own future intentions?' Maddox sat back, trying his utmost to be casual and unfocussed. 'I mean, is he going to resume work at UCT, is he taking a sabbatical, is he moving on?'

'To be truthful, I was worried. He was scared and defensive. He said that he was even more evil than his brother and that there was a ghastly spell over the Chetty family. He said he needed time to reflect about how wrong it had been for him to avoid the family after a violent death but he was uncharacteristically incoherent – he is typically logical and ordered. He ended by saying that his sins would probably atone for the multiple wickedness of Ravi. It was all a bit weird, to be frank. I told him to go to a counsellor and talk it through.' Ami pursed her lips while smiling – it seemed there was nothing else she was going to add to her conjecturing without a nudge from Maddox, who took the hint.

'Very odd. What did you take this to mean, if decoded?

'Do you really want to know? To be honest, I was terrified that he was more involved in the whole thing than I thought. I couldn't work it out. I put it down to some cult thing that I'd never understand. I was glad to back off, quite frankly.' Ami stood up and passed round some quixotic delicacies. 'Richard, how about another drink please?' Despite her frostiness, Maddox judged that she was glad to unburden her discomfort about Ashwin.

*****

De Vries fumed as his staff slowly unfurled the bad news but once the full story had been told to the half-dozen Dutchmen in the bare offices in Den Haag's Hofkwartior, he fell sullen and quiet.

'So Chief, to sum up. All the investments we've made, whether through the initial accounts in the Cayman Islands, Hong Kong, Singapore or transfers to South Africans have been identified and named in the Johannesburg Restraining Order. In total they amount to around twelve million Euros. They've been frozen on government authority pending a High Court hearing in four weeks. You are named to appear to contest the order. If you fail to appear, they will initiate forfeiture proceedings. If we win, the assets will be recovered unless further claims are made against us. If we fail, we can appeal through South African and probably European High Court but it seems likely that they'll deal with forfeiture proceedings immediately, because of the size of seized assets. That will mean a criminal trial in South Africa, answering charges of fraud and contravening their Organised Crime Act. A guilty finding carries between five and twenty-five years imprisonment.' The chief accounting officer paused, knowing De Vries would have questions.

'So what have you done to get Jali to say the Restraint was issued on wrongful evidence? How can they be so sure of where the cash flow came from? Have we got a friendly voice talking to us from the Prosecutions office – since when are clubs illegal?' De Vries sounded tired and lost.

'Chief, we haven't. All that dried up the moment Chetty was killed. But we've asked questions about Thailand and South African differences with girls on the game. It's only illegal in Thailand, funnily enough, if it's promiscuous but there's nothing private or shy about our sex clubs, Chief! The whole thing is based on laundering and they've done their homework, it seems, by peeling off our front companies and transit banks.'

'And what's Jali saying?'

'Chief, his office is being very uncooperative. Forgive me, but I think he's running scared now. We've turned the screw a bit on Nhleko and Jali and they're up an alley now. The tide has changed a bit, Siyeza is half-built and the government has actually chipped in five percent ownership into the main fund. I guess that Jali knows he'll get smacked about and lose his job. And if you go over and your appeal fails, what then? You'll go down but so will they – big time! So he's happy for you to stay away, forfeit the money and carry on with the next sponsor.'

It was inevitable that De Vries cracked. He leapt up and grabbed the accountant's shirt collar and swiped him viciously with first a backhand and then the full might of his palm, his showy rings splitting the skin on the young man's forehead and eyebrow.

'You're fired! You useless idiot! You sit and spout this crap at me, having done nothing to see it coming and snuff it out! Are we exporting flowers or something? What business do you think we're in?' He began to kick his victim before being pulled off by the others.

*****

Maddox pulled his chair a little nearer General Mthembu's desk, smiling broadly. 'Khanyisile, I have an offer for you that you cannot possibly refuse!' Their respective looks reflected the warmth and trust between them. 'I know who killed Ravi Chetty. It was his brother, Professor Ashwin Chetty. I persuaded Ami Kirkside to admit privately to me that she has been in regular touch with him. She told me how Ashwin Chetty seems deranged but relies on her as a source of maternal fondness. Having put two and two together over the last few weeks, I've produced a report for you here that points conclusively towards Ashwin anyway, but my gut feeling was that a confession was likely. Ami has told Ashwin that there is strong evidence against him and that there is no point remaining in hiding. The Kirksides have put him in touch with a reputable shrink in the city and he is now prepared to hand himself in, providing his medical condition is fully assessed beforehand. I know this is totally unprofessional but it solves a lot of problems, don't you think? If I was you, I'd get a senior Indian officer to arrange a meeting and eventual accompaniment to somewhere neutral to take statements. Ami says the medical assessment should be complete within a month. Now how about that for a favour?'

'Not bad Maddox, not bad. Quite extraordinary – that peace-loving little professor, who wouldn't say boo to a goose! In fact it's too good to be true – there's more to come, isn't there?' The corpulent Khanyisile kept her smile but knew Maddox too well – Katie was right to sense the affection she showed for him. 'Come on, what's the deal?'

'Funny you say that, Khanyisile, since it would be another favour – certainly not a condition!' Maddox kept his beaming smile in place. 'It's simple really. As you know, Katie and I are getting married and like most of you girls, she's spring cleaning beforehand. She's hoping my SAPS commitments could end, now that you've completed the makeover in this place?' Maddox hesitated before adding, 'The help you gave Gary and Joost is a case in point – to be truthful, your boys almost completed the investigation without us and showed great skill and patience with forensic findings.'

'Okay, Maddox. I don't want another fancy meal out of this but I do want an invitation to the wedding – can you fix that?'

'I can, yes, but it looks like it'll be in Australia!' Maddox roared with laughter on seeing Khanyisile's alarm and disappointment.

'Ooh, I've always wanted to go! My sister has been and says it's wonderful. Maybe I could get leave? My boyfriend would worry about the Aborigines – he's not happy with Zulus, you know.'

'No worries there Khanyisile – the Zulus are not happy with the Zulus, either!'

*****

'Any other business?' The Reverend Nicholas Mahlambi's voice rose above the hubbub that signified the end of a long council meeting. It had covered several important issues, including the almost certain demise of De Vries from future Siyeza involvement and the verification by the government to double its five percent holding in the project by the beginning of the forthcoming Financial Year. Additionally, the video of the "topping out" ceremony of the thousandth Cape Flats' new house had been shown – cleverly introduced by Harry Reynolds as a progress milestone. The entire project's completion date was brought forward to coincide with the country's next General Election, which would serve as a double-edged sword for any future political opposition. Mahlambi glanced around. 'None? Fine. Well, I have just one request to make myself, particularly of the Mayor and the TDC Chairman.'

'No more God Squad marches, I hope, Mr Chairman?' quipped Kobus Labuschagne irreverently.

'I will forgive you your heathen indiscretion, Mr Mayor, because you are quite close to hitting the proverbial nail on the head!' The clergyman gave him a radiant smile. 'I refer to the vacant plot and the land previously ring-fenced for San City development. You'll recall how we felt there was a surfeit of sports grounds and how the Municipality Planning Committee was being asked by the Director to shelve the idea of building two sports centres within a kilometre of each other? Well, it falls to me as your pastor and political advisor to consider the erection of a Christian church, where unlike sports facilities, the nearest one is five kilometres away in a traditionally different cultural community. As you know, I've been having a ministry in Ottery every month, attracting a thousand souls each time in the open air. There is clearly a deep love of God in the community, cleansing itself from its demon past! So my proposal is to build a Christians United church to house fifteen hundred worshippers on that vacant site!' Mahlambi became impassioned, with a hint of his infamous menace surfacing. 'After all, my party's part in steadying the ANC ship and my congregation's peaceful demonstrations against former violence suggest that this would be a natural and fulfilling outcome, don't you feel?' Mahlambi froze his grin, his teeth gleaming against his shining black skin.

Kobus and Harry exchanged glances. Mahlambi had tied things up convincingly, with consummate timing and sense of place. Neither wanted to commit on the spot as the question hung in the air.

'I think it's a very creditable idea, Mr Chairman. If the Mayor and Director were to give qualified approval now, I suggest the matter is moved to the Planning Committee straight away. I can see no insurmountable difficulty in raising benefactors, obviously steered by your lay elders.' Richard Kirkside seemed at his incisive best, as he stared down his old friend Harry, who opened his mouth without speaking.

'Thank you, Richard. That's just what I hoped you'd all say. May you all receive the Lord's Blessing! Let's record that in the Minutes please and unless there are further thoughts on this wonderful response, I will declare the meeting closed!' The pastor sat back in stunned amazement, having previously considered the chances of outright acceptance extremely remote. He was already visualising two thousand congregants assembling on the proposed site for worship each weekend.

Chapter Sixteen

Malusi Jali felt extremely uncomfortable. His Minister of Justice had asked for a private discussion between Jabu Nhleko and themselves, accompanied by three Constitutional Court judges. He had forewarning, due to the increasing anxiety over the Restraining Order on De Vries' assets, but now the Day of Reckoning hovered above Nhleko and himself, not De Vries. As he had feared, the Siyeza law and accountancy teams had eventually unearthed all the transactions, payments and sources of funds connecting them through a welter of front companies and banks to De Vries and his money laundering activities abroad. So when the final outcome from the Asset-Forfeiture Unit's investigations was leaked to the media, which was an imminent certainty, the court would hear the case against De Vries and all complicit or participating parties, which included Nhleko and himself. The informed word was that De Vries would plead illness preventing travel to a South African hearing, but however long he played that card, or if he declined to attend, the court would award forfeiture of all assets concerned. They would use international courts to lay charges of fraud and practising organised crime both abroad and in South Africa.

'So talk about damage limitation my friend – some of you here owe me gratitude and loyalty for your advancement and survival! If we keep De Vries out of the country – effectively forever – and he doesn't plead one way or the other, then what are the implications for Mr Nhleko and myself? I'm trying to get it into your thick skulls, my honourable judges, that we've lived in a world of family favours – or cronyism as the white press call it – since 1994. All of us in power are infected and are spreading the virus. But what we are supposed to have produced in parallel is a defensive structure to immunise us until the Apartheid and Colonial legal practices are neutralised. So why, a quarter of a century on, are you reading a solemn Last Testament to your Deputy President, for God's sake? Are you saying you have put on the white man's cloak and wig, but done nothing except struggle with a law system that is way beyond your understanding? Wise up, you old fools and tell me why I should not feel nervous!'

'Deputy President, you are demeaning your position, which we all respect but none of us can protect you from the law. As judges, we're indeed dedicated to doing better for our race by removing bias and increasing access to high quality lawyers. But we're here today to point out how Mr Nhleko and you are tainted with international corruption, theft and fraud. You acted as accomplices to an overseas criminal who used you to subvert government, in return for personal aggrandisement and political power. Never mind the small-time favouritism – this is complicity to international organised crime, Mr Deputy President!'

'You're still playing the prosaic old fool, Ndebele! We can smell the dung on our feet well enough! How are we to apply the precious ANC adage of silence, denial, counter-charge and ignore? Never, never, never admit guilt, my friend! Go on, think on your feet – what is your collective advice?'

There was murmuring among the three learned judges, who withdrew into a huddle away from the table, ignoring the vexed politicians and their note-scribbling young assistants. After a few minutes, they returned to the table, where their senior member spoke again.

'Mr Deputy President, we are of the opinion that this meeting be termed a formal tribunal – we can arrange the technical aspects of that. Furthermore, we firmly recommend that both Mr Nhleko and yourself admit through sworn statement that although you were involved in receipt and payment of assets knowingly originating from Mr De Vries, you nevertheless, in total good faith, understood that this was an introduction to full-scale government participation in Siyeza – witness today's 10 percent ownership.' The judge looked down to flick through his sheaf of notes, appearing to be flustered. 'Yes, now then. At no time did you participate in the knowledge that this might promise personal gain. The subsequent promotion of the primarily De Vries sponsored proposals for San City verified this. You learned with shock of Mr De Vries being arraigned on criminal charges and his assets being frozen.' He glanced down again, removing his glasses to point with them. 'But gentlemen, here is your escape clause: mindful of the public discontent over De Vries and the potential fall-out against a government dedicated to making Siyeza Africa's most ambitious social regeneration project ever, both of you volunteered to make good any sum considered appropriate by the Treasury. Do you see what I'm getting at? This same tribunal can meet downstream to determine a favourable amount gentlemen. The important point is that this will only be released as public knowledge when pressure against you is considered intolerable. Then we will be able to say retrospectively that although you deny involvement, nevertheless you undertook confidentially to repay sums that might have featured had you been brought to court.'

The judges waited, fully aware of how far they were bending every rule in the book to preserve their five mutual positions. The politicians had no way out of the cul-de-sac and had to eat humble pie, probably for the rest of their government terms. The liberal dosage of favours was almost an expectancy in post-1994 South Africa, but when an ignorant politician overstepped the fine line and insulted his intellectual brethren, where meritocracy still played a part, he had to expect retribution.

*****

'Annabelle's asking whether we'd consider postponing our wedding until after the baby is born. They'd rather not travel all that way with a tiny baby for a couple of years and she's keen for us to see it before it becomes much older. What do you think?' Katie was looking up from her iPad as they sat on Maddox's veranda, drinking tea after an hour's gardening.

'Really? Well, she's got a point. Are you sure you don't want your chums from Cape Town and elsewhere to come to your wedding?' Maddox knew the rehearsed reply but wanted to be absolutely sure that there would be no later regrets.

'Absolutely Maddox. Look, combined, it's our fifth wedding, we'll both be grandparents and there's something posed about middle-aged weddings, don't you think? I'd far rather get away somewhere private and exciting, with a bit of romance to spice up the marriage formalities, wouldn't you? We've never seen Australia or been away together and it would be lovely to do it around a new grandchild.'

'Glad we haven't booked the flights yet!' Maddox chuckled mischievously. 'And don't forget Khanyisile wants to come, but I think she's coming on a different flight!' Maddox avoided a rebuke by hurrying indoors for his diary, shouting over his shoulder, 'When's Annabelle's baby due, by the way?'

*****

With around eighteen months to run, Kobus Labuschagne's ambitions to lead the DA into the next General Election became increasingly focussed. In many respects, he would never be in a better position. His popularity as Mayor was high, the Siyeza achievements were seen as a feather in his cap and his voting attraction as a married father with a baby daughter – curiously called Clara Khanyisile – had gone down well. His attractive wife Rita was similarly popular in the city, playing a prominent role in Siyeza welfare projects. They were the right age and tri-lingual Afrikaners, at a time when the party was searching to avoid another first language English-speaking incumbent. The party leader had lost popularity and was blamed by the "kingmakers" for allowing the ANC to survive relatively unscathed, despite the condemning leadership revelations that had dominated headlines.

So it surprised neither him nor his strong caucus within the party's main branches when he was elected as party deputy, with a view to assuming leadership one year before the election. Having spent all his political career in Cape Town, he worried about his Gauteng urban savvy, but more than that, he worried about his successor. Siyeza would need significant skilled management for some time, as new ideas were absorbed and fresh funding sought. Its corporate municipal requirement was already managed independently from the city, meaning a high-quality mayor and council would need establishing within the next year. All of this pointed fair and square at Lesebo Bafokeng in Kobus' eyes, although she occasionally declared that she would never consider a political career.

'Look, Kobus, we're not an item,' Harry Reynolds reminded him. 'We're great friends and I love her company. She's got an unreal pick-up – hellish imaginative and resourceful. And frighteningly driven, as you know. She's also not half bad as an operational manager, which usually comes from experience and exposure to a hundred challenges. So I stick to her like glue when I'm over here but I'm not casual about such things and I'm not sure we're ready to team up – I live a peripatetic life and Lesebo is still a rural African at heart. I know you've just got married but I've just got divorced! Anyway, what's on your mind?' Kobus had broached the subject of Lesebo's future during one of their regular meetings and knew Harry well enough to broach the subject.

'No, man, don't get me wrong. I'm only asking because I wondered how vital Lesebo is at the Directorate these days – is all that energy and ambition still being soaked up?' Kobus had to come to the point to avoid appearing prurient. 'I tell you what it is. Between you and me, they've picked me as the next DA leader to take them into the next election. They don't want me stuck here like Teddy Kollek, mayor of Jerusalem for thirty years while trying to rule the world, so in the way of politics, it would help if I could pick my successor. You can see what I'm getting at, can't you? How about Lesebo joining the DA and taking over as Mayor – they all think she walks on water round here? They've got used to her being clever, young and black.' Kobus watched Harry carefully as this sank in. The imperturbable Englishman let his eyes wander as he thought it through.

'Selfishly, we've both eased up from the crazy stuff of a year or two back, but we're probably more effective operators as a result! I don't come over as often as I used to and I know Lesebo has developed delegation skills too. There are ongoing high-profile people and proposals coming in regularly but we've all become more relaxed. It's mostly stakeholders or entrepreneurs trying to find shoulder room and trade, rather than space and civil engineering, town planning and all that. Thanks to you, the politics has gone out of it, I suppose. So I'm trying to see a Directorate without Lesebo and a Municipality without you!' Reynolds laughed easily. 'It's too easy to say "yes" straight away, Kobus! Maybe Lesebo could grow into your shoes but replacements for her don't fall off trees either. There are some bright young things forcing their way through the Trustcore bursaries but they're not ready yet. Maybe we'd have to go to the head-hunters to find someone?'

'Well, can I ask you to think about it, Harry, please? You've probably got more influence over her than the rest of us. In many respects, it doesn't represent a huge upheaval in her life, does it? From a professional point of view, I'd say your relationship could work just as well, given a few sensitivities about access to a political appointee – but it's worked for us, so why not with her?'

Harry knew that Lesebo would buy the idea. It would be a clear signal to her that Harry was not yet ready to develop their relationship to anything ultimate like living together, a business partnership or eventually marriage. This would prompt her to concentrate her energies into new challenges to overcome and prevent disappointment discolouring her existence at Siyeza. It would also feed her insatiable ambition – being a Cape Town Mayor in her late twenties would not harm her CV. Yet they would continue to rely on each other as working friends and confidants. He rang Lesebo and invited himself round to talk it through with her.

*****

Lennie Steinhoff ushered Richard Kirkside and Kobus Labuschagne into his sombre chambers. He had summoned them to be briefed on the outcome of recent court hearings concerning the Restraining Order on De Vries' assets. After curt pleasantries, he began his usual monologue that brooked no interruption.

'Gentlemen, as my summonses suggested, I think we need appraise our strategy following some recent legal developments. Firstly, the presiding judges hearing the Provisional Restraining Order reported receipt of a formal refusal to attend either the hearing or any other legal summonses to a South African court from the De Vries attorneys. They summarised a lengthy statement that refused to accept the legitimacy of either the National Director of Public Prosecution obtaining the urgent provisional order or the seizure of assets by the Asset-Forfeiture Unit. It sought to obtain acceptance of non-complicity due to the unproven audit trail of deposited investments to original sources of funds. As a consequence, the court ruled the submission as inadmissible without statutory attendance and converted the Order to permanent status.' Steinhoff waited for this to sink in.

'So we can go after De Vries?' said Labuschagne in unrestrained excitement.

'Precisely gentlemen. It means two things. One, summonses were issued and charges of fraud and contravention of organised crime laws were laid against De Vries. In acknowledging receipt, The Hague lawyers repeated how their client declined the invitation on the grounds already outlined. This meant that the charges remain extant and will be pursued internationally at governmental level for a period of time. If no convincing argument is made or willingness to attend a court hearing here is indicated, then a judgement will be reached, with a foregone guilty verdict against Mr De Vries. Appeals procedures notwithstanding, this means that international warrants for his arrest will remain extant.' Steinhoff allowed himself to glance through his miniature spectacles at his two silent listeners.

'And secondly, gentlemen, the rules of forfeiture will apply regarding the two billion Rands deposited in the SPF account. There is a slightly tortuous procedure that comes into play, whereby the funds are technically under national Treasury control. Only they may sanction their redistribution. This is only because most forfeitures are made from front company accounts that conceal the process of illicit activities. In such cases, funds are transferred to Treasury accounts. In your case, this need not apply, providing we obtain approval to proceed without inhibition. In lay terminology, the government is under legal remit to refund any account that received the sum in good faith and can prove disassociation with any guilty investor or agency identified in law. I don't foresee any impediment here, without wilful or criminal interference, gentlemen.'

Richard was looking thoughtful. 'So there are presumably convoluting rules conditioning later expenditure of the funds? Or can accountants put their heads together and demonstrate through, say, projected budget forecasting and expenditure that the funds were part of a larger whole that was bespoke and fundamental to the entire Siyeza undertaking?'

'Precisely my point, Mr Kirkside. This is an essential technical accomplishment, if I may remind you. We must obtain Treasury approval to a carte blanche continuation of existing Siyeza operational budget and plans, allowing your agents to continue to complete their separate contracts and roles without any piecemeal interruption or inspection process. To my knowledge, the Treasury have already indicated that such approval is forthcoming. Once formally in place, I will send you official authority to proceed. Now, this means no windfall funding of course, but merely protects you in using funds obtained from illegal sources. Needless to say, the court found in your favour for all court costs, legal expenses and defray of incidental costs. Our own accountants will be in touch.' Stenhoff made a rare gesture of removing his glasses, his task complete. Labuschagne got the impression that this was as far as he allowed himself to unwind, like an ex-Army friend he had who always wore his regimental tie on Fridays.

*****

Lindiwe Nhleko [nee Mthembu] was undergoing resuscitation. She had led an unhappy existence after her departure from Cape Town to accompany her husband to the Presidency. The consequent failures and embarrassments suffered as Deputy President were painful to her, as she clung to her sinecure appointment as Minister of Women in the Presidency. Her gold card status as the wife of two successive government Deputies, first Jabu Nhleko and now Malusi Jali, was indisputably tarnished. She was considering resigning her post, leaving Jali to his concubines and embezzling cronies and going into business with her sister, now General Khanyisile Mthembu, boss of Cape Town police.

As she agitated for fresh opportunities for herself, she heard in a cabinet meeting that the DA were making Kobus Labuschagne their leader and moving him out of Cape Town. The ANC spy network revealed that his probable replacement as Mayor was Lesebo Bofokeng, the Basotho wonder child. Lindiwe Nhleko lost no time in double-checking the detail and satisfied herself that there was one last chance for the government to wrestle Siyeza from the DA's grasp for election and voting benefits. But there was no time to waste and she would begin tonight.

Lindiwe confronted Malusi Jali that evening. She knew that the way to Malusi's heart was not through his stomach, contrary to what his hanging belly suggested. He had told her that he had a business dinner but her informers denied this, saying that bodyguards were taking him to the Crown Avenue safe house.

This was used by the Presidency for covert visitors, private meetings and in Malusi's case, for entertaining his most recent "Clinton Intern", as the departmental officials called his girlfriends.

'Malusi, my poor boy! You're wandering around looking so sad. What's wrong?' She leant over his chair and pushed her breasts into his neck, as she ran her hands down his corpulent belly. 'I know you're going to see your girl now but too many others know as well. Ooh, look how my little man has grown so big.' Malusi squirmed but did not push her away. 'They're saying in Cabinet that you are a public disgrace; your money is frozen and maybe you and Jabu are going to be dragged into court over the De Vries scandal?' She pushed her hands into his fat thighs and kissed and whispered into his ear. 'I would like you to take me now and see if you are still strong enough for your girl!' She stood in front of him and began to remove her clothes while he sat immobile in the armchair. 'If you are not strong enough, my little bull, then I want a big favour instead – are you listening?' Malusi was beginning to resist but Lindiwe's size and weight prevented him from pushing her away. 'Close the Mahlambi Council immediately and start another ministry in its place – the Ministry for Siyeza Affairs. I will resign from my stupid ministry here and start in Cape Town. You can stay here with all your young girls and sort out your court case problems, my naughty boy.' As she unbuttoned him, she whispered in his face. 'There we are, you can still do it when you try, can't you? Do as I ask, Malusi, my little boy, or all the dirty pictures from Crown Avenue will go on the web, do you hear?' Malusi shuddered and collapsed, only opening his eyes to find himself alone with a maid coughing loudly to wake him up.

The cunning Lindiwe did not pause. From her private bedroom, she managed to call Jabu Nhleko on Skype. He was looking haggard and thinner than when they last met. She relayed her latest plan to him, reminding him how their ex-married partnership survived in terms of loyalty and favours. She intended to appoint Jabu as Director of Siyeza in place of Lesebo Bafokeng. Having persuaded Malusi to create a Ministry to replace the Council, they would regain political control over Siyeza, despite the Municipality and provincial opposition. At a stroke, all the damage by the ANC would be completely repaired with astute selection, loading of official appointments and award of public service contracts.

With only Lesebo Bafokeng to contend with as a young Mayor badly out of her depth, it would be plain sailing. His first job was to annex and rename a large property as "The Lindiwe Nhleko Orphanage" for child victims of drug abuse and AIDS. Jabu was speechless. No wonder this woman left him trailing in marriage. He nodded agreement and promised confidentiality; what she promised would only improve his position if the ghastly court case loomed over Malusi and himself. But as a discarded and disgraced ex-Deputy, what had he got to lose?

*****

It had been announced at the Siyeza's Council's last meeting, following the government fusillade that had left its members shell-shocked. It seemed a familiar coup attempt to that tried by Nhleko with his hi-jacking of the funds and the control mechanisms some years before but despite the speed this time, the story did not seem so crude. The explanation was simple, they were told; following the personality reshuffle of the two most powerful influences at Siyeza – Labuschagne and Bafokeng – the government had decided to use the opportunity to rationalise the management of Siyeza as it stabilised and lived up to its reputation as a "Metropolitan-in-waiting". It coincided with a Cabinet reshuffle, which made Lindiwe Nhleko available – once a Capetonian resident and an experienced minister with knowledge of both departmental and presidency working practices. The newspapers called it "The Cuckoo's Nest Eviction", saying that this time, rather than fight head-on with big business and the DA, the government had waited until the job was nearly done before claiming the title deeds.

'Well, we've been here before, haven't we?' bemoaned the Reverend Nicholas Mahlambi. 'Because I think you avoided catastrophe by using calm heads before, I thought it best we call in those same wise men to give ideas. So welcome Harry and Maddox.' There were smiles and handshakes exchanged with Kobus, Richard, Khanyisile and Lesebo. First, I think the intelligence from Kobus, whom we are lucky to catch in post before he claims immortality!' Kobus smiled but not appreciatively; his departure and that of Lesebo now seemed the cause of the problem.

'Well I'm glad about my personal fortunes but very worried about Siyeza, rather than the Municipality. Lesebo has enlisted as an electoral candidate with the DA, as some of you know, and I think her selection as Mayor will be uncontested in the All-Party Appointments Committee. I don't want to pre-empt anything there, so let's consider the Directorate instead. If it is subsumed, as is proposed, it will pass under direct government control, answering to a national minister. The Director's replacement becomes irrelevant in management terms because the minister will merely appoint a deputy with special responsibility to oversee all ex-Directorate affairs. They will remove the key positions under guise of cost efficiency. Since Jabu Nhleko and Malusi Jali have been lapdogs to Lindiwe for twenty years between them, I cannot foresee them denying her anything.'

'Them? You said "them"?' interrogated Harry.

'Sorry, haven't you heard? Oh my God, okay! Well hold on to your seats – Jabu Nhleko has just been gazetted as the new Director as it is absorbed into the Ministry of Siyeza Affairs, no less!' Kobus felt guilty that this information, obtained by privy means that morning, had not been passed to the council members. There was an uncharacteristic interruption of incredulity; Jabu Nhleko had been named Public Enemy Number One and The Scarlet Pimpernel in his time but there had been general belief that his prospective charges of fraud and organised crime would be served on him shortly.

'How the hell can he get away with that?' asked Harry. 'If De Vries is guilty, then Jabu must be at least complicit?'

'Well, it's funny that you say that,' interrupted Richard, 'because so did all of us! But Lennie Steinhoff, our senior counsel, got in touch yesterday, saying it appears both Jali and Nhleko filed statements before a Tribunal a couple of months ago denying guilt but admitting a willingness to repay amounts judged fair and appropriate by an independent authority – the Treasury presumably. Steinhoff said that the case against Nhleko was weaker than Jali's because of his physical and business removal in dealing with ZPF as it was then – Jali did all the dirty work as Nhleko's subordinate at the time. I can vouch for that, I suppose. So who knows? Our friend Jabu just might wriggle or at least get away with rapped knuckles, which is a Long Service and Good Conduct medal in today's cabinet, let's face it!'

'Well, that takes the wind out of my sails Richard!' exclaimed Kobus indignantly. 'I've heard nothing about Jabu being born again. That puts an uglier complexion on things. He'll be right back to his old tricks without any restraint. How are we going to prop up Lesebo, with Harry gradually winding down TDC mass involvement?' Kobus looked despondent as he gestured with outstretched palms. 'The government interference and dirty tricks will flood into Cape Town after I go. They'll make a concerted effort to win back the Western Cape, hook or by crook, during the election run-up. I know I sound like a political party manager, but it will affect us all and reverse the benefits that Siyeza is already bringing to thousands of former Flats citizens. In other words, they'll turn the clock back ten years and dismantle and abuse all the genuinely social good that's spreading everywhere. It'll disintegrate within a year!' Kobus looked spent, anything other than the indestructible giant, as he raised a hand to his forehead, leaning forward over the table.

*****

The Cape Town mayoral inauguration was traditionally a full-blown political opportunity to appeal to all sections of the city community, which had steadily billowed in recent years to ape a Latin carnival. The term "Mother City" was its boastful and assertive tag, lending it a licence to compete with Rio and Sydney as the world's premier seaside capital, in a league far advanced from its ordinary and drab sibling cities. Its inferiority complex as the junior partner to Johannesburg and its envy of the blessed climate and laissez faire attitude of Durban, had made Cape Town increasingly combative. It fought tirelessly to declare and exhibit any prevailing social conscience issue, be it gays, ethnic minorities, abused women, xenophobia, crime and corruption, drugs, nudism, neo-colonialism or even the "Establishment". So while the institution of a mayor for his or her term of office was the actual purpose of the occasion, the enthusiastic and imaginative metropolitan and commercial high jinks was the main attraction.

Lesebo Bafokeng was keenly aware of this. The media and the DA party machinery had whipped up a worship cult that matched a Madonna following in her prime years. The international social media and tourism industry seized on the event with an insatiable frenzy, promising pageantry and global media coverage that was previously seen at the likes of Mandela's funeral and the Soccer World Cup's opening evening. It developed a force of its own, settling on a plateau that promised the coronation of an iconic beauty queen – a modern Nefertiti, without king or suitor. Lesebo's advisors smothered her with ever more extravagant proposals and requests. She was to reflect an ecumenical approach, acknowledge the Praise Speaker, welcome the traditional leaders, be gracious to the diplomats, wear this, say that, do this. Her acceptance speech was continually re-drafted, shortened, reduced, included and excluded with a choreography of laser effects, fireworks, choirs and dance troupes. She endured it for a while, but with ten days to go, she decided the time had come – maybe the third or fourth such step-change moment in her young life – to reassert her individuality.

Kobus Labuschagne was now the party Heir Apparent and his judgement and decisions reflected this. Harry Reynolds was her unrequited lover; she had told him that if he did not propose to her on her thirtieth birthday – eighteen months hence – she would consummate their relationship, and Harry suspected that she meant what she said! Maddox was always her moral rock and true sage but this time, she could predict his fatherly line. She thought of escaping to her real father to draw strength, but although she spoke to him often, she felt a better source of inner conviction lay with Ami Kirkside, whom she agreed to meet for lunch at the Cape Point restaurant.

They met alone, as Lesebo suggested. As Ami drifted through the idyllic landscape from Muizenberg to Simon's Town and crossed into the windswept green and fawn vynbos coverage of the Cape of Good Hope Nature Reserve, with the Buffels Baai and False Bay attractions to her left, she was at peace. The Kirksides were overawed by the whole Lesebo story and could not place themselves comfortably in the mainstream hullabaloo that was buoying her to Hollywood fame and fortune. Had Lesebo asked her to meet as an act of contrition or apology? The sixty kilometres passed fast without hurrying her powerful sports car, her hair blowing around her huge sunglasses, with the canopy folded back. She turned many eyes as she passed through Simon's Town and small habitations, a coveted symbol of wealth and privilege. Lesebo anticipated Ami's incurable extravagance and selfishness and drove a tiny Fiat, the smallest car she could find within the Municipality's crowded stable of limousines. Her own appearance but more importantly, her identity, was concealed behind the darkened windows. She arrived before Ami and realised how difficult it had become to find privacy or loneliness; several local visitors wanted her captured alongside them on their "selfie sticks". Thousands saw her on social media clips at Cape Point before Ami arrived.

They met warmly, hiding as well as they could behind sun glasses and large floppy hats. Lesebo suggested they stroll to the Dias Cross, which was a popular item in the tourist's Cape Point itinerary. They talked about each other, avoiding the hype and excitement of Lesebo's imminent inauguration. Ami's natural assertiveness fitted this bill perfectly, with her engaging Lesebo with a seemingly endless account of Tristan's academic achievements. When there was a pause, and as they reached the monument, Lesebo saw her chance.

'Ami, I had to come here with you. Somehow, I had to claim myself back again before this tidal wave swept me away forever, a bauble for a hundred market men!'

Ami was momentarily quelled by Lesebo's ambient strength and attraction. It was indeed absurd that these market men felt they could improve this woman's natural imagery; she had read in a girlie mag how Lesebo had been offered some film parts and had ridiculed the moguls with contemptuous scorn. Ami could see how she didn't need them.

'We both do our homework and trust our own opinions, don't we? Well, we're at Dias Cross because it reminds us all that the Portuguese sailor Bartholomeu Dias was the first to round these treacherous African rocks in 1488 – that's five hundred and thirty-odd years ago. He traded with Khoi-Khoi, who had been pastoralists for nine hundred years by then, and whose ancestors arrived in the Cape around the same time as Christianity began. The Khoi-Khoi in turn had predominated over their predecessor race, the San people.' Lesebo sat on a rock and looked out to sea, knowing that Ami would not stay quiet.

'What is your pitch though, Lesebo? We both know the history and the subsequent interpretations of European influence. Does this join or separate us?'

'Whichever you want. You know, the greatest ignorance passed on by whites is to believe that blacks had no religion. One way or another, most major sub-Saharan African faiths have startling fundamental similarities to Christianity and its junior cousin, Islam. My ancestors believed that good and evil – and all nature's ambiguities – were governed by Tsui/Goab, the omnipresent and powerful force of good who provided benefits and wisdom. He struggled with Guanab, the spooky one who dispensed war and evil, sickness and death.' Lesebo turned to stare at Ami. 'Isn't that God and Satan, or the good and evil, of the Old Testament? But through real power and innate avarice, the European introduced the religio-political Dutch imperialism to the indigenous people here! You know this – you still teach it! What false arrogance, driven by greed and ambition, when condemned in the Ten Commandments?'

'All right Lesebo, you're lecturing me now. Why are we here?'

'Don't worry, I've never been saner! We're here as women. You are the mother of Tristan, for whom I was once tutor. Your husband raped me as a virgin when my whole purpose was to further my knowledge and return to my land to do better for my people. I would give my body to the man I wanted for life, not a one-night stand or a cheap thrill on the kitchen floor – again, echoed in the Bible's Ten Commandments. My compromise between Western and African ethics and beliefs was ripped to shreds in three minutes.' Lesebo knew she would not hold Ami's attention or sympathy unless she spelt out her purpose. 'Ami, this has all been a salvation, believe it or not. I was yesterday's victim, trampled for gain. My woman's survival instinct saved me. I manipulated the powerful, the white and the male. I was weak, black and female and fought back – with them, not against them.'

Lesebo stood in front of Ami, moving her forearms in throwing motions for emphasis, her eyes wide and hypnotic. 'Equality to me, Ami, is the eradication of past mistakes and distortions. I want a level playing field in Cape Town, with meritocracy to sieve and use our multi-cultural talents. So we inculcate the Indian ethic of self-improvement into coloureds and the white's respect for gender into blacks. For the whites, for the next generation, the blacks can lend them their Ubuntu formula and ask them to reform it for our universal good – business, schooling, medicine, land and a competitive spirit. The whites have come far in retribution but not far enough – we are living out a charade society, still of white design and teaching, with a sprinkling of "transformation". The Afrikaner still talks of 'the new dispensation' and measures his tribal decline by the non-white faces in the Springboks. Ami, I want – and we must have soon, to avoid implosion – competition and pride from a stable and just society that is ingrained with good education, health and jobs, not government hand-outs and cronyism.' Lesebo half-crumpled as she drew near to Ami and sobbed deeply in her arms. Ami looked over Lesebo's shoulder and clasped her tight.

'Your mind is your most precious asset, Lesebo!'

Lesebo raised her voice and stamped a foot for emphasis. 'And what I forgot to say is that I want Tristan on the balcony with me at the Inauguration, holding my hand. He will never know how much he's meant in my life! I'm so proud of him too, you know – he's cleverer than us both!' They clung together as they cried. Ami felt weightless as self-pity and anger lifted from her.

*****

Maddox had been as disheartened as the others following the swansong Siyeza Council meeting. This time, there seemed no way out from a stifling government stranglehold on Siyeza control and accompanying avalanche of promotional activity in readiness for the election. His departure to Australia drew nearer following the birth of a son for Annabelle but he had hesitated over booking flights as this new controversy emerged. Government factionalism reared its ugly head once more, threatening to expose Deputy President Malusi Jali as leading a breakaway group, focussed principally on Siyeza. The opinion polls seemed stacked against him as the Lesebo fever reached an ecstatic crescendo during her magnificent Inauguration performance. Maddox thought he would consider one last idea before placating Katie by booking flights and arranging a day and a venue for their wedding – 'it's not meant to be *that* low key, darling!' was her latest retort.

With the bit between his teeth, Maddox agreed to one last rendezvous with General Khanyisile Mthembu at the Waterside restaurant at the upmarket Kelvin Grove Club. It was a risky undertaking, since the venue was invariably noisy and crowded, with flat screen TVs showing recent sports highlights as a light lunch was enjoyed. But Maddox wanted relative anonymity among a younger clientele, despite them struggling to hear each other.

'Well, Khanyisile,' said Maddox raising his glass, 'this is truly our swansong appearance!' They toasted each other and laughed.

'I doubt it somehow Maddox. Since I didn't come running to you, it seems I'm to be asked a favour?' The plump policewoman, looking immaculate in a new turban and wrap-over floral dress, had long since lost her inhibitions with Maddox.

'It's about the Siyeza nonsense that's resurfaced with your sister and her ex-husband. I want you to use some good old-fashioned family influence as her older sister!' Khanyisile giggled appreciably; Maddox wasn't in the mood to pull punches either, it seemed.

'The cards are stacked against her, my dear. First, the Reverend Nicholas Mahlambi is a fully fledged sangoma, which he kept practicing as a priest until he formed his political party. This isn't widely known but you need to know now. Secondly, whatever they might think, Messrs Jali and Nhleko are in for a big shock now that the Supreme Court has ruled that De Vries must answer charges of fraud and money laundering. I don't know what your lawyers are telling you, but my information is that although he won't appear, his conspirators Jabu and Malusi must do so – it looks like charges will be issued shortly. All right so far?' Maddox paused to stab at some bacon and feta filling in his salad, watching for Khanyisile's reaction.

'What you're saying is that my cherubic sister has jumped the gun?'

'Oh yes, to the point of disqualification, I'm afraid. But as ever, help is at hand. We needn't call on Nicholas' sangoma services to exhort advice from your ancestors – I think you would prefer not to! But we can suggest to Siyeza Council's attorneys that providing De Vries' charges remain in perpetuity, then the charges relating to Jali and Nhleko could be held over in obeisance and related to any De Vries development. What do you think?' Maddox smiled like a poker player turning an ace. Khanyisile remained thoughtful.

'I can try Maddox – they are due to set up shop in a fortnight and it's already a running sore I can do without. The Cape Town police deserve a break – we've all been there and suffered heavily!' She pushed her unfinished prawns to one side. 'But one good turn deserves another, Maddox.'

'Ever keen to oblige, General!'

'I hear you plan a very quiet wedding in Australia. I want you to ask Katie whether she needs a bridesmaid or maybe just a reliable witness. You see, I have a male companion who is as hard to nail down as you. Not only would I catch Katie's flowers but I'd carry them for her and never let them go!' Khanyisile revealed her brilliant teeth as she laughed. 'Maddox, three's a crowd, don't worry. But I sit on a Commonwealth Police Service Standing Committee on drug abuse. I have been mandated to go to Brisbane at my earliest convenience and would be given carte blanche chauffeur-driven service during my time there. If you are as clever with GPS as you are with hidden cameras, there should be no problem meeting up!' Maddox scarcely believed what he heard but nothing surprised him about Africa after twenty-five years in Cape Town. He remembered his manners.

'I'm sure she'd be delighted. But more importantly, I congratulate you on your romance and future wedding plans. Anything we can do to help will be a pleasure. I will let you know about dates and places, don't worry!' As Maddox left the club, he wondered about the best time and place to tell Katie his happy news too.

Chapter Seventeen

One powerful attribute of Lesebo's acceptance speech at her tumultuous Inauguration was the largesse she was able to dispense. Having been bounced by the Reverend Nicholas Mahlambi into building a church for his faith, Harry Reynolds and Kobus Labuschagne were keen to make arrangements before the latter's departure. In order to avoid another surprise request for donor sponsorship, they set aside sufficient space and redirected funding for at least two such building enterprises. This was noticed by the alert Lesebo who persuaded Harry to ring-fence the new bonus area for developing a prospective Politics and Economics Academy with UCT affiliations.

Ami Kirkside was easily enrolled by Lesebo as a compliant agent in managing the academic community's sensitivities. She never lost touch with Professor Ashwin Chetty, who continued his existence as a psychiatric in-patient at a prison hospital. He had undergone innumerable treatments and tests and had attended one special legal and medical board for assessment. Richard had agreed to fund an attempt to plea for a reduction in sentence if medical specialists were confident that he was not responsible for his actions when he killed his brother. Ashwin had improved considerably since then under careful treatment. There was talk of a plea being assembled within two years, when doctors forecast a full recovery. The tests and the legal implications were forbidding but the shrewd Ami stored away the hope that Ashwin would one day be readmitted into the academic community and judged a fit candidate to be the first principal of Lesebo's P and E Academy.

The Siyeza Council never went into permanent suspension. The Ministry of Siyeza Affairs evaporated before it took root and Jabu Nhleko was not seen in Cape Town. The Deputy President was deemed by the body of the ANC to have eaten one humble pie too many and lost the majority of his bloc votes that he would require for caucus re-election a year in advance of the election. The opportunist Lindiwe Nhleko fell on her face too, without either her new or old ministry appointments. It seemed she would fall far too low in the rankings to be considered as a senior candidate again.

With flights booked and Katie fully sympathetic about her unexpected bridesmaid, Maddox felt ready for the changes that lay ahead. He was given a bachelor's night out by Richard, Nicholas, Harry and even Kobus, who insisted on being there. "Night out" meant what it said, with rooms booked at a luxurious vineyard lodge. Harry revealed that he and Lesebo were considering becoming engaged before the end of year, which prolonged festivities further into the night.

Lesebo had committed herself to a five-year term of office at Cape Town. Richard told them about Ashwin's circumstances. He also revealed that he and Ami had slipped away to California to refresh their marriage vows, which left them all joyful but poignant. It seemed that Ami and Richard planned to alternate as minders in Oxford while Tristan completed his first year of studies. Maddox was voted "Brain Teaser of the year" for his uncanny ability to reduce the insoluble to workable answers. Kobus was confident of gaining Gauteng and the Eastern Cape provinces in the election, giving the DA nearly 40 percent of the national vote. He also reported happily that Moses Sithole, Lesebo's understudy at the Directorate, had succeeded her as director and was doing a brilliant job, according to Lesebo. As the steam ran out, they all retired to bed contented and calm.

Maddox had one more duty to complete before departure. Gary and Joost had waited patiently while Maddox chopped and changed his departure date to Australia, but having seen the E-tickets, arranged an office farewell party for Maddox and Katie in Sea Point. Maddox reflected on how the deadly Curmudgeon had to be tied down before he would come out to celebrate his sixtieth birthday. Now, holding Katie's hand, he couldn't be restrained as the party's life and soul.

'We don't do this often enough, but I don't know about you lot, but I'm pleading overwork!' There were howls of "Shame" and "Slave driver" as the staff, now numbering over forty, clapped their popular leader. 'But then, I'm a born-again character, about to take on my third wife. I'm so old that I can assure you that this one is for keeps – I'm thinking about buying her my second bottle of Angostura bitters!' Katie went through some mock theatricals as they roared and jeered. 'But I'm a plausible liar, like all coppers. I'm the luckiest bloke in the world too, to have found Katie and to have kept such a magnificent bunch of loyal and skilled operators together – you could all take better jobs anywhere in the country. But our dear old Employed Stock Ownership Plan, or ESOP, has come up trumps, it seems. We've all worked our backsides off for the last four years or so and it shows. I'm told that 65 percent of you have already paid off your loan fees in full and that all bar the most recent two employees are investing cash for shares – that's awesome!' There were loud cheers and clapping. 'It must be right because our wastage rate has dropped from 15 to just 2 percent per year. That makes me happy too. Now when I get back from Down Under, I'll be talking about easing up myself and seeing what you need for the future. But as it stands, Maddox Private Investigators has never been so large, busy or prosperous. Or held in such good esteem – I salute you all!' To the strain of 'For he's a jolly good fellow,' Gary worked his way to the front.

'As ever, thanks, boss from us all. We'll give you a wedding present when you get back and we have seen a ring on Katie's finger!' Hooting and American whooping now. 'But we have a little token for you to entertain you as you travel. Karin, where are you please?' The voluptuous Karin, unchanged by her motherhood and several more thousand miles zipping around the Cape Town thoroughfares, wobbled forward on high rise shoes, bringing whistles from the younger men present. She planted a kiss on Maddox's cheek and handed him a small parcel.

'Don't know where it turned up, boss!' The parcel had "Missing DVD" crudely scratched over it, which brought long laughter and a string of vulgar suggestions. Maddox was genuinely caught off guard – the offending stolen item was extremely sensitive and "need to know" information. He glanced anxiously at Gary, who was enjoying his dilemma.

'Don't worry, boss. Not that one. But I'd still keep this one to yourself if I was you!' The speeches over, proceedings subsided as an excellent supper was served.

'What's on that DVD, then?' Katie murmured quietly across the table.

'Haven't a clue. Let's look when we get home. Whenever they went home together, Maddox reminded Katie that he needed a Steady Eddy equivalent sex therapist. Being seen going home together kept tongues wagging about them being "an item", which was a source of private fun. But then nobody saw and nobody was told as they fell asleep, wrapped in each other's arms. They played the DVD at Maddox's house, having settled down with a nightcap whisky. To their astonishment and amusement, it was a video recording of Maddox taking tennis instruction with Steady Eddy, Maddox at a Virgin Gym, Maddox losing a doubles match with Katie, Maddox having lunch with Khanyisile, Maddox choosing shorts at Woolworths, Maddox gardening and cycling and Maddox eating a crispbread lunch in the office.

*****

Lesebo insisted on her driver taking them to the airport, much to Katie's embarrassment. As they approached the final slip road, they were flagged down in a police speed trap. The driver protested innocence, supported by Maddox who seriously thought they were driving well within speed limits. The police sergeant smiled at Maddox, handing him a brown envelope.

'Courtesy of General Mthembu, sir.' Maddox unfolded the summonses which read: *MASQUERADING UNDER FALSE PRETENCES AS MAYOR OF CAPE TOWN. THIS TIME YOU WILL BE ADMONISHED AS A BACHELOR BUT NEXT TIME YOU WILL BE EXPECTED TO BEHAVE LIKE A RESPECTABLE MARRIED MAN.*

'Well how exciting Maddox, we're off at last!' Katie squeezed his hand across the plush arm rests in their Business Class seats. 'What's in store for us in Australia, darling?'

'Not sure. I don't know what's in store when we get back, either!'

CPSIA information can be obtained
at www.ICGtesting.com
Printed in the USA
LVHW021010040121
675397LV00008B/572